Rowe is a p

𝕏𝕏𝕏

## Praise for Not Quite Dead

"[Rowe] has penned a winner with *Not Quite Dead*, the first novel in her new NightHunter vampire series...an action-packed, sensual, paranormal romance that will captivate readers from the outset... Brimming with vampires, danger, resurrection, Louisiana bayou, humor, surprising plot twists, fantasy, romance and love, this story is a must-read!" ~ *Romance Junkies:*

𝕏𝕏𝕏

## Praise for Darkness Possessed

"A story that will keep you on the edge of your seat, and characters you won't soon forget!" - Paige Tyler, *USA Today* Bestselling Author of the X-OPS Series

"*Darkness Possessed*...is an action-packed, adrenaline pumping paranormal romance that will keep you on the edge of your seat... Suspense, danger, evil, life threatening situations, magic, hunky Calydons, humor, fantasy, mystery, scorching sensuality, romance, and love – what more could you ask for in a story? Readers – take my advice – do not miss this dark, sexy tale!" ~*Romance Junkie*s

𝕏𝕏𝕏

## Praise for Darkness Unleashed

"Once more, award winning author Stephanie Rowe pens a winner with *Darkness Unleashed*, the seventh book in her amazing Order of the Blade series...[an] action-packed, sensual story that will keep you perched on the edge of your seat, eagerly turning pages to discover the

outcome…one of the best paranormal books I have read this year."
~*Dottie, Romancejunkies.com*

## Praise for Forever in Darkness

"Stephanie Rowe has done it again. The Order Of The Blade series is one of the best urban fantasy/paranormal series I have read. Ian's story held me riveted from page one. It is sure to delight all her fans. Keep them coming!" ~ *Alexx Mom Cat's Gateway Book Blog*

## Praise for Darkness Awakened

"A fast-paced plot with strong characters, blazing sexual tension and sprinkled with witty banter, Darkness Awakened sucked me in and kept me hooked until the very last page." ~ *Literary Escapism*

"Rarely do I find a book that so captivates my attention, that makes me laugh out loud, and cry when things look bad. And the sex, wow! It took my breath away... The pace kept me on the edge of my seat, and turning the pages. I did not want to put this book down... [Darkness Awakened] is a must read." ~ D. Alexx Miller, Alexx Mom Cat's Gateway Book Blog

## Praise for Darkness Seduced

"[D]ark, edgy, sexy … sizzles on the page…sex with soul shattering connections that leave the reader a little breathless!...Darkness Seduced delivers tight plot lines, well written, witty and lyrical - Rowe lays down some seriously dark and sexy tracks. There is no doubt that this series will have a cult following. " ~ *Guilty Indulgence Book Club*

"I was absolutely enthralled by this book…heart stopping action fueled by dangerous passions and hunky, primal men...If you're looking for a book that will grab hold of you and not let go until it has been totally devoured, look no further than Darkness Seduced."~*When Pen Met Paper Reviews*

XIXIX

## Praise for Darkness Surrendered

"Book three of the Order of the Blades series is...superbly original and excellent, yet the passion, struggle and the depth of emotion that Ana and Elijah face is so brutal, yet is also pretty awe inspiring. I was swept away by Stephanie's depth of character detail and emotion. I absolutely loved the roller-coaster that Stephanie, Ana and Elijah took me on." ~ *Becky Johnson, Bex 'n' Books!*

"Darkness Surrendered drew me so deeply into the story that I felt Ana and Elijah's emotions as if they were my own...they completely engulfed me in their story...Ingenious plot turns and edge of your seat suspense...make Darkness Surrendered one of the best novels I have read in years." ~*Tamara Hoffa, Sizzling Hot Book Reviews*

XIXIX

## Praise for Ice

"*Ice*, by Stephanie Rowe, is a thrill ride!" ~ Lisa Jackson, #1 *New York Times* bestselling author

"Passion explodes even in the face of spiraling danger as Rowe offers a chilling thrill-ride through a vivid--and unforgiving--Alaskan wilderness." ~ Cheyenne McCray, *New York Times* bestselling author

"*Ice* delivers pulse-pounding chills and hot romance as it races toward its exciting climax!" ~ JoAnn Ross, *New York Times* bestselling author

"Stephanie Rowe explodes onto the romantic suspense scene with this edgy, sexy and gripping thriller. From the very first page, the suspense is chilling, and there's enough sizzling passion between the two main characters to melt the thickest arctic ice. Get ready for a tense and dangerous adventure." ~ *Fresh Fiction*

"Stephanie Rowe makes her entry into Romantic Suspense, and what an awesome entry! From the very first pages to the end, heart-stopping danger and passion grab the heart. ... sends shivers down the spine... magnificent... mind-chilling suspense... riveting... A wonderful romance through and through!" ~ *Merrimon Book Reviews*

"[a] thrilling entry into romantic suspense... Rowe comes through with crackling tension as the killer closes in." ~ *Publisher's Weekly*

<hr/>

## Praise for Chill

"*Chill* is a riveting story of danger, betrayal, intrigue and the healing powers of love... *Chill* has everything a reader needs – death, threats, thefts, attraction and hot, sweet romance." ~ Jeanne Stone Hunter, *My Book Addiction Reviews*

"Once again Rowe has delivered a story with adrenalin-inducing action, suspense and a dark edged hero that will melt your heart and send a chill down your spine." ~ Sharon Stogner, *Love Romance Passion*

"*Chill* packs page turning suspense with tremendous emotional impact. Buy a box of Kleenex before you read *Chill*, because you will definitely need it! ...*Chill* had a wonderfully complicated plot, full of twist and turns. " ~ Tamara Hoffa, *Sizzling Hot Book Reviews*

<hr/>

## Praise for No Knight Needed

"*No Knight Needed* is m-a-g-i-c-a-l! Hands down, it is one of the best romances I have read. I can't wait till it comes out and I can tell the world about it." ~*Sharon Stogner, Love Romance Passion*

"*No Knight Needed* is contemporary romance at its best....There was not a moment that I wasn't completely engrossed in the novel, the story, the characters. I very audibly cheered for them and did not shed just one tear, nope, rather bucket fulls. My heart at times broke for them. The narrative and dialogue surrounding these 'tender' moments in particular were so beautifully crafted, poetic even; it was this that had me blubbering. And of course on the flip side of the heart-wrenching events, was the amazing, witty humour....If it's not obvious by now, then just to be clear, I love this book! I would most definitely and happily reread, which is an absolute first for me in this genre." ~*Becky Johnson, Bex 'N' Books*

"*No Knight Needed* is an amazing story of love and life...I literally laughed out loud, cried and cheered.... *No Knight Needed* is a must read and must re-read." ~*Jeanne Stone-Hunter, My Book Addiction Reviews*

# Acknowledgements

Special thanks to my core team of amazing people, without whom I would never have been able to create this book. Each of you is so important, and your contribution was exactly what I needed. I'm so grateful to all of you! Your emails of support, or yelling at me because I hadn't sent you more of the book yet, or just your advice on covers, back cover copy and all things needed to whip this book into shape—every last one of them made a difference to me. I appreciate each one of you so much!

There are so many to thank by name, more than I could count, but here are those who I want to called out specially for all they did to help this book come to life: Leslie Barnes, Alencia Bates, Jean Bowden, Shell Bryce, Holly Collins, Ashley Cuesta, Maureen Downey, Denise Fluhr, Sandi Foss, Teresa Gabelman, Loretta Gilbert, Valerie Glass, Tamara Hoffa, Heidi Hoffman, Jeanne Hunter, Rebecca Johnson, Dottie Jones, Janet Juengling-Snell, Deb Julienne, Bridget Koan, Jan Leyh, Phyllis Marshall, Mariann Medina, D. Alexx Miller, Jodi Moore, Anita Nallathamby, Mary Lynn Ostrum, Judi Pflughoeft, Jenn Shanks Pray, Kasey Richardson, Caryn Santee, Dana Simmons, Julie Simpson, Summer Steelman, Sharon Stogner, Nicole Telhiard, Rachel Unterman, and Denise Whelan. You guys completely rock!

Special thanks to Michael James Canalas at MJC Imageworks for a wonderful cover. Mom, you're the best. It means so much that you believe in me. I love you. Special thanks also to my amazing, beautiful, special daughter, who I love more than words could ever express. You are my world, sweet girl, in all ways.

# Dedication

For Jeanne Stone Hunter, a dear friend and a great supporter.

# Darkness

# Seduced

An *Order of the Blade* Novel

# Stephanie

# Rowe

# Chapter 1

The weight in her soul was becoming almost too heavy to bear, and that fact terrified Lily Davenport even more than her current situation did.

That kind of thinking would doom her. It would get her nowhere, and she had to rise above it right now.

Even if it was true.

Fighting exhaustion, struggling against despair, and trying desperately to hold onto the hope that had kept her going for the last two years, Lily leaned back against the cement wall of her cell, not even caring how hard and cold it was. She just needed something to support her head for a minute. Just until she found her way back to the tough, indomitable woman who had survived two years (and counting) of hell at the cruel hands of Nate Tipton, the sociopathic Calydon warrior who'd taken her prisoner when she'd shown up at his house to interview him for her latest research paper.

Calydons were immortal warriors, descended from a crazy, evil male who'd taken one too many doses of demon-tainted water and nearly brought down the world. His legacy was thousands of immortal warriors who were cursed with both a natural instinct to protect innocents, and the horrific destiny of going rogue and destroying the very innocents they were born to keep safe. Each male was chosen by his weapon, and he carried its mark on his forearms where the weapons would wait, ready to be called out during battle to do his bidding.

Nate, however, had no such excuses. He wasn't rogue,

and yet somewhere in the tainted recesses of his mind, he'd lost the need to protect innocents. Instead, he thrived on causing pain and death simply because it fit in with his plans, whatever they were. After two years at his non-existent mercy, Lily hadn't figured out what his intentions were, other than to inflict upon her a steady course of abuse designed to break her soul.

Her eyes at a weary half-mast, Lily studied the crusted bagel sitting on the cardboard box that served as her dining room table. That was all the food she had left. One pathetic piece of dried-out bread that she once would have tossed into the garbage without a thought. Today it was an agonizingly tempting feast that was making her mouth water.

Should she try to conserve it a little longer, or eat?

Oh, who was she kidding? She had to eat, or else she'd disintegrate into a pathetic ball on the floor and be unable to save herself when someone finally opened the locked door of her cell.

"Okay, Lily. Up you go." Lily wrapped her hand around the frame of the metal cot that had cushioned her for so many nightmare-laden nights. With a groan, she pulled herself to her feet. Her legs were trembling, aching with exhaustion, making her almost want to laugh.

If only the world could see her now. The internationally renowned Calydon expert, celebrated around the globe while she delivered shocking information about the reclusive immortal warriors, violent males who lived and died by their blades. How far she had fallen from the serious and staid professor who had stared down hundreds of annoyed Calydons in her lifetime, refusing to be cowed. Today, she could barely manage to hobble across the floor to bask in the delight of eating a stale bagel.

Honest to God, she felt a little defeated right now.

Dammit, no. She couldn't afford to think like that. Wearily, Lily rubbed her hand over her eyes, willing away the exhaustion. She'd survived this long. Why not try to make it another day? You know, because she'd invested so much time and effort into staying alive and all. It would be a shame to waste it, right?

She almost laughed. God, the things she said to herself to try to stay sane.

"Okay, Lily," she said aloud, trying to break the debilitating silence that had been closing down on her with increasing intensity. "How about a lovely candlelit dinner just for one?"

Fabulous idea.

Lily pulled her shoulders back and walked across the dirty floor, her legs shaking with weakness as she fingered one of the fading bruises on her arm. She eased herself down to the floor beside the cardboard box. Sitting beside the bagel was a tin can of water. Even though the bagels were stale, at least the water was fresh, or as fresh as whatever was coming out of the faucet in the crumbling cement wall. She preferred to think of the water's orange tint as a rose-wine color, as opposed to something more unpalatable and probably more accurate.

Nate thoughtfully left Lily eight bagels to gnaw on while he gallivanted about the Pacific Northwest murdering more people. He thought it was hilarious and ironic to leave her with bread and water each time he went out on a mission.

She, however, wasn't feeling the joy and delight of the irony nearly as much.

Nate had been due back after one day, but now it was day eight, and there was still no sign of him. Good, because it had given her a chance to recover from his latest assault. Good, because it made her hope he'd finally been killed. Bad, because it left her locked in a basement waiting for his brutally terrifying partner to come and get her. As always, he had taken all his guards with him when he went out on his killing spree, so there was no one left in the house to make sure she didn't die of starvation. If Nate was dead, his partner was the only one who would be coming for her.

Lily shivered as she recalled the ice blue eyes of Frank Tully, so cold, so chilling, and so terrifying. As much as Nate had brutalized Lily over the last two years and, as terrified as she was of him, Nate's effect on her was nothing in comparison to how badly Frank had unnerved her the one time he'd come by the house.

Nate had isolated her, used physical force to manipulate her, and had kept her captive for some future grand plan she had been unable to figure out, but he'd never managed to take away her determination to stay alive and fight until she could find a way to escape.

But one look into Frank's eyes, and Lily had known he had plans for her. Plans that would make her beg for death long before he'd ever give it to her. She'd met Frank only that one day, and it was after he had left that Nate had done truly horrific things to her—

Tears welled up with such unexpected suddenness that Lily was caught off guard before she could will them away. Tears that were tainted with memories long past, long-buried nightmares brought to the surface by her thoughts about Frank.

God, no. She couldn't afford to think of her past right now. She had no resources left to deal with it. She had to hold tight to her emotions and carefully direct her thoughts, or she'd lose it. She knew she was so close to the edge, barely hanging onto hope, sanity and strength. "The past is gone," she announced. "Let it go."

But she was still blinking hard against the tears as she took the last remaining bagel out of the plastic bag and set it next to the tin of water. "Ana will come," she told herself. "Have faith in her."

Nate had kidnapped Ana Matthews several months ago, but Lily hadn't managed to get in to see her until two weeks ago. God, that moment when Lily had seen another human being, a woman, a friend, it had almost been too much. It had been so overwhelming after the isolation of the last two years.

Nate had taken Ana with him on this latest killing spree so he could use Ana's powers to help him murder. Lily and Ana had devised a plan—if one could call it that—for Ana to escape and send help back for Lily.

Lily had to believe Ana was still alive. *She had to*. Because if Ana was dead or even incapacitated, the only one coming for Lily was Frank, because Lily was becoming increasingly convinced that something had happened to Nate. She was too important for him to risk leaving her behind to possibly starve to death. With Nate gone, even if Ana *were* alive, it wouldn't matter if Frank made it here first...

"God." Lily pressed her forehead to her palms and squeezed her eyes shut against the sudden swell of tears, unable to stop a sob from wrenching out of her throat. She'd battled to stay sane, to stay positive, and to believe that someday she'd go home. She'd worked so hard to maintain some semblance of herself—how could it end with her dying of starvation in a basement? Or at the brutal hands of a madman like Frank? Two years of hopelessness surged over her, crushing her, and that last shred of hope slid out of her grasp as she finally gave in—

"No!" She lifted her head and took a shuddering breath. "It's not over yet. It's never over." She lifted her head and glared at the ceiling Nate loved to stomp on whenever he thought she was sleeping. "You aren't stronger than I am," she shouted. "I'm going to win."

Silence.

Her throat tightened, but she resolutely broke an inch off the end of the bagel and put the rest back in the plastic bag for tomorrow. Because there would be a tomorrow for her. *There would be.*

She picked up her tin can to toast herself—

There was a loud thud from the hallway, a shudder so forceful the floor shook beneath her. She froze, and then her heart burst into frantic life.

Lily bolted to her feet, the tin can hitting the cement floor with a clank. Water splashed over her bare feet, but she didn't move, staring at the door as adrenaline pounded through her. Was it Nate? Frank? Or had someone arrived to snatch her out of hell?

A loud crash reverberated through the basement and the door shuddered. Someone was trying to break her out! Not Nate, because he had a key. *It wasn't Nate.* Tears of relief flooded her eyes. Someone had come to rescue her? "I'm in here," she shouted as she ran to the door. "Help!"

There was no answer, just another thundering crash and the glaring din of metal against metal as the steel door shook this time. Someone was trying to beat the door down? "Hello?"

Again, no response, just another violent blow against the door.

A sudden chill shot down Lily's spine, reality rushing with agonizing clarity into her mind. If someone were there to rescue her, they would be yelling for her, giving her reassurance, or trying to ascertain if she were alive behind that steel door. Whoever was trying to break down the door didn't have rescue in mind. The door trembled again as something metal slammed into it with a shattering clang...metal against metal.

*Frank.* He had Calydon warriors working for him, Calydons who sported steel weapons that would be able to take down her cell door.

Oh, *God.*

Bile rose in Lily's throat as she whirled toward the corner where she'd hidden the one item she'd been able to turn into a weapon during her sojourn in hell. She grabbed the metal rod that used to frame the underside of her cot, nearly dropping it as another crash exploded through the basement.

Her ears ringing from the noise, she clutched the metal rod, making sure the end with the splintered spike and the two inch pieces of wire hanger was pointing away from her, and then ran back across the room.

She almost whimpered when she saw a metal blade pierce the steel door. Then it was yanked back and slammed again, this time coming through further. Far enough for her to see the intricate design on the blade, a design typical of a Calydon warrior's weapon.

She stared at the shiny metal blade, her chest so tight she couldn't breathe. She'd never be able to take down a Calydon. *Never.*

The blade was wrenched out of the door and slammed into it again, this time coming through a good eight inches, nearly stabbing her in the chest. She leapt back and threw herself against the wall next to the door. She clutched her spear tightly, holding it at the correct angle to stab a six and a half foot tall warrior in the eye.

One chance. She'd get one chance to blind him and run. She'd mapped out her escape route precisely, and she knew exactly how long it would take her to get to the kitchen to grab Nate's car keys, and then make it to the garage.

She knew the odds of her escaping were miniscule, which was why she'd never tried it before. But now it didn't matter. She'd rather die trying to escape than let Frank take her. Staying alive was no longer her number one goal. Ever since

Frank had fixed his sights on her, she'd known her options had changed. Ana had been her last hope...

The door shook again, and Lily leaned her head back against the wall, her whole body trembling as she waited for the door to succumb to the assault. She didn't have to kill the Calydon. She needed him out of commission for only three minutes. She'd run the calculations dozens of times, and she knew three minutes were all she needed for a head start. *Three minutes, Lily. You can do this.*

She had to take him by surprise. Attack before he had a chance to consider defending himself. No warrior would ever think that the refined Professor Davenport would go on the offensive. He wouldn't be ready. *Please, God, don't let him be ready.*

The next blow rattled the wall so badly she had to lift her head off it to keep her teeth from clattering. The door strained at its hinges, and Lily gripped her spear tighter, her heart pounding. *This is it, Lily. Your chance.*

There was a brutal crash, and the door exploded out of the frame with violent force. It catapulted across the room and smashed into her cot, decimating it with the furious shriek of metal being ripped to pieces.

She held her breath and tucked herself further out of sight, waiting for the Calydon to step through the doorway and into range so she could spring at him before he was ready.

But he didn't come in.

He didn't even take a step.

Silence.

Sweat trickled down between her shoulder blades, and she realized he'd be able to smell her sweat if he took the time to scent her—

She felt a humming in the air, and she silently cursed, realizing that the Calydon was reaching out with his preternatural senses to find her. He would hear her heart pounding and know exactly where she was. Even holding her breath wouldn't keep her silent enough, not with him this close.

She had to act *now*.

She tightened her grip on her spear, then lunged forward and jammed it around the doorframe, striking blind.

Gauging where his head would be, she aimed upward and to the right, throwing her whole weight into the thrust. It slammed into something and thudded to a stop. Target!

Elated, she jumped around the doorway, and her heart froze with terror.

*She'd missed.*

Her spear was harmlessly wedged in the shoulder of a dark-haired Calydon warrior, one who she'd seen with Frank. Blood was trickling down his shoulder, and he let out a roar of outrage and grabbed the handle of the spear to yank it out.

Lily ducked past him and sprinted up the cement stairs, her bare feet slapping on the concrete, her heart thundering in her ears as she vaulted up the steps toward the open door. She jumped through it then whirled around and threw it shut, catching a glimpse of the Calydon as he came after her. She slammed the bolt home then tore down the hallway. There was a shuddering explosion behind her as the Calydon burst through the wooden door. She skidded around a corner as her mind whirred. She'd never make it to the kitchen. She needed to stall him—

She screamed as a heavy, sweaty body tackled her and her chin smashed on the wood floor. Her head rattled with the impact as he grabbed her and flung her onto her back. He leered at her chest as he pinned her beneath him. Lust flared in his eyes, the raw, uncontrollable sexual greed of a Calydon. She jerked her gaze down and realized he'd torn her shirt when he'd tackled her.

Terror, raw visceral terror, tore through her, and for a split second, she was too numb to move, too terrified by the memories, by the moment, and by what had happened before. Just like this. Again. God, not again.

He reached for her breast, and the sight of that hand coming toward her jerked her out of her stupor and galvanized her into frantic self-defense, a chance she hadn't had all those years ago. "No!" she screamed. She slammed her foot into his crotch as hard as she could.

Her attacker shouted and doubled over, and Lily scrambled out from under him, lurching to her knees—

He grabbed her ankle, his grip crushing her leg. "I have to bring you back alive and able to perform," he ground out as he tried to catch his breath from her blow. "But those are all the orders I have."

She fought, she kicked, she tried everything, but she was no match for his strength as he yanked her across the floor, back toward him, toward the lust gleaming in his eyes—

Oh, crap. *His eyes.* They were glowing red, pulsating with evil, and her heart stuttered.

*He'd gone rogue.* He'd crossed the line from sanity into raging, crazed killer, a beast who would feel no pain, have no empathy, ravage mercilessly until there was nothing left. There was no compassion, no humanity left in this warrior. No matter what his orders, she was doomed now. He wouldn't be able to stop himself. He would kill her.

Again. It would all happen again. Just like before—

"Get off me," she screamed, scrabbling desperately for a handhold to try to get away from him. Her fingers hit a table leg and a cord. Tears streaking down her cheeks, she yanked on the cord and covered her face as a lamp crashed down on both of them, shattering glass everywhere. Oblivious to the glass, he grabbed her other calf and hauled her until her legs were around his waist, her back slicing across the broken glass as she fought him, desperate, frantic—

"Get the fuck off her!" An enraged bellow blasted through the hallway.

Her attacker didn't even flinch, lunging for her with the furious insanity of a rogue Calydon. She pounded on his shoulders, then heard the whoosh of wind behind her. She looked up as a throwing axe spun past her head and slammed into her assailant's chest. The fatal blow flung him backward against the wall, a gaping wound opening over his heart.

She scrambled back, barely noticing the glass sinking into her hands and feet as she struggled to get away from him. He hit the floor with a thud, and the axe yanked itself out of his body and sped back past her head. She heard the slap of it hitting someone's palm.

Another Calydon.

She whirled around, and her breath caught. At the end of the hall stood the largest Calydon she'd ever seen. He had to be close to seven feet tall, and he was wearing all black, even his heavy boots and the tee shirt that barely covered his broad shoulders.

Everything about him was dark, except his dusty blond hair hanging raggedly about his angular face and the metal throwing axe in his right hand, stained with blood on one of its blades. His face was wrenched with fury, his blue eyes raging, his stance wide and ready, prepared to take on all threats. He was darkness, he was danger, and he was death.

His eyes weren't red, but she could sense he was far more dangerous than the Calydon that lay motionless behind her. He radiated with danger, heat, and something she couldn't identify. Something that eased the terror beating at her. Something that calmed her need to flee. Something that made her want to rush over to him and throw herself in his arms, just to feel his body against hers...

*Oh, crap.* What was wrong with her?

He held up a hand for her silence and cocked his head. She realized he was listening for others. Oh, God. Others?

She lurched to her feet, staggering as a wave of dizziness caught her and she nearly went down. She braced her hands against the wall, holding herself up as she stumbled away from him, toward the kitchen. Glass cut through her feet, and a cry of pain slipped out.

"Lily!" he commanded. "Don't move!"

*Lily?* He knew who she was? Was he also working with Frank? Had he killed her rogue assailant to ensure she made it back to Frank alive?

The Calydon was striding toward her, his face dark with fury. Energy was swirling off him, and his well-defined muscles were flexed with rage. He was terrifying, but at the same time... he was pure, elemental beauty. Filled with a fantastical grace that reminded her of a wild cat, loaded with sinewy muscle and a lightning-fast strike that would bring instant death to his enemies. But one that would also curl around her and protect her, keeping her safe, claws carefully sheathed just for her.

He was all male, a testosterone-laden specimen of strength and aggression, and a threat to all she was as a woman. He was a ruthless temptation to her deepest, darkest desires, the ones she'd hidden away even from herself. In his presence, everything that made her female flared to life, longing for this man, this warrior, this *enemy*.

She backed up as he neared, holding out her hand in a pathetically useless attempt to stop him.

"My name's Gideon. I'm here for you." His voice was forceful and unyielding, but to her surprise, he eased himself to a stop several yards away from her. He spread his hands as if he were trying to appear harmless. There was no chance he could ever be mistaken for anything harmless, and it wasn't simply because of the weapon in his right hand or the axe-shaped brands burned into his forearms. Danger bled from his pores, darkened his expression, and weighted his broad shoulders. "Don't run," he said. "You'll slice your feet."

Her stomach lurched. There was no remorse in his face for the body on the ground behind her, yet at the same time, heated desire brimmed in his eyes as he studied her intensely. He was a Calydon, a warrior of hot passions and cold death, both of them hopelessly intertwined. His overwhelming presence was stirring up heated feelings of longing deep within her, even as her heart froze in fear at all he was, for how her life could fall at his hands in a split second.

She tugged her torn shirt closed over her chest, knowing it would do nothing to protect her from the raw sensuality pulsing from him, from the painfully intense yearnings rising within her, responding to his call, desperate to fall into the fire he was already kindling between them. She'd met dozens of Calydons in the past. She'd always felt their pulsing sexuality, their intense stares that made desire rush through her, preying on her heritage and how it called her to their kind, but this was *different*. With all those others, she hadn't felt anything for them. It had been easy to turn them away, to ignore the beastly desires of her kind.

But Gideon was different. He was stripping her raw, branding her with his gaze, making her body ache with need for him, for all that he was and could offer her.

His eyes darkened, and she knew he could sense her attraction, the need pulsing so strongly within her.

Her cheeks flared with embarrassment, and she began to slide along the wall away from him, using it as a support to keep herself vertical. She winced as her foot landed on something sharp, and she jerked it off the floor, brushing off the glass by running her sole over her calf.

His jaw tightened, and his hand went up as if to grab her, but he stopped himself when she flinched. "Lily. There are more Calydons outside that my teammate is dealing with." There was an urgency to his voice. "We need to go." He snapped his fingers impatiently. "Come on. Now."

She gritted her teeth against the almost uncontrollable urge to drop her shields, bolt into his arms and give herself over to him. He was death, but he was also temptation. As she stared at the hand he was holding out to her, she felt an unshakeable conviction that he was safety. For the first time in years, she could be safe, if she would just reach out and take what he offered: his violence, his sensuality, his overwhelming desire, his *protection*.

But she'd trusted Nate, and she'd wound up his captive for two years. Despite all she knew about Calydons, she'd forgotten all her lessons and walked into Nate's house, and she'd paid dearly for it. She wasn't stupid enough to trust a Calydon again.

Never, ever again.

Not even the warrior who'd killed to save her. Next time, it could be she who fell victim to Gideon's weapon. Or next time, it could be Gideon who turned that uncontrollable lust onto her.

And if he didn't turn on her next time, he would eventually. Of that, she had no doubt. The warrior standing before her was her salvation, her passion, and also her ultimate destruction.

# Chapter 2

Gideon Roarke was lost, swept away by the woman he'd come to rescue.

The world fell away as he stared into Lily's moss green eyes. The violence of the battle faded, the clash of metal weapons fell silent, the cold chill of the Oregon high desert disappeared.

Thick lashes framed those sea-colored depths, giving them a sensuality that awakened every cell in his body. But it was the emotions in her eyes that reached inside and seized him by the gut, ripping him out of his role as the warrior and catapulting him into the unfamiliar place of a male consumed by a woman.

Deep fear was etched in her eyes, ingrained so deeply it had become a part of her. The raw loneliness. The aching despair. The desperate courage striving so hard to be strong, to fight, to survive. Her cheeks were still streaked with tears, her face lined with worry, but there was a passionate beauty to her, a depth of spirit, a fascinating play of femininity and fire to her features.

*Son of a bitch.* Gideon's axe burned in his hand, fierce with the need to kill Nate for a second time, to destroy him for putting that pain on Lily's face. He wanted to behead the bastard still lying on the ground beside her, punishing him for putting his hands on Lily, for daring to threaten her, for bringing those tears to life.

Gideon didn't know Lily. He'd never met her before this moment. He'd never spoken to her. He knew nothing about this woman he'd been sent to rescue from this hellhole. He hadn't given any thought to her, other than that she was his next mission, and for that reason, she was important.

But as Gideon stood there, riveted to the floor, feeling the heat of her gaze as she stared at him, everything shifted. No longer was it just another mission, another job to do for the Order of the Blade, the elite group of warriors who were sworn to protect innocents from rogue Calydons. Now, the mission had become real. It had become a woman. It was about an achingly beautiful female with curves, a broken soul, and a battered body.

Now, it mattered. It had become personal. Lily was no longer simply an assignment. She was *his* to protect.

With sudden possession and a fierceness foreign to him, Gideon swept his gaze over her, swiftly cataloguing everything he needed to know about her. Her shoulders were thin beneath that torn and filthy blouse, narrow enough that a raw anger began to swell inside him at the underfed state of her body. There were bruises on her wrists and red marks on her throat.

Beneath the injuries, however, was the steady, courageous resilience of a woman who would not be brought down. There was a determination in her gaze as she stared at him, and his attention was drawn mercilessly to the fullness of her mouth, to her high cheekbones, and to the delicate slant of her nose.

Her dark blond hair was tangled and matted around her shoulders, but he could imagine the softness of those strands, the delicate femininity of how they fell forward over her collarbone. Her hands were trembling, her breath an effort with each inhale. The fine line of her jaw as she raised her chin was compelling as hell, and he knew immediately she was a survivor, a warrior whose weapons were her courage and her mental strength.

She was all female, vulnerable, and unprotected, a warrior who had reached the end of her reserves. Lily needed him, and a fierce excitement raced through him as he started forward to retrieve her—

A squeal of terror ripped from her, and panic flared in those beautiful eyes as she scrambled back.

Gideon stopped instantly, viscerally aware of her fear and recognizing instantly that she was going to flee. He could feel it in his chest, in his mind, and in every fiber of his being. Her terror was so intense, almost overwhelming, shocking him for a moment. His mentor, Dante Sinclair, had taught Gideon long ago to turn off his empathic abilities. It was so automatic he hadn't thought of it in centuries.

Until now.

Until every breath of pain, fear and torment Lily was feeling bore into him like the dark twisting of an ominous storm, raging through him, threatening his control—

He shut it down. Just shut the damn thing down. Cut off all his emotions, and severed his connection to hers, swiftly reclaiming the calm, focused state that he lived by, the one so necessary for him to do his job.

Still sweating from the sudden onslaught of emotion, Gideon focused on the woman before him and he searched for the words she needed to hear to ease her fear. He wasn't soft. He wasn't gentle. He wasn't kind. His dominant mode of operation would be to haul ass over to Lily, toss her over his shoulder and break like hell for freedom, regardless of how terrified she was. Comfort and gentleness had no place in battle.

But he made no move to lunge for her. Instead, for reasons he couldn't fathom, he stayed right where he was, refusing to inflict any more terror onto those heavily weighted shoulders. "Lily," he said quietly, his voice soothing and gentle. "You can trust me."

Her eyes widened. "No."

*No.* He was shocked by the first sound of her voice. It was like the most beautiful spring breeze, caressing his skin. Musical, as if dozens of tiny bells had taken flight when she'd spoken. Her voice was rich and full, laden with emotion, with pain, and with the vibrations of a female who lived and breathed with more passion than Gideon had felt in centuries. It burst through him, right to his gut, thrusting into him like a fierce stab of passion and desire.

He became truly aware of her in that moment. He saw the tiny pulse hammering at the base of her throat. He noticed the swell of her breasts beneath her tattered blouse. He felt the rush of desire emanating from her, like a raging tide of passion. Her cheeks flushed with need, her gaze riveted to his as her sensual reaction to him crashed past his shields, flooding him with the intensity of the emotions consuming them both. His body responded instantly, shockingly and he swore.

Lust? Now? In the middle of battle, when Lily was barely hanging on, broken and battered? What the hell was wrong with him? He was here to do a job, to rescue Lily. Nothing else.

It was time to focus. It was time to be the warrior he'd sworn he would be.

Not the sensual, lustful male pulsating with hot desire that made him want to haul her against him and consume her until they were both too sated to move.

Yeah, he definitely didn't have time to be that guy, but damn, it was tempting as all hell. And then some.

❧ ❧ ❧

"It's time to go. Now," Gideon said firmly, his hand tight around the handle of his axe.

Go? With him? Fierce longing flooded Lily, chased by the icy chill of real terror. Dear God, what was wrong with her? Why was she responding to him like that?

She forced herself to shake her head, her legs trembling as she willed herself to keep moving away from him, even though every instinct she had was screaming to run to him and take all that he offered, and more. "I'm fine here, thanks, now that I'm out of the basement. You go do your thing and I'll call a cab."

Gideon's jaw tightened, and she thought for a second he was going to simply grab her. She froze, awareness flooding her body at the idea of his hands on her. It was a dark, sensual awareness that terrified her.

When he didn't move for her, relief and dismay warred ruthlessly inside her, intense emotions fighting to be heard.

"Ana told us you were here," he said, his deep voice wrapping around her like strong arms and hot flesh.

"Ana?" Lily paused in her retreat, her mind whirling as she tried to make sense of what he'd just said. "*She's alive?*" Her mind flashed back to the woman who'd been imprisoned with her. She recalled with vivid clarity all the gashes on Ana's body, and the fierce fire in Ana's silver eyes when the two women had plotted Ana's escape, a desperate attempt that had been their last chance before Nate and Frank could kill them both. "She got away? Is she okay? Is she hurt?"

Gideon nodded, his blue eyes softening at her barrage of questions. "We retrieved her. She's safe."

"Safe." The word taunted Lily, laughed at her. God, she wanted to feel safe again. Just for a day. For an hour. For even a minute. *Gideon will keep you safe.* She winced at the unbidden thought, at the desire raging within her for him.

She forced herself to meet his probing gaze, stunned by how utterly cold it was. For a brief moment, she thought she'd seen fire simmering in his deep blue eyes, intense passion that had awakened an answering response in her. But the heated desire was gone now, replaced by the impersonal visage of a warrior on a mission.

Had she imagined it? Had she been so desperate for some kind of humanity that she'd created feeling and fire in this emotionless warrior? Or had it been there? Was he really both, stirring hot desire and icy cold fear deep inside her?

She shook her head, trying to clear thoughts that made no sense. She knew what Calydons were like. She knew how dangerous they were in general, but especially to her. Oh, how terrifyingly dangerous to her, specifically. "Safe is an illusion." She met his gaze. "No one is safe with a Calydon. Not even if that Calydon is you."

Frank knew she'd be worried about Ana. Frank would know that the best way to get her acquiescence would be to pretend Ana had sent the warriors. The fact that Gideon knew to use Ana's name with her didn't mean he was really on her side.

Lily couldn't be a fool. She had to count on herself. No one else. She couldn't trust anyone, especially not a Calydon who had somehow awakened the sensual side of her that she tried so hard to hide from his kind.

A muscle ticked in his cheek, and she saw a silent acknowledgement in his eyes, that she'd struck upon a truth he hated. A truth he couldn't deny, that no one was safe from him.

The glimpse into his vulnerability broke through her walls, and she suddenly wanted to cry for this warrior who could do no more than let out the merest flicker of humanity. Emotions crashed through her, too much to hold back after all she'd been through. She was losing control, losing sanity, losing everything. She steeled herself against the need to fall to her knees and offer herself into his protection, to show him that she trusted him, to heal him... God. Heal *him*? What was *wrong* with her?

She needed to focus and stay firm in her goal to escape, even from him. She was almost to the kitchen door, almost close enough to slide inside...

His gaze flicked to the doorframe she was reaching for, and he shifted slightly, readying himself to grab her if she bolted.

Fear and desperation made her eyes burn. She would never get away from him. He would be too quick, too strong, and too determined. Freedom, so close, was nothing but an illusion. Her heart began to hammer again, panic setting in. Nowhere to go. Nowhere to hide.

"Lily," Gideon interjected, warmth rolling through his words. His brow was furrowed in concern, as if he could sense the panic closing in on her. "Ana said you told her about the stone. She said you could read the writing on it."

Lily paused at his comment, searching his face for the truth. "She did?" Lily *had* told Ana about Nate's stone, and no one else had been present when she'd done so. She'd never believe Ana was weak enough to tell tales to people she didn't trust. Disbelieving hope flickered through her. Was Gideon telling the truth? Was he really here to rescue her?

She couldn't believe it. After two years of praying for freedom, life was playing a cruel trick, teasing her with illusions of liberation. "No—"

"Yes." His voice was urgent, and he took a step toward her. "You can trust me, Lily. Ana told us where to find you." He laughed softly. "She almost took my damned head off, demanding that I rescue you. She chose me to come get you. You think she'd send someone she didn't trust?"

Lily's steely resolve faltered. His description fit Ana and how Lily would have expected her to behave, ordering Gideon to retrieve her. Was it true? Was he truly here to rescue her? To keep her safe? Was he the one Calydon she could actually trust, at least for now, for this moment, until she could get home?

Lily's defenses began to crumble and exhaustion pressed at her. She leaned her head back against the wall, too tired to hold it up any longer. "You're really not here to hurt me?"

"I'm not here to hurt you." He started walking toward

her, ever so slowly, like he was afraid to spook her.

She noticed his approach, but she was too tired to flee. Too fatigued to fight her need for him, her desire to have him fold her into those heavily muscled arms, to let him chase the nightmares away with passion that would make her body come alive in ways she'd never dared try. She wanted Gideon, craved all he could give her, and she could no longer summon up the strength to resist her need for him. Her instincts told her to trust him, to turn to him for help, and she simply didn't have the will to fight any longer.

The strategic, logical mind that had kept her going for the last two years faded, leaving her with nothing more than the basic human need to be taken care of. She couldn't talk herself out of trusting Gideon. She couldn't muster the energy to assemble the facts and analyze them. All she could do was accept her trust for him, her need to stop fighting and let him help her, to simply let go.

Lily watched him approach, using all her energy to hold herself vertical, her body prickling with awareness as he neared. *Lily. He's too dangerous to you. Resist him.* "No closer," she mumbled, fighting to find the strength that had kept her alive for so long. She couldn't trust him. She knew she couldn't. Even this amazing, powerful warrior who stirred things in her she hadn't felt in so long. "Don't touch me."

Fierce possessiveness glittered in his blue eyes, like hot sparks of lightning igniting a centuries-old instinct in him. "You're under my protection now, Lily. No one's getting another crack at you."

"Your protection? Meaning what?" God, she was so exhausted. Her feet hurt. All the cuts from the glass pricked at her. So tempting to just sit down. To let him take over.

*Stop it, Lily. You're stronger than this. You know better than to turn yourself over to someone else.*

She pulled herself straighter, her body trembling with the effort. Anger flashed in Gideon's eyes, anger that struck deep in her heart in the most beautiful way. It warmed her, because she realized it was anger on her behalf, fury at Nate for what he'd done to her. It was the same anger that she'd channeled for the last two years to keep herself from giving up. Her own emotions, reflected on the face of this handsome stranger. A man outraged by what had been done to her. A powerful warrior who was on her side.

There was a sudden howl of rage outside, and she flinched, fear ricocheting through her. "There are more out there," she gasped. "Who else is here?"

"It's a whole party, sweetheart. You're one popular woman." Gideon studied the wall, his brow furrowed as if he could see right through it. Then he cursed. "You stay here. I'll be back for you." Then he slammed his shoulder into the wall and plaster went flying as he burst through it and raced out into the night.

*I'll be back for you.*

They were the same words Frank had spat at her when he'd left, words that had filled Lily with terror, desperation and the foreboding of a terrible death.

But with Gideon making the same promise, Lily just felt vast relief. He would be back for her. To rescue her. To bring her to Ana. To freedom.

Lily leaned against the wall as Gideon loped out into the night, his muscles rippling with a lithe grace. Then she saw one of Frank's Calydons charge up behind Gideon, moving too fast for her to scream a warning—

Gideon whirled around and sank his axe into his attacker's gut. The warrior dropped to the ground, dead. Two more Calydons approached. They circled Gideon to try to distract him, then she saw one of them glance in her direction.

The warrior caught her gaze for a moment, then he jerked his head toward her and charged Gideon. The instant Gideon turned toward him, the Calydon's partner sidestepped the skirmish and bolted toward Lily, his knives clenched in his hand, deadly intention etched in the hard lines of his face.

"Oh, crap!" She whirled around but he tackled her before she could even take a step, slamming her to the floor, pinning her beneath his massive body. He was instant dead weight on her. She struggled out from under him, her pulse hammering frantically as he lay inertly on top of her. She wiggled free and looked down at the back of his neck in time to see a double-sided axe work itself free and whip through the air back to Gideon's palm.

Gideon had saved her. Again.

Gideon gave her a quick wink, as if slaughtering attackers was everyday business, which she knew it was for a man like him. Then he spun around to take on more assailants.

Her stomach retched at the thought that a man had died on top of her, then a scream of death jerked her attention back out to the battle again. Gideon and another Calydon were back to back, defending against dozens of Calydons. There was no way Gideon and his teammate could win against such odds.

Frank's warriors would kill Gideon.

For a split second, Lily felt such an unexplainable heart-wrenching grief for Gideon's death that her legs actually gave out and she fell to her knees, gasping for air. Her hands went to her throat as bile churned in her belly. Her body shook violently as the devastating image of Gideon's death loomed in her mind and she pressed her hands to her head, gasping as she fought to keep herself from falling apart.

*God, Lily! Get it together!* She threw up emotional barriers against the pain. Staggering, she wrenched herself to her feet, taking one last glance at Gideon as he fought, his muscles bulging and blood running down his arm. His face was tight, coiled with deadly purpose as he took down another warrior, not even flinching as he claimed another life.

"This is your truth," she whispered to herself as she watched Gideon and his partner in their lethal battle. "He isn't safety. He isn't some passionate lover who will heal your scars. He's death, destruction and violence, as all Calydons are."

Blood sprayed as bodies fell, the death screams hammering at her as the warriors succumbed to Gideon's blade. He spared her no glance as he turned on another assailant. He was a warrior utterly focused on one goal, one mission. There was no mercy in him. Lily knew his passion would be nothing more than the typical all-consuming lust of his kind, sweeping any and all women under its spell. No tenderness, no emotion... with Gideon, there would be no safe place.

Lily knew that. She'd known that, and yet she'd somehow still responded to him.

Damn her and her foolishness. She knew better than

that!

Lily ratcheted her emotions back under control, forcing herself to turn away as his blade fell once again. If Gideon was killed—she stumbled at the idea before she caught herself—there would be no one to protect her from Frank's retrieval team. *Run, Lily. This is your chance.*

She spun back toward the hallway and sprinted into the kitchen, barely able to breathe through the tightness in her chest at her fear of what was happening to Gideon outside. Damn him! She didn't even know him! How could he affect her like this already?

It was because he'd saved her from a fate worse than death from both Calydons. They hadn't been planning to kill her. They'd been planning worse, so much worse, but Gideon had stood by her. He'd given her the first offer of protection she'd had in so long. He was her first breath of hope. How could that gesture not overwhelm her? It had been too long, too arduous, and too heartbreaking, her wait for freedom, for kindness, for someone to hold her hand and show her she didn't have to fight on her own.

It made sense, her reaction to Gideon, and she accepted her feelings as logical, not indicators of something more dangerous. *Please don't die, Gideon. I owe you my life.*

Able to focus on her escape now that she understood her intense attraction to Gideon, Lily grabbed the hammer from its place under the sink, and slammed it into the lock on the drawer next to the fridge.

The lock stayed intact.

Lily swung again, and still it didn't break.

She jumped at a loud crash from outside, the hammer sliding out of her trembling grip. She lurched for it, wrapped her fingers around it, and *swung.* "Come on!" She slammed the hammer down as hard as she could, and the metal lock snapped. *Dear God, thank you.*

Lily threw the hammer aside, ripped the broken lock off and tossed it. The metal lock clanged as it bounced on the tile floor, and she yanked open the drawer, nearly sobbing with relief when she saw the keys exactly where they were supposed to be. She grabbed the set of keys with the Hummer keychain, her hand shaking so badly the keys slipped free and landed on the tile floor with a clatter. She swept them up then bolted across the kitchen. Her fist clenched around the cold keys, she fumbled with the deadbolt to the garage, unable to get it open. "Focus, Lily!"

She forced herself to slow down enough to concentrate, and this time she got the deadbolt to turn. She jerked the door open, holding her breath that Nate's pride and joy would still be there, the vehicle he would never soil by taking it on his murder runs and staining the interior with the blood from each attack.

It took a moment for her eyes to adjust to the dark, but she didn't dare turn on a light. After an interminable pause huddled by the door, she finally saw the sheen on its black paint and the outline of the huge SUV, and tears pricked her eyes.

*It was there.* All her years of planning, believing that someday she would have this chance, it was really happening.

Lily ran down the four steps into the garage, sprinted across the three empty parking spots and pressed the button on the remote to unlock the Hummer. She flinched as the beep seemed to bounce off the walls and ceilings of the garage, horrifyingly loud. Any Calydon within five hundred yards would have heard it, if he were listening.

She hoped they were too distracted by the fight to notice, too occupied by their battle with Gideon.

Sudden grief consumed her, terror for what was happening to Gideon outside, and she screamed in frustration at the way he was affecting her. "Come on, Lily! You can't afford to fail!"

There was a roar and the clash of metal on metal from outside, and she scrambled up into the truck, praying no Calydon would come rushing through the garage doors for her.

Her hands were shaking so much she missed the ignition with the key twice, then she stopped and closed her eyes. "Calm down, Lily. You can do this."

When she opened her eyes this time, she shoved the key directly into the ignition. She yanked her seatbelt on and whispered a prayer, knowing that once she turned the truck on, they would come running for her.

She located the garage door opener incorporated into

the visor. She poised her left index finger over it while she tightened her grip on the ignition key, getting everything ready before she took action that would alert the warriors outside. She wiped her forearm over her brow. The cuts on her arm burned as the sweat stung her skin.

Emergency brake off, she knew where the gearshift was...she was ready.

She took a deep breath and started the truck. The engine rumbled to life with a ferociously loud roar. She hit the button to open the garage door, then slammed the truck into reverse and floored it.

The truck smashed through the half-open garage door, and she winced as the truck slammed into two Calydons who were running straight at the doors when she burst through, splintered boards flying. The truck lurched as the tires bounced over the warriors, and she stared in horror as they appeared on the ground in front of her, lit up by her headlights, men that she'd run over.

Then one of them lifted his head and rolled to his feet, barely staggering.

"Oh, *shit*." She shifted the truck into drive and jammed her foot onto the accelerator. The tires spun frantically in the sandy drive as she peeled through the mass of warriors. She jumped as they came at her, wincing when each warrior bounced off her truck as she barreled through them.

Grunts of pain rang in her ears, and she felt the truck shudder from the collisions. Oh, God. Was she killing them?

A machete flew at the windshield directly toward her face, and she screamed, ducking down—

Gideon's throwing axe smashed into the machete and both weapons crashed onto the hood of the truck. She stared in disbelief as the two weapons sat harmlessly on the hood for a split second. He'd saved her again.

Both weapons flew up into the air and disappeared into the night, summoned by their owners for another attack.

"Go, Lily!" She clutched the steering wheel as she barreled down the gritty driveway, flinching at each clash and bump as weapons slammed into the truck.

The back window shattered. She ducked as glass

fragments flew everywhere, but she forced herself to keep the gas pedal floored, to stay focused on the winding driveway. The truck skidded around a corner, and she sucked in her breath as she felt the right wheels come up off the ground.

Lily jerked her foot off the accelerator and the truck dropped back down on all four tires. She hit the accelerator again, and nearly cried with relief when she finally reached the main road. She took a hard right and sped out onto the two-lane highway, the sounds of battle finally beginning to fade in the night as she retraced the path she'd taken two years ago when she'd walked into Nate's house and changed her life forever.

# Chapter 3

Gideon grinned with satisfaction as he watched Lily's Hummer disappear down the driveway. She'd blown off his orders to wait for him, and he was damned impressed with that fact.

She'd decided to save herself, using Gideon for cover while she escaped. She'd done it well, and he had to admit, he admired the fact she'd taken charge of her own destiny. Yeah, he'd be catching up with her as soon as he and Ian had finished taking out the rest of the crew and making sure no one would follow them, but he was still impressed.

He tracked her vehicle carefully as she sped down the road, making sure she got away safely as he instinctively blocked another assailant going for his head. He was well aware of how broken she was. He'd felt her pain, her anguish, her terror. The extent of her exhaustion had been evident in every breath she took, in the trembling of her body and the weariness of her eyes, and yet she'd hauled ass out to that damn truck anyway.

She shouldn't have had to do that. It was his job to take care of her. Gideon's smile faded as he recalled the intensity of her pain in that hallway. Her fear of him. Her refusal to trust him.

Anger began to build inside him. How much had she suffered? He'd seen how bad Ana's condition had been when they'd retrieved her. What had Nate done to Lily? A fierce fury built inside him, intense anger that had no place in a battle that required a cool, controlled warrior.

But he couldn't help it. He was royally pissed.

Gideon hurled his axe at a warrior coming at Ian from behind, and tried to evaluate his burning need to protect Lily. He needed to understand why he'd responded to her physically, with so much intensity. He'd been so far from all-business in that hallway, it was an embarrassment. He had one job. One goal. One promise to keep, and that was to fulfill Order business every damn time.

It was not to look at a woman and imagine how silky soft her skin would be, to envision what it would be like to feel her body against his, to hear her whisper his name with trust. Shit, just the thought of her now, and he was already getting worked up. What the hell was wrong with him?

Gideon caught a glimpse of movement out of the corner of his eye and spun to the right as two Calydons broke from the battle and sprinted down the driveway after Lily's Hummer, so fast they were mere blurs even to his enhanced eyes.

Adrenaline leapt into high gear. Fuck. They were Runners. They'd be able to catch up to Lily's truck, and fast. All amusement gone, Gideon hurled both his axes after them. One axe slammed into the back of the Calydon on the right with the deadly precision of an Order of the Blade warrior, knocking him down. But the other warrior blocked the axe with his machete and then disappeared into the night, a dark streak hunting the woman Gideon had come to retrieve.

Son of a bitch. *He'd missed.* How the hell had he missed? He never missed. But he had, and now the bastard was on Lily's tail. What the fuck? "Ian! We're going after her!"

"I saw him." Ian swung his flange mace with fierce intensity, taking out a Calydon charging Gideon. "Let's go."

Gideon's axes returned to him, and he sprinted for his truck, oblivious to the battle raging around him. All he could think of was Lily in that Hummer, alone in the middle of fucking nowhere, and that bastard finding her. Gideon swore and yanked open the door, leaping behind the wheel as a dagger flew at him. He swung at it with violent force, driving it to the ground as he gunned the engine. He had the truck in gear and moving before his door was even closed.

Ian leapt in as Gideon peeled past him. The tires spun

out on the sandy driveway, then they caught traction. The vehicle leapt forward, leaving behind the eight remaining Calydons who were still alive.

It was against Order protocol to leave a situation unmanaged like they were doing right now. They needed to break down those attackers, find out who they were, and why they were after Lily. Proper strategy would entail taking another five minutes to secure the situation before going after Lily. They were not following protocol, and they both knew it.

But Lily was too important. They needed her too badly to let her go.

They needed her for the mission, yeah.

But as dark tension fueled Gideon's pursuit, he knew it was more.

Much, much more.

He just fucking needed her.

❦ ❦ ❦

Lily tensed as the Hummer skidded around a corner and the rear slid out, sending the front end straight toward the ditch.

She hauled the steering wheel to the left as her right tires careened down the incline. The truck bounced back up on the road and shot across the lanes from her overcorrection. She jerked the wheel back to the right, slamming on the brakes as the truck swerved back across the road and skidded toward the embankment. She clenched the steering wheel desperately as the truck slid down the ditch. "Come on!" she shouted. "Stop!"

The truck skidded to a stop, partway into the gully.

For a moment, she didn't move, didn't breathe, didn't blink, terrified the earth would give out and the truck would fall the rest of the way into the ditch. The only sounds in the truck were her panicked breathing and the thundering of her heart.

It took a full minute before she finally realized the Hummer had stopped. It was over. She hadn't crashed. "Oh, God." She shoved the gearshift into park, her body shaking so badly she could barely make the lever move. "It's okay, Lily. You're okay."

She draped her arms over the steering wheel and

dropped her forehead to the cool leather, trying to catch her breath. But it was too much.

The two years of despair and hopelessness that she'd kept locked up for so long broke free. The fear, the terror, the loneliness, she couldn't hold it off anymore. It welled up and burst out, like a dark night of doom and loss crushing down on her. Gone was her strength, her courage, her rigid control.

Emotions consumed her, stripping away her defenses, piercing her with an intensity she didn't have the resources to fight off anymore. Lily moaned and pressed her palms to her eyes, rocking back and forth as the sobs shattered her defenses. For two years, she'd never cried, and now that it was over, she couldn't stop. She cried for all that she'd lost, for all that she'd suffered, but most of all, she cried for how scared she'd been for so long. The relief was overwhelming. After holding on so tight, she didn't have to do it anymore.

It was over.

But even as those words she'd been dreaming of for so long filled her mind, denial flooded her with cold warning.

It wasn't over. She wasn't safe yet. She had to pull herself together again. No sobbing. No crying. The time for that would be later.

Lily scrunched her eyes shut and took a shuddering breath, willing the loneliness, the fear and the uncertainty back into the box she'd kept it in for the last two years. "Only a little longer," she whispered. "Just keep it together a little longer." She fought to find that strong woman she'd been, but it was so hard to go back there.

She didn't want to be strong. She didn't want to be brave. She just wanted to cry.

Lily lifted her head and took another breath, this one less shaky than the last. Her throat thick with emotion, she peered out at the dark night. A sliver of moonlight danced in the black sky, thousands of stars sparkled across the horizon, and hundreds of miles of barren Oregon high desert stretched in all directions.

She was stunned by the vastness of the sky and the endless expanse of earth. No fences. No walls. No constraints. Just space to run as far and as long as a person could go. She'd forgotten what it was like to stand outside the walls and breathe in the wildness of nature. It had been so long since she'd had the choice of when to eat, when to sleep, and when to wake.

Inhaling the clean air into her starved lungs, Lily rolled down the windows. She closed her eyes as the cold desert breeze tickled her face, sweeping across her skin as if it were wiping away all the sweat, grime and fear. Fresh air. Owned by no one. At liberty to fly wherever it wanted.

This was what freedom felt like. This was what she'd craved so desperately for so long. Yes, she'd missed her family. She'd longed for her home, her career, and her books. But more than anything, Lily had burned for the simple ability to choose for herself.

And here she was. Sitting here. Enjoying the desert air. Simply being.

It was a gift.

Something moved in the bushes, and Lily jumped when a shadow darted across the road. Its striped tail dragged as the furry creature waddled across the asphalt, pausing to study her with its little masked face. Lily groaned softly and leaned back against the headrest, trying to calm down. "Okay, Lily. Chill out. It's just a raccoon." Not a Calydon, ready to drag her back into hell. Not yet, at least, but she knew they were coming.

There was no safety here. She was less than twenty minutes from Nate's. Not far enough. She still had to get over the mountains and back to western Oregon. More than eight hours from home.

Until she was home, until she was truly safe, it wouldn't be over.

Then grim reality began to set in. Would she even be safe at home, or would Frank find her there? Would she ever be safe again, or would this nightmare haunt her forever? How would she know when she was free?

Exhaustion crept over her again, and suddenly Lily felt like it was too much effort to pick herself up and slog onward. She had so little energy left to fight with. So little chance by herself. Maybe she shouldn't have left Gideon. Maybe she would have been better off trusting he would survive—

A gaping loneliness swelled up inside her at the thought

of Gideon dying in that battle, and she fisted her hands on the steering wheel, dragging her thoughts away from the warrior who'd unsettled her so badly. "Come on, Lily. You have to pull yourself together. You can do this. Just take it one step at a time. Drive the truck. That's all you have to do right now. You can do that."

Yes, she could do that. That much she could manage.

Lily wiped her sleeve resolutely across her damp cheeks, and winced at the sharp pain. Her whole body started to hurt, pain shooting through her. She realized that she still had glass in her back, hands and feet. Adrenaline had kept the pain at bay, but now... God, it was excruciating.

"Get over it, Lily," she ordered herself.

It was no worse than anything Nate had done to her. She could handle it. It was almost better that way, to be reminded about how bad everything would be if she didn't keep it together. A little glass in the back was such a helpful kick-in-the-pants. Thank goodness for small favors, right?

Right.

Rolling her eyes at herself, but feeling stronger now, Lily sat up straighter to keep her back from touching the seat. She shifted the truck into drive again and started to pull forward, the tires spinning as they tried to fight their way out of the muddy ditch. Her heart tightened, but she clenched her jaw and she shifted into four-wheel drive. She rocked the truck back and forth, then the tires found solid ground and the Hummer popped up out of the ditch with a lurch.

Tears of relief pricked Lily's eyes, and she pulled out onto the road, forcing herself to keep to a safe speed.

There was no way she was going to crash the damn truck and make it easy for them.

She simply wasn't that agreeable of a person.

❦ ❦ ❦

Gideon's truck catapulted down the driveway, his body coiled with rage at the thought of the Calydon finding Lily.

The image of that Calydon pinning Lily to the floor kept racing through his mind. The look on his face...fuck. Gideon knew what that look was. He'd seen it on the faces of too many

Calydons when they'd gone rogue, when Gideon had pulled the battered and bloody body of the innocent out from under them, too late yet again.

Rogue Calydons were warriors who had, at one point, been men of honor. Then they'd succumbed to the darkness that pulsed in all Calydons, reduced to beasts who destroyed the innocents they'd been born to protect. If Gideon had arrived a minute later, Lily would have been just like those other innocents, and now she was unprotected again. "Fuck!"

Ian was perched on the edge of his seat, a flange mace clenched in each hand. He was ready and burning for action. The three-foot long steel staff was ringed with a spiked ridge on the end. The weapons were humming with energy, primed for their owner to set them free against the enemy. "Try not to crash the truck. I just got it waxed."

"Fuck off." Gideon didn't question his raging terror at the thought of that Calydon finding Lily. He'd didn't waste time trying to understand his driving need to get to her, a compulsion far deeper and more powerful than the mission that had brought him and Ian in search of her. Gideon simply knew, without question, that he *had* to reach her in time.

There was no other option. *Do whatever you have to do to stay alive until I get there, Lily.* He shouted the words in his mind as the truck peeled out of the driveway and he opened it up on the main road, somehow knowing, with absolute certainty, which way she'd gone.

⚜ ⚜ ⚜

Lily rounded a corner and yelped when she saw a dark shape looming in front of her in the middle of the road. A man? She slammed on the brakes, then saw the moonlight glint off a blade in his hand.

It was a machete. The same machete that would have taken her out if Gideon's axe hadn't intercepted it. He'd beaten her here. He'd come to take her back to Frank.

Terror screamed through her at the thought of going back to that hell after being so close to escaping. No, she couldn't. She couldn't do it. She hadn't come this far to lose her chance for freedom now.

Before she could register what she was doing, she jerked her foot off the brake and gunned the gas, the truck skidding as she tried to straighten it out, aiming right for the Calydon. Her mind recoiled in horror as she bore down on him, but she couldn't make herself stop. It was as if something else was compelling her, her need to survive driving her to do something out of her own worst nightmares, as if she'd finally snapped. As if Nate had finally turned her into the demon he was. "God, no, don't let me kill him."

Her fingers clenched on the wheel, she stared at her target, horror rising in her throat at what she was about to do. Then he shifted into a ready stance, and too late, she realized she was doing exactly what he wanted.

The truck careened across the road as she tried to swerve away from him. She was going too fast to redirect! He sprang onto the hood and smashed his machete through the windshield.

She screamed and slammed on the brakes, but he grabbed the frame as the truck spun out. Then the tires caught and the Hummer flipped, sailing through the air. It landed on its roof with an agonizing impact that whipped her head back and skidded across the asphalt as the earsplitting shriek of metal being ripped apart rent the night.

Hanging upside down in the inverted truck, Lily fumbled with the seatbelt, her numb fingers struggling to push the release button. "Come on!" How close was he? Was he still on the truck? Had he been thrown off? The scenery was spinning too fast as the truck whirled. She was dizzy, disoriented, and nauseous. She squeezed her eyes shut, trying to regain her equilibrium as she frantically worked on the seatbelt.

She found the button and jammed her thumb into it, the truck still screaming its protest as it spun across the road on its roof toward the ditch. The seatbelt released with sudden force and Lily dropped out of the seat, thudding onto her shoulders, her feet tangled in the steering wheel. Frantically, she tried to free herself. She had to hurry. She knew he was still out there. *Please, God, give me time to get away.*

With a fierce kick that sent pain spiraling through her knee, Lily finally got her feet free. She hastily rolled to her knees and hunched low to peer out the windshield, searching desperately for her assailant. The trees were rushing past, the white lines on the pavement whipping like undulating snakes, sparks leaping off the road as the truck tore its way across the asphalt. There was no way she could get out while it was still moving. Damn it! Where was he?

She peered up toward the front bumper, trying to see him. There was a shadow near the right headlight. His foot? She leaned closer, straining to identify it—

He swung down from the left front wheel, hanging by one arm, inches away from her, like a beast sprung from the night, his teeth gleaming in the darkness. His eyes met hers, and for a split second, she was overwhelmed by the ruthless promise in his dark eyes. They were the windows into the soul of hell, a bottomless pit of violence and death, without morals, ethics or humanity. He wasn't rogue. He was simply a monster. And he was after her.

"Crap!" She jerked back.

He lunged for her, springing off his perch with terrifying ease. His fingers latched around her wrist with violent force and he yanked, jerking her through the shattered windshield.

"No!" She grabbed for the steering wheel, but her fingers slipped uselessly off the slick leather as he dragged her out of the truck.

He tossed her away from the spinning vehicle. She sailed through the air and landed with agonizing force on the pavement. The asphalt tore at her skin as she slid across it, her bones thudding against the hard ground as momentum flung her across the road.

The Calydon landed beside her, grabbed her arm and jerked her to a brutal stop. She gasped, but he gave her no respite, hauling her to her feet immediately.

He grabbed her shoulders, holding her ruthlessly as if she were nothing but a puppet. His cheekbones were high and fine, his hair short, his black pullover made of finely woven wool. He was clean-shaven, not a scar to behold, and the white collar of a starched dress shirt peeked above the V-neck of his sweater. Except for the gritty determination in his eyes and the sheer size of him, he looked like a man who should be spending his time with a bourbon and a stock report, not streaking through a midnight desert, chasing down Hummers and innocent women. What in God's name was he doing working for Frank? "Why?" she blurted out. "Why are you after me? I didn't do anything."

Something flickered in his eyes. For a split second, she thought she saw a flash of humanity, the agony of a man torn by his conscience. Hope leapt through her. "Release me," she urged. "Please!"

"Never." And just as quickly, the assassin was back. His eyes were a bottomless black. Not rogue, but violent and deadly, a merciless willingness to do whatever was needed. Whatever humanity had been trying to surface had been denied.

He grabbed her around the waist and she realized he was going to pick her up and cart her away into the night like some chattel to be disposed of as Frank saw fit.

"No!" She slammed her fist into his throat as she scrambled away from him.

He swore, and she saw in his eyes a promise of hell.

He held out his right arm. She saw the black brand of his kind on his forearm, in the shape of his weapon. The machete glowed for a split second, then there was a flash of black light and an explosive crack. The machete appeared in his hand, a stainless steel weapon that he'd called out of the brand into reality.

"Oh, crap." She could see in his eyes that he was going to use it on her. Anything to make her behave. Panic rifled through her, and she leapt backward.

He smiled as she stumbled, the face of a predator who was enjoying watching his prey try to flee, knowing he could stop her at any second.

It couldn't end like this. So close to freedom, only to fail like this. God, she couldn't go back into captivity. She couldn't do it again. She couldn't—

He grabbed for her and she dove out of the way. He caught her ankle and she kicked at him, her bare feet useless against his hard body. She twisted frantically, her ankle rotating in his hand, but she knew it was too little, too late—

His head jerked up and he stared down the road. Taking advantage of his distraction, Lily yanked herself free and sprinted behind the Hummer as he scented the air. He cursed, and then spun toward her.

She froze as he crouched, ready to launch himself at her.

He looked down the road again, then back at her. What did he sense? What was coming?

He took a step toward her, then swore again, spun around and bolted up into the sand hills, so fast he was nothing but a blur.

The night swallowed him instantly, leaving her alone on the dark road. Gone? He'd really left? He hadn't taken her?

She stared blankly after him, trying to regroup, trying to comprehend that he'd simply left her there. Something had scared him. A threat. What was it?

Chills raced down her spine and she lunged for the driver's door before she remembered the vehicle's state. Her only way home: upside down, the roof half-torn off, its tires spinning aimlessly. The beams from the headlights were pointing haphazardly across the deep grooves the SUV had carved into the road.

No way home. No way to safety. No more choices.

Tears pricked at the back of her eyes, and she stared at it, watching the expensive hubcaps whirring. Her head ached, her vision blurred, and she realized how completely screwed she was. *I can't take this anymore. I can't.*

Then she heard the rumble of an engine. She turned and saw headlights lighting up the night as a car raced toward her. She realized the Calydon had heard the car coming, and that's why he'd bailed: because the occupants of the car had scared him off. She stared into the approaching headlights, and suddenly knew who was in the vehicle. *Gideon.* Just the thought of him made desire and fear thrum through her, nearly staggering in its intensity.

She needed to run. To hide. To get away.

But something deep inside her told her she didn't need to run anymore. Not now.

She fought against it, tried to order her body to flee, but her legs gave out and she sank to the road as the truck peeled around the corner. She flinched as brakes squealed and the truck spun wildly, but the driver managed to keep the enormous black pickup from flipping. It finally skidded to a stop inches from the overturned Hummer. Gideon leapt out of the truck and raced toward her, his face raw with fury that should have terrified her.

But it didn't. She was simply too depleted to fear him, too weary to overcome her need to stop fighting and put her well-being in someone else's hands.

"No." She summoned up all her willpower and held up an exhausted hand as he neared her. "Don't touch me."

He hesitated at whatever he saw on her face, and for a moment, she thought she'd won. He wasn't going to help.

Then she suddenly was overwhelmed with such grief and despair that she doubled over, her arms wrapped around her belly, and she knew then that she'd finally lost the battle.

# Chapter 4

Gideon swore as Lily let out a soft moan that blistered his core. Her head was bowed so low that her tangled hair was draped on the asphalt. She hugged herself as she rocked back and forth, trying to hold in the low moans of distress. The white cotton of her blouse was streaked with blood, and fresh rage coiled through Gideon at the sight of her distress. He wanted to scoop her off the ground and into his arms, but he'd seen her fear as he'd approached, and knew instinctively that grabbing her wasn't an option. Not with her, not now.

Instead, he kneeled in front of her and bent his head so his cheek was right next to hers. "Lily." He kept his voice as soothing as he could, having never tried to be soothing in his life. "I won't hurt you."

Gideon was aware of Ian moving around him, searching for signs that the Calydon had been there, but he didn't look up. He was too consumed with the woman in front of him, desperate to ease her pain. "Lily," he repeated. "Nate's dead. It's over."

A strangled sob escaped. "He's really dead? Truly? I can go *home?*"

"Yes." Fuck. The anguish in her voice tore at him. He felt her pain in every cell of his body, in each breath, and in the very beat of his heart. He was so accustomed to feeling no emotions and never setting roots. He was simply a shadow, slipping through life but never connecting. Emotions were destructive. They caused chaos at best, and death at worst. He knew that.

He'd been there. And he'd learned. As an empath, he'd had to shut down not only his ability to sense other's emotions, but also his own. There was no way to do his job and feel, and he had to do his job.

Gideon was used to living in a precise, controlled void, but Lily was delving right past his shields. He could feel every agony within her, every torment she'd suffered, every vulnerability. It was like this miasma of bright colors flooding his senses, and he couldn't stop it. It was as if he'd come alive, truly alive, for the first time ever, and it shocked him. It felt brilliant, and at the same time, violently dangerous and out of control.

Gideon knew he had to pull it back, to get her out of his body, to reclaim his steady state, but he couldn't. Not with her beautiful, earthy scent drifting through him, her slim shoulders trembling so violently, and her heart beating so wildly to survive. Instead, he instinctively accepted her turbulence and sent out his own calming energy. He gave her his strength, his power, and his confidence that he could handle anything.

"Lily," he said softly. He didn't know how to comfort her. He'd never tried to offer support. He'd never been comforted. It made no sense in his world. To need comfort or offer it was weakness and vulnerability in a world held firm with protocol and duty. And yet, he had to do it. Now. For her.

Gideon grasped her shoulders, intending to support her, but the contact shocked him. It was like an electric spark leaping from her body to his. Lily sucked in her breath and she stared at him in shock. Her skin was hot, so decadently soft, so feminine and alive beneath his hands.

Her eyes widened, and he felt her sudden flush of desire. It was the same crash of physical awareness that had hit them both at Nate's house. It was more intense now, so much more, because of the physical contact between them. Fear rippled through her, and Gideon tensed, certain she was going to pull away. Every impulse in him roared with refusal to allow her to pull back, his unwillingness to lose contact with her.

But she didn't retreat.

To his shock and utterly male satisfaction, she leaned slightly into his touch, accepting his offer.

Gideon immediately closed the distance between them,

sliding his hands down her upper arms. He could feel every curve of her muscles and the angle of her bones. She was so thin, but at the same time, there was power vibrating beneath her skin. Lily was far from human, pulsing with power that roared through him like great temptation.

There was the thud of footsteps as Ian suddenly took off across the pavement and sprinted into the desert. Gideon didn't follow, knowing Ian would have let him know if he needed help. He stayed right where he was, shielding Lily with his body, accepting her violent emotions, and running his hands over skin that was too precious to be marred with so many bruises.

"I've got you," he said simply. There were no more words to say. Nothing more he could offer. That was all he had to give: his protection. His ability to protect was what defined him, and he gave it to her.

Lily turned her head slightly, so her cheek rested against his, and he felt a pulse of absolute rightness at the contact. She smelled sweet, delicate. Innocent. Desire hit him hard in his gut again, and he had to force himself not to turn his head to kiss her. It would take only one move to capture her lips with his, to taste her, and to claim her.

"Gideon." His name was a whisper in the night, almost angelic the way it drifted off her lips.

"Yeah, it's Gideon." His voice sounded rough and raw in comparison to hers.

"Why?"

He rubbed his thumbs over her arms, not sure whether he was touching her for his sake or hers. "Why what?"

She pressed her face more tightly against him, nuzzling into the crevice between his shoulder and his neck, as if she was trying to crawl inside him and hide. He loved her instinct, her natural inclination to use him for safety.

"Why did you come for me?" Her voice was muffled, her breath warm.

"Ana sent us." It wasn't the entire story, but it was enough for now. "We're not here to hurt you. Trust me." He slid his arms slowly around her waist, needing desperately to hold her, driven mad by the feel of her nestled against him. He felt like the heat from her skin was burning through her thin shirt, and he wanted to tear it off her, destroying that which the rogue Calydon had shredded when he'd violated her.

"I can't," she said. "I can't trust you." But even as Lily spoke, she untangled her hands from her belly and found the front of his shirt, clenching tightly. A small sob broke free, twisting his gut into knots. "I'm so tired," she whispered. "I'm so tired of fighting. I want to go home. My family must think I'm dead—" Her voice broke and anger roared through him at her pain.

Lily tensed, and he knew she'd felt his fury. He swore and forced it aside, drawing upon five hundred years of practice to pull his shit together. "I know, Lily. I know." He gently lifted her up and eased her onto his lap, unable to accept the sight of her battered knees on the hard cement any longer.

Despite the fear he could still feel emanating from her, Lily curled into a tight ball, her bare toes tucked between his thighs, her knees snug against her chest, and her face tucked against her knees as she hugged her legs.

God, yes. This was right to have her against him, turning herself over to him.

Gideon pressed his face to her hair, inhaling her scent, drinking it into his soul as if he'd never get another chance. This was his moment: right here, right now, with this woman he didn't even know in his arms, trusting him when she had no trust left in her soul.

He started to rub her back, then jerked his hand off when she yelped and twisted, trying to get away. "Shit, sorry." He cursed himself for pushing too hard.

"No, it's okay." Those mossy green eyes were filled with agony and apology. "Sorry. It wasn't you."

Apology? Shit, he deserved no apology. "It's okay," he said quietly. "Come back." He pulled her on his lap and rested his cheek against hers, hoping it would work again to soothe her. He needed it to work. He burned to reconnect, to feel her body yield to him again. Her cheek was cold, but her skin was so soft and delicate. So utterly female.

After a minute, she relaxed and let herself sag against him. He closed his eyes at the contact, at the feel of her body sinking into his. God, it felt good.

"Glass," she whispered. "In my back."

"Glass?" Gideon couldn't keep the fury out of his tone, but Lily didn't flinch this time. She just leaned against him, as if she were too exhausted to fight anymore. He lifted his head to inspect the back of her shirt, scowling at the speckles of blood from when she'd been dragged across the floor by the Calydon. He cursed and clenched his fists against the need to go back and punish the Calydon for what he'd done to her.

He was dead. That was enough.

But, fuck. It wasn't. Nothing would be enough.

Growling, Gideon gripped her shirt, then paused when he felt her tense. "I'm going to look at it, okay?"

She nodded, but said nothing, so Gideon gently tugged her shirt up to expose her back. The soft tones of her skin glistened, and he was so tempted to drop his head and press his lips to each injury. Her back was liberally sliced, and he could see glass fragments glittering like diamonds. Outrage tightened his jaw, but he forced himself not to react, not with her so fragilely clinging to sanity on his lap. "We need to get those out." He brushed her hair back from her face so he could see her. "Is that okay?"

She lifted her head and looked at him. Gideon was shocked by the total exhaustion in her eyes, the absolute depletion, and the desperate need for help buried deep beneath her shields, as she fought to maintain her strength and her independence.

His fingers tightened in her hair. "You're not alone anymore," he growled. "I swear it."

Lily shook her head. "I don't want to need you," she whispered. "Don't make me need you."

He couldn't help but smile at her courage. Who was she kidding? She was at the end of her resources. And damned if he didn't like the fact that he was the one who was going to catch her.

At that moment, Ian came loping down the hill and out onto the street. "Lost him. The bastard's fast. The last eight are on their way. I could hear them." Ian's gaze flicked to Lily, thoughtful curiosity on his face. "They're fools to come against Gideon and me, with only eight of them left, but they're coming after you anyway. They must want you badly."

Lily sat up so quickly, she almost lost her balance. Gideon caught her as she stumbled to her feet, wincing as if every muscle in her body hurt. He caught a glimpse of a dark bruise on her upper thigh before her skirt fell back into place, and he felt a darkness fester inside him at the sight.

Lily didn't seem to notice his reaction. All her weakness and vulnerability seemed to vanish, replaced by a woman who was focused, clear-minded and ready to fight. "How close are they?" she asked Ian urgently.

"Five minutes. They're closing fast." Ian raised a brow at Gideon. "Fight or bail?"

Gideon's first instinct was to stand and fight, to take them down and try to keep a few survivors for questioning, but he saw the way Lily hugged herself as she searched the dark night for their pursuers. Yes, she was ready to defend herself, but she was running on fumes for sure.

She was trembling, clad in nothing but her thin blouse and skirt. Her eyes were shadowed with the trauma she'd already been through, and he winced at the blood on her hands and shirt from the two warriors he'd killed on top of her. No more for her. Not tonight. "We bail. Lily's our priority."

"Then let's go." Ian turned and started loping toward the truck they'd arrived in.

Lily's gaze shot to him, her eyes wild. "Why am I your priority? It's more than because Ana sent you. You wouldn't waste your time on me. Why do you need me?"

Gideon touched her shoulder to acknowledge her question, but he didn't take time to answer. Instead, he reached out with his senses to assess the threat. He caught the scent of their sweat almost immediately and felt the beat of their black hearts. He picked up their single-minded focus on Lily. They were close and moving quickly. Gideon cursed and grabbed her hand. "Later. We need to go."

She hesitated, and he remembered the haunted way she'd looked at him in Nate's house. As if she knew all his blackest secrets and was terrified by them, scared in the way of someone who knows her fears are grounded in the ultimate truth and complete reality.

He knew she was ready to dig in and refuse to accompany him and Ian. "Lily." He met her gaze. "I'll keep you safe, but I can't do it if you don't come with me." He would take her if she didn't go willingly, but he didn't want to push her. He could sense that she needed to make the choice for herself. Gideon forced himself to give her time, trusting that the intelligence he'd seen in her eyes would trump her fear and her independence.

Lily slowly shook her head, but he could see the torment in her gaze, her instinct to trust him warring with her fear of all that he was. She fought to overcome the traumas that had taught her not to trust *anyone*.

Gideon moved closer and cradled her face between his hands, probing her with his gaze. "I *promise* I will protect you. I won't hurt you, I swear."

Lily stared up at him, then her gaze flicked down the road, in the direction of the approaching Calydons. She gripped his wrists, resolution setting on her features as she breathed strength and determination back into her body. "They work for Frank, and you killed them to keep them from taking me," she said, her voice desperate, but strong. "I have to believe in that. Right now, I have to choose you."

Gideon felt such an immense sense of relief and satisfaction at the look of trust on her face that his insides snapped. Possessiveness swirled through him. Her eyes widened at whatever she saw on his face, and she jerked back. "You're so dangerous to me." Her words were replete with a horror that left him cold, a rejection that struck straight to his core: it was a truth he deserved.

Lily whirled around and tried to run toward the truck, limping painfully with each desperate step.

Gideon recovered a split second later. Screw that. Yeah, he was a cold bastard, but that didn't change the fact that he was all she had right now. As hell was his witness, the Order needed her, too. He ignored the whisper in the back of his mind that suggested that he also needed her, and it had nothing to do with the Order.

Gideon strode after her, caught up to her in a heartbeat, and swept her up in his arms, not even giving the exhausted female a chance to fight her battle alone anymore.

To his surprise, she didn't resist. Lily simply wrapped her arms around his neck as he tucked her against his hip and sprinted for the truck. Rightness settled through him at the feel of her body against his, and he tightened his grip protectively as he ran. *You will be safe with me, Lily.*

She frowned at him, and for a second, he thought maybe she'd heard him. Something leapt in his chest, but then they were at the truck, and it was time to focus.

Gideon set her gently in the back, climbed in next to her and yanked the door shut as Ian peeled out, whipping past the upturned Hummer and out into the road, just as their pursuers rounded the corner behind them.

※ ※ ※

Lily twisted around in the seat, her hand instinctively going to Gideon's shoulder for balance as Ian swerved back onto the right side of the road. The headlights behind them were closing fast, and she dug her fingers into his broad shoulder. Her mouth was dry with fear as she watched their pursuers approach. God help her. Would it ever end? "Is that them?"

Gideon turned, his shoulder wedged up against her side. He was far too big to fit in the back seat comfortably, and he had no business trying to share it with anyone. There was nowhere for her to move that didn't result in her being pressed up against him. Every inch of his body emanated heat and danger, and she couldn't keep from noticing, not with him invading her senses so thoroughly.

He peered out the back window, then cursed. "Any ideas, Ian?"

"A couple." Ian glanced at them in his rearview mirror, and Lily could tell from the look on his face that she was not going to like his idea. "You want to flip a coin?"

He and Gideon exchanged silent looks that were heavy with information she couldn't interpret, and she realized they were communicating mind-to-mind. Gideon nodded and shoved open the oversized pass-through to the back of the truck and climbed though the opening.

She groaned and closed her eyes, letting her head flop against the seat. "I'm not going home, am I?"

"Not yet." Ian tightened his grip on the wheel as they careened around a corner.

The truck whipped around the bend in the road, and the momentum tossed Lily across the seat. She grabbed for the door handle as the right side of the truck lifted off the ground. "Ian!"

"I've got it," he said calmly as the tires squealed, and she hit the side of the truck hard as they bounced back down.

There was a curse from the back of the truck, then a medium sized duffel bag flew from the pass-through and hit Ian in the back of the head. "Fuck, Gideon. Watch it!" The truck skidded, and Lily sucked in her breath as Ian fought to keep control of the vehicle. He jerked the bag off the back of his neck and hurled it into the back seat, where it landed with a thud next to Lily's hip.

Gideon stuck his head through the pass-through. "Why are these Calydons after you, Lily?" He tossed another bag at her, and this one landed on the floor next to her feet instead of on Ian's head. "I know you smell good, but *hell.*"

She stared at him blankly, so surprised by his comment that it took a moment to even understand what he meant. She smelled good? Was he serious with that? They were on the run from the most terrifying man she'd ever met, and Gideon was actually thinking about how she smelled? And what in God's name was she doing actually noticing his comment and feeling all ooey-gooey inside from it? Had it really been that long since anyone had said anything nice to her?

Well, yeah, it had been. She should let herself appreciate it, even if it was just a compliment on her body odor while she was on the run from certain death and torture. A girl had to take what she could get, and she hadn't lasted two years in hell without taking advantage of opportunities to feel positive. So, yay for the big, manly man who thought she smelled good, even though she hadn't showered in God knew how long.

"Lily?" Gideon apparently didn't like having his question ignored, a grim reminder that these were two deadly, determined Calydons she'd entrusted her life to. God, what a choice to make.

"I don't know specifically why they're after me." She

fumbled for the seatbelt and yanked it around her as Ian took another sharp turn. "I think they work for Frank Tully, a partner of Nate's. Frank seems to have an interest in me." She shivered, unable to keep the fear out of her voice. The desperateness of her situation came crashing down, and she leaned forward. "Can you drive faster?"

Ian met her gaze in the rearview mirror. His answering grin didn't hide the deep anguish haunting his eyes, or the torment that had brought hollows to his cheeks. "A woman who likes speed," he said. "My kind of gal."

"Frank Tully?" Gideon repeated as he hauled himself through the pass-through and dropped onto the seat next to her, his bulk crushing her into the corner of the seat. He smelled like leather, woods, and man. Like freedom. Like safety. "Who the hell's Frank Tully?"

She found the receptacle for the seatbelt and shoved hard until she felt a click. "A scary bastard. I couldn't figure out who was in charge between Nate and him." She leaned back against the seat, gripping the handle above her head to try to keep from slamming into Gideon as the truck careened down the twisting road. "He wanted Nate's stone. I heard them arguing."

Gideon threw an arm out to brace himself against the front seat, and hauled her against him with his other arm, anchoring her to his side. He and Ian exchanged glances. "So you think this Frank guy is after you?"

"Probably." Lily shuddered at the thought of being at Frank's mercy. The way his eyes had fastened on her... Her head started to spin and she bent over, hanging it between her knees. "I can't deal with this."

Gideon shifted, setting his hand on her head, his fingers tangling in her hair. "Sure you can." His voice was quiet and confident, his touch warm and reassuring. "You think he wants you, or the stone?" he asked, continuing his urgent questioning.

She closed her eyes and concentrated on his touch, letting it ground her. God, it had been years since someone had given her physical comfort. It made her want to crawl into his lap and give up all pretense of being able to cope. To let someone else take care of her. For a day. Or even an hour. Just to be able to stop fighting for a minute...but it wasn't an option. Not now.

She clenched her fists and willed herself to be strong. "I don't have the stone, so I'd have to think he wants me specifically."

"Why?"

She winced as the tires squealed, but Gideon kept her anchored against him, and she barely slid in the seat. "Because of my charming personality, of course. Why else?" No way was she going to admit who she was to them. Never could a Calydon be trusted with the truth of what she was. Never.

His soft chuckle made her belly curl. "Why else, indeed?"

"Seriously, I don't know. I don't know why Nate kept me, either, but he had a reason. I tried to find out, but he kept his secrets locked up." Lily had some ideas, but she wasn't about to share them with Calydons she couldn't trust. "He had big plans, and I think Frank is trying to take over now that Nate's dead." She felt the truck tip again, and she sucked in her breath. "We're going to die right now, aren't we?"

# Chapter 5

"You might, but we're immortal."

She glared at Gideon. "What kind of comfort is that?"

He grinned and brushed his thumb over her cheek, an affectionate, playful gesture that seemed so incongruous for the situation they were in and for the power of the man who'd done it. "Just trying to distract you. The time to worry about dying is after you've beaten death, not when you're about to take it on."

She blinked as panic surged through her. "We're really about to take death on? I thought you were exaggerating." She moaned and bent over to the floor again as the interior of the truck started spinning again. "You couldn't have told me that *later*, and just let me be mad at you right now?"

"I can see down your shirt."

Sudden heat flared through Lily, and she sat up, holding the collar of her shirt against her chest. "Letch." But she didn't feel like he was a letch. She felt dangerously tempted by his comment, by the way his gaze roamed over hers. Her response to him was so unfamiliar and unsettling. She'd spent her entire life being careful to hold all Calydons at bay and suppress her magic's response to them. Having a Calydon look at her as a woman had always made her uncomfortable, and for good reason. But her response to Gideon was like a raging inferno he was stoking with each look, each comment, and each touch.

It was terrifying to feel herself respond to him, but at the same time he made her want more. Which she couldn't do. Ever. No matter how heroic Gideon had been thus far, he would never be able to handle who she was. She had a sudden vision of Gideon caught up on the high of her power, and she went cold. A warrior with Gideon's power would destroy her. It would be a thousand times worse than before—

Gideon gripped her tighter as the truck bounced high over a rut. "I could distract you with sex."

Lily swallowed at the pulse of desire that coursed through her and the sudden clenching of her belly. How was it possible that those words didn't make her want to run screaming from him? Her mind logically knew she should be afraid, but her body didn't. Why? She didn't understand, and it scared her to think that Gideon could strip away the years of self-preservation she'd worked so hard to erect. "Are you kidding with the sex talk?"

His grin faded. "Not really. Ever since I saw you in that hallway, I've been completely fixated on getting you naked. Inappropriate as hell, but I can't fucking help it." His blue eyes darkened with utterly masculine heat, and she felt her body burn in response.

"Cut it out," Ian snapped. "I can smell your lust all the way up here, and I don't need to deal with that shit right now."

Lily started with surprise, then felt her cheeks flare with embarrassment. Gideon winked at her, and she realized that Ian wasn't the only one privy to the desire coursing through her at this ridiculously inopportune time. "God, this sucks."

"It's not you he scented." Gideon touched Lily's hair, his fingers drifting lightly over the ends. Then he clapped his hand on Ian's shoulder in a silent apology that got a nod from Ian, and the tension was gone from the air as suddenly as it had appeared.

"Bridge construction up ahead," Ian reported. "Three minutes."

"Ready." Gideon released Lily to unzip one of the duffel bags.

Lily peered out the windshield, then gasped when she saw the red brake lights lining the street several miles ahead and the floodlights from the road crew as they worked on the bridge. "Oh, no." Behind them, their pursuers were closing in quickly.

They were trapped. Lily's heart began to race. "I can't go back there," she whispered. "I can't."

"You won't." Gideon thrust a black jacket at her. "Put this on and zip it up. Fast."

She didn't ask for a reason; she just jerked off the seatbelt then yanked the jacket on. Her fingers were shaking so badly she barely managed to get her arms in the sleeves. Gideon had his on and zipped before she'd managed to get the ends of her zipper matched up. The sleeves hung way past her hands and she had to shove the collar away from her face so she could see. He took care of her zipper, then grabbed a nylon harness out of the duffel on the floor. "Turn around."

She bit her lip and spun around as he quickly fastened the harness over her shoulders and around her chest, looping one strap between her legs, moving so fast that she didn't have time to be embarrassed by the flood of heat that rushed through her when his hands brushed against her bare thigh, the skirt riding up from the straps.

"Two minutes." Ian flicked a button on the dash, and a police siren began wailing from the truck. Blue lights reflected on the hood.

Up ahead, Lily saw people begin to scatter, clearing the way for the truck speeding toward them, so no one would get hurt. What ordinary Calydon would have a truck equipped with a police siren?

Suddenly, all the pieces fell into place. The way Gideon and Ian had fought with such dominance when they'd been so outnumbered. How her attacker had vanished into the desert rather than risk Gideon's wrath. She realized Gideon's protective instincts weren't actually that he had some special connection with her. It was what he was trained to do, what the Order of the Blade was trained to do.

"Protection of innocents at all costs," she whispered. Was that what Ian and Gideon were? *Order members?* Her stomach turned. "You're with the Order of the Blade?" Her blood ran cold as Gideon checked her harness, and she shoved his hand away frantically. "You're Gideon Roarke? You're *that* Gideon?"

The warrior who had destroyed her family? The murderer who had haunted her nightmares for years? *That Gideon?*

"Yeah, I am." His blue eyes hardened as he donned the mask of the cold, heartless warrior she knew he was. Gone was that rush of heated connection between them. He sucked it all back in, and became the man who killed so ruthlessly. "I don't know what you've heard about me, but I'm your only damn chance to evade the assholes chasing us, so get it together and stay with me. You can hate me later."

Lily's breath was racing and her chest was starting to close up. How had she not figured it out? Ian Fitzgerald. Gideon Roarke. Order members for the last five centuries. She knew everything about them. About Gideon. About the man who'd murdered her family.

This man she was entrusting her life to was *Gideon*. She batted at his hands as he reached for the harness again, and she tried to pull the harness off. She had to get out. Not Gideon. She couldn't put her life in *his* hands. "No, you don't understand. I can't—"

He grabbed her shoulders and forced her still, his blue eyes penetrating. "For hell's sake, Lily, *cut it out*. I'm on *your* fucking side! I'm trying to keep you *alive*, so stop fighting me." He growled. "I swear I'll knock you out if that's what it takes to keep you safe."

She stared at him, into his intense eyes, and saw the truth of his words. He wasn't going to hurt her. Not right now. He was her only chance. Oh, God. She *had* to trust him. But how could she? "I don't know if I can trust you—"

"What do you know about the Order of the Blade?" Ian asked.

She shot a wild glance at him, grateful for the interruption as Gideon grunted and went back to adjusting her harness, muttering about how it was too loose. "Order of the Blade," she recited, using the opportunity to try to calm down, to shut out all she knew about Gideon. To stop thinking about what he'd done to her family— *No. Don't think about that. Not right now.* "The Order is an elite group of Calydon warriors who've taken an oath to protect innocents from rogue Calydons. The Order members are ruthless killers who are willing to trade the life of one innocent to save many." Her mouth became dry as her gaze slid involuntarily toward Gideon.

He scowled as he yanked on the buckle. "I'm not about to trade your life for anything right now, so stop worrying about it."

"It's so much more than that," she said, her voice raspy in her throat. "You killed—" She couldn't even say it. Not with her life in his care right now. She couldn't afford to think about it. "Rogue Calydons are at least insane when they kill innocents, but you guys do it on purpose."

"You're too damn skinny." Gideon ignored her comment as he unbuckled the harness, tied a couple knots in it, then buckled her back up. "Next time you get kidnapped, find someone who will feed you better." The nylon cut into the glass still wedged in her back, but she was too freaked to protest.

Lily swallowed. "Yeah, sure, I'll try to keep that in mind." She focused on his eyes, on how intensely he was concentrating on securing her into the harness. He'd come to her rescue tonight, more than once. She reminded herself that Ana had trusted Gideon enough to send him after her. He was *Gideon*, but he was also more than that. And it was this extra bit, this protector side, that she needed to focus on right now. *Let him help you, Lily. You need him.*

Ian had turned his attention back to the road, trying to work his way around the stopped cars. Behind them, the headlights of their pursuers encroached ruthlessly, getting closer and closer. She was trapped, sandwiched between two demons closing in on her.

Gideon tugged at the front of the harness, the back of his hand brushing against her breasts. "Shit. Still loose. It'll have to do. Try not to fall out of it."

"Try not to fall out of it?" Oh, that just didn't sound promising. Her gaze snapped to his grim face. "I really don't think I liked that order."

Gideon flashed her a grin as he fastened the other end of the harness around his wrist, giving it a hard yank to test the buckle. "I doubt you like any orders."

"One minute." Ian's voice rang out.

Lily's heart started hammering out of control, thundering in her ears. "One minute until what?"

"All you need to do is trust me. I'll take care of the rest."

"Trust you." God, to ask the impossible of her. "I can't—"

He glared at her. "You have to, Lily. You have no other choice." His voice was hard and confident, almost arrogant.

It pissed her off, but at the same time, it eased some of her panic. For some unknown reason, Gideon had taken her well-being as his mission. As brutal as he was, he was the best at what he did, and she knew it. He could kill with ruthless ease, but right now, he was turning that same competence in her favor.

She had to take it. She wasn't a fool, and she knew what her choices were. Gideon was her only chance. "Don't kill me," she whispered.

Outrage darkened his features, and he leaned forward, his blue eyes blazing with an intensity that had no place in the cold warrior he was supposed to be. "I will never fucking hurt you. Do you understand? *Never.*"

He meant it. This brutal, deadly killer meant it. She felt his promise in her very heart, in the intensity of the emotion he was pouring into her. Tears filled her eyes, and she was suddenly overwhelmed by the gift he'd just offered. Protection. Safety. Help. She knew enough not to trust him long term, to know that there were limits, but right now, in this terrible moment, in a twist of events that she never could have foreseen, Gideon Roarke was there for her. "Thank you," she whispered.

His face softened, and he brushed his fingers over her cheek, the softest, most intimate gesture. She wanted to cry for the offer of that kindness.

"Thirty seconds," Ian said.

The emotion vanished instantly from Gideon's expression and he sat back. He strapped the other duffel around his upper body, and she realized it was far more than a simple bag. It was well stocked, secure against his body, a good eight inches thick all the way around. A fanny pack for warriors. Perfect for dangerous outdoor activities she wanted no part of.

"Twenty seconds."

"Turn around, Lily," Gideon ordered. He jerked his head toward Ian. "Have Quinn contact me once it's safe."

"Will do."

Quinn Masters? Another Order of the Blade member? She sucked in her breath as realization hit her. She was part of an Order mission? How had that happened? *Please, God, let me survive them.* Gritting her teeth, Lily turned so she was sitting sideways in the seat, facing the door. She tensed when Gideon locked his arm firmly around her waist and pressed himself up against her back. His body was flush with hers, pinned against her as if he was using his body to protect her from something terrible.

The road flashed past, and he pushed them both closer to the window, until they were right up against it. Oh, man. She did not like what her instincts were telling her. "Tell me we're not going to jump out of a moving truck."

"We're going to jump out of a moving truck."

Lily's heart kicked into overdrive, and she gripped his wrist. "This is going to suck, isn't it?"

He braced his free hand on the doorframe above her head. "Depends on your definition of suck."

"It's pretty broad."

"Then yeah, this is going to suck."

"Five seconds," Ian announced, sending chills down Lily's spine.

The truck tires bounced over the entrance to the bridge, smacking hard on the rough pavement as Ian whipped around the stopped cars. He drove straight over the part of the bridge that was being worked on, driving perilously close to the edge that was currently without a railing.

Gideon reached around Lily and shoved the door open.

"Seriously?" Lily jerked back as the road flew past the bottom of the truck, the night dark beneath the bridge, the edge of which was only inches away. "You've got to be kidding." She dug her fingers into the doorframe, her heart pounding so loudly she could barely hear the crashes as Ian smashed through the safety barrels.

"Not this time, sweetheart." Gideon's arm tightened around her, his thighs scooted under hers, and he pried her hand off the door and pinned her arms around her belly.

"Are you sure we can't outrun them?" She was a professor, damn it. Not the kind of woman who leapt out of moving trucks in the middle of the night. Or in the middle of the day, for that matter!

"I'm certain. Don't scream. We don't want anyone to

notice we're doing this. The Calydons on our tail need to follow Ian so we can get away."

"Oh, God. This is a terrible plan." Lily shrank back against Gideon's chest, fighting to get her hands free so she could grab the doorframe. The stubborn man didn't let her go. Suddenly, the fact he was built like a solid wall of muscle and was twice her size didn't seem like such an appealing trait. "I'm not going."

"Go." Ian's voice was so calm she almost didn't hear him.

But she did hear him. So did the arrogant, crazy warrior holding onto her, apparently, because Gideon grabbed the doorframe with his free hand and shoved them both out.

A scream welled up in her throat, and it took every last bit of restraint she had to hold it in as they free-fell into the blackness. She scrunched her eyes shut, her fingers digging into Gideon's arm as he controlled their jump.

"Hold your breath." His voice was quiet, his lips brushing her ear.

She had no time to ask, sucking in her breath as he turned them in the air, so he was below her. The impact shook her as his body hit, and then she was sucked under water so cold it shocked the breath right out of her.

Panic seized her as the world descended into silence, then Gideon jerked her to the surface. Her head popped out of the water, and she gasped with relief even as the rapids crashed into her face, nearly swamping her.

There was a hiss of air, and her jacket inflated, covering her face and mouth. She clawed at the collar, trying to get it out of the way as she was tossed against Gideon, who still had her locked down against his body. He shouted something, but she couldn't hear it over the roar of the water, an all-consuming noise flooding her senses. She got the jacket out of the way, and sucked in a breath a split second before a wave filled her mouth. "Gideon," she screamed.

She might have heard an answer, but then there was a brutal impact that wrenched her out of Gideon's arms. She scrabbled for the rock that had separated them but was ripped away, tossed ruthlessly by the raging river.

The harness tugged at her chest, and she grabbed at

it, shocked by how loose it was, even with the inflated jacket beneath it. Another wave crashed into her and Lily sucked in water, a cough ripping through her as she tried to clear her lungs.

Then she was yanked beneath the water, the icy coldness closing over her head. Her body slammed into another rock, knocking the wind out of her, then the jacket popped her back up to the surface, and she gasped in air the instant her head was free.

The collar of the jacket rose over her face and she tried to pull it down. The harness tightened around her chest, as if Gideon was pulling on it. She grabbed it, holding so it couldn't slip off, trying to lift her chin high enough out of the water to catch another breath.

She bumped against another rock, hitting it so hard she lost her grip. Her head ringing, she felt the harness slide down her shoulder and dig into her upper arm. "God, no!" She coughed as more water poured into her mouth, and grabbed the harness, her fingers so cold she could barely hold onto the slippery nylon.

Something brushed against her fingers, and she almost jerked away before she realized it was a hand closing around her arm. "Gideon!"

He grabbed her wrist, locking his grip tightly around her. She caught a glimpse of his face, his light brown hair plastered to his head, water streaming down his cheeks. Elation rushed through her, and she felt like crying with joy as he dragged her to him with fierce strength.

She slammed into him and then his arms were around her again, trapping her against him. Her back was against his chest, his arms tight around her upper body. His grip was unwavering as the river flung them about. "We're going to ride for a while," he shouted. "Hang on!"

She gripped his arm with one hand and used the other to tug the collar of her jacket out of her face so she could breathe. She sucked in air, then pressed her lips shut as another wave crashed in her face. Water stung as it flooded up her nose.

They were tossed into another rock, but this time Gideon took the hit and kept his grip, cushioning the blow. Then they were out in the middle of the river again, the water crashing in her ears, against her face. It sucked them both beneath the surface, the icy cold water closing over their heads.

Gideon shoved off another rock and they shot upward, breaking through the surface as a huge log careened toward them. Gideon threw up his arm to block it, and it smacked into his forearm a split second before it would have crashed into Lily's head.

Then they were off again, the raging waters tossing them violently as she gasped for air each chance she got, bouncing off rocks as Gideon fought to control their ride.

Finally, after what felt like an eternity, the water began to calm. The roar eased and the waves stopped trying to swamp her. Lily let her head fall back against Gideon's shoulder as they were carried down the river, her body shaking so hard she couldn't stop her teeth from rattling.

"You doing okay?" he asked.

"Fantastic."

His arm tightened around her. "That's my girl."

"I'm not your girl," she mumbled. "I've been owned by Nate for two years. I'll never be anyone's girl again."

"He didn't own you. He might have tried, but he never did." There was a fury in Gideon's voice that warmed her.

She closed her eyes, suddenly too exhausted and too cold to keep them open. "That's what I kept telling myself, but now—"

"Fuck that. He's dead. You're not. You win."

"I win," she murmured as the gentle swirls of the water lulled her to sleep. "Yay, me." *So tired. Just need to sleep...*

"Lily!" He shook her hard and she jerked awake. "Stay with me. I'm taking us to shore."

She let her eyes fall closed again. "Tired..."

He shook her again. "Lily! You need to stay awake." His voice was laced with such urgency she felt it prick through her exhaustion. She forced her eyes open, staring up at the vast starry sky. "Freedom," she mumbled. "No boundaries. Stars are free."

"Like you." His body jarred against her as his feet hit ground, and he swung her up into his arms as he slogged his way out of the water. "You're no longer his prisoner."

The cold air hit Lily's bare legs, and she shuddered,

realizing how much her body was shaking. The cold had penetrated to her core. So very cold.

"Hang tight, Lily. We'll get you warm in a second." Gideon broke into a jog, holding her tight against his chest as he loped away from the river, until she could no longer see it, and could no longer hear the soft waves lapping at the rocks.

He dropped to his knees and set her on the ground. "Get out of that harness and jacket."

"Okay." Lily sat up as he quickly unfastened the pack that was still strapped around his body. Her fingers fumbled with the buckles, aching with cold as she tried to free herself. Her hands shook, and she couldn't even feel the metal as she tried to grip it. Her stomach was shivering so hard it hurt, and her brain felt slow and thick. "Can't..."

Gideon cursed and took over, his fingers flying over the buckles as he freed her and eased the harness off her shoulders. He unzipped the jacket and helped her get it off. Her white blouse was plastered to her, and she vaguely noticed that Gideon would be able to see her nipples clearly though it.

But he was already unzipping the pack he'd brought and he pulled out a thick sweatshirt. He set it on the ground then flicked his fingers toward her blouse. "You want help getting that off?"

"No," she mumbled through her chattering teeth. "I've got it." She tried to unbutton it, but her fingers slid off the smooth plastic.

Gideon made a noise of aggravation, then grabbed the edges of the blouse and ripped it off her. "Trust me, although I think you're unbelievably sexy, I have enough self-control not to try to seduce you right now. I need to clean your back." He turned her gently, and she felt his hands probing the cuts on her skin. She bit her lip, preparing for the pain, but her back was so numb with cold that she felt nothing.

Gideon grunted with satisfaction. "The river washed the glass out. You're good." He grinned. "Nothing like class five rapids to flush out a little glass, right?"

"Class five?" She mumbled. "You carried us through class five rapids? Aren't those deadly?"

"Nah. Just a little bit of recreational activity." He

grabbed the sweatshirt and tugged it over her head, guiding her hands through the sleeves and tucking the hood around her head. "Let's get you warm."

He grabbed her hands and helped her to her feet. He yanked her tattered and drenched skirt and underwear down over her hips. She braced her hands on his shoulders, leaning on him for support, her legs too exhausted to support her. She held tight to him as he slid her feet into a pair of thick sweats and tugged them up her legs and over her hips. He eased her back down to the ground and pulled a pair of thick socks over her feet.

She watched Gideon numbly, his muscles bunching as he took care of her. How was it possible that the first kind word she'd heard in ages was from the man she'd vilified for so long? How was it possible he even knew how to offer kindness and support? It didn't make sense, and she was too tired to figure it out. It was all she could do to simply hold herself upright and accept his help.

Gideon yanked a thin blanket made of dark, shiny material out of the pack and tossed it at her. "Here."

Her freezing fingers stung as the slippery material landed on her hand. "You fit all that in there?"

He peeled his wet jeans off. "I prioritized my packing list. You needed clothes."

She wanted to watch as his jeans slid over his legs, but she was too tired. Too cold. Her eyes fell shut as she curled into a ball and tugged the blanket over her, her body aching as she shook with cold and exhaustion. She was vaguely aware of Gideon moving around her. She heard the sound of branches crackling, and wondered if he was making a fire.

Probably not. Too much exposure.

Then his hand was on her shoulder. "That blanket is actually a sleeping bag," he said, his deep voice soothing. "It's a special material that traps heat."

She didn't open her eyes as he pried the foil out of her hand, curling herself tighter into a ball as he shook out the blanket. She heard the burl of a zipper and the soft sound of it being spread on the sandy ground, then he gently clasped her shoulders and rolled her over onto it. She felt the slippery coldness of the blanket under her cheek, her body still shaking violently as he flipped it over her and zipped it back up.

"Move over." He nudged at her, and she realized he was climbing in with her. "You need my heat to warm up."

She tried to scoot, but she couldn't make her body move. Too cold. Too exhausted. "Can't."

"It's okay." His hands slid down her back and gently shifted her to the side, then he wedged himself into the bag with her. He pulled her hood up, then snaked his arm around her and threw his leg over hers, enveloping her with his bulk, tugging her into the curve of his body. "Shit, you're still shaking."

Lily couldn't believe how good it felt to be tangled up with him. Nothing had ever felt as amazing as his body wrapped around hers. He was warm, burning hot, infusing her with fire. But it wasn't just that. He was so powerful, so strong, and so dominating in the way he tucked her against him. She felt like she'd burrowed into some secret hideaway, complete with her own personal immortal guardian who would keep all the nightmares away.

All the hell that had been chasing her fell away, unable to penetrate the cocoon that Gideon had created for her. She breathed deeply, basking in his musky male scent, like leather and smoke mixed with the warmth of a hot summer day. The aching tension in her body began to ease, tension she'd been holding for two years. "Don't even tell me you're going to pull the old 'we both have to be naked to warm you up' thing," she mumbled.

He chuckled. "No, just me."

"You?" She untangled her hand from the oversized sleeve of the sweatshirt and felt for his thigh where it was draped over her, sucking in her breath when her hand landed on his bare skin, the sinews of his muscles flexing beneath her touch.

He was blistering hot, resonating with strength and power, and she couldn't bring herself to pull her hand away. He felt so alive, so warm, so *there*. Her fingers dug into his leg, as she felt her throat tighten, overwhelmed by his mere presence. By the fact he was there, for her, protecting *her*. For the first time in so long, she had help. She wasn't alone. Not anymore. Not for this moment.

On the road, she'd had that moment where she'd tasted safety, but it hadn't been real. She'd still been exposed, alone, and vulnerable, only minutes ahead of her pursuers. There had been no time to stop and fall apart. But now, in Gideon's arms, with the heat of his body easing the tension in her muscles, his strength wrapped around her so securely, and the quietness of their solitude in the woods, the urgency faded.

There was no battle to fight right now. It was over for the moment. Lily didn't have to stay strong anymore, and her heart knew it. Her eyes began to sting and she scrunched them shut, trying not to cry, afraid to let go and feel all the emotions she'd been holding at bay for so long.

"I didn't have space to pack dry clothes for me, and it wouldn't have made sense for me to get in here wet," Gideon said. "There's nothing sexual about me being totally naked in a sleeping bag with you. Absolutely nothing." But there was an undercurrent in his voice that made her snort.

"Liar," she managed to say, barely able to keep the tears out of her voice.

"Yeah, okay, so I'm not exactly thinking saintly thoughts right now." He laughed softly and tightened his arm around her, pulling her even more securely against his body. "But right now my biggest concern is making sure you actually survive." He rested his cheek against her head. "How do you feel?"

The concern in his voice plucked at her, and she felt her walls begin to crumble. "Exhausted." Her voice broke, and she clamped her lips shut against a moan that echoed deep inside as her anguish finally broke free. The hopelessness she'd been fighting for so long, the loneliness, the fear, and the uncertainty that she'd kept ratcheted down in order to survive—she couldn't hold any of it back anymore. She pressed her palms to her eyes, trying to hold herself together.

Gideon brushed his lips over her hair. "Let it go," he whispered. "You don't have to be strong anymore."

"God, yes, I do." She shuddered as grief wracked her body, as the first tear burst free, trickling down her cheek. "I can't fall apart," she whispered. "If I do, I'll never get it back."

Gideon nuzzled aside the hood of the sweatshirt and kissed the side of her neck. "Yeah, you will."

Tears spilled over as she wrapped her fingers around his wrists, holding him tight so he couldn't let her go. "I can't let Nate defeat me. Don't you see? I have to be stronger than he is."

"You are. You survived. He didn't. It's over now, Lily. It's over. You're safe right now. I've got you. Stop fighting."

*It's over.* The last of her walls shattered at his words, and the sobs burst free, as two years of fear, grief and loneliness poured out of her, raking her with pain, consuming her.

Lily rocked back and forth as the sobs shook her. Through the tears, the pain, the debilitating exhaustion, she was so aware of Gideon's arms tight around her, of his lips against her ear, whispering to her, soothing her. She didn't even know what he said. It didn't matter. The mere fact he was there was enough, and she latched onto his voice, drank in his reassurances, and cried until she was certain she'd never be able to stop.

# Chapter 6

It was hours until Gideon felt Lily finally relax against him, until the sobs quieted and her body stopped trembling. Her breathing evened out and he knew she had finally fallen asleep.

He groaned softly and let his head drop to her shoulder, completely exhausted by her grief. Emotional turmoil so wasn't his thing, but he had been unable and unwilling to shield himself when he'd realized she was crumbling. Her emotions had been so intense, so vibrant, so alive, that he'd felt like she'd thrust life into him, like she'd made his heart start beating.

He'd swallowed her anguish, he'd bled for her pain, and he'd been consumed by a need to fill the gap in her soul and heal the wounds that were so open and raw. It had been more than Nate, more than her last two years. The damage to her soul ran far deeper than that, with roots that scattered in so many directions, pain that had cut so deeply that her only way to survive had been to shut it down, just like he did. There had been no healing for her, just survival, made more difficult by every day in Nate's hell.

Gideon wanted to heal her. He wanted to ease that pain and weave hope and peace back into her tattered being. He wanted to breathe in and absorb every emotion she had, to let it fill him the way it filled her, and to come alive for this woman he held in his arms.

The minute her first tears had fallen, he'd been slammed with all her pain. Every last bit of it had crashed into his gut until he'd felt the tears glistening on his own cheeks. He didn't know how to feel. He'd never allowed emotions into his life. But when Lily's soul had crashed into his, it had felt incredible to be that alive.

Gideon rolled onto his back and pulled her on top of him, letting his forearm rest against his forehead as he felt her warm breath on his throat. He ran his other hand over her back, needing to touch her, to hold her, to feel her. She had such courage and strength. Lily was a survivor, but at the same time, there was an enormous vulnerability within her that awakened every protective instinct he had.

Like that moment when he'd lost her in the river…Shit. Gideon had never felt fear in his life. Fear was an emotion that had no place in a warrior's existence. Fear had never even crossed his mind in five hundred years…until Lily had been wrenched out of his arms in the rapids. He'd felt like his own soul had just been ripped out of his body.

He never should have lost his grip. For hell's sake, he'd worn the float jacket so he wouldn't have to think about anything but hanging onto her and keeping her from hitting the rocks, but he'd still lost her. What the hell?

When they first hit the water, he'd thought he'd heard music. Not just music. Magical, surreal bells that had vibrated through his entire body and filled his mind with a chorus of music so beautiful he'd thought for a second that he'd finally made a fatal mistake and died. He'd never even understood the concept of beautiful before that moment. The word meant nothing to him, to the warrior who had one goal, and that was to fulfill his oath and do his job.

And yet when he'd landed in the river, he had, for a split second, been cast into a place he'd never been in his life. The moment Gideon had heard that music, he knew he'd finally been shown what beautiful truly meant. He'd been so startled by the noise that shouldn't have been there that he'd lost his concentration for a split second. It was in that instant that they'd collided with the rock and he'd lost his grip on Lily. That slight moment of distraction had nearly killed her, and he'd nearly lost his mind trying to get back to her.

What the hell was wrong with him? Yeah, the Order

needed Lily, but it had felt too fucking personal in the river when he'd lost her. And when he'd ripped off her blouse, he'd nearly gone to his knees at the sight of her body. Blue with cold, bruised, with cuts on her hands, he'd nearly tackled her right there, desperate to claim her and offer her his ability to heal. To nourish her body and spirit back to life, to feel her skin against his in the very personal, very private way of a man and a woman.

"Fuck." That was the talk of a Calydon who'd met his *sheva*, the one woman who was his true mate. Every Calydon was destined to meet his *sheva* and bond with her, singing poems of true love and eternal happiness, and of course, mind-blowing sex.

But the minute they completed all the stages of the bond and sealed their fate, they were destined to destroy each other and everything they cared about. Both of them dead, utter destruction, no happy ending for anyone. The male would go rogue, and his woman would have to kill him to stop him, and then die herself. Destiny. Fate. Hell. Yeah, one couple seemed to have skated through, but that exception meant nothing, not when there were two thousand years of destiny winning.

Of course, the couple would make it to the point of mutual destruction only if the Order didn't find and kill them first, before they could complete the bond and bring down everyone around them. Preemptive strikes were part of the Order mission. Kill the warrior, not the woman, unless it was an Order member, in which case he was deemed too valuable to eliminate and his *sheva* would be the one to die.

Yeah, he knew all about *that* fucking rule.

Gideon tangled his fingers in Lily's knotted hair, trying to work out the mats. She shifted against him, and her sweatshirt rode up beneath his hand. His thumb brushed against her bare back and he felt his body harden instantly. He set his hands on her hips, drinking in the feel of her body in his grasp, as desire built inside him, a raging, powerful need that actually hurt it was so intense.

He cursed and dropped his hands before he could do something he'd never do to a woman who was passed out from exhaustion, to a woman who'd summoned the internal strength to trust him when there was no trust left in her soul.

His need for Lily was so beyond anything he'd ever felt before...it was too intense. Unnatural. Or was it? Maybe it wasn't a big deal. He was a Calydon, after all, and Calydons had a thing for women. His need for her could simply be lust. Or it could be admiration for her strength, or even his Calydon instincts surging to the surface to protect an innocent in his care. She wasn't his destiny, knocking at his door to bring utter destruction to both of them.

He knew that, with absolute certainty, because there was no way she could be his *sheva*. He'd already met his *sheva* five hundred years ago, and she'd been killed by another Order member, per their oath. As much as Gideon wanted Lily, it didn't mean a damn thing, no matter how intense it felt. She wasn't his *sheva*, and anything else was something he could manage.

He felt relief settle in his bones. *Everything was under control.*

Gideon raised his hand to her hair again and fiddled with the tangled strands. He got one knot out and went to work on another, her damp hair so fragile in his callused fingers.

She moved restlessly in her sleep, her knee falling against his groin in the most seductive of temptations. Lily sighed and nuzzled against his neck, and he turned his head to press his face into her cheek. Washed free of the mud and the blood, she had a scent of freshness, a delicate sweetness that teased him. It promised a tenderness and a softness that had never been a part of his life, that he'd never even thought about.

He cursed and dropped his hand from her hair. What was he doing, thinking about emotions and beauty and tenderness? That wasn't him, and it wasn't acceptable. It would only weaken him, and he'd made a promise five hundred years ago. That promise went deeper than his oath to the Order. It had been a promise offered on the soul of the woman who'd died for him, and he would never do anything to violate that oath. Deviating from his role as a focused, cold warrior would compromise his ability to fulfill his promise.

There was no room for the way he was reacting to Lily. He had to shut it down now—the emotional side that was. He had no chance of stopping his intense physical desire for her, nor would he try. She simply felt too damn good to him.

But if anything happened with Lily…no, *when*, things became physical with Lily because he knew there was no other alternative, it would be sex only, no matter what her scent did to him. He wasn't interested in anything more than that. Didn't want it. Couldn't afford it.

None of them could.

The clock was ticking even as she slept.

 ❧ ❧ ❧

Lily woke to a feeling of warmth, of utter and complete security. Her body was completely relaxed as sleep began its slow retreat. It was a decadent luxury, the gift of peace. She smiled and snuggled more deeply into the heat, wanting to retreat into her dream, to this amazing, perfect place where she woke without fear.

She tucked herself against her pillow and sighed happily…then she became gradually aware of the steady thump beneath her cheek. A heartbeat? Someone was lying next to her? She realized a heavy weight was draped over her, pinning her to the ground. A man. Crushing her. Trapping her. Awareness came screaming back to her, and she shot awake, panic surging through her. She grabbed for the arm, trying to get it off. It was too heavy. He was too strong. She clawed at it, fought, struggled. "Get off, get off, get off—"

"Hey." Strong hands cupped hers, lightly squeezing her fists. "It's okay, Lily. Everything's all right."

"It's not all right!" She lurched upright, trying to get free. Her legs were tangled, caught. Her feet bound. *She was tied up!* Oh, dear God! Not again! A scream welled up in her chest, a scream of such true terror—

"Lily!" Gideon was suddenly in front of her, his blue eyes full of concern as he held her shoulders, forcing her to face him. "Look at me. Look at me now!"

She stared at him, trying to understand. "Gideon?" she whispered. She tentatively reached up and touched his face. His whiskers prickled against her fingers. He was real. He was there. Not Nate. Not those others— "It's just you?"

"Yeah, it's me. Only me." His grip on her shoulders softened, and he rubbed his hands down her arms. "It's over,

Lily. You're not at Nate's. You're with me."

She let his deep voice fill her and resonate through her like a warm blanket of protective strength. His voice was steady and calm. Reassuring. It charged through her like a deep pulse of thunder. Lily drank it in, the sound of kindness, of safety, of a power meant to protect.

"There you go." He brushed her hair off her face, his touch tender and endearing, his brow furrowed with concern. "See me, not the monsters in your head. Do you see me?"

She nodded and swallowed. It felt so good the way he was touching her. Gentle. Kind. Not a threat. Not a danger. His hair was flopped over his forehead, disheveled from sleep. He looked harmless and human. Not scary.

"You with me?" he asked.

She was. He'd brought her back. "*Gideon*." She moaned and flopped back down on her back, pressing her hands to her face as she tried to regroup. "I'm so sorry about that."

"Hey, no problem." He kept stroking her hair, and she didn't pull away. It felt too good. "Women often react that way when they wake up in my bed. I'm used to it."

She snorted then pulled her hands down so she could look at him. His eyes were bright blue in the early morning light, studying her intensely. "When I woke up pinned down like that, it made me remember—" No, she didn't want to remember.

Anger flashed over Gideon's face, but it was instantly contained. "It's okay. I should have thought of that. My fault."

"Yours? Yeah, you should totally be prepared for me to become completely irrational and fall apart on you..." Her voice trailed off as she recalled the hours of tears she'd dumped on him last night. Where was the woman she used to be? The one who was methodical, orderly, and always in control. The one who didn't dwell on what had happened to her when she was seventeen. The one who didn't let Nate get to her. "Sorry about the meltdown last night."

"No, it's fine." Gideon shrugged it off, and then propped himself up on his elbow so he could look at her. She liked looking up at him, seeing him leaning over her, like he was her shield from the world. He made her feel small and feminine, but not in a vulnerable way. She felt cherished and protected, as if she didn't have to be strong anymore. Not that she had a problem being strong—she liked it—but it felt good not to *have* to be strong.

Gideon grinned. "It made me feel like a man to have you go all weepy on me. Feel free to stroke my ego anytime."

She almost laughed at the absurdity of his response, and her reaction startled her. When was the last time she'd laughed? She couldn't even remember.

Gideon shifted next to her and the silver sleeping bag slid down his hip, revealing a broad expanse of taut skin. She realized it had unzipped when she'd been panicking, revealing far more of Gideon than she'd been in any state to notice last night. Heat flared in her cheeks. "Are you still naked?"

He grinned. "Hell, yeah. Wanna see?"

"No." But she couldn't quite keep herself from sneaking a peek at his shoulders. They were heavily muscled, broad and entirely bare, and her body heated in response. Not just heat. A burning, calling, *needing* for him. For his touch, for his kisses, for his body to rub against hers, skin to skin—

He leaned over her, his eyes a turbulent blue. "Liar," he whispered.

She tensed as his breath fluttered over her lips, clenching her fists against the compulsion to tangle her fingers in his hair and tug him down to her.

*Her attraction to him was too intense*, she realized suddenly, her body going cold with the shock of that comprehension.

She should have realized it last night at Nate's house, but she'd been too freaked out about everything. But now...it was so obvious. No wonder she'd been so certain he was her destruction. God, what an idiot she was! How could she have gotten herself in this situation? She couldn't even get away from him, stuck in the desert like this... She'd spent her life preparing for this moment, but still been totally blind-sided by it!

"Lily?" He touched her cheek. "Talk to me."

She met his gaze, her heart racing. "Aren't you worried about being alone with me?"

His eyebrows shot up, and for a moment he looked adorably confused. She would never have imagined Gideon

Roarke with such a vulnerable, human expression on his face, but he looked ravishingly handsome with his hair disheveled, his body still relaxed from sleep, and those blue eyes uncertain. This was the side she never would have expected of this cold, deadly warrior, and it made her heart melt just a little bit.

"Why would I be afraid of you?" he asked.

She had to say it. Had to lay it out there. Now, before others from the Order came around. Now, while they still had a chance to fix it. "Because I might be your *sheva*." Her heart was thundering when she said it. Dear God, even after preparing a lifetime for that possibility, to actually say those words was shocking. Scary. Exhilarating, which was, of course, terrifying in itself.

His face relaxed. "Oh, *that*."

"Yes, that. It's a big deal, and that might explain why I can't stop thinking about you..." Oy. She couldn't even say it, unable to keep the worry out of her voice. "I'm too smart to be attracted to you, but I am. So much. I need you so badly..." She wet her lips as his eyes darkened with a sensual heat that burned deep inside her. "I've done my research. I know my need for you is beyond what's natural. We're..." She stumbled over the word. "I'm your *sheva*."

"No—"

Lily interrupted him, her words tumbling over each other in her rush to get them out. "We could part ways right now before the bond starts forming. No one would have to know..." Her hands went to his shoulders, gripping him, as if she could force him to understand, her voice desperate. "I don't want to die just when I got free. You have to let me go so your Order members don't kill me. You *have* to." She wasn't ready for this. She wasn't prepared. She hadn't figured everything out yet. She didn't have her plan prepared!

He shook his head, his eyes hardening with memories he didn't share. "I already met my *sheva* a long time ago, and she was killed by the Order."

"You did? But that's impossible. I would have known that—" Oh, God. She did know that. How had she forgotten that? She'd spent her life researching Calydons, ferreting out all the information she could in order to avert the hell that had already been brought onto her family twice. Three times. She knew everything about Gideon. *Everything.* The fact he'd lost his *sheva* was part of what made him so legendary. How on earth had she forgotten?

But she knew why. Because she was barely clinging to the edge of sanity, and she was so strung out that she couldn't even think rationally anymore. Because the one fear that had haunted her for her whole life, the terror that had defined her and everything she'd done, was the very real possibility that she was genetically predisposed to being a *sheva.*

She'd been waiting for it, watching over her shoulder for twenty years, waiting for that fate to snatch her up and spit her out. The way she'd responded to Gideon had been so precisely what she had been dreading that it had triggered her deepest terrors. She'd panicked, dismissing all the information she'd worked so hard to acquire to give her power.

Gideon was right. He'd already met his *sheva.* So, then what was going on? Was she imagining her response to him? Maybe it was just some reaction because he rescued her, right? A little bit of relief, combined with her magic's natural attraction to Calydons? Yeah, maybe—

"I'm safe, Lily. Destiny isn't coming after us, no matter what we do." Gideon's gaze went to her mouth, and she felt heat flare inside her.

Not just heat. A burning, raging need that threatened to consume her. She felt the enormity of his presence. His raw masculinity crawled beneath her skin, wrapping its way around her, and drawing her toward him.

Oh, crap. This wasn't good. "If I'm not your *sheva,* then there has to be an explanation for how I feel—" She gasped as he dropped his head and pressed his lips to her throat. She shoved at his shoulders, writhing at the intense need that small action had raised inside her. What was wrong with her? Why couldn't she resist him?

Fear licked through her, the first real fear she'd had. What if she couldn't stop him? What if it happened again, like before? She went cold, ice cold, and the scars on her wrists and ankles began to throb, as if they were still fresh, as if she was bound again, just like she'd been all those years ago. "Stop!"

He lifted his head, his blue gaze intense. "What's wrong?"

"You scare me!" She wriggled out of the bag, wincing when she accidentally brushed his erection with her hand. "Oh, God. Sorry."

Gideon pulled back, and let her go, but she saw the tension in his body and knew how difficult it had been for him to release her. He wanted her just as badly as she craved him. The last time anyone had looked at her with that much interest, it had ended so terribly. So awfully.

"It's not just that I want you." She hugged herself as she stood on the arid ground, the sand leaching through her thick socks. "I feel like I'll lose total control if you kiss me even once, and you've got this look in your eyes…you'll do the same, won't you? Lose control? You're *sure* I can't be your *sheva?*" Maybe it would be better if she were his *sheva*. If she were, then his instincts would prevent him from hurting her. They might be strong enough to keep the situation from spiraling. Without that protection, without her ability to keep him at a distance, there would be no stopping him once he got a taste of her magic. He would kill her. It would be just like before—

"I'm absolutely positive you're not my *sheva*." He pulled himself out of the bag and rose to his feet, starkly magnificent in his nudity. His body was lean, yet heavily muscled. His stomach was carved, his shoulders wide with a power that made her shudder. She could see cords of muscle beneath the skin drawn tautly across his thighs, and the dark hair on his chest teased the golden hue to his skin. He made no attempt to hide how badly he wanted her, and her stomach knotted with desire as her gaze fell below his waist.

"Lily." His voice was husky, curling into her belly and sending liquid heat coursing through her.

Fire burned through her at the raw lust on his face. Passion and fear. Hot and cold. He was twisting her up, and she couldn't resist him. She was losing the battle. She knew she was. Despite everything she knew and all the lessons she'd learned… she was falling…

"I *know* I'm going to lose total control if I kiss you, and I don't care." He slowly crossed the hard ground, coming to a stop just before her.

Her breath started coming faster. "But I do care. I—"

"I've never felt like this. You make me feel alive." He cupped the back of her neck with his hand and tugged her toward him. "I won't hurt you, Lily. I swear it."

She braced herself and her hands went to his chest to block him, to try to keep distance between them, but the minute her hands touched his bare skin, her resistance vanished, consumed by her need to feel him against her. "Gideon—"

His mouth was hot and wet as it closed over hers in a kiss designed to make her his in every way.

The moment his lips touched hers, she knew she was in trouble.

# Chapter 7

The instant Lily's lips parted for him, a fierce possessiveness roared through Gideon. He wrapped his arms around her and pulled her against him. Her body was warm and alive, pulsing with life and igniting flames inside him that had been dormant his entire life.

He growled her name and tunneled his fingers through her hair, the silky locks sliding over his skin like the most decadent of temptations. Soft, sensual, breathtaking. With the groan of a man falling out of his depth, Gideon locked his fingers in her hair and deepened the kiss, pouring everything he had into the unbelievable sensation of her lips, her tongue, and her breath mingling with his.

Lily made a noise of surprise at his invasion, then she threw her arms around his neck and tumbled recklessly into the kiss. She gave him everything: her body, her passion, the bright spirit that made her who she was. She clung to him, her tongue crashing into his mouth with the same desperation grinding so deep in his soul.

*Yes.* He kissed her again and again, deeper and harder. He was unable to consume enough of her, needing more than what he could get, even as she met every kiss with equal passion and heat. Her hands were pure seduction, the way she was running them over his shoulders, his arms and his back, as if she couldn't get enough of him, as if by some unfathomable miracle, she wanted him with every bit of the same heated passion.

Gideon slid his hands beneath the waistband of her

sweatpants, groaning as he kneaded the soft flesh of her bottom. Passion licked through him, like a tidal wave of pure desire, igniting every cell as it shot through his body. Her hips were curved and round beneath his hands, her body aching for him. He kissed her again, his mouth frantic to taste more of her, to somehow catch up to the desire racing through him.

Lily made the most beautiful, feminine sound in her throat, the sound of a woman at the edge of her control. Her desire flooded him, like white-hot blades lacerating his self-control. He could feel her need for him, a crushing, uncontrollable heat threatening to overwhelm them both. He was shocked by his ability to feel her passion, and her desires, and even more stunned by how it ignited his own. The intensity was beyond anything he'd ever experienced, more than he could control, more than he could contain.

Gideon kissed her harder, but heaven help him, it wasn't enough. It was a tease, a taste, but his core burned for more. He needed her skin against his, her breasts against his chest, his hands over the bare skin of her hips. He needed to be inside her making her his, and only his, binding them together for all eternity. And, God help him, he needed her hands on him. He needed to feel her stroke across his chest, her mouth kiss his stomach, her bare legs against his. Nothing between them. Nothing holding them back. He wanted it all.

Lily mumbled his name as her hands went to his hair and she pulled him down toward her, kissing him frantically. He could feel Lily's desperation, internalizing it until he didn't know which were her emotions and lust and which were his. All Gideon knew was that it was wrecking him, torturing him because he couldn't get enough. Couldn't satisfy it. Couldn't get his brain around how badly he needed her. Every inch of her body...he had to touch her, to taste her...

"I need you." He fumbled with the hem of her sweatshirt, his hands shaking as he spread his palms over her ribs, a soft groan falling from his lips as he felt her heat beneath his hands. Her skin was soft and fragile, so perfect he couldn't stand it. "I have to taste you."

"Yes," she whispered, her voice a throaty tremble that rolled beneath his skin like the hot wind on a summer night.

Gideon dropped to his knees in the sand and tugged up her sweatshirt. The flat expanse of her belly... hell and damnation. All his. This unbelievable, amazing woman was his. He flanked her waist with his hands and slowly, reverently, kissed her belly.

She made a noise of passion, a small, sexy whimper of desire, and wrapped her arms around his head, holding him to her stomach.

*Hell, yes.* Gideon tightened his grip on her hips, holding her captive as he kissed his way across her torso. She smelled like woods and the fresh scent of spring water...but that wasn't all. She smelled like desire, like a woman on fire. He knew her desire was only for him. He could feel it in her emotions, her intense connection to him and no one else. His name was imprinted in her soul, his scent swirling through her body, his kiss calling to the part of her that made her a woman.

"God, Gideon," she whispered. "Don't stop. Please don't stop."

"Never." Her stomach quivered under his touch as he swirled his tongue into her navel, his hands roaming her back, her stomach, and her ribs. He slid his palms upward over her smooth skin to the soft curves of her breasts. Lily sucked in her breath as he rubbed his thumbs over them, and her nipples hardened. Raw heat rushed through him, not just his, but both of theirs, mixed, on fire—

His lower body jerked, and he realized he was about to lose it. Literally. Son of a bitch. "Hang on." He jerked his mouth off her and set her back away from him, trying to regain his control before he made an ass of himself.

"No, no, don't stop." Lily reached for his shoulders, and he felt another pulse jolt through him as he grabbed her hands, intercepting them before she could reach him.

"Don't touch me," Gideon gritted out. Hell, he had to get control of himself. Desire and lust were plunging through him. Hers, his, five hundred years of holding his shit together was all coming down around him, driven by her, by her kiss, by his need to take her, to kiss her, to make love to her—

"I *have* to touch you." Lily's throaty whisper caught him in the gut, and he yanked her down to him to kiss her again, unable to resist her. She fell to her knees before him, her body slamming against his chest, and her hand going between his legs before he could stop her.

Her fingers clasped around his cock, and his body's response was instant, totally out of control. The orgasm shot through him like a sword lancing him right through the chest. "Lily—" He dove into the kiss, taking her, owning her as the climax roared through him.

He roared and bucked against her, knocking them both to the ground. Their kiss was frenzied and frantic as she kept her grip on him. Helpless in her grasp, Gideon kissed her desperately as his body shuddered again and again. The final crest tore through him, and he bellowed her name as he locked her down against him and rode the orgasm out. The waves continued to ride him relentlessly, taking him until there was nothing left.

For a long moment, minutes, hours, he didn't even know how long, they were still, both of them breathing heavily. Sweat trickled down his back as his body fought to reclaim itself from her. Gideon swore and dropped his head, leaning his forehead against her throat. His arms wrapped around her waist as he sagged on top of her, utterly spent.

Lily's arms were around his head, holding him to her. Her heart was hammering as rapidly as his, a frenzied beat against his chest.

They didn't speak. They didn't move. Just two beings trying to find their footing after being stripped of everything that made them who they were, after connecting with the other so intensely that there had been no dividing line between them.

Gideon swore under his breath as the reality of what had just happened began to settle in. With a groan, he lifted his head to look at her. Her moss-green eyes were at half-mast, the face of a woman still caught in the throes of desire and passion. His cock became hard again, growing against her belly. "All you did was touch me, and I went," he said, still shocked by the realization. "I feel like I'm fifteen again. One touch by you and all my control vanished." His muscles were still spasming from the orgasm. What the hell had just happened?

Lily smiled, a smug little grin that reached inside him and plucked at something soft. Something warm. Something that made him want to smile back. He liked that arrogant look on her face, the one that showed the courageous woman inside that battered body.

Of course, that didn't change the fact that he'd been completely derailed by what had just happened. He'd had every intention of making love to her, and instead, he'd jumped off the ship early. Early! What the hell? Where was the rigid control he'd owned for the last five hundred years?

Lily trailed her fingers through his hair, and then she lightly kissed his temple, a tender, affectionate gesture that rocked him as much as the orgasm had. No one was tender with him. It wasn't a part of his life, and he didn't need it.

But with his skin still tingling from her kiss, he wanted her to do it again. And again.

"Did this happen to you a lot when you were fifteen?" Lily sounded amused, and a little proud of herself.

"Yeah, it did, actually," he admitted, unable to keep anything from her. "It completely humiliated me every damn time." It had happened every time he'd gotten it on with a girl, triggered by the intensity of the emotions and lust racing between them. It had continued until he'd figured out how to shut down his emotions and separate himself from what was happening around him. Once he'd learned that, sex had become a tool to sate his Calydon instincts, something he could engage in with the impartiality of an outside observer.

Since then, sex had never been something he couldn't control, but that one kiss with Lily had triggered an intense reaction that he'd been completely unprepared for. Even all that shit he dealt with when he was fifteen was nothing compared to what he'd just felt. This hadn't just been sex. It hadn't just been his empathic abilities taking over. This had been something else entirely. "I lost it from kissing your stomach. I can't believe it."

Lily laughed softly and patted his cheek. "Don't look so upset. I've been told I have a very sexy stomach."

Yeah, well, that bit of news sure helped his mood. "Who's been checking out your belly?" he growled.

Her eyebrows went up. "You're jealous?"

"Hell, yeah. I wanted to impress you with my great sexual prowess and I went off early." Gideon groaned and dropped his head to her neck again and inhaled. "You smell so damned good, I'm getting hard again already."

What in hell's name was going on? He had no defenses against her scent, against the way her body felt against him. He had no resistance to the way those green eyes glittered with so much emotion. "I'm not like this," he muttered. "I don't react this way to women. Ever. I can't stop myself when I'm with you."

Lily didn't move for a second, then her muscles tensed up. She shoved at his shoulders. "Get up."

He wrapped his arms around her. "No way. I need another chance to prove myself."

"No, you don't." She shoved harder, and he could feel the palpitations of her heart. Nervous. Worried. Panicked.

Shit. He didn't want her afraid of him. He immediately loosened his grip, allowing her to scramble free. The moment he lost contact with her, a cold feeling of loss settled over him. Being separated from her felt wrong. His instincts shouted for him to reclaim her, to bring her back beneath him, to finish what he'd started.

But he made no move to go after her. She'd spent too long being trapped, and no way would he make her revisit that hell, no matter how badly he wanted to vault up and go after her. "You don't need to fear me," he said, unable to keep the heat out of his voice as he watched her stand up. Her body was lithe and athletic, those long legs stretching as she rose to her feet. Even in those baggy sweats and that huge sweatshirt, she was sexy as hell.

"No?" Lily hugged herself. "I'm fully aware of your virility, and I feel like I just dodged a bullet. You just admitted that you have no control with me. That's not good!"

He rolled onto his back, trying to get his muscles functioning again, but they were still spent from that short interlude. Hell. Was he getting that old? "Most women would take that as a compliment that you were the only female in five hundred years to break my control." He kept his voice even and low, trying to figure out what it was he'd said that had spooked her.

"I would have had sex with you just then, Gideon."

Something carnal and male pulsed through him, and he sat up. "I'm guessing that's a problem?" His voice was dangerously low, throbbing with the desire thickening inside him.

Lily's eyes widened, and her cheeks flushed. Then she raised her chin and set her hands on her hips. "Yes, it's a problem. You're a *Calydon*."

"So?" He couldn't take his eyes off the curve of her mouth. He knew what she tasted like: sin, temptation, and all the colors of the damn rainbow. Not that he'd ever tasted a rainbow, but he *knew* that it would taste like her.

Lily threw up her arms in frustration. "So, you're dangerous! I mean, I knew I responded to any Calydon, but that...that was so far over the top I can't even deal with it." She grabbed the sleeping bag and threw it over his hips, covering his erection that was already primed for her. "And stop tempting me by lying there naked. Damn all of you Calydons and your sexuality." She stalked a short distance away and sat down on a boulder.

He scowled, something dark and not so playful rumbling through him at her comment. "You respond to any Calydon? What does that mean?" She was his. He knew it in every cell of his body. There would be no other Calydons for her. Ever. "You respond only to me."

He wasn't saying it as a threat or a warning. He was saying it as the truth. Just as she was the single force that had penetrated his walls, he knew it was the same for her.

This was a first for both of them, and any further thought of other warriors needed to be off the table. Now.

"Well, yes, that's my point. You're different." Her cheeks were still flushed, and he could smell her arousal, felt it pulsing through her, still seeking fulfillment. He knew, with absolute certainty, that it would take only one kiss and she'd be his again. And this time, he'd make sure he lasted long enough to take her.

"Oh, no, you don't." Lily's eyes widened and she pointed her finger at him as she scooted to a boulder a little further away. "I'm not getting caught up in some crazy sex thing with you. Stay right there and tell me why you came to get me. Even if Ana sent you, I know the Order has more important things to do than rescue random women. You have a reason. I want to know what it is." Her words were heavy with desire, but he sensed the determination behind her questions.

She wasn't simply avoiding talking about sex. Gideon could tell she actually needed answers, as if information would give her strength.

And shit, she was right about what they needed to focus on. He groaned and rubbed his hand over his eyes. How the hell had he forgotten about that? He didn't have time for a sex marathon with anyone, even Lily. Because that's what it would be. Once he got another taste of her, he knew he wouldn't stop until they were both too tired to move.

"Gideon?"

"Yeah." He tossed the blanket aside and stood up, ignoring his erection as he walked over to the clothes he'd tossed over a branch last night. Still wet, but he didn't care. He needed to pull his head back together and get focused. He ditched the idea of wet boxers bunching under his jeans and grabbed his pants instead. "What do you know about the stone?"

"The one in the handle of Nate's knife?" Lily eyed his chest as he pulled his jeans up over his hips. The yearning on her face was evident, and Gideon had to steel himself to keep from marching over to her and finishing what he'd tried to start.

"Yeah," he said. "What's so important about the knife?"

Lily frowned. "I don't know anything about it. All I know is that both Nate and Frank wanted it, so I figured it was important. Is that how Ana got free? Did she get it?"

Gideon cursed and ignored her question. "Seriously? You know *nothing*?"

She stiffened at the frustration in his voice. "That's why you came to get me? So I could give you answers about the stone?"

He met her gaze. "I came to get you because you needed help." It was the truth, and he knew it. Yeah, he'd been sent there on Order business once the team had realized Lily might be able to help them. But that wasn't *why* he was there. He was there because the night they'd rescued Ana, when she'd told him about Lily and begged him so desperately to retrieve her, Gideon had been consumed by a fierce, burning need to find Lily and save her. No woman could suffer what Ana had suffered, and he'd known instantly that he was the one who had to retrieve this woman that Ana had entrusted to his safekeeping.

He'd come for Lily, pure and simple.

# Chapter 8

Lily's face softened, and she smiled. "Thank you," she said quietly. Something passed between them. A connection. An understanding.

He nodded. Nothing more needed to be said. They both got it.

Shit. He'd never been so in tune with anyone before. Yeah, sure, he'd done a blood bond with two of his Order brothers so they could connect telepathically, but he'd never been hit with their emotions like he was with Lily.

He *knew* what she was feeling, even when he tried to block it, which was damned inconvenient when he was trying to concentrate on his mission. Shit. He had to focus. The mission was critical. "We have to find out what the deal is with the stone," he said. "There's writing carved on it. Ana said you would be able to tell us what the writing means."

"Oh…" Excitement lit up Lily's face, giving such a spark of life to her that Gideon was riveted. "I never had an opportunity to decipher the carvings, but I think I could if I had time. I'd love to have the opportunity to study it. Do you have it?" She leaned forward with eagerness. "I mean, do you have it with you now?"

Hell, she was radiant, the way her eyes were glowing with anticipation and intelligence. "Damn, you're beautiful."

Lily's cheeks flushed, but her fear of him was gone, chased away by her enthusiasm about the stone. "Seriously, Gideon. Can I see it? I know a lot about Calydon history, and I bet I can figure it out."

Gideon picked up his damp shirt, energized by the excitement emanating from her. "Yeah, I noticed that you knew a lot about us. How do you know so much?"

Wariness flashed across her face. "You don't know who I am?"

He raised his brows. He knew a hell of a lot about her, actually. He knew she was afraid. He'd felt the demons from her past. She'd shown him her fear and her courage, and he knew she was spooked by his kind. He was also well aware of her intense sensuality and the heat that lit up between them. It was actually sort of surprising to realize that he didn't even know her last name. "No. Who are you?"

She cleared her throat, looking slightly uncomfortable. "I'm Lily Davenport."

He rolled the familiar name around in his head for a minute while he tried to place it, and then he figured it out. "You're Dr. Davenport? The leading expert on Calydons, who travels the world to lecture about us?"

"Yes." Lily watched carefully, wondering how much Gideon knew. How much had the Order paid attention to her? How much did they know about what she'd spent her life doing?

Lily knew the moment Gideon realized *exactly* who she was. His face darkened and a scowl creased his features as everything clicked into place in his mind. "You're the crazy professor who's been vilifying Calydons for twenty years," he growled as he yanked his shirt over his head. "The one who screwed up some of our missions by telling secrets we didn't want told." Realization flickered in his eyes, and his voice softened. "The one who disappeared two years ago. Shit, Lily. We had no idea what happened to you."

She was surprised by his ability to offer honest sympathy. Lily hadn't expected him to be the kind of person who could communicate such a heartfelt apology simply with the tone of his voice. He was sorry for not realizing she'd needed help, when she'd never even met him? This was the man she'd spent her life accusing of being so cold, so merciless, so heartless?

Standing here with Gideon, with her skin still tingling from his kisses, suddenly all Lily's convictions about the Calydon lack of humanity seemed so unfounded. He wasn't the remote, faceless monster she'd spent her life cultivating. He was real, he was living, and he was the most passionate person she'd ever experienced. "Did I really screw up some of your missions?"

"Yeah." His expression was deadpan. "We have a dartboard with your face on it, and if we weren't bound by our oath to protect innocents, you'd be dead. Until you disappeared, we were all hoping you'd wind up being an Order *sheva* so we could kill you."

She blinked. "Are you joking?"

Gideon walked over to her, his bulk intimidating and daunting. "You've been stalking me for years." His eyes were relentless and hard, exactly how she'd imagined he would be. This was the Gideon she'd expected, not the passionate lover who could evoke so much desire in her. "Why?"

A sudden sense of dread welled within her as she sat up more stiffly on the rock, realizing what he'd just asked. "You knew I was focused on you, specifically?"

"Of course I knew. You weren't just seeking information about the Order or Calydons in general." His gaze narrowed. "You wanted *me*." He crouched down so he was level with her, his quad muscles flexing like rods of steel beneath the wet denim. "That's why you freaked in the car when you realized who I was. Because you're Lily Davenport, famous researcher with an agenda when it comes to Gideon Roarke." He caught his fingers under her chin, his touch light, his blue eyes intense. "Tell me, Dr. Davenport, why do I matter so much to you?"

Lily felt her stomach roll at his direct question, at the searing heat from his touch. The Gideon she'd spent her life researching was a man so ruthless that no one was safe from him if he thought killing you would fulfill his mission. He was death. He was destruction. He was utterly without mercy. He took women with ruthless pleasure to satisfy his own needs, free to indulge all the lustful urges of a Calydon warrior, without restraint since he'd already found his *sheva*.

He was the only Calydon in history who had stood back and watched his *sheva* be slaughtered without remorse. Most Calydons couldn't even survive the loss of their *sheva*, yet Gideon was so hard that he'd watched her death and walked away unaffected.

How could that stoic warrior possibly be the male kneeling before her, his touch so electrifying she could barely keep from closing the distance between them? His eyes searched hers so intently, as if he could feel every emotion churning inside her. But it was the same Gideon. She knew him so well, from years of research, and from the intensity of his emotions, which she could feel so clearly.

Lily brushed her finger over his jaw, unable to keep herself from bridging the distance between them, despite all she knew about him. "I can't believe you're...him."

Gideon's hands went to her knees. His touch was firm and steady, a caress that sent heat spiraling up her thighs and right into her belly. "Who exactly do you think I am?" His voice was husky and deep, his blue eyes churning with intensity.

Lily wanted to push him away and shove his hands off her legs, but instead, she slid forward, unable to deny the intensity of her response to him. "You murdered my grandmother," she whispered as his hands slid further up her thighs. "You're the warrior who destroyed my family."

Gideon's hands stilled on her legs. "What are you talking about?"

"My grandma was Elizabeth Ridley. She was the *sheva* of an Order member named Cade." Lily lifted her chin, forcing herself to say the words that had haunted her for so long, that suddenly didn't make complete sense anymore. She couldn't reconcile the past and the present. "They had a son named Trig. You killed both Cade and my grandma, leaving Trig without any parents. You murdered my grandparents, Gideon, in cold blood, in front of their children."

For a moment, Gideon looked confused, then she saw him remember. He cursed and ran his hand through his hair, looking utterly at a loss for what to say. "Yeah, I remember," he said finally. No apologies. No excuses. Just the grim truth of what he was.

Long-held anger boiled through Lily at his lack of remorse and at his ability to look her in the eye and not apologize. "My grandmother was happily married before Cade came into her life. He used the bond to force her to leave her husband and daughter, who was my mom. Cade took her away, then he got her pregnant."

Gideon's eyes narrowed. "I'm sure he treasured her."

"Treasured her? Are you kidding?" Lily shoved at his chest, wanting space from Gideon and from her confusing attraction to the man who had haunted her for so long. "He stole her from her family. My grandpa went to their house to get her back, and Cade murdered him."

Gideon's jaw tightened. "Cade went rogue when another man tried to claim her. That's the *sheva* destiny. He will be destined to lose her—"

"What happened next, Gideon? Do you remember?" Lily leaned forward, anger pulsing in her, fury at this man who had torn apart her family with so little remorse. "You showed up and killed not only Cade, but also my grandma, leaving her seventeen-year-old daughter to raise Trig herself."

His eyes met hers without flinching. They were hard, cold, unfathomable oceans of darkness. "Your mom was there? She saw it and told you?"

"Yes." Tears suddenly filled Lily's eyes. "Trig was only two years older than me. My mom raised the two of us together. He died when he was eighteen because he didn't survive the dream that would have brought him into his powers as a Calydon. Your race destroyed my family, at all levels." Lily closed her eyes for a minute against the pain of losing Trig, who had been her best friend and brother. Yes, technically, he was her uncle, but in her heart and soul, he was her brother and he always would be.

She felt Gideon's hands on her shoulders, and she wrenched her eyes open to look at him. His eyes were dark, and his face was raw with emotion. "I am truly sorry."

She was startled by the intensity on his face and by her belief in his words. "But you...you couldn't be. You believe in your mission. You have no mercy. You regret no action if it serves your oath. You simply aren't capable of remorse or any kind of human emotion."

His grip tightened. "You know so much about me, do you?"

She swallowed. "Yes, I do. I've studied you for twenty years."

He looked disgusted. "For someone who's obsessed with Calydons, you know very little."

She tensed. "I'm not obsessed."

He gave her an impatient look. "Not obsessed? Exactly how many articles have you published on the Calydons? Somewhere between six and seven hundred maybe, starting when you were about five years old?"

She felt her cheeks turn red, realizing his guess wasn't that far off. "Okay, maybe a little obsessed." She gave him a hard look, trying to hide the fact that she wanted to do nothing more than slide into the heat of his body and hug him, burying her pain in him, trying to take his away. Because she felt his pain. She really did. But it simply didn't make sense. He wasn't capable of it. "I researched the Calydons because I wanted to understand why my grandmother had died, why my mother was so freaked out about Calydons that she was warning me off them since birth, why my brother had to die. I wanted to understand how to survive it if I became someone's *sheva* like my grandmother." She met Gideon's gaze. "I needed to understand, so I could find a way to keep the nightmare from repeating itself, from having someone like you destroy everything I cared about."

Gideon growled and grabbed the back of her neck, yanking her toward him. She tumbled off the rock and fell against him, her hands bracing on his waist as he cupped her hips with his hands. He glared down at her, his face inches from hers.

His eyes were dark, bubbling with a rage that made her stomach ripple with fear...and excitement. He was every bit as dangerous as the fictional Gideon who'd haunted her dreams and nightmares for years. And twice as handsome. "Lily." His voice was harsh, a growl worthy of the brutal warrior she'd studied for so long.

She swallowed. "What?" As terrifying as he was, she wasn't afraid of him anymore. She should be, on so many levels, but she wasn't. Why not? Where was her sense of self-preservation? Her intelligence? Her ordered world?

Gideon's voice was low, vibrating through her body, his breath warm on her mouth. "You're right that I never regret anything I do to fulfill my oath, even if it's killing an innocent. I do what I have to do, and I stand behind it."

"Even murdering my grandmother?" she challenged, desperate to have him do something to enable her to pull back from him and remember that he was the enemy.

"Yes. Even that. I do what I have to do." His voice became harder. "But my Calydon heritage demands I protect innocents at all costs. It doesn't understand the concept of sacrificing one innocent to save millions, so every time I go against our heritage and kill an innocent, it's..." A muscle ticked in his cheek. "It sucks to kill an innocent, and that's the truth."

Lily swallowed hard, unable to deny the harsh reality in his voice and his eyes. He meant it. She could feel his regret and his anguish beating at her, twisting the air like some poisoned taint. "Oh, Gideon." She touched his arm, staggered by the pain rolling off him. "I'm so sorry," she said quietly. "I had no idea."

His tight grip didn't loosen. "It's brutal what you endured. I get that, and I wish you hadn't had to deal with it. I really do. But if I hadn't killed them, you wouldn't be here today. Cade would have killed your grandmother, their son, and her daughter. Your mom would have died before you were ever born, and you never would have existed."

She bit her lip at the flash of agony on his face, at the way he pulled her closer, as if he were afraid she would disappear right then. "Gideon—"

"Cade would have destroyed everything he or your grandmother cared about, and any innocent that came within reach would have been brutally murdered. It was his destiny, Lily. Once bonded, the Calydon will go rogue. The only way to stop him is for his *sheva* to kill him, then she dies utterly broken, knowing she took the life of the man she loved." He shook his head. "Until you've seen a rogue Calydon on a rampage, you'll never understand how bad it gets. My job is to protect the innocents from them, and I'll do whatever it takes."

In Gideon's expression was a coldness that made Lily shiver. He was showing her that lack of emotion he'd culled so expertly to be able to do his job. But she also saw heat. She saw pain. She saw the man she'd never really seen, even after all those years of research. A man she wanted to cradle in her arms and comfort, even as the blood of her own grandmother dripped from his hands. "Damn you," she whispered.

He raised his brows. "Now what?"

"You'd kill me, if you needed to."

He said nothing.

"I know that. I know what you are. I've lived through the destruction that you've left behind..." She closed her eyes. "And yet, I still..."

"You still what?" His voice was softer now, curling through her.

She pulled out of his grasp and walked across the clearing, out of his reach. "I can't get involved with you."

His eyes narrowed. "Too late, Lily. You're not only involved with me, you're involved with the Order."

Her belly tightened. "Didn't you hear what I just said? There's no way I can get involved with you or the Order. *No way*. I have *issues* with you, the Order, and Calydons in general. Big issues beyond even my grandmother and my brother—" Her heritage, her background...it made her so vulnerable to Calydons.

Especially to one as powerful as Gideon. Her magic was linked to Calydons. She was a source of energy destined to be linked to the powerful warriors. An expendable fuel that had always been lethally harvested by Calydons for two thousand years—

Sudden realization flooded her with terror. If she wasn't his *sheva*, then there was only one other explanation for her intense response to him: her magic had selected him for her. He was the one her Satinka magic had been searching for: the Calydon meant to be her mate, the only one who could truly mesh with her power and use it for all it was.

Lily went cold, ice cold at the thought. When she was seventeen, six Calydons had nearly killed her when they'd raped her for her magic because they'd been driven insane by her gift. What would it be like with Gideon, the male that her magic *wanted*? Lily's wrists began to burn from the damage of chains long gone, scars in her soul as much as on her skin. Her breath caught in her chest, and suddenly she was back there, in that god-forsaken dump, tied down, at the mercy of those six Calydons for three days—

"Lily?" Gideon turned sharply toward her, his brow furrowed. "What's wrong?"

She stared at him, at his massive shoulders, at the sheer, untamed power emanating from him. She'd had no defenses against her attackers ten years ago, and they had been young men with a fraction of the power and strength that Gideon had. What would Gideon do to her if he got caught up in the thrall of her Satinka magic? With his strength, and the way she craved him so badly?

Dear God, if Gideon knew what she was, if he learned that her magic had chosen him, he would kill her for it.

Not on purpose. She knew that about him now. But he would kill her, because he wouldn't be able to stop himself, and she wouldn't be able to resist him. No warrior could resist that kind of call. No wonder she'd been so drawn to him. It hadn't been because of the *sheva* curse. It was because her magic had selected him as the warrior it wanted, the male it would feed with power until Lily was dead.

"Lily?" Gideon walked toward her, his strides long and powerful across the sand. "Talk to me. I can feel your fear. What is it?"

She shook her head. "Nothing. I—"

He caught her shoulders, his grip solid, secure, and unbelievably tempting. "Listen to me. I know Nate betrayed you. I get that. I understand your fear. I feel it in every cell of my body. But you need to understand that I've given you my protection, and that's unshakeable. I swear on my Order oath that you're safe with me. Do you understand? You're working for the Order now, and that means you have our protection. Not just the Order. Mine. *I will protect you.*"

"I'm not working for the Order!" Dear God, she could never walk into that room and put herself at the mercy of the warriors meant to destroy her. Yes, Lily felt Gideon's fierce determination pulsing at her, his commitment in every word he spoke. She wanted to believe it, she wanted to just crawl into his circle of safety and trust him. But she wasn't a fool, and there was no way he could keep that promise, not if he was the one her magic had chosen. "I just want to go home—"

Gideon didn't back down. "Do you remember the eyes

of the Calydon who would have raped you at Nate's? Deep pits of evil?"

She shuddered at the unwelcome memory. "Yes."

"There's a Calydon far more evil than that who has been in a metaphysical prison for two thousand years. The magic that sealed his walls is fading, and he's about to get out. As the Order, our mission is to stop him at all costs, but we don't know why his walls are weakening and we don't know how to stop it." Gideon's grip tightened so much it hurt, but it wasn't aggression. It was his unshakeable instinct to do his job, the same drive that had enabled him to kill innocents for five hundred years. "This Calydon, named Ezekiel, nearly destroyed the world once. If he gets out, he'll do it for real this time, because there's no one alive who can stop him once he's free."

Oh…she knew exactly how deadly Ezekiel had been two thousand years ago. And he was getting free? Lily couldn't help the chill that ran through her at his words and at the starkness of the emotions he was sending into her. "What does that have to do with me?"

"Nate was orchestrating it, the stone is involved, and it sounds like Frank is taking over now that Nate's dead." Gideon's eyes glittered. "You're our only link to all three, and with your knowledge of our history, you might have the answers we need."

Her stomach churned and she shuddered. "Frank? I can't—"

"Yes, you can. And you will." He drew her up against him until their bodies were touching from chest to thigh, until he was all over her personal space. "I'm incapable of letting Ezekiel destroy countless innocents, and as long as you might be able to help, I'm not letting you go."

"So, I'm a prisoner again?"

Regret flickered in his eyes. "Only if you refuse to help. It's your choice."

"Oh, come on, Gideon. Don't insult me like that. There's no choice here!"

He gritted his teeth. "There's always a choice, Lily, even if it doesn't feel like it."

She shoved his arm off her. "Damn you, Gideon. That's a lie, and you know it."

Sometimes, there were no choices.
Sometimes, there was only hell.

# Chapter 9

Gideon felt like hell when Lily ripped herself out of his grasp and stalked away from him, her shoulders hunched and her eyes haunted. All because she'd become a prisoner again. His prisoner, this time.

He had no right to take her, but he knew he would do it anyway. He had to do what was right. Personal freedom meant nothing if Ezekiel got out. They would all die if he did, and the greater good took priority.

It had to. That was his oath.

But shit, it was a hell of a lot more difficult to do when his actions were mired down with the burden of emotions. Where was his control? Gone since he'd met Lily. She'd stripped away his defenses, and he couldn't get them back.

Gideon knew why he couldn't pull his shit together and shut down his emotions. As inconvenient and distracting as it was to be wading through all this emotional shit, it felt incredible to feel his heart beat again. It was as if he'd broken out of some dark cavern into the sunshine, and damned if he didn't want to stay outside.

But he couldn't afford to. He had to get himself back where he needed to be. Yet, as he felt the waves of tension emanating from Lily, he couldn't shut her out. He wouldn't. He liked feeling her. He damn well got off on knowing she was pulsing beneath his skin.

"Hell." He ran his hand through his hair, forcing himself not to close the distance between them, to drop to his knees and offer her whatever she damn well wanted. "Lily. I'm sorry. If there were any other way, I'd do it. But we need you." The apology felt foreign on his tongue, words he so rarely spoke, because he could not afford to question what he did to fulfill the promise he'd made so many centuries ago.

Lily turned her back on him, walked up to a fir tree and wrapped her arms around it. She pressed her cheek to the rough bark and closed her eyes, as if she were gaining solace and strength from nature itself. "I can't be a prisoner again," she whispered, so quietly he wouldn't have heard it if it weren't for his enhanced hearing. "I can't do this." Tears squeezed out of her eyes, and he felt like she'd torn his gut right out of his body.

"You can do it. You're not a prisoner, not like before. I swear I'll—" He started to walk toward her when he felt the mental presence of Quinn, his blood brother of five hundred years and a fellow Order member.

Quinn was the one remaining Order member with whom Gideon had performed a blood bond, which enabled them to communicate telepathically over any distance. Elijah had been the third part of their trio, but Elijah was dead. He'd been slaughtered by the bastard who had held Lily hostage for two years.

Gideon flexed his jaw against the pain that wanted to spring up at the thought of Elijah. His death was so recent that the pain was still raw, culling grief so powerful that it was resistant to Gideon's iron-willed attempts to bury it.

*You up yet?* Quinn asked.

*Yeah, we're fine. Could use a ride. Is Kane available to teleport us back there?* Gideon walked over to Lily, unwilling to leave her isolated. Her head was bent, accentuating the bones in her too-thin shoulders. She'd suffered so much already, and he was going to bring more down on her.

He really was the bastard she'd accused him of being, wasn't he?

*You want to bring Lily here?* Quinn hesitated. *You want to risk exposing her to Kane? I thought we weren't bringing her in.*

Every female was a risk for an un-bonded Order member, and if she were Kane's mate, the connection would flare up the minute they connected. Something dark and dangerous spilled through Gideon at the idea that Lily might be Kane's *sheva*.

Lily turned sharply toward him, as if she could feel his response. She raised her eyebrows at him, showing no fear.

Gideon ground his jaw and touched the ends of Lily's hair, needing that contact between them. He knew he had no choice about whether to bring Lily in. His oath required he take advantage of all resources, and that included Dr. Davenport. But it wasn't simply his oath. It was the promise he'd made five hundred years ago, a promise drawn in blood and innocence. *Kane's the only one who can teleport, and I need to show her the stone. She might be able to decipher the writing on it. She's Dr. Davenport.*

He felt Quinn's surprise at Lily's identity. *Damn. You're right. She could be the expert we need. I want the stone protected here, so I'll send Kane as soon as I can. He's out right now checking on a couple things, but he'll be back shortly. You safe there?*

Keeping one hand on Lily, Gideon tuned his senses to the forest around them, searching for any sounds or scents that were off. He caught nothing out of the ordinary. A cluster of ferns was brown and dying, a grim reminder of how Ezekiel had decimated even nature when he'd been free two thousand years ago. *We're fine. Keep the others away until I get her sequestered.* He sent Quinn a mental image of their location, then cut off communication.

He turned his attention to Lily. "I have someone coming to pick us up and take us to our temporary headquarters."

She lifted her head from the tree to look at him. "An Order member?"

"Yeah."

Her hair was dry and clean now, flowing over her shoulders in rich blond waves that caught the morning sunlight. Even wearing the baggy sweats, even with the tense set to her body, she was beautiful. He knew how soft her hair was, how silky her skin was, and it was taking all his self-control not to haul her against him and bury himself in those decadently soft tresses.

In her very essence.

He met her gaze and for a moment, desire flared in her eyes. It was quickly chased away by a cold wariness. "I can't go." She turned to face him, leaning her back against the tree. "I'll make a deal with you, Gideon. I'll help the Order research the stone, and I'll try to translate the writing on it. But you have to let me keep my space."

His eyebrows shot up at the undercurrent of tension in her voice. There was more to her request than she was admitting. He could feel the cool drift of her evasiveness. "Why?"

She met his gaze. "In my research about Calydons, I discovered that certain families are more likely to be mates for Calydons. My grandma was an Order *sheva*, which means there's a good chance I'll be one too." Caution flickered in her eyes. "Since I'm not yours, I could be someone else's. I refuse to put my life at risk like that." She lifted her chin, new strength surging into her stance. For the first time since he'd retrieved her, he saw indicators that she was reclaiming her old self, the strong, intelligent woman who had traveled the world, undaunted by the enemies she stirred up. "I won't give the Order a reason to kill me, and I refuse to get sucked into the *sheva* destiny."

Gideon was in complete agreement with her about not getting her hooked up with any other Order members. Just the thought of her being with Kane... Yeah, no thanks on setting her up to bond with anyone else. "We're stranded in the desert. You have any other suggestions, I'm all in."

"I want to go home," she said. "I just want to go home."

He closed his eyes against the sudden crash of her loneliness in his gut, and his body ached for her. Her emotions tugged at him, ripped through his shields until he couldn't think straight.

He opened his eyes and looked into her face, saw the desperation in her eyes, felt the years of despair welling inside her and knew exactly why he'd worked so hard to shut down his emotions. His mentor, Dante, had taught him to build walls to keep himself emotionally detached from the hell he inflicted on others.

But Gideon had no defense against the kind of pain she was feeling right now and sending into his core. He cursed and ran his hands through his hair, trying desperately to figure out how to raise his shields against her.

But he couldn't.

Lily turned away again, folding her arms over her chest as she walked a few yards, putting distance between them. He felt her fear. More than fear. Terror, ingrained over years and years. Of him. Of his kind. Of his mission. Of his team. He cursed, realizing why Dante had worked so hard on his training. It was absolutely fucking impossible to do his job when he could feel her emotions.

She turned to face him, her forehead furrowed. "Stop it."

He frowned. "Stop what?"

"You're making me feel bad for you."

He blinked. "What are you talking about?"

"I can feel how upset you are." She pressed a hand to her belly. "Right here." Her gaze went to him, her eyes wary. "It makes me want to come over and hug you. To tell you it will be okay. To do whatever you want me to do, just to ease your torment." She laughed softly. "Imagine me needing to comfort an Order member."

He was so shocked by her statement that he didn't know how to respond.

Her face became even more cautious. "Why are you looking at me like that?"

"Are you an empath?" he finally asked.

"Me? No."

"But you're feeling my emotions? You're internalizing them?"

She nodded. "You've been inundating me with them this whole time. You're projecting them onto me—"

"No, I'm not. I don't have that capacity. I only receive others."

She stared at him, her eyes widening. "That's impossible. I wouldn't be able to feel your emotions, unless—"

"No. You aren't my *sheva*. There's no chance. We both know that." He ran his hand through his hair anyway, unsettled. "You *must* be an empath."

She shook her head. "I'm just...human."

He heard the hesitation, saw the question in her eyes,

and all his senses kicked into alert mode. "You're more than human, aren't you? What are you?"

She lifted her chin. "Just human."

He cocked his head as things began to click into place. "That music was you, wasn't it? In the river?"

Her eyes snapped to his. "*What music?*"

"Bells."

She paled and sucked her breath. "*Bells?* You're sure?"

"Dead sure." He narrowed his eyes. "Why?"

"Bells," she whispered with a groan, muttering to herself as she turned away. "He heard *bells*. It had to be *Gideon* who heard my bells. I was hoping I was wrong."

"What are you talking about?"

She said nothing as she closed her eyes and lifted her face to the sun. The sun glinted through her hair, making the strands come alive, as if they were glowing.

"*Your* bells?" He frowned as he thought about that, studying her as she pulled off her thick socks and buried her toes in the damp sand of the Oregon high desert. Bells. Why was that significant? Memories tugged at his mind, and he tried to recall what he knew. "How do you create the music of bells?"

"Don't ask. Let it go." She pressed her palms against the tree. Her body visibly relaxed as her feet sank into the earth, and he heard a distant, faint tinkling of bells again.

"Bells again," he said, a thought beginning to tug at his memory. He'd heard about those bells before. But how? When?

"Damn it." Her voice was throaty, almost musical. "I can't stop them."

"You can't stop the bells?" The call of her glistening hair was too strong. He walked across the sandy ground until he could touch the silkiness, until he could thread his fingers through the strands. Longing heated her eyes, and she didn't move away as he slid his arms around her waist and pressed his face to her hair.

He pressed his body against her backside and set his hands on her hips, nuzzling her neck as he started to sway back and forth. He breathed in her scent, this time recognizing it for what it was. The delicate scent of new earth, the freshness of spring, the emergence of the sun after a rainstorm.

And then he knew. The earth. The music. His response to her. He just knew. It all made sense. "You're Satinka, aren't you? That's why I want you so badly. Earth magic."

Lily stiffened. "No, of course not."

"No?" He kissed the side of her neck, grinning when she let out a small noise of desire. Yes, he felt it now, the intense power growing between them. "Calydons and Satinka. Each powerful on their own, but together...they are so much more." He nudged her hips, coaxing them to sway in a slow seduction. "Every Calydon's fantasy, but extremely rare after all the Calydons drained and killed them off hundreds of years ago..."

She shivered, and he felt her resistance fade as she accepted him. She began to move with him, her hips swaying with an invitation that sent awareness spiraling through him.

"Not just Satinka." Her hands went to his hips, her touch a sensual caress as she held him to her, synching the slow sway of her hips with his. "Your Satinka."

"Mine? What do you mean?"

"My magic seeks out a Calydon who is worthy of it. I'm extremely powerful, so no Calydon has ever awakened it, even though my magic has tested every one I've ever met. Until you. You heard the bells." Her voice had gone soft and throaty. His body began to hum in response.

Gideon ran his hands down the front of her thighs and inhaled as she leaned back into him, letting her head rest on his shoulder. "Sing to me, Satinka." He pressed his lips to her neck. "Share the music with me."

"No," she whispered, even as she reached behind her and cupped his butt, her body moving with his as if there was music dancing around them. "It's too dangerous. Neither of us would be able to stop. This can't happen." She wiggled her butt into his pelvis, making her words a lie.

"So, it's not all Calydons you're attracted to. You were just looking for me." Gideon was intensely pleased by that fact. He ran his hands over her belly, up her ribs and over her breasts, groaning when she arched against him. He began to sing. It was a melody he didn't know, but it fell from his lips anyway. A language he'd never learned, words he didn't understand, a tune he'd never heard, but the music still came.

Untapped, decadent desire flared inside Lily as Gideon began to sing to her. They were Satinka words he should never have known, an ancient song he could never have been taught, and yet he knew them. His deep baritone was haunting in its beauty, curling through her body, reaching deep inside her. She felt something inside her begin to unfurl, and she closed her eyes, absorbing the magic he was spinning around her.

His hands moved across her body, gliding, caressing, never stopping, over her breasts, across her belly, along the inside of her thighs, then back up. She could feel the heat from his touch through the thick cotton of her sweatshirt. Pressing her back against the front of his body, she reached back and wrapped her hands behind his head, pulling him down toward her.

"Sing to me, Gideon," she whispered, burning for the music that was hers, that was somehow inside him now. God, it felt amazing, the way he was bringing her to life. Never had she felt like this, as if the earth had begun to dance, as if magic was filling the air and the sky, up to the heavens and out to the furthest reaches of the horizon.

Gideon continued to sing, the notes rumbling deep inside his chest as he slipped his hands beneath her sweatshirt, flattening his palms on her belly. Heat caressed her as she began to move, as his song touched that place inside her reserved only for music. His lips were warm on the side of her neck as his hips moved with hers, a slow sensual dance of indulgent pleasure, of timeless seduction.

His hands slid up her ribs and over her breasts, and she let out a low moan as desire licked through her veins, arching her back against him, her hands still locked behind his neck.

His song whispered through her mind as his hands slid down her belly, easing beneath her sweats and down to her thighs, his thumb a mere brush against her most intimate parts before it was gone. A tease, like the music he was still singing, his breath warm against her neck as he breathed life into words with his song.

They began to sway more, their bodies moving in unison, following the magic of his song, drawn into its misty web as his hands moved over her body once again. He paused to cup her between her legs for a teasing instant, and then his hands were gone again, sliding up over her belly to her breasts again, his palms branding her nipples the way his voice was searing her soul.

"Lily," he whispered, his voice raw with a sensuality that made her shiver. "Sing to me."

"I can't." Her voice was throaty and raw. "It's too dangerous." But God, she wanted to. The music inside her was straining to be released, to be allowed to soar. To mesh with Gideon, to tap into the power he carried. To ignite them both with the intensity between them.

He began to sing again, another tune of words that plucked at her memories, words that felt so familiar, but she couldn't quite understand or interpret, but she knew it was a song of seduction, of passion, and her body burned in response.

His hands moved down again, sliding beneath her pants and brushing along the inside of her thigh, so close, teasing. Hot desire pooled beneath his touch, and she knew she was lost to his song, to his caresses, knew she could never turn away from the magic he was waking up in her. She could feel the music taking root within her, and then she began to sing, matching her voice to his.

The instant their voices melded, she felt her body truly come alive for the first time in her life. The wind began to swirl, licking at them. The sand shifted beneath Lily's feet. Heat rose within her, between them. She felt the tingling of her magic as it began to rise, to truly rise, within her.

Gideon's hips undulated, taking her with him in time to the music, his fingers sliding over her, a tease, so close as she felt something begin to vibrate in her, something light and musical—

Gideon rubbed his chin against her cheek. "I have no defense against you," he whispered, his voice raw.

Her fingers dug into the brands on his forearms as desire pulsed within her and her music danced around her. Her body called for Gideon, and he pressed his groin against her backside. She felt his hardness against her as his hands slid down her thighs again, parting them as his body undulated to the music. "I can't let you go," he said, his voice hoarse with unbridled lust and raw need.

Lily heard the words and, on some level, she realized their danger. Gideon was succumbing to her music, but she couldn't make herself care. Not with her body tingling with magic, not with her legs parting as he slid his hands higher along her inner thighs, his fingers a sensual caress on her skin. She groaned and let her head fall back against his shoulder, her cheek resting against the bristles of his whiskers as her magic roared to life, taking over the song they were both singing, drawing them to a place where neither of them had control, climbing and climbing until the music was rising from the world around them.

His lips trailed over her neck and his teeth caught her skin as his hands moved higher and his finger slid inside her. Her body jerked with intense pleasure and she leaned back against him, boneless and at his mercy. The ground began to vibrate, and the music became louder. It wasn't simply the two of them singing. The wind joined them, the rumbling of the earth was their bass, the branches crashed against each other…the power of nature pounded at them as the very Mother herself joined in.

Gideon's fingers began to move within her, his teeth grazing her neck as his deep voice began to vibrate with power and intensity. Her voice blended with his, beat with the rhythm of the earth, and his broad hands palmed her waist and he spun her around, then sank his mouth down onto hers, taking, taking, taking.

She welcomed him, pressing against him as the rhythm of the earth made her vibrate with life, as her skin tingled with magic and desire and him. The kisses were deep and hot, gaining strength, increasingly desperate and intense. She could feel Gideon soaking through her pores, melding with her. His voice was magic as it filled her, winding through her soul. She knew she wanted him. She needed him. Inside her. *He was power.*

As if he'd read her mind, he grabbed the edge of her sweatshirt and yanked it over her head in one swift move, and then his hands were tracing her ribs, cupping her breasts as he held her tight against him, his hips driving against her.

So much heat from his body. So much *magic*. Her womb tightened with heat and magic and hot desire—

"Get down!" He suddenly threw her to the side.

She hit the dirt hard and whirled around in time to see a mace slam into the back of Gideon's head with a loud crack. His body jerked at the impact, and then he collapsed on top of her, blood pouring from his wound and into the sand. He didn't move. "Gideon!"

Several Calydons stepped out of the trees. She recognized the one from Nate's who had the machete, and three others. More kept coming out...eight, nine...ten...*Too many.*

*They were there to take her to Frank.* That's when the grim truth hit her. There was no going home for her. Frank would follow her there and take her. Her only chance was to align herself with Gideon and the Order. She had to help them fight their battle and defeat Frank and Ezekiel.

She had to go to war. Adrenaline and determination surged through her. A calm, focused presence. No more the victim. No more hiding. She was taking her life back, and she was doing it *now.*

Gideon groaned and tried to lift his upper body off her, his body trembling with the effort as blood continued to gush from the back of his head. She knew he'd never recover in time to beat them. They would kill him and take her. She and Gideon had no chance.

Screw that. She wasn't going down, not when she had access to the most deadly warrior the Order had ever had. A warrior who had made an art of being cold and impassive, of controlling his emotions more than any other living creature could do.

Gideon lifted his head, his blue eyes glazed with pain as he fought to sit up. Lily grasped his face in her hands, fighting off all her instincts that were screaming not to do it, not to risk it. She'd been a passive victim for too long, thinking that simply getting up in the morning was some great victory. Screw that. She wanted it all. She wanted her damn life back, back to what it was like before the abduction when she was seventeen, before Nate's kidnapping, before the fear had taken root in her heart.

Gideon swore and tried to lever himself off the ground, but she knew the blow had been too hard, too precise. He met her gaze, and she saw in his face the man of honor who had saved her already. The man who burned for her. The warrior that her magic had chosen.

He grimaced with pain, and she felt the darkness as the other Calydons closed in. Their time was up. She had one choice to make: either trust Gideon to be stronger than any Calydon had ever been, or turn herself over to Frank. Gideon was the first strength that had been extended her way in a lifetime, the first kindness she'd felt in years. He was her chance. Her only chance, if she was brave enough to use it.

For a split second, her mind flickered back to that hell ten years ago when the team of Calydons had fed off her magic, and a deep, long-accustomed fear rippled through her. But as she looked into Gideon's eyes, she knew that he was a man of honor. Frank would prey on her like those men had before, and it would be a repeat. Gideon was different. She knew that. For the first time since her brother, she knew she'd met a Calydon she could believe in.

There was only one choice worth making.

Lily wanted to fight, so she chose Gideon.

She gave him her magic. She gave him the tools to save her life or to kill her.

She gave him something that she thought she'd lost forever: her trust.

# Chapter 10

Gideon's arms were numb and he felt like his head had been split open, but he had to get up. Had to defend Lily. Her body was warm under his, and he could feel her skin tingling against his from the magic they'd already started to build. He could hear the whispers of fabric as their assailants approached. He could feel the darkness of their thoughts. He heard the whisper of their fingers sliding over the handles of their weapons. He caught the bitter scent of their desperate sweat.

Danger prickled over him and his weapons burned in his arms, warning him of the threats. *Come on!*

Gideon shoved himself to his knees as he heard one of them laugh. "The Order's not so big and powerful now, is it?"

He tried to turn his head to look at them, and he nearly went down at the pain. They'd clipped him good. He'd been so caught up in Lily that he hadn't even heard them coming. They'd caught him dead in his tracks. The legendary warrior caught not looking. *Crap.*

He had to fight. He had to save her. Gideon braced himself and summoned all the energy he had, preparing to lunge to his feet—

"Gideon." Lily's arms went around his neck, holding him down. "Try not to abuse this gift."

"What—" He barely had time to register the gritty determination in her eyes before she pressed her lips to his in a searing kiss that thrust an obscene amount of power into him. The music was instant, deafening, and blinding. Bells, drums, a blistering rhythm that sent him down to his elbows as he cradled his head against the din.

But then, through the noise, Gideon heard Lily's voice. Strong and mesmerizing, calling to him, singing to him, and only to him. He became aware of her mouth still kissing him, her hands skimming over his body, and her hips moving against him in a sensual, seductive motion. "Lily," he growled.

He grabbed the back of her hair and held her head, plundering her mouth with his as the music rose louder and louder. All he could hear was her voice, weaving through his body, through every cell, making his body come *alive*.

"Go now," she whispered. "We're connected. Be quick." She broke the kiss, and his mind returned to him, and he sensed the whisper of pressure behind him. He whirled instantly, his hand closing over the handle of a machete a split second before it sank into his back.

He and his assailant both paused in shock at the sight of Gideon's hand wrapped around the weapon he'd intercepted in mid-flight. Then Gideon switched his grip and hurled it back at his opponent. It sank into the Calydon's chest and dropped him instantly.

Gideon stared at the dead Calydon in surprise. Calydon weapons didn't work for anyone but their owners. *Ever.*

He should never have been able to do that.

There was an outraged cry, and his attackers charged. With Lily's song vibrating in his mind, Gideon leapt to his feet and called out his axe. His assailants unleashed their blades. Weapons came at him from all directions, and Gideon reacted with blinding speed, defending himself against the assault.

Power consumed him. Strength and indestructibility screamed through his body. Gideon's mind processed everything so quickly that it was as if the weapons flying at him were moving in slow motion, lagging uselessly behind his reflexes.

The world seemed to glow with brightness as Gideon wielded his axe, blocking each weapon before it could touch him or Lily. Twenty weapons, flying at him simultaneously, with the precision of the Calydons, and yet they were powerless against him. He took them out of the air, one by one, like he was swatting softballs instead of defying all the laws of the universe.

The weapons clanged into his axe and fell to the earth. Gideon snatched others out of the air before they hit the ground and hurled them back, finding their owners with deadly precision in an impossible task that was ridiculously simple.

Attack. Defend. Counter-attack.

Effortless. Easy. Child's play.

It was over in less than a minute, eleven dead Calydons strewn around him. Gideon threw back his head and roared, drinking in the power consuming him, the strength, the utter and complete indestructibility of his body.

"Hell, Gideon. Where'd you learn to do that?" Kane was standing on the side of the clearing, his double spike flails clenched in his fists, the spiked balls dangling at the end of the studded chains. As always, Kane was naked from the waist up, his torso completely covered in scars, intricate carvings and designs. He was wearing black leather pants that were tight across his hips, black boots and a thin leather cord around his throat.

Gideon blinked and tried to focus on Kane, but his body was pulsing with such power he couldn't bring himself down from the high. He couldn't stop the pounding of his heart, the headiness of killing so many, so easily.

"Hey!" Kane hurled the flail at Gideon's face, and Gideon caught it without even blinking. "Hell, man, what's happened to you?"

"The music." Gideon let the flail drop to the earth so he could drink in the power as Kane called his weapon back. "Do you hear it?" The bells were pounding in his ears, the earth vibrating beneath him. "Earth magic. For me."

"Earth magic?" Kane echoed. "You mean Satinka?"

The music began to fade, and Gideon opened his mind, trying to absorb the last remnants of the magic. Needing more.

Kane cursed and raced toward him. "You're killing her! Stop draining her!"

*Killing her?* Gideon spun around as Kane dropped to his knees beside Lily.

*Lily.* She was stretched out on her back. Her body was rigid. Her skin was deadly white. Her lips were ashen, and her eyes were staring blindly. The sight of her yanked Gideon back from his high and he sprinted over to her. He crouched beside her and pulled her onto his lap. "Lily! Shit." Her skin was ice cold under his touch, so brittle he felt like it would crumble under his fingers.

"She's not dead." Kane had her wrist in his hand. "I can hear her pulse. Stop draining her now, or you'll finish her off."

He knew Kane wasn't exaggerating. He could feel the life fading from Lily with every breath. Gideon swore and tried to sever his connection to her, but the music was still dancing in his head. He couldn't stop himself from hearing it. He reinforced his mental shields and tried to shut down his mind, but nothing worked. The music was still there, calling to him, feeding him. There was no time to figure it out. He had to cut himself off from her instantly. "Knock me out."

Kane didn't hesitate. He swung his flail into the side of Gideon's head. The blinding pain was instant and then there was blackness.

※ ※ ※

When Gideon woke up, Kane was pacing the small clearing, his hands clasped behind his back, his body rigid.

*Lily.* Gideon jerked upright and looked wildly around for Lily.

She was lying right beside him in the sand. Her eyes were closed now, no longer gazing blankly. Her skin had returned to its normal shade, and her body was no longer rigid.

The music was gone from Gideon's mind. It was over. "I'm so sorry, Lily." Gideon gathered her in his arms and pulled her against his chest, rocking her gently as he felt his insides begin to unclench. Her body was limp, but warm, and he knew she was going to recover. Relief coursed through him and he rested his head against hers.

Kane stopped pacing and turned to face him. "You almost killed her."

"No shit." Gideon understood now what Lily had been talking about, her fear of tapping into her magic. He'd heard the tales about how it was impossible for a Calydon to resist the siren call of Satinka magic, but he'd never understood the true intensity of the power.

The grim reality of what he'd done settled on him. Lily

had trusted him, and he'd failed her. Two women he'd failed—

Gideon suddenly noticed her sweatshirt was back on. Darkness swirled through him at the realization that Kane must have dressed her. Kane's hands must have been on Lily's body, touching her skin. Gideon slowly turned his head toward Kane, lethal danger taking root inside of him. "You put her shirt on?"

Kane was watching him intently, his flail in his hand. "Yeah. I did. Does that bother you?"

Gideon narrowed his eyes at Kane's challenging tone, his hackles rising in aggression. "What are you talking about?" He kept his voice even, trying not to let Kane know how badly he wanted to rip his head off for looking at Lily half-naked. "Is she your *sheva?*"

Kane's brows went up. "If she were, would you kill her?"

Gideon instinctively shifted Lily so his body was between Kane and her. "It would be my job." But it was a lie. He knew it was. There wasn't a chance in hell he'd kill Lily if she were Kane's *sheva*. He would kill Kane. The realization that he'd turn on his Order teammate so readily shocked him, but he managed to keep his face expressionless, not revealing the traitorous turn of his thoughts.

"That's not what I asked." Kane walked over and squatted beside Lily, his eyes dark with challenge. "I asked whether you'd be able to kill her."

Gideon's brands began to burn, his battle axe reacting to the threat of Kane too close to Lily. "What's your problem, Kane?"

"Look at her arm."

"Her arm? You're claiming her?" If Lily was Kane's *sheva*, Kane's brands would appear on her forearms once they began to bond. Aggression churned inside Gideon, and he wanted to shove his axe through Kane's throat. "She wouldn't carry your mark yet," he ground out. "You haven't done any of the stages—"

Kane grabbed Lily's wrist and shoved her sleeve up. "For hell's sake, stop being such a thick-headed ass. *Look.*"

Gideon jerked his gaze down to her arm, and then his whole body tensed at the silver lines on her skin. "That's *impossible.*" He grabbed her wrist from Kane, holding her arm out for a better look. But there it was. Thin silver lines on her skin. Intricate designs.

The lines didn't match Kane's brand.

They matched Gideon's.

Numbly, Gideon turned his arm over and laid his arm next to hers. The lines on her skin were a perfect match for the outline of one of the blades of his brand. The first stages of bonding between a Calydon warrior and his *sheva*—his brand beginning to appear on her arm.

Lily was his *sheva*.

"This is wrong. It's a mistake. A joke." Gideon rubbed his palm over her marks, as if he could wipe it off. Her skin became red, but the marks didn't fade. Even as a cold dread claimed him, intense satisfaction pulsed through him, a deep-seated possessiveness that made him want to claim her like some ancient cavemen. *His.*

Shit. He was screwed.

Kane inched closer, watching Gideon carefully. "Did you kill to save her when you guys plucked her out of Nate's?"

Gideon swore. "Yeah, I knocked off a couple Calydons who were trying to take her out."

Kane nodded. "It's one of the stages of the bond. Killing to save the other."

"I know what the damn stages are," Gideon snapped. "This can't be happening. It's *impossible*. I had my *sheva*. She's *dead*. Dead!" He gently set Lily back on the ground and jumped to his feet, pacing a small circle around her, not willing to get too far away in case more of Frank's men showed up, but needing space.

Kane sat back on his heels. "Theoretically speaking, I should kill her."

Gideon whipped around and had his axe at Kane's throat before the other warrior could move. "Don't. Touch. Her."

Kane's eyebrows went up. "Five hundred years ago, you stood there when Dante killed your *sheva*, and it didn't bother you. It's never affected you since. What's different this time?"

Gideon had to work hard to keep his face impassive, to not correct Kane's assumption. His *sheva's* death had haunted him his entire existence; it was his motivation for everything he did.

He wasn't interested in going through that again. Couldn't go through it again. He couldn't let another *sheva* die because she was unlucky enough to get paired with him. The guilt he'd been holding for five hundred years coursed thick and deep, breaking free of the dark place he'd kept it locked up in for so long.

Kane didn't move away from Lily, carefully watching Gideon for any indication Gideon was going to try to attack him. "I'm not going to kill Lily," Kane said.

It was part of their Order oath to kill the *sheva* of any Order member before the bond could turn him rogue. Order members were deemed too valuable, so their lives were always honored over their *sheva's*. It was a brutal choice for warriors driven by their need to protect innocents, but they all did what they needed to in order to ensure the survival of those who could protect the world from rogues.

Gideon couldn't keep his gaze from sliding back to Lily. She looked so vulnerable lying in the sand. Beautiful. Like an angel sent from the heavens to claim his soul. How in the hell had this happened? "Why are you willing to let her live?" Gideon had to know how much he could trust Kane.

"Because Dante's dead. I'll do whatever it takes to avenge his death." Kane slowly stood up, his eyes blazing with rage at the mention of their downed leader who had been murdered by Nate less than two weeks ago. "If Lily can help us find those responsible for Dante's death and stop Ezekiel from escaping, then I'm not killing her. Avenging Dante and protecting innocents from Ezekiel is what matters. If you and Lily want to destroy each other by getting up close and personal with the *sheva* bond, do it after I avenge Dante's death."

Gideon felt the intensity of Kane's words, and knew Kane was telling the truth. He wouldn't kill Lily as long as she could help them.

Gideon knew why Kane had been able to make that choice: Quinn's *sheva*, Grace Matthews, had changed things for the Order. For the first time in the two thousand year history of their race, Quinn and Grace had managed to bond without succumbing to destiny and destroying everyone around them.

Grace had been instrumental in taking down Nate, and the Order had been forced to adjust their views of her as a *sheva*. Between Dante's death and Grace, Kane had new priorities other than killing Lily for being a *sheva*.

Lily was safe from Kane, for the moment. Gideon let the axe fall beside his thigh, and then he crouched beside her again, studying her closely, with the eyes of a man who was looking upon the woman destined to be his.

Her hair was golden and soft, tangled, but beautiful. Her face relaxed in sleep made her look even younger. Younger. Hah. He was over five hundred years old. Five hundred years of war compared with what? Twenty-six years of life?

Gideon noticed the faint yellow on her throat, and he hooked a finger over the collar of her sweatshirt and tugged down slightly to reveal an angry yellow and purple bruise. Anger roared through him, but he placed his palm over the bruise, forcing himself to remain calm.

He needed her to tell him who made every single mark on her body, and he'd kill each and every asshole who'd touched her.

Shit. That wasn't the cool, collected warrior he needed to be, was it?

"Are you going to kill her for being your *sheva*?" Kane asked.

Gideon traced his thumb over her bruise, trying to rub away the pain that had caused it. "She's suffered enough at Calydon hands."

"So?"

Gideon glared at him. "No. I'm not going to kill her."

"Me neither." Kane spun the flail restlessly, the spiked balls singing through the air. "So, I guess we better figure out how to keep her alive, then, huh?"

Gideon brushed stray grains of sand off Lily's cheek. "What are you talking about?"

"I may be willing to forego my Order oath to kill your *sheva*, but I doubt the others will feel the same. Just because Grace and Quinn are doing okay doesn't mean that the curse is lifted. One win out of two thousand years isn't exactly enough to bring confidence. If I bring you guys back to the Order, someone will take her out."

"No one will touch her." Gideon tightened his grip on his axe.

Kane's hand fell on his shoulder, his fingers digging in. "You'd really fight an Order member for her? What the hell, man? You're ice."

Ice. Ha. Gideon was a seething cauldron of anger, possessiveness and heat right now.

But Kane was right. He had to find his way back to the cold, focused warrior who had triumphed for five hundred years. Gideon sheathed his axe, rapidly assessing how to handle the situation.

They still needed Lily to help them with the inscriptions on the stone. He had to take her back so she could do that. "The plan was to keep her isolated from the other Order members in case she's someone's *sheva*." The word stuck in his throat. *Sheva.* How in hell's name was it possible that she carried his brand? It was impossible. *Impossible.*

But as Gideon ran his fingers over the brand on her arm, he knew it was the truth. Somehow, some way, destiny had come back for him. "We keep to the plan," he said. "We'll take her back long enough to check out the knife and pick her brain about everything she knows. We'll keep everyone else away while we're there. Then we take her home—"

But even as he said it, Gideon realized he was wrong. Frank was still sending Calydons after her. Until the Order stopped Frank, Lily would be at risk. She had to stay with Gideon until Frank was dead.

His skin chilled at the risk of staying with her, of risking her by tightening that bond, but at the same time, he knew there was no other option. He would not leave her to stand alone against the nightmare she was facing.

"What about Ian and Quinn?" Kane asked. "They've both met their *shevas* so they'll be safe with her. They'll want to talk to her, and the minute they see you two together, they'll know what's going on."

"If I can meet a second *sheva* so can Ian. He's not safe with a woman either." Ian's *sheva* had been killed by Elijah less than six months ago, and Ian still hadn't recovered. Gideon wasn't sure he ever would.

"Shit. You're right." Kane frowned. "Ian would lose his mind if he met another *sheva*. He'd never survive. We need to warn him to be careful." He looked at Gideon. "But we can't tell Ian he's not safe, not without revealing Lily's status as your *sheva*. What excuse are you going to use to keep them away?"

"I'll think of something." Gideon knelt down and scooped Lily up. "I have to get her out of the woods. Let's go."

Kane set his hand on Gideon's shoulder. "You aren't going to turn into Ian when this one dies, are you?"

"She isn't going to die."

Kane raised his brows. "Of course she's going to die. You've met each other. Your destiny is sealed. I'll let her live because we need her right now, but someone has to kill her before she takes you out."

"What about Grace and Quinn? They survived the bond."

Kane snorted "You really think they beat fate? Look at you. Your *sheva* already died, and destiny gave you another one. As long as Quinn and Grace are alive, they're not safe. Destiny's just gearing up for another attack. There's no way to beat it, Gideon. Lily dies, or you die. It's the only way."

Gideon tucked her more closely against his chest, her body so light and fragile in his arms. He shifted her so his sword arm was free, ready to defend her if needed. "So I won't bond with her."

Kane snorted. "Now you sound like Quinn with all that denial crap. You'd be better off if you'd just acknowledge what you're facing and deal with it, instead of living in denial—"

Gideon grabbed Kane by the throat and yanked him close. "I stood back and watched an innocent woman be slaughtered for no other reason than she was my *sheva*. She didn't do a damn thing to deserve it, and she died anyway. I know exactly what I'm facing right now, so back off."

Kane's eyes narrowed, and Gideon could see the realization in Kane's eyes that Gideon wasn't the cold, unfeeling machine he'd presented to the world for the last five hundred years. Not by a long shot.

Shit. Gideon couldn't afford to be reacting like this. He

had to pull his shit together. Now. He had another *sheva* to be responsible for, and this time, he was getting it right.

Kane flicked Gideon's hand off his neck, his eyes flashing. "I'm all for keeping Lily alive because I think she'll help us find the mastermind behind Dante's death. But the minute I sense she's turning you rogue, I'm taking her out. So *don't* grab me by the throat again because I won't wait to strike."

Gideon nodded in acknowledgement, realizing that Kane was right. He needed to pull himself together and fast. How had Quinn managed to stay sane when he'd met his *sheva?*

Not that he could ask.

Gideon was on his own, and the first time he'd been through this, he'd failed completely.

He wouldn't let it happen again.

# Chapter 11

Lily frowned at the murmur of voices penetrating her sleep. They were soft and feminine, not the familiar harsh tones of Nate and his Calydons. She cracked her eyes open cautiously. She was in a bedroom with beige walls, white crown molding, and towering bookshelves loaded with hardcovers. The room felt light and airy, not dangerous. The sheets were soft and silky against her body, and they smelled fresh and clean. Confused, she looked around, trying to understand where she was. Not at Nate's. Not at her home.

Two women were standing by the door whispering in low voices.

Lily realized she recognized one of them. "Ana?" She tried to sit up, but her body ached too much, and she sank back down in the bed as both women turned toward her.

"Lily!" Ana ran across the room with an obvious limp and pounced on the bed, hugging Lily tightly. "I'm so happy you're okay!"

Dear God. She was safe. It was real. Tears filled Lily's eyes as she clung to Ana, holding tightly to the one friend she'd had in the last two years, even if their connection had been for the briefest moment in time. "I can't believe you're alive, Ana. Gideon said you were, but—"

"The Order came after Nate." Ana released her and bounced in place, her eyes brimming with warmth. Her dark hair was pulled back in a low ponytail, and her silver eyes were glistening with life that hadn't been there when they'd met at

Nate's, after he'd beaten Ana so severely. Ana was wearing jeans and a pale pink cotton tee shirt. A thin gold chain hung around her neck, and she was even wearing some mascara. She looked beautiful, a woman with an indomitable spirit who was already recovering from her ordeal. "They kicked his ass the way he deserved." Ana crossed her legs, and Lily saw a cast around her ankle.

Empathy filled Lily. "Nate hurt you again?"

Some of the light left Ana's eyes. "Who else?" Then she grinned with forced cheeriness and tugged open a drawer in the nightstand. She found a red marker and handed it to Lily. "Sign it. Write something happy."

Lily hesitated. "Happy?" God, she didn't even know what that was anymore.

"Happy," Ana said firmly. "We're moving on. My bruises will be gone in another week or so, the cast will be off shortly after that, and I'm never thinking about him again." She lifted her leg and set her foot on Lily's lap. "Happy."

Lily inspected the cast, surprised to see Gideon's name on it. He'd drawn a goofy smiley face next to his name, with the eyes crossed and the tongue sticking out, as if the happy face was giving her a raspberry. He'd even used a pink marker.

Gideon. She suddenly recalled everything that had happened in the clearing. How he'd almost killed her. She'd thought he was going to. Where was he? Clearly, he'd managed to get them both back here, so that had to be a good sign, right?

"Lily," Ana urged. "Sign my cast."

"Yeah, okay." Lily scrawled her name under his and then wrote something about looking to the future, but her mind was too scrambled to think. What had happened after she'd passed out? "Do you know where Gideon is?"

"He's been with you the whole time, but he had to run downstairs to talk to the rest of the Order," Ana said. "He asked me to stay here in case you woke up." She smiled. "I would have offered to stay with you anyway, of course. I was so happy when he brought you back from Nate's."

Lily sensed the pain underneath the surface of Ana's cheerful persona, and felt an answering weight swell inside her. Nate had forever changed both of them. "He's really dead?"

Ana nodded. "Dead as a cockroach under a hammer. My sister saw him die."

Relief filled Lily at the confirmation that Nate was truly gone. It felt so right, so perfect to have Ana sitting beside her, alive and healing. Lily felt hope, real hope, that the future could be okay. "When you didn't come back for so long, I didn't think you'd made it," she admitted. "I was afraid you'd died."

Ana hugged her again. "Oh, Lily. I'm so sorry it took so long. I sent them after you as soon as I could, but I was unconscious for a while."

Lily couldn't help but smile as she leaned back against the pillow, sinking into the plush softness that felt so decadent after two years in Nate's basement cell. "How dare you be unconscious? You're so insensitive."

Ana giggled and scooted next to her on the pillow, two women who'd found solidarity and hope from each other in a harsh and brutal life. "Okay, yeah, I guess I have an excuse, huh?" She gestured to the other woman, who was waiting by the door. "This is my sister, Grace. She's the one who got the Order on my case." Ana beamed at her sister. "She saved me."

"Hi." Grace nodded from the door, and Lily was amazed at how much the sisters looked alike. The same silver eyes, the same golden skin tone, and gorgeous black hair that practically glistened. Ana was shorter, with more luxurious curves, and her eyes slanted down at the corners, giving her an exotic, sensual look.

Grace's dark hair was tumbling down around her shoulders, and she was wearing a pair of slim-fitting jeans that made her legs look long and toned. She looked relaxed, and her long silver earrings were delicate and feminine, but she gave the impression of strength, a woman who somehow combined everything soft with everything strong.

Lily sat up a little straighter and touched her own hair, realizing she still hadn't showered. "Where am I?"

"The temporary headquarters of the Order, the home of their leader Dante, who Nate killed," Ana said. "You're in isolation so none of the men accidentally stumble across you. Gideon seems rather determined that you not be turned into a *sheva* and killed, not that I'd let them kill you, of course." She held up her pinkie finger. "We've suffered together, and I'm here for you." She grabbed Lily's pinkie and shook it. "We're sisters, Lily. You and me."

"If you guys are sisters, then I guess you're part of my family now." Grace reached the bed and held out her hand to shake Lily's, smiling with genuine warmth. "Nice to meet you, Lily."

Lily reached for her hand, then froze when she saw the silver outline of a sword on Grace's forearm. Grace was sporting a brand that would no doubt prove to be identical to that of her mate, the mark of a fully bonded *sheva*. Lily's heart constricted and her gaze jerked toward Grace's face. "Your mate was killed by the Order?"

"No." Grace smiled. "He's actually an Order member."

Lily blinked. "But you're alive?" How could an Order *sheva* be walking around the halls of their headquarters? They would never allow it.

Grace nodded. "It appears Quinn and I beat destiny, at least for now. They're letting me live."

"You're serious?" Lily frowned, trying to reconcile that news with all that she knew about Calydons. She'd never seen any kind of indicator that destiny could be thwarted, not in all her years of research. "Really? I've never heard of anyone defeating the bond. It's impossible."

"It is impossible, but it's not." Grace looked happy and relaxed, like a woman comfortable in her life and with her mate. She definitely didn't have the fearful demeanor of a woman worried that some Calydon was going to leap through the door and take her down. "They had no choice with me," she said with a wink. "I wouldn't recommend testing them again. They're a little prickly about changing their ways."

Ana held out her arm. "I have one, too."

Lily grabbed Ana's wrist and peered closely at her arm. There were faint silver markings up by her elbow, the first outlines of a weapon. It was the earliest stages of the bond. "Who?"

Ana's eyes saddened. "Elijah. Another Order member. He died trying to save me from Nate. By giving his life for me, he satisfied one of the stages of the bond, so I developed the mark. Since he's dead, I'm no danger, so the Order doesn't mind if I live." Ana rubbed her hand over the mark, a caress so tender that it almost made Lily believe Ana was connecting with her dead mate.

Lily thought of Gideon, and she glanced toward the door, wondering how soon he'd return. Hearing Ana and Grace talk about their mates was stirring something inside Lily. She felt restless and unsettled, and she wanted Gideon there by her side.

Grace set her hand on her sister's shoulder. "Trust me, Ana. I'm sorry you never got to know Elijah, but it's easier this way. You don't want to go down that road."

Ana glanced up at her. "It worked out for you."

"For now," Grace acknowledged. "Who knows what the future will bring, though? I wouldn't have chosen it if I had a choice."

Lily looked at Grace. "But you didn't have a choice. No *sheva* has a choice about whether she will bond with her mate." Lily thought she heard footsteps in the hall and looked sharply at the door. Gideon?

No one entered, and disappointment surged through her.

Grace pressed her hand to her mark. "No, I didn't have a choice, though I certainly tried. I refused to believe in destiny and the whole bonding thing, but destiny didn't really care what I believed." Her face softened. "But now that I'm here, it's so worth it."

Ana grinned, her silver eyes sparkling with amusement. "Grace is in love. Isn't it cute? She's been this hard-edged miserable person for the last ten years, and then she meets some Order member who has to kill her, and boom, she remembers how to smile."

Lily felt a pulse in her heart at the genuine affection between the sisters, and suddenly she missed her family so much. Her throat tightened. "Is there a phone here I can use?"

"I'll get mine." Grace smiled again. "Nice to meet you, Lily. We're so glad you're here." She squeezed Ana's hand, and then strode out of the room, carefully closing the door behind her.

Ana settled down beside Lily and propped herself up on one of the flowered throw pillows. "So, before she comes back, I have to ask you something."

Lily grinned and settled down next to Ana. It felt good to have girl talk, to be sitting in a real bed, not afraid, knowing that Gideon was somewhere nearby, making sure she was safe. "What's up?"

"Do you remember the man who visited me in my cell that time?" Ana's face became shuttered. "Frank Tully."

Lily shivered and glanced at the window, all her peacefulness quickly dissipating. Frank would be coming for her. She knew he would. Would he be able to breach the Order headquarters? She shifted again, restlessness building inside her. Where was Gideon? "What about Frank?"

Ana leaned forward and lowered her voice. "I dream about him."

Lily frowned. "Nightmares?" She had plenty of those.

"No. Dreams like I'm drowning and he saves me." Ana fixed her gaze on Lily's face, her eyes desperate for information. "Who is he? Do you know?"

Lily shook her head. "No, but I know he's more dangerous than Nate was. Smarter, too."

"I sensed that...but I think there's something else." Ana hugged her legs to her chest, resting her chin on her knees. "Like maybe he was pretending to be a jerk when Nate was around so Nate would trust him?"

Lily frowned, not liking Ana's questions or her apparent desire to see something good in Frank. "Trust me, he wasn't pretending. You met him. Didn't he scare you?" Scare was too gentle of a word. Frank had looked at Lily with such evil, such threat, and such mercilessness that she'd known that if he ever got his hands on her, he would destroy her, and death would not come fast enough.

"Yeah, he did unnerve me." Ana sighed and rubbed her forehead, suddenly looking exhausted. "I just feel like...I don't know. Confused. Like I should know more about him, but I can't remember. I just feel like he's not who he seems."

"He's worse than what he seems." Lily remembered how Frank had seemed concerned about Ana's injuries and how Nate had been treating Ana. She recalled how he'd made a gallant show of protecting Ana from Nate's violence. Was that what Ana was remembering? "Listen to me, Ana. Nate messed you up, and I'm sure Frank seemed like a chance for escape or something, but he's a really evil person. I felt it. Didn't you feel it when you looked into his eyes? They still haunt me."

Ana chewed her lower lip. "I did feel it...but something else too." Her face was lined with worry. "He scares me so much, but at the same time...I feel drawn to him."

Lily set her hand on Ana's shoulder, squeezing gently. "He did something to you, then. He can affect emotions." She swallowed hard as she recalled when Nate had tried to call out her magic, and Frank had done something to make her respond to Nate physically even though she reviled him. "Don't be fooled by Frank. You're finally free, Ana. Don't go back. Do you hear me?"

Ana looked away, picking at a stray thread on the comforter. "It's not like I even know where to find him, so it doesn't matter."

"Ana! That's not an answer! Promise me you'll stay away from him!"

The door opened and Grace walked in, carrying a stack of items that looked like towels, clothes, and some toiletries. She set it on the bed. "I know you don't have any of your own stuff here, so here are some of mine. I think we're about the same size." She frowned, looking back and forth between Lily and Ana. "What happened?"

"Ana is—" Lily began.

"Don't say it." Ana was on her feet suddenly, her cast thunking to the floor. "I'm fine. I'll resist him." Her eyes pleaded with Lily. "Everyone here is already treating me like I'm some fragile doll. Don't make it worse. Please. I just want to forget all of it."

Lily knew how strong Frank was. Ana would have very little defense against someone that powerful, if he truly were trying to influence her. "I think we should tell Gideon—"

"No!" Ana's eyes flashed. "I sent them after you, Lily. You owe me. Let it go." She whirled around and stalked out the door, limping with each step.

Grace sighed as Ana limped down the hall. "Ana's been struggling. She's always had a positive view of the world, but everything she went through with Nate really shook her up. She's been having difficulty finding her equilibrium again." She looked at Lily. "I won't put you in the position of asking you to betray her secret, but do you feel it's important?"

Lily nodded. "I think she's in danger." If Frank had his sights set on her, Ana was definitely in trouble, especially if Ana didn't want to believe how awful he was. Lily supposed it made sense: after what she and Ana had been through, it was hard to figure out how to move forward.

Grace's eyes flickered with worry. "I won't allow anything else to happen to her. I'm going to go talk to her." She flicked a finger toward a closed door. "Bathroom's in there. Oh, and here's my phone." She tossed a cell phone to Lily and walked out, pulling the door shut behind her as she called Ana's name.

Lily stared after them for a minute then looked down at the phone. Her heart pounding, she dialed her parent's phone number and pressed the phone to her ear, her hands shaking.

There was a click, and then Lily heard her mom's voice. "Hello?"

Tears filled Lily's eyes and she started to cry, obliterating any chance she had at talking. Her mom sounded exactly the same as she'd remembered. How many times had Lily played this moment over in her mind, trying to believe that someday she'd hear her mother's voice again? And it was real. It was happening. *Mom.*

"Hello? Who's there? What's wrong? Who is this?" Her mom's voice rose with concern.

Lily cleared her throat, clutching the phone. "Mom? It's me. It's Lily."

"*Lily.* Oh, dear God. Lily!" Her mom screamed. "Gerry! It's Lily! She's on the phone! Lily! Where have you been? Dear Lord, is it really you?"

"It's me." Lily could barely even talk, she was crying so hard. "Mom...I love you."

"Oh, Lily. I love you too." Her mom was crying now, as well. "I can't believe it's you."

There was another click, and then her dad's cautious voice. "Lily?"

Her throat filled up again. "*Dad.*"

"Oh, sweet Jesus. *Lily*." Her dad's voice filled with tears, and she heard him sobbing.

❧ ❧ ❧

"When are you coming home? Can we meet you somewhere? I have to see you," Lily's mom said ten minutes later, after Lily had filled them in on some of the less gruesome details about what had happened to her. Her mom and dad had been asking questions about Nate that Lily didn't want to answer. The information would just burden them and give them no peace. And the answers would involve things Lily didn't want to relive.

"We have to see our baby," her dad agreed.

Lily leaned against the polished cherry headboard and studied the huge window that was so open and inviting. Where was Frank? Was he out there right now, trying to figure out how to breach the headquarters and get her? Was he watching her condo, waiting for her to reclaim her life? "I can't come home yet."

"What? Why not?"

Lily rubbed her palm over her forehead. "It's not safe for me. The man who held me..." She paused, trying to figure out how to explain it without worrying them more. Without telling them that an even more dangerous psychopath was now pursuing her.

There was no need for them to know Frank's Calydons were probably sitting outside her parents' house, waiting for her to show up. There was no way she could tell her mother that Gideon was the one who had saved her. Gideon. What was she going to do about him?

But even as she thought about him, fierce longing pulsed inside her, a need to connect with him. Was her magic crazy? Or was it her own truth and her own heart that had looked into his eyes and believed he was worthy of her trust? She needed to see him again, to figure out what was going on between them. To determine what was real, and what wasn't.

"Lily? What about the man who held you? You said he was dead?"

"He is. I'm working with the police," she lied. "They need my help to catch the guy's partner."

"Tell them no," her mom said. "You've been through too much. *We've* been through too much. Come home. I'll make your favorite stew and Grandma's Dutch apple pie."

Lily closed her eyes at the mention of her grandma, who Gideon had admitted to killing. "Mom? I have a question about Grandma."

There was a tense silence. "What is it?"

"Before Gideon..." Lily swallowed. "Before Gideon killed her, was she acting...weird?" She needed the truth. She had to know who Gideon truly was. She had to know if she could really trust him, or if it was her Satinka need for him that was making her want him. Had he really killed her grandma in cold blood, or had he been justified?

"No, not at all," her mother said quickly. Too quickly. "She was her same sweet self as always."

For the first time, Lily didn't believe her. "Mom. Tell me the truth."

"Tell her, Maggie," her dad said. "After what Lily's been through recently, I know she can handle the truth."

More silence, and then Maggie finally began to talk. "I had stopped by my mother's house to pick up Trig for the afternoon while she and Cade had some private time. But when I got to the kitchen, I saw Cade standing over my father, Cade's spear lodged in my dad's chest. My mother was sobbing, screaming at Cade for killing him, and Cade was yelling at her, telling her she was a slut for defending another man when she was Cade's mate."

Lily nodded. She'd heard this part before, and it still gave her chills. Her mom had explained that Grandpa had come to find his wife and beg her to leave Cade and come back home. Cade had returned home, and he'd gone crazy with rage when he'd found another man with his *sheva*.

"I freaked out," Maggie said. "Cade saw me and went crazy. He started yelling that I had come there to steal his son, and he called out his weapon and I thought for sure he was going to kill me."

Lily hadn't heard this part before. In the rendition she'd heard, Gideon showed up at this point and killed both her grandma and Cade without justification. "What did you do?"

"My mother—Grandma—yelled at him to stop, to leave me alone. When he turned toward her, I thought he was going to attack her, so I grabbed a knife and threw it at him."

Lily felt her jaw drop at the thought of her non-confrontational mom throwing a knife at a Calydon warrior. "You did? He ducked, I assume?"

"I wouldn't know. My mother grabbed a kitchen chair and slammed it into my head. It knocked me out for a split second, and when I awoke, she was bringing it down again, screaming at me for trying to hurt Cade. She broke my arm and my shoulder."

A cold chill crept up Lily's arms at the image of a mother turning on her seventeen-year-old daughter. "Oh, Mom—"

"She stopped attacking me when Trig came into the room and Cade went after Trig, screaming about how Trig was stealing my mother from him," Maggie continued. "My mother hit Cade with the chair, and he whirled around, threw her against the wall, and then called out his spear to plunge it into Trig's chest, cursing Trig for coming between Cade and my mother."

Lily's hand went to her chest. "Oh, God—"

"That was when Gideon showed up. He killed Cade and saved Trig, but then my mother grabbed the knife I'd had and charged Gideon. So he killed her, too. Then he left, without another word. The bastard just walked away, leaving Trig crying and me with a shattered arm and shoulder." Maggie's voice grew bitter. "He didn't need to kill my mother in self-defense. There's no way my mother could have killed him. He did it because of what he is, a cold-blooded assassin poisoned by the Order."

Lily's stomach churned, reeling with her mother's brutal disclosure. "He had to kill her, Mom," she whispered, her voice raw. She now understood why Gideon had simply turned away. It wasn't because Gideon had felt nothing. It was because shutting down his emotions was the only way he could survive what he'd done. "Your mother was lost, Mom. She wasn't your mother anymore. She would have killed you." Lily had done enough research on Calydons to know it was true. By the time the bond got that far, there was no hope.

"Only because Cade warped her mind and turned her into something crazy. Once Cade was dead, she would have recovered, I'm sure of it. She would have been my mother again," Maggie said. "Between Cade and Gideon, they destroyed everything I had, everything Trig had, though fortunately, he was too young to remember any of it. If I hadn't met your dad a couple months later...I don't know what I would have done. I was seventeen, Lily. Still in high school. No girl should ever go through what I went through that day."

Lily closed her eyes and leaned back against the headboard. "How come you never told me all this? You just told me that Gideon came and killed them both."

"Oh, Lily, how could I possibly tell you a story about a mother turning on her own daughter? It would have given you nightmares, and I didn't want that. I just wanted you to know enough to make smart decisions and to stay away from Calydons. There was no need for more."

Lily swallowed. "Before Cade, was Grandma good to you?"

"She was the most wonderful, loving mother in the world," Maggie said, her voice full of warmth. "I loved her more than anything. She was so devoted to me and to my father. That was all that mattered to her. When she met Cade, she walked away from all of it. Just like that."

Just like that. Because she was Cade's *sheva*, she'd left the family she loved and tried to murder her own daughter. Lily knew that a Calydon and his *sheva* were destined for destruction. She'd read the stories and heard the tales, but having it happen in her own family made it real in a way it had never been before. How horrific for a mother to turn against her own children. Lily couldn't even imagine what damage had been caused to her grandma's brain and soul to make her do that. The horror her mom had to deal with..."I'm sorry, Mom. I'm sorry you had to go through that."

"Oh, sweetie, now that you're back, and you're fine, none of that matters." Maggie sighed, and there was audible contentment in her voice. "You've brought my life back."

Lily's throat tightened. "I'm so sorry you had to think I was dead."

"No," her mom said firmly. "Don't talk like that. It's in the past."

"Mom's right," her dad said. "We can't dwell on the past, or life gets unbearable. You're safe, and we'll see you soon. That's what matters."

Lily managed a smile, marveling at their strength. "Is it any wonder I turned out okay? You guys are amazing."

"We take full credit, of course," her dad said with a chuckle. "Damn, it's good to hear your voice, Lily."

The door opened, and Lily looked up to see Gideon walk into the room. Her belly did a little flip at the sight of him. He had changed clothes, and was wearing a pair of faded Wranglers, a rough cotton black button-down shirt hanging out of his jeans, and he had on a pair of work boots that were battered and broken in. His clothes looked old and worn in. Almost as if they were his comfort clothes…as if a warrior like Gideon needed comforting.

He gave her a long look, and she realized how cold his eyes were. He'd retreated back into warrior mode, and she could suddenly envision him as the warrior in her mother's story. There was nothing kind or gentle about him at all…yet at the same time…she felt herself relax, knowing that she was safe, now that he was in the room with her. No longer did the window seem to be a big fat invitation for Frank to come get her.

Gideon came to a stop at the foot of the bed and fixed his gaze on her. He reminded her of a predator, waiting for her to flinch before he leapt on her, claws out, teeth bared. His eyes were dark, and there was anticipation on his face. Tense anticipation, and not in a good way, but at the same time, there was unmistakable desire rising from him, that same need that had leapt between them at their first meeting.

Lily's skin flushed with heat under his intense gaze. "Okay, I have to go," she said to her parents, unable to tear her gaze off Gideon. "The police have some questions for me."

"Can we call you back on this number?" Maggie asked.

"You can try. I borrowed it from one of the cops. I don't know if they'll let me keep it. Love you guys."

They both assured her of their love, and Lily had to hang up over her mom's pleas to talk longer, knowing Maggie would never let her go. She folded the phone and set it on the bedside table, then turned to face Gideon.

# Chapter 12

Gideon wanted her.

There was no way around it.

Yeah, he should cut and run before they could bond any more, but with Lily sprawled on that bed, her cheeks rosy, her eyes bright with anticipation as she looked at him, there was no chance he was going to bail.

He was sunk, and he knew it.

The huge pillows dwarfed Lily, and her hair was tangled around her shoulders. There were faint gray shadows under her eyes, and her skin looked drawn. But there was a flush of pink to her cheeks, and he'd caught the scent of her arousal the moment she'd seen him walk in the room.

Gideon was absolutely stunned by the fact she'd responded to his presence after the story her mother had told about him.

He'd heard the entire conversation with her parents, courtesy of his enhanced hearing. He'd listened to all the details, and he'd felt the pain that her family had endured. Yeah, he finally understood why Lily Davenport had spent her life searching for answers about his race. Why being thrust into this situation with Nate and Frank and the Order would be against everything her life was built upon.

Yet, there was no accusation in Lily's expression as she waited for him to speak. If anything, there was a level of understanding that hadn't been present before. And fear... No, not fear. It was more like respect for how dangerous he was.

Wariness. But she was also projecting a certain level of calmness. Her energy had become increasingly focused and controlled as she'd listened to the story about her grandma's death. Instead of upsetting her, the information had empowered her.

Her reaction made Gideon realize that knowledge was Lily Davenport's greatest weapon. Her security blanket. For Lily, knowledge was power, and the quest for information gave her strength.

Gideon could tell from the heated expression on Lily's face that she hadn't looked at her arm yet and seen his mark on her skin. Once she knew, there would be no calm.

He needed to tell her about the bond, but first he had something to say that he hadn't had the chance to say to his first *sheva* after he'd failed her. He leaned forward, gripping the footboard. "I'm sorry."

Lily's eyebrows went up. "For killing my grandmother?"

"No. I did what I had to do there." He couldn't step down from that commitment to his mission. The moment he began to get personal with what he had to do, he'd be unable to do it. "I apologize because I almost let you get taken by Frank's Calydons, and then I almost killed you." His fingers dug into the footboard as he recalled the sight of her sprawled on the ground, immobile, half-naked, *dying*. "I promised you I'd keep you safe and I fucking blew it."

Lily's face softened, and she crawled across the bed toward him, a slow, seductive movement that made dark, forbidden desire pulse deeply inside him.

Gideon tensed as Lily rose to her knees and laid her soft, gentle hands on either side of his face, a gesture of tenderness that made him want to stay right where he was for the rest of his damned life.

"I didn't die," she said softly. "I'm okay." She slid her arms around his waist, and he froze, afraid to touch her.

He had to stop himself from getting involved with her. It was too dangerous to connect with her in any way, even if it wasn't officially one of the stages that would wind the noose tighter around their necks.

Lily nuzzled her face into his chest and he felt her soul reach for him, needing to connect with him after the story her mother had told, after he'd nearly killed her. *She needed his touch.*

Gideon groaned and wrapped his arms around her, hauling her against him. No one had ever craved his touch before, not like this, and he couldn't resist the call. He kissed her hair, and then buried his face into the curve of her neck, drinking in her scent, her touch, her life. "I'm so fucking sorry. I blew it. When I saw you there...and I couldn't stop draining you. I'll never forget it."

Lily shook her head. "No. It's not your fault. I knew it would be a risk feeding you my magic. I gave you no warning, and I didn't try to protect myself. I knew the risk."

Gideon shook his head, refusing to absolve himself of responsibility. "The only reason you had to do it was because I was so busy trying to have sex with you that I stopped paying any attention to anything else. I've never fucked up like that before. I...shit." He realized suddenly that he was shaking, and he held her tighter, trying to prove to himself that she was really there. Alive. That he hadn't killed her. "Jesus, Lily. How can you even stand to touch me? I heard the story your mother told. I'm a monster. You know I am."

"Because I've seen what a monster really is." Lily sat back on her heels, and he felt her pull her energy inward, as if she were amassing it to protect herself. "I need you to understand something about me, Gideon."

He frowned. "What is it?"

She swallowed. "When I was seventeen, I met a boy. A Calydon."

Oh, Gideon could tell he wasn't going to like this story. "I don't think I want to hear about you dating some other guy," he muttered.

"No, listen." Lily put her hand on his lips. "It was right after Trig had died. I was lonely and I missed having a Calydon in my life since he was gone. So I let this boy win my heart. He was nineteen, and he'd already come into his powers. I wasn't his *sheva* so I thought it was safe."

Dark foreboding began to pulse through Gideon. "What happened?"

"I went camping with him." Lily closed her eyes for a

split second, and Gideon felt her gathering strength.

Fierce possession shifted inside him, and he tightened his grip on her. "What did he do?"

Lily looked up at Gideon, and in those green eyes, he saw acceptance, a realization of exactly how bad the world could be. "When we got to the 'campsite,' he had five of his friends waiting for me. He'd figured out that I was a Satinka, and they wanted to see what it was like to get a high off me."

Gideon swore, and she felt black fury rising hard and fast in him.

"I had no chance to stop them." She hadn't let herself think of it for so long, but suddenly, just like that, she was back there. She could smell the rot of the nearby garbage dump, the dampness of the muddy ground, she could hear the distant hum of the highway, so close, and yet so hopelessly far. "They chained me up by my ankles and wrists, and then they started the music." Lily rubbed her wrists, feeling that sharp pain of the metal digging into her skin.

"Son of a bitch, Lily." Gideon's hands slipped beneath hers, loosely bracketing her wrists, his warm grip protecting her from the chains she could still feel. Fire raged in his eyes, helpless fury, and she stared at him, losing herself in the fierceness of his gaze. "Satinka magic is sensual in nature," he growled with vivid understanding of exactly what her captors had done to try to bring her magic. "Those fucking bastards—"

"Three days," she said quietly, struggling against the old terror fighting to surface, striving to take over. "Three days they kept me. They never slept, because they were on such a high from my magic. They were like manic beasts, fighting for more."

"Jesus, Lily." Gideon pulled her into his arms, and she went willingly, needing to feel his strength, the protective warmth of his body, to keep the memories from taking hold of her.

She closed her eyes, breathing in the woodsy, pure male scent that was Gideon, letting it drown out the memories of sweat, fear, and pain. "In the end, there wasn't enough of me to go around, and they fought each other." She still remembered their death screams, the thuds of their bodies hitting the ground beside her, the dark stains in the dirt as their life bled into the earth. "They slaughtered each other. It took another two days for anyone to find me." Six bodies, rotting in the heat, while she'd lain there, still bound at her wrists and ankles, praying with every fiber of her soul that someone would find them, helpless to do anything but wait. Never again would she ever feel as powerless as she did during those five days.

"Son of a bitch." Gideon's arms tightened around her, his voice raw with fury. She was locked down against him, trapped against his body, in a helpless position that she'd avoided ever since that horrible kidnapping.

But Gideon wasn't triggering her fight or flight instincts. For some reason, for some beautiful reason, the warmth of his embrace just eased away the panic and the fear, and made her feel solid and grounded. Was it because he'd saved her life so many times already? Or because he'd used her magic to defeat the enemy, instead of abusing it? He'd done what he was supposed to do when she'd fed him. Yeah, sure, he'd almost taken it too far, but given how much magic she'd thrust into him without any guidance or warning, the fact she was still alive and he'd been able to channel it against the enemy was extraordinary.

"Did any of them live?" Gideon asked, his voice low and lethal.

Lily almost laughed at his fury. "You're going to kill them?"

His face was deadly fierce. "Yeah, I am."

Her smile faded at the intensity of his expression, and awareness pulsed deep inside her. Here was the man who would do anything to keep her safe. God, it felt brilliant. "They're all dead," she said. "They killed each other."

"Damn." His fingers flexed. "I need to kill someone for that."

Lily could tell he wasn't joking, and a thrill of excitement ran through her. Yes, she should be horrified, but it was sort of cool to be linked with someone who could do all the things she couldn't, someone who was willing to do them. "Thank you."

Gideon's gaze flicked to hers, and she saw such respect in them. Anger and deadly intent, yes, but also respect. "How in the hell did you trust me enough to give me your magic, after that?" he asked. "How did you let me touch you? And sing to you? *How?*"

Lily bit her lip and absently rubbed her hand over his shoulder, needing to touch him. "At first, I thought I was going to die." She held onto him, using his strength to help her deal with the memories. "I was so terrified I couldn't even think. I cried, I screamed, and I begged, but it didn't matter. They were insane, and they were brutal. Nothing I did mattered, and eventually I became numb to the fear. I was too exhausted to be terrified anymore, you know?"

Gideon brushed her hair back from her face, his blue eyes boiling like a seething ocean. "You went into survival mode."

Lily nodded, sensing that he understood. "My only focus was to survive, to try and hold back enough of my power that I could stay alive. I refused to think of anything but home, no matter what was happening to me. It was like I wasn't even there."

"But you were."

"Yes, I was." She rubbed her wrists again, trying to wipe off the scars that only she could feel. There were no marks on her skin anymore, but those chains were still tight around her wrists and ankles every day, every moment, no matter how hard she tried not to think of it. "I did survive, and nothing I'll ever encounter again will be as horrific and terrifying as those five days."

"Shit, Lily." Gideon took her hand and raised it, pressing his lips to her invisible scars. One kiss, then another, making a bracelet of his protection around her wrist. "I swear on my soul that you will never, ever have to be afraid again."

Tears filled Lily's eyes at the intensity of his words, the raw commitment in his eyes and the tenderness of his kisses. "You mean that, don't you?"

"Hell, yes." Gideon swore, realizing that he would never rid his mind of the vision of Lily and her kidnappers, a brutality he would forever remember, because it was part of what made his woman who she was. To honor Lily, he would never forget.

He was burning with the need to protect her, to do whatever it took to strip her of that past, to honor that courage and strength that she held so bravely. How could this one woman have gone through so much and still walk with her shoulders back and her head held high? But he knew the answer. "Some people break under that kind of hell," he said quietly. "Others use it as proof that they can survive anything." She was a survivor, a courageous warrior who fought with her heart, her soul, and sheer force of will. "That's how you made it through Nate's, wasn't it?"

Lily nodded, and in those beautiful green eyes, he saw the woman he'd been meant to find for the last five hundred years. A woman of courage, hope, and beauty. There was no resentment in her for the life she'd been handed, for the losses she'd suffered. Instead, she was full of passion and emotion, openly feeling everything life brought her, even if it hurt. She felt pain, yes, but Gideon had heard the warmth in her conversation with her parents, he'd felt her love for her brother, and he'd experienced the absolute trust she'd given him at the river.

Somehow, Lily had faced the worst and still found a way to keep her heart open. Unlike Gideon, who lived in a cold shell of survival, Lily wasn't afraid to feel pain, to offer herself to love, or to set herself up for hurt. Lily lived and experienced life with every last bit of her soul, and that was why she was standing before him, in his arms, showering him with the gift of feeling and living for the first time in five hundred years.

No wonder Gideon's shields hadn't been able to hold up to protect him from feeling Lily's emotions. She was so powerful that nothing would ever hold her down. "God, I admire you."

Lily smiled and snuggled closer to him, her breath hot through his shirt. "I don't need much," she said, "and I've worked hard to be independent, but I'll admit that I'm at the end of my resources. I want to feel safe, Gideon, even if it's just for a day." She slipped her arms around his waist, her touch tentative and unbelievably vulnerable. "It feels good to be with you, Gideon. You make me feel safe."

"Me?" He wrapped his hand around the back of her head, sinking his fingers into her tresses as he brushed his lips over her silky soft hair. He was raging with the need to kiss her, to fill her with his passion, to chase away all the memories of the hell she'd faced, so all she would ever think of again was how it would feel to be with a man who treasured everything about her very soul. "How is it possible that I make you feel safe? You know what I am. You're insane, aren't you?" he murmured. "That has to be it."

She lifted her face to look at him, and he saw true fear in her eyes. Not fear *of* him. Fear she was sharing *with* him. "I've spent my life researching you. Researching Calydons." Lily didn't pull away or even hint at retreating. "I understand you, Gideon. By killing Cade and my grandmother, you saved my mother's life. Trig's, too."

Gideon frowned, listening to her repeat the words he lived by. That all the lives he took were justified for the greater good. People outside the Order never understood that, certainly not when he was taking the lives of people they loved. How was it possible that a woman who'd suffered so much violence understood him?

"No matter how it happens," Lily said, her voice clear and true, "you're true to your mission to protect innocents. There is honor in that." Her fingers dug into his hips, keeping him close. "My brother was a Calydon. He was a good person. I loved him with all my heart. I knew he was strong, he was good, and he was honorable, even though he was also burdened by being a Calydon. Like you are. I wanted to hate you. I did. I tried." Lily met his gaze. "But you're like my brother. You do horrible, horrible things without remorse, but you have honor."

Gideon tangled his fingers in her hair, knowing he should stop her and tell her about the mark, but he couldn't bring himself to do it. For this one moment, he wanted her to look at him like he wasn't a demon, because she made him almost feel human when she looked at him like that, and that was a gift.

Because he was a monster. Yeah, sure, he'd tried to atone for it over the last five hundred years, but he *knew* he was. The instant Lily realized she was bound to him, she'd know it, too. She'd never again look at him the way she was right now: with trust, with tenderness, and with desire so pure and so intense that it brought everything inside him to a roaring crescendo.

Gideon felt something flicker inside him at the honesty on her face, at her belief in him, calling upon the one thing he didn't have, would never have, and had spent his life trying to make up for. "Lily, I don't have honor—"

"You do—"

"No." Gideon ground his jaw, unable to accept her accolades when he knew what a bastard he was. He couldn't lie. He couldn't deceive her. Not anymore.

It was time to show her the truth about what he was.

Silently, Gideon took her hand and pressed his lips to her palm, keeping his gaze fastened on her eyes. Then he took her sleeve and gently pushed it up her arm, knowing that everything would change between them the minute she saw the mark. Lily could forgive him for killing a grandmother she'd never met, because of her love for her brother. She could forgive Gideon for almost draining her dry, because she took responsibility. But she'd never forgive being bonded to him. Not with her history. It would be too personal to her.

Which was fine.

He wasn't going to forgive himself either. He should have known. Somehow, someway, he should have known and prevented it. That was his duty, to protect her, and the only way to keep her safe would have been to keep the bond from beginning. He'd failed once, and he'd failed a second time with her.

The sleeve was up, baring Lily's arm, and Gideon laid his hand over the mark, her skin pulsing with the warmth of his brand.

Questions flickered in Lily's eyes, and she glanced down at her arm, but he was covering it.

He felt her body tense, and she sucked in her breath. Her hand shaking, she peeled his fingers off, and he allowed her to move his hand.

# Chapter 13

Lily's stomach plummeted as she stared at the marks on her arm. "That can't be—"

Gideon shoved up his sleeve and laid his arm next to hers.

They matched. His brand was on her arm.

Lily shoved away from him, stumbling off the edge of the bed, still gaping at her arm. "That's not right. It can't be right." She jerked her gaze to him. "You already met your *sheva*. It can't happen twice."

His jaw was rigid, his blue eyes blazing with regret, but also with a possessive heat that made her body leap with desire. "Apparently, it can."

"No!" Lily whirled around and ran into the bathroom, turned on the faucets and shoved her arm underneath, scraping at it with her fingernails. Clawing at her arm. Visions of her grandma trying to kill her own daughter crowded her mind, Trig convulsing in his bed as his Calydon destiny claimed him, and she started shaking violently. "It's wrong. I can't—"

"Lily!" Gideon walked up behind her, his body crowding hers as he reached around her and grabbed her hands, prying her fingernails out of her skin.

"No! I have to get it off!" She tried to rip free of his tight grasp, her heart pounding so hard, her ears ringing, her stomach churning.

Gideon's muscles bunched as he wrapped his arms around her, immobilizing her against his chest. "Lily." His voice was calm. So calm it made no sense. "You can't get it off. It's there forever."

She stared at him in the bathroom mirror, at his broad shoulders dwarfing her, at his intense blue eyes, at his muscled arms pinning her to his chest. Her gaze drifted down to his forearms, and she saw the black brands on his skin, burned into the flesh.

Her stomach lurched and she jerked free of his arms and fell to her knees. She lurched over to the toilet, grabbing the seat as she vomited. Tears streamed down her cheeks and she couldn't stop.

Gideon knelt beside her, holding her hair off her face, rubbing her back as her body heaved again and again until there was nothing left. But still her body kept trying until she was shaking so violently she was afraid she'd shatter.

Gideon kept stroking her, his head bent next to hers. He was murmuring words, but she couldn't hear them, couldn't think about anything other than her grandma, her brother, and the fate she was locked into... *I can't do this. I can't—*

*Yes, you can.*

She moaned and held her forehead with her hands. *You can hear my thoughts now.* She stumbled to her feet and grabbed the sink. She turned the faucet on full, splashing water on her face, in her mouth, on her arms, trying to get herself to feel clean. But she couldn't. She just couldn't. "Dammit!" She gripped the sink and bowed her head, fighting off another surge of tears.

*We were both resisting so hard before that we were blocking our connection. It's open now.* Gideon's arms went around her and he pulled her onto his lap.

Lily tried to shove off him. "Let me go!"

He tightened his grip and kept her locked against him. "No."

"Gideon—"

"I don't even know the name of my first *sheva*." His voice was quiet, so quiet that she had to stop struggling to hear his words. "I was walking down the street with Dante and two other Order members. We were going to get food." He snorted in disgust. "Food. So mundane. So innocuous."

"Let go of me," Lily whispered, her fingers sliding around his wrists to try to pry his arms off her. "I know the story." She didn't want to hear it again. She didn't want to hear how he stood back and let that innocent girl be killed. She didn't want to hear how he was going to do it again, this time to her.

"Listen to me, Lily. I need you to hear this." Gideon's voice was raw and bitter, and she shivered at the harsh edge to it. "I need you to hear the story from my point of view. You're locked into me now, and you need to know the type of male you're burdened with."

She hesitated, realizing she wasn't going anywhere until he released her. And a part of her wanted to know. From him. She sighed and stopped fighting, but she couldn't relax, not with his powerful arms wrapped around her with such unyielding strength. "What happened?"

"I saw her across the street," Gideon said, gazing at the wall as if he were reliving the moment in his head. "She was walking with two friends. I think she was maybe eighteen, if that. I was nineteen, and I'd come into my powers only a few weeks before. I was reeling with my new powers, and Dante was having difficulty controlling me. My muscles were twice the size they'd been before my change, and I was getting stronger every day."

Lily said nothing. She knew all about the transition. About the dream the young Calydons had where they were fighting for their lives in a battle on another plane. If they survived the dream, they woke up with their brands. If they didn't, they died in their sleep. Trig had died. Despite the fact she'd spent her whole life searching for ways to ensure he survived his dream, he'd died.

"I saw her," Gideon continued, "and I knew instantly that she was my *sheva*. I wanted her so badly, but it wasn't just sex. I needed to protect her, to hold her, to bring her into my world and make her mine."

Lily's jaw tightened as jealousy slammed into her. "I don't want to know—"

"I could have kept walking," Gideon continued relentlessly. "No one else saw her. I could have walked past her that day and let her disappear. I knew the implications, but I thought she was so beautiful and I wanted her to see me. See my muscles. Feel my power. I wanted to see her face light up in awe for who I was. So I crossed the street and introduced myself." His arms tightened around Lily, and he pressed his face into her hair before continuing.

Lily felt a small ache in her chest, and her grip on his wrist softened. "Gideon? Are you okay?"

He lifted his head from her hair. "Dante followed me over there, and the minute she smiled at me, I went down on my knees. Literally. She knocked me over with her voice." His voice grew harder. "Dante grabbed her in one hand and me in the other and carted us both around the corner into an alley. He threw me down on my ass and told me I was a total fuckup and I'd better turn out right or he'd be making the wrong choice. Then he called out his spear and he killed her."

Her forearms searing hot in response to his confession and torment, Lily twisted out of his grip to face him. His eyes were haunted, his face tight. Where was the cold, stoic warrior who'd been unaffected by his *sheva's* death? It had been a lie. All this time, he'd been living a lie, and she'd bought it.

He glanced at her, then averted his eyes and leaned back against the bathroom wall, his arms draped over his knees. "She looked at me the split second before Dante's blade sank into her and she said 'Why?'. That was her last word. Why." He met Lily's gaze, and she saw the coldness in his eyes that he was so well-known for, the detachment that she now knew was simply a shield. "The answer to her question was because I was too fucking arrogant to keep walking when I should have."

"Gideon—"

"Dante handed her body to me, and he told me I'd better make myself worthy, because an innocent had died to keep me alive. Then he left." A muscle ticked in Gideon's cheek. "I held her for the next ten hours. I just stood there in that alley, with this dead girl in my arms, and I couldn't move."

Tears began to sting at the back of Lily's eyes for his pain, even though his eyes were hard, and his body was rigid. He believed he felt no pain. He'd erected a shield around himself for five hundred years, but she knew all too well that that kind of anguish never left. It was always inside, fermenting and poisoning.

"Quinn and Elijah, who were rookies with me at the time, came back and found me. I was covered in her blood. Together, we buried her. We sat on her grave for six days. All three of us. They knew I would have killed myself if they'd left. So they didn't. They stayed with me, until they finally helped me realize that the only appropriate response was to make her death worthwhile." Gideon's fingers traced the inside of his wrist.

Lily saw he was rubbing a small scar on his skin, and she knew that Calydons scarred only from other Calydon weapons.

"I cut myself and bled onto her grave. I swore on her death that I would never waiver in my oath to protect innocents against rogue Calydons. I promised her that I would be worthy of her death, that thousands of lives would be saved because she sacrificed her life." His gaze flicked to Lily. "And then we got up, and we never talked about it again." His eyes grew bitter. "And the legend of Gideon was born."

She moved between his knees, and he let her, his hands finding her hips, palming her waist.

His gaze went to her. "And now, I have another *sheva*. Another responsibility to carry. Another choice to make."

Lily didn't need to ask what he was going to do. She already knew. His need for her was burning in those blue eyes, in the fierceness of voice. He hadn't walked away from his *sheva* before, and he wasn't going to now. He was going to keep her, devil be damned.

Gideon's grip tightened on her hips. "I can't stand back and let you die. There's no *fucking* way." His chest expanded with a deep breath. "But if I end up going rogue or dying because of the bond, or even just fuck up the one thing I truly care about, which is to keep innocents safe from rogue Calydons, then I've violated my promise to a dead girl whose name I don't even know. How do I make that choice?" He lifted his hand to her hair and fisted the strands. "Hell, Lily. I'm not prepared for this. I'm not prepared for *you*."

Lily braced her hands against the rough cotton of his shirt, feeling the thud of his heart against her palms. It was a steady, strong beat, but it was uneven. Irregular. Damaged. "I'm not prepared for you, either."

Gideon pulled her closer. His mouth was inches from hers, heat rising furiously between them. "I don't know what to do."

His confession was so raw and desperate, she knew only tremendous pain would have prompted him to admit something like that, and suddenly she felt so ashamed for all the horrible things she'd written about him in her articles. For her accusations of how cold and brutal he was. She lifted her face to his. "I'm sorry for judging you."

He managed a small smile and brushed her hair out of her face, his fingers snagging in the tangles. "I worked hard for that reputation. You helped me spread the word. Don't be sorry."

Lily leaned against him, reveling in the hardness of his body. He was her enemy in so many ways, but he was also her only ally. Now that she was his *sheva*, she knew his commitment to her safety would never fade, never die…until he went rogue, of course. But right now, she was in the arms of a man who would destroy the world to protect her, and that was a pretty incredible feeling for a woman who'd been hiding from shadows for too long. "I spent my life trying to learn as much about the Calydons as I could, so when Trig had his dream, I could save him."

Gideon kept playing with her hair. "He was lucky to have you care about him so much."

"Yes, well, it didn't seem to make a difference." She tangled her fingers through Gideon's, watching his hand dwarf hers. "I thought I could save him. I thought I knew how. I danced for him when he was dreaming, trying to feed him my power. I stayed in his bedroom all night, dancing and singing until my feet bled, watching his body convulse on the mattress as he fought for his life. And he died." Lily lifted her chin, refusing to revisit that horrible moment, the aching loss of realizing she'd lost her brother. "Until I figure out how to ensure a Calydon survives his dream, I can't have a son."

Gideon's hand paused in the slow caress he was doing on her back. "If you mated with a human, you wouldn't have a Calydon for a son."

"I've done my research, Gideon. Being a *sheva* runs in the family, and I've known since I was little that the odds I'd be one were high. So, that was part of the other reason for doing my research. To figure out how to control the situation. To prepare myself if it ever happened. To stop it from happening. I've been careful not to get too serious with a human male, because I didn't want to abandon my family if I got sucked in by a Calydon." She groaned. "The best laid plans—"

He stiffened. "You have a man?" His voice came out a low growl that vibrated in his chest.

Lily lifted her head to look at him. His eyes had gone to a blue the shade of midnight, and his face was heavily lined with anger. She laid her hand on his face. "It's difficult to believe I ever thought you were ice."

His scowl didn't lessen. "You didn't answer my question."

"No, I don't have a man. And if I did, I'm sure he'd be long gone. I've been missing for two years, remember?"

His arms tightened around her and the scowl slowly faded, replaced by regret. "Shit, Lily, I don't know why I just reacted that way."

"I do. It's the bond. We're not even close to being fully bonded, and you're already turning into the man Cade became. A man who was ready to murder his own son in a jealous rage."

His face darkened. "I would never murder my child."

His voice was so resolute with conviction, she knew he believed his words, and she did too...for now. "Did you know Cade?"

"Of course, I did. He was younger than I was, but I'd known him for three hundred years."

"Would you ever have believed he'd try to murder his own son? A thirteen-month-old toddler?"

Gideon's jaw worked hard and finally he shook his head. "No."

"And my grandmother tried to kill her own daughter." Lily needed to get off his lap. Retreat from their intimacy. Start to build the walls, like she'd been planning since she'd first realized she could be someone's *sheva*.

But Lily couldn't bring herself to pull away from Gideon. His body was warm, his muscles hard, and his hand was reassuring as he caressed the small of her back. They weren't doing anything that could increase the bond, but being this close to him was giving her strength. Grounding her. He was giving her security, and she needed that right now.

She gave up resisting her need for him and snuggled up under his jaw, as if he could keep all the monsters at bay. All but the monster he himself brought to the table.

"So, you believe this bond will turn us into people who kill the ones we love?" Gideon asked as he rested his chin against her head. "You buy into the legend?"

Lily nodded. "I haven't found anything that will stop it, and I've been trying for a long time." She nuzzled against his neck, inhaling the warm scent that was him. He still smelled like freedom and heat and man, but there was something else there now...vanilla. He smelled like vanilla. The faintest hint of chocolate chip cookies. "God, I haven't thought of cookies in two years."

"Cookies?"

"You smell like contentment and security." She closed her eyes and concentrated on the vanilla, letting it curl through her and drift into her cells, relaxing her body and giving it a sense of completeness and safety. Even happiness. "How can you make me feel better, when you should be terrifying me?"

"The bond." He pressed his lips to her hair. "You don't think Cade knew the danger the minute he met your grandma? He knew, and there wasn't a damn thing he could do to stop it. It just feels too damn good. You and I both know, yet all I want to do is slide my hand under this sweatshirt—" He slipped his hand beneath the waistband and flattened it over her belly, his light touch sending sparks of heat through her body. "And seduce you until you can't think of anything but my body between your legs, my mouth on your breast and my scent all over you." His hand moved upward until it brushed against the underside of her breast.

She sucked in her breath as desire rushed through her.

His teeth grazed over her ear. "You make me feel again, Lily, and I hate that. I can't deal with it. I don't know how to deal with it and it pisses me off. Emotions make me weak. But at the same time..." He paused to nibble on her earlobe. "God, it feels brilliant to feel alive again."

Lily moaned softly and lifted her head so his lips could

find her throat. She began to hear music dancing in her head, and she felt him tense, and knew he'd heard it too. "Be very careful," she whispered. "I don't think I can bring the full magic without earth, but you call it in a way it's never been called before. I don't know how it will work with you."

His mouth stopped moving along her neck, but he didn't pull away. He simply hovered there, as if he were fighting an internal battle. "So, the attraction between us...Satinka or *sheva*?" His voice had dropped a couple octaves, and was smoldering with a fire that licked at her insides.

"Both." Lily swallowed hard, suddenly aware that she was curled up between his thighs. She could feel his manhood hardening beneath her left hip, and her body quivered in response.

Gideon ran his thumb over her lip. "So, if we succumb to the Satinka attraction, I drain you dry and kill you. If we succumb to the *sheva* bullshit, all hell breaks loose. Double the risk."

"And yet we've got twice the forces trying to pull us together."

He nodded once and let his head fall back against the pale blue wall, his hand still buried in her hair, as if he couldn't quite let go. His face was strained, and there was a single bead of sweat on his temple. He closed his eyes. "The simplest thing would be to pack you off to your parents and call it a day."

She stiffened. "Frank—"

"I know, babe, I know." His hand caressed the back of her neck. "He'll come after you, and I couldn't live with that." His jaw tightened, and she saw the warrior come out. "Plus, we still need your expertise to find out what the hell's going on." He opened his eyes to look at her. "I owe it to my *sheva*...my first *sheva*...to see this thing through. Ezekiel can't be allowed to get out."

Lily nodded. "Frank has to be stopped. I'm not free until he is, so I guess that means we have the same goal, then." She bit her lower lip and started to think, falling back into her old patterns of trying to strategize when the situation became too unbearable to handle. She'd done a lot of thinking during the last two years. "Okay, so I can look at the stone and see what the writing says and then—" She stopped at the expression on his face. "What?"

A faint smile toyed at the corners of his mouth. "You. Knowledge is power with you, isn't it?" He slid his hand over her arm and lightly squeezed her biceps. "You might not have the muscles of a warrior, but you have strength. So much strength."

Her belly tightened at the respect in his eyes. "Most people consider me a geek."

He shrugged. "Who gives a shit what most people think?" He cocked his head. "How'd you survive for two years under Nate? I saw what he did to Ana, physically and emotionally. She's a mess, and Grace is worried she'll never recover. But you—" He laid his hand over her heart, his palm infusing heat into her chest "You survived intact, didn't you?"

Something in her chest began to ache at the expression in his eyes. They weren't cold anymore. Not at all. They were hot with hooded desire and something else. Respect? Affection? "Intact might be a bit optimistic, but yes, I survived."

He tapped her heart. "With this. You willed yourself to win, didn't you? Argued yourself into not giving up, or giving in?"

Lily thought of the nights she'd paced her cell, spending hours talking to herself, rationalizing her fears, focusing on her plans, buoying herself up, trying to learn from everything Nate said and did, so that someday she'd be able to take advantage of some slip up and escape. "I guess."

Gideon cupped her chin and raised her face to his. "Kane asked me why it was different with you. Why I could let my other *sheva* die, but not you."

"Because you're not the arrogant idiot you were back then?"

He smiled. "Yeah, that too, but also because—"

There was a knock on the bedroom door. "Gideon?" It was a male voice. "Let me in."

Gideon cursed, shoved Lily off his lap and leapt for the door. He slammed it shut just as the doorknob was turning. "She's not decent," he growled.

There was silence. "Hell, Gideon. What have you done?"

Gideon dropped his head against the white paneled

door, his blue gaze not leaving Lily's. "Leave the stone, Quinn. I'll have her look at it."

"I can smell her from out here," Quinn said impatiently. "Anyone who walks down this hall is going to know you've bonded with her. You have two seconds to make sure she has clothes on, and then I'm coming in."

Lily scrambled to her feet, her breathing tight in her chest as she hurried toward the bathroom. "He's going to kill me."

Gideon grabbed the stack of clothes and toiletries Grace had left on the bed and shoved them at Lily. "Take a long shower, and don't come out until I get you. I'll deal with this." He grabbed the bathroom door, paused to give her a hard look, and then yanked it shut.

# Chapter 14

Gideon pulled the bathroom door shut a split second before Quinn stepped into the room. He heard Lily lock the door and almost smiled at her action. They both knew the lock would do nothing against a Calydon. But knowing Lily, it was important because it was symbolic of her taking action. Lily needed to be in control, and he understood that part of her now that he knew about her past.

His smile faded as he recalled her story about when she was a teenager. He expected anger to surge through him again, fury at what had been done to her. But the emotion that touched him was sadness, a deep, aching sadness that was unfamiliar and unsettling. It made him want to turn around, head right back into that bathroom, scoop her up and...

Gideon's gaze fell on the bed, the covers still askew and the pillows still dented from Lily's head. He could imagine her hair spread across those pillows, her arms reaching for him...

Yeah, well, maybe the sadness he was feeling was just another excuse to justify why he wanted to get up close and personal with her so damn badly it felt like his blood was running hot.

Quinn flung open the door, and Gideon positioned himself in front of the bathroom door, blocking access to Lily.

Gideon's blood brother strode into the room, flipping the bedroom door shut behind him. His dark hair was tightly shorn, and his jeans and boots were well-worn and still caked with mud. Quinn had been out on another mission, no doubt trying to get a handle on the situation with Ezekiel. Clearly, he hadn't bothered to change before tracking down Gideon. "What the hell's going on in here?" Quinn demanded.

Gideon let his hands dangle beside his hips, his fingers flexed as Quinn got closer to Lily. The brands on Gideon's forearms burned, his axes ready to be called forth. He was prepared to strike to defend her, if he needed to, even if his target was the man who'd stood by his side and fought off death with him thousands of times over the last five hundred years.

Quinn stopped at the aggression emanating from Gideon. For a moment, the two men froze, at a standoff.

"Are you going to kill her?" Gideon asked, opening his mind to Quinn's, searching for any sign of betrayal. He picked up the buzz of tension and adrenaline, but not aggression.

He didn't relax. Never would he relax when there was a potential threat to his woman.

The Order's interim leader wasted no time answering Gideon's question. "It smells like you've bonded with Lily." His dark brown gaze settled heavily on Gideon's. "Tell me she's not your *sheva.*"

"She is." There was no point in denial.

Quinn swore and ran his hand through his hair, the action of a man who was agitated, not ready to strike. "You already had a *sheva.* You dodged the bullet already. *You paid your price.*"

"I did," Gideon agreed. "You were there. You know. She was buried with my mark on her arms because she gave her life for me. The death stage."

"Then Lily can't be your *sheva.*" Quinn swore, his fists bunching when Gideon said nothing to support Quinn's statement. His dark eyes were seething with tension. "You're absolutely positive? There's no chance you're wrong?"

"She carries my mark." Gideon shifted restlessly, adrenaline racing through him in response to Quinn's agitation. "You will let her live," he said quietly. "The same way I allowed Grace to live."

"Fuck!" Quinn stalked over to the window, making no move toward the bathroom. He yanked it open and leaned on the sill, scowling out into the woods that stretched behind

Dante's mansion. He closed his eyes to the damp air, fighting for control. Only the tautness of his shoulders and the white of his knuckles indicated his true mood. "Does Grace know?"

"That Lily's marked?" Gideon didn't move from his position blocking the bathroom door, not yet certain whether he could trust the man that he'd trusted with his life for half a millennium. Shit. Had he really just thought that? Was he really questioning loyalty bonds that had supported him for centuries?

He thought of Lily, and the courage in those sensuous green eyes, and knew the answer was yes.

Quinn jerked his head once in acknowledgment. "Yes. Does Grace know you have another *sheva?* "

"I have no idea. She's the one who told me Lily was up." Gideon's brands were on fire now, burning with the need to come to life and protect his *sheva.* "What's your problem? Talk to me before I attack first to defend her." Since he had his own *sheva,* Quinn would understand that comment. He'd grasp the protective instincts surging through Gideon, the raging aggression threatening to shred all his self-control and launch an assault at Quinn before he could turn on Lily.

Quinn turned to face him, his gaze hollow and... worried. Shit. Gideon had never seen his blood brother look worried before. Order members assessed facts and analyzed weaknesses and strengths. Then they made a plan and took action, sometimes doing all of the above in a fraction of a second. Worry was weak, inefficient, and debilitating. They had no time for that.

But there was no mistaking the fluttering and instability of Quinn's energy.

The dude was worried.

"If you've met a second *sheva,* that means Grace and I aren't safe," Quinn said. "Destiny came back for you, which means she'll come back for us. Fuck! I thought we'd defeated the curse. I thought it was over."

Gideon slowly began to relax, finally understanding Quinn's agitation. "You're not going to kill Lily, are you?"

Quinn shot him a resigned look. "Who would I be to kill your *sheva* when I wouldn't let you kill mine?" He stalked across the room, his hands clasped in his hair. "What do we do now, Gideon? What the hell do we do now?"

"We continue forward," Gideon said. "We get Lily to translate the writing on the stone in hopes we can find Frank, or find out why Ezekiel's prison walls are weakening, and we try to find Drew." Frank had kidnapped Dante's son, Drew, the night the Order had rescued Ana and killed Nate. They all believed Drew was a key component to freeing Ezekiel, and they had to retrieve the young Calydon before he could be used. "And when destiny comes to find you and Grace, you stop her again."

Quinn spun toward him, his expression fierce and raw with fear. "Grace almost died last time we fought off our destiny. I can't lose her, Gideon. *I can't.*"

"I know." Gideon softened his voice. "I was there. I remember."

Quinn took a deep breath and settled his gaze on Gideon. "What are you going to do about Lily? Are you going to complete the bond with her?"

"And go through what you went through with Grace? No chance." The words didn't sit well for Gideon as he spoke them. Logically and morally, he knew that completing the bond with Lily was to be avoided at all costs. But centuries-old male instincts were growling with displeasure at the very thought of letting Lily go.

Gideon heard the shower turn on, and suddenly envisioned her clothes sliding off her body and hitting the floor, the water caressing her skin—

Quinn let out a soft chuckle of irony. "Not so easy to walk away from her, is it?"

Gideon groaned and paced across the room to the window Quinn had opened, sticking his head outside to catch the fresh air and listen to the damn birds, instead of getting a high off the faint hint of lilac coming from the bathroom. "No. It's not."

"I tried to resist. Grace tried. And we failed." Quinn came to stand beside him, shoulder to shoulder. "You want my advice?"

"No."

"Your only chance is to get her out of your life. If you guys stay together, you have no shot at keeping your distance."

"She needs my protection." Gideon ground his jaw, knowing Quinn spoke the truth. He wasn't a dumbass, and he knew full well that the longer he spent with her, the harder it would be not to throw her down on the nearest horizontal surface and stoke the fires between them until she was his, completely and forever. "I can't walk away from her."

"You think it's hard now? It just gets worse."

Gideon slanted a look at Quinn. "You regret staying with Grace?"

"Hell, no. It ripped me to hell and back when she almost died, but it's worth every fucking minute of it." Quinn was quiet for a minute as he propped his shoulder against the wall. "There's no going back for me, Gideon, but you don't have to go down that road. Grace is the best thing that has ever happened to me, and also the worst. And it's not over." He cursed softly and rubbed his hand over his own brand. "I can't believe you have another *sheva.*"

"Me either." It sucked, yeah. It was wrong, sure. But damned if Gideon couldn't help feeling an intense, powerful satisfaction each time he thought of Lily carrying his mark. He wanted it. He wanted her. He wanted to complete the damn bond. When he'd met his first *sheva,* it had been about sexual need and a cocky instinct to be the man for her. With Lily, it was so much more, so much deeper, so much more intense. Shit. He was in trouble, wasn't he?

Quinn shot Gideon a knowing look. "You dealing okay?"

Quinn was one of the rookies who'd stayed with him on the grave. Quinn and Elijah had stayed with him. They were the only two beings on the earth that knew what that experience had done to Gideon the first time. Elijah was dead, but Quinn would know how having another *sheva* would affect him.

Gideon gave Quinn a look and said nothing.

He didn't need to.

Since they'd blood bonded five hundred years ago, Quinn could get into his mind, and he into Quinn's. And Elijah's. None of them ever bothered to lie to each other, or to hide their emotions. There was no point, not between the three of them. Others were a different story. Gideon kept the rest of the Order out of his damn head, except for the terse commands during battle. Hence Gideon's legendary reputation as an ice-cold killer. Quinn knew better.

"Do you think if I separated from her, that would really work?" Gideon asked. "Or would destiny find a way to bring us back together? Is there really any way to win? To stop our fate?"

"There has to be." Quinn's voice was strong, firm. "I have something I'm not willing to lose, so yeah, I have to believe there's a way to beat destiny. Or at least beat her back each time and win the small battles, so you never lose the war."

Gideon worked his jaw. "You and Grace are the only ones in history to have made it this far. Two thousand years, and only one couple has survived a complete bonding." His gaze flicked to the bathroom. "Lily and I could crash and burn like everyone else."

"Yeah, you could."

Gideon thought of Lily's strength and knew if anyone had a chance to win, it would be her. Except for the Satinka... Shit. He'd forgotten about that.

"She's *Satinka?*"

He grimaced at the thought Quinn had picked up from his mind. "Not just Satinka. I heard her bells." He sensed Quinn would probably know what that meant, and when Quinn cursed, he knew he'd been right.

"Jesus, man. You'll kill her."

"No shit. Already would have if Kane hadn't been there."

"You have to separate." Quinn turned to face him. "You *have* to, and it has nothing to do with the *sheva* bond. I'll put someone else on her, and you stay away from her."

"I can't—"

"You *will.*" Quinn's jaw flexed. "We need her for Order business, and you don't have the right to drain her. I'll violate my Order oath and not kill her for the mere fact she's your *sheva,* but I'm damn well using her to stop Ezekiel from getting out."

Gideon stared at Quinn as his words settled in, as the pieces started to fall in place. "That's what he wants her for," he realized. "He wants her for her magic."

"Who?"

"Frank Tully. Nate's partner. Lily gave me his name. We

know who we're looking for now."

"Frank Tully," Quinn repeated. "He's the one who was manipulating us? He's taken over?"

"Seems that way." Gideon paced the room, thinking. "He's after Lily, even though she doesn't have the stone. He must want to use her magic." He looked at Quinn. "Somehow, he's going to use her to free Ezekiel. She's part of the plan, along with the Calydon weapons he harvested from all the dead Calydons Nate murdered over the last couple months."

Quinn let out a low whistle. "He'll be coming after her, then. It's just a matter of time until he realizes where she is. We need to be ready." He strode toward the door, his concern about Grace subordinated to the warrior who had a job to do. "Meet me downstairs with Lily as soon as she's done in the bathroom. We need her to read the inscriptions on that knife. I'm going to go alert the team to be on the lookout for Frank or his Calydons coming after her. Then we'll put Kane on her and you take off." Quinn's eyes glittered. "And don't worry if you can't bring yourself to leave her. I'll make sure it happens."

"You mean, you'll knock me out so you can take her?"

Quinn nodded. "Trust me, Gideon. It's the right choice."

Gideon scowled as Quinn strode from the room. Quinn had raised his mental shields at the last minute, but it had been a fraction of a second too late. Gideon had caught his teammate's thoughts: if Lily really was a necessary key to Frank freeing Ezekiel, then the only way to truly stop Frank might be to kill Lily so he couldn't use her.

Gideon had seen the determination in Quinn's mind, and knew Quinn was already steeling himself to do what would need to be done, if it got to that point. Such a neat solution: to kill one of the critical components to Frank's plan. Sacrifice one innocent to save millions.

It was an easy, automatic choice. It was a decision Gideon had made hundreds of times in order to make the world safe, to protect the thousands who would have died otherwise. It was the essence of who Gideon was, of his oath to the Order and the girl who'd died so he could live five hundred years ago.

It was who he was.

Lily, quite simply, might be too dangerous to be allowed to live.

Then Gideon heard the soft sound of singing coming from the bathroom, and he closed his eyes, allowing the beauty of it to fill him. It spread through him like a violet light, the scent of spring, and the warm rays of a summer sun, reaching into the parts of him that had been dark, cold, and silent for so long.

Gideon Roarke, Order member, would do his job.

Gideon Roarke, bonded male, had different priorities. Damn.

❀ ❀ ❀

Lily lifted her face, letting the hot water wash over her as she scrubbed her hair with the shampoo Grace had left for her. It smelled like lilacs.

Lilacs.

After two years of deprivation...lilacs just smelled... decadent? Frilly? Silly?

Silly.

That was it.

She used to care what her shampoo smelled like. She used to pay money for highlights and a flattering haircut. There was a time when she made certain to put only all-natural products on her skin.

Now, things like that just seemed...silly. It felt foreign, like some confusing world she didn't understand anymore.

Lily turned and let the hot water wash the soap out of her hair. She wanted to care about her hair. She wanted to fill her brain with little thoughts, like whether the conditioner was adequate, and whether the shirt she was wearing was flattering. She wanted to be the woman who hounded her publicist to find out whether enough tickets had been sold to her upcoming lecture.

She didn't want to be thinking about the heat pulsing in her forearm, about turning into a murderer like her grandmother. She didn't want to be consumed with the reality of being bonded to Gideon. She didn't want to recall having Frank's ice-cold eyes focused on her, and wonder what he was planning for her.

Lily dumped conditioner in her hair and mechanically worked it through the strands, her belly aching. She'd thought a leisurely shower would be wonderful. Healing. Purifying. She'd been in Gideon's sweatpants in the woods for so long. She'd been in her skirt and blouse at Nate's for two years. Now that she'd been able to shed them, to cleanse all the vileness from her body...it should have been invigorating, right? Healing?

But she felt no relief. In fact, she almost felt more vulnerable and more naked, as if the filthy skirt and blouse had been her armor against becoming soft or weak. Now that she smelled like lilacs and had been undone by the kisses of a man who made her entire soul shift when he walked into the room, she didn't know who she was anymore. She felt like she was straddling two worlds: the woman in battle fighting to be strong and to survive, and the female who wanted to be delicate, pretty, and consumed by a strong, powerful man whose entire being was focused on her safety and her world.

Gideon was out in the bedroom, negotiating for her life with another Order member. He was her barrier against evil and death, but he was also her ticket to hell.

But she couldn't stop wanting him.

Lily was too smart, too educated, to fall into the trap of being a *sheva*. She'd spent her life intellectualizing all that Gideon and his race were. She'd tried to control their power by learning about it and understanding them. She didn't react emotionally to things. She didn't have some burning female wooziness when it came to men, especially male Calydons.

And yet the things she felt for Gideon had nothing to do with her mind. It was her body. Her soul. A craving for him so deep it hurt.

She knew her feelings for him couldn't be healthy. It was too intense, too desperate. Too needy. He made her feel like a woman, but it was sexual and sensual, reverberating in her core. Not light and frivolous, like wearing a cute outfit for him and exchanging flirty glances...not that she'd ever been flirty or frivolous in her life. She had no idea how to do that, or be that kind of woman.

Her desire for Gideon made her body pulse with longing. It was a relentless calling that made her not care if she was covered in mud and blood, because the attraction and the need were so deep inside her—

A thud from outside the shower curtain made her jump. "Lily."

She caught her breath at the nearness of Gideon's voice, realizing that he was in the bathroom. "I'm still in the shower."

He yanked open the shower curtain and she jumped back with a yelp. His eyes were burning, so dark.

Her heart started pounding and she grabbed the shower curtain to cover herself. "Gideon! This is so not a good idea."

He said nothing as he stepped into the shower, the water pounding on his clothes, like tears darkening the cotton of his shirt. Dirt swirled off the treads of his boots, turning the water a light beige. Water teased his blond locks, dampening them to his head, changing the shade of his hair to a dark brown.

Gideon grabbed the shower curtain and ripped it out of her hand, exposing her. Yet still, he didn't look at her body. His gaze was riveted to her face, so intense she felt as if steam were rising off her.

He was every bit the warrior, the dominating Calydon who took what he wanted and wasted no thought on the needs of others. The marks on her forearms began to pulse, searing her skin as if they were on fire, and she couldn't make herself turn away from him. She didn't want to make herself leave, even as her mind was screaming at her to run.

She wanted to stay right where she was, igniting under the intensity of his sizzling gaze.

Lily swallowed hard, trying to break the spell she felt like she was under. "You wanted something?"

Still he stood, his clothes getting drenched, water streaming down his face, staring at her.

"Gideon?"

"I'm thinking."

God, *she* should be thinking. Thinking would be smart. So much smarter than letting herself ride the wave of heat building inside her. But she couldn't think of a single thing other than *him*. He was simply the entirety of her mind, of her being. His aura, his power, and his maleness were consuming her.

His gaze finally went to her body, and his jaw tightened

at what he saw. His hand moved, and she knew what he was going to do before he did. She pressed her lips together as his fingers brushed over a bruise on one of her breasts. She watched his expression tighten, letting his growing anger be her shield against the memories of how she'd gotten those injuries.

"Hell, Lily," he whispered, his voice raw. "You're covered in bruises."

She lifted her chin, refusing to look down at what he was seeing. She didn't want Gideon to regard her as damaged goods. She wanted him to look at her as a woman who was beautiful, strong and desirable. She wanted to be who she was today, not what she'd experienced in the past. "It's over. I'm moving on."

He slid his hand over her skin, his touch soothing and stirring at the same time, moving down until he laid his palm over a large, yellowing bruise on her inner thigh. Sadness flickered in his eyes. "You've suffered too much already."

She felt her throat thicken. "Don't give me sympathy, Gideon. I can't take it right now. I have to focus on what I need to do. I need to be strong."

"Turn around." He gently cupped her shoulder and turned her even as he spoke.

She let him spin her and leaned her forehead against the cool tile of the shower as she felt his gaze on her back. His fingers traced the cuts from the glass. The glass had been washed out in the river, but the slices still stung. She could only imagine how awful her body looked right now.

Gideon's curse was a whisper as he caught her wrist and turned her around to face him again, touching her jaw with the pad of his finger before dropping his hands to his sides. He was intentionally not touching her, and she ached at the distance between them. The few inches seemed like a tremendous gulf, a chasm that made her feel alone and desperate for connection.

"Stop worrying about my injuries. We have much bigger things to deal with now." She gestured at her bruises, forcing herself to stay focused. "These matter only if I get more of them. As long as I can stay safe from here on out, I'm good—"

His eyes narrowed ever so slightly, and she had a fraction of a second to realize he'd made a decision before he moved. He was on her so fast she didn't even realize he'd moved until she felt the rough material of his shirt against her breasts, until the wet denim of his jeans scraped across her belly, until his hands gripped her bare hips. He pinned her against his body for a brief moment, his eyes searching hers, as if for confirmation.

Oh, wow. This was going to be some kind of kiss. "Don't—"

He slammed his mouth over hers before she could finish her protest.

# Chapter 15

The heat was instant, debilitating, and overwhelming. Gideon devoured her, kissing her so deeply Lily couldn't breathe. He claimed her with every thrust of his tongue. He stoked fires in her, relentless with his almost violent kisses, as if he couldn't control himself, couldn't withstand the need driving him.

Lily pressed her hands against his chest, as if somewhere deep inside her she knew she had to stop him, but she couldn't bring herself to push him away. He gave her no chance to stop, to think, to assess. His onslaught of seduction was merciless, driving rational thought from her mind. His hands were everywhere, sliding over her wet skin, hotter than the steaming water still streaming down over them both. He kept up the sensual assault on her mouth until her arms finally went around his neck and she pulled him down to her, pressing her body against his.

"That's it," he whispered into her mouth. "Just like that. Just don't sing."

She almost laughed at the desperation in Gideon's voice, then forgot what was funny when he cupped her bottom and lifted her up, sliding his hands down her bare thighs and forcing her legs around his waist, still kissing her, his tongue scraping over her teeth, so hot, so wet, making her want more. *So much more.*

Lily leaned into him, kissing him back as desperately as he was kissing her. She didn't resist as he carried her out of the bathroom into the bedroom. He tasted so good, like mint and the warm breath of spring and something else...he tasted like the scent of vanilla.

And...something more ominous. Something dark and controlling. Something that tapped into the ancient power pulsating through him, the legend of the Calydons. She started to pull back. "Gideon—"

"You're mine." He set her on the bed and crawled on top of her, pressing his hips between her thighs, his erection nudging against her through his jeans, making desire flare so fast she couldn't breathe. He kissed her, so deeply, so thoroughly. His hands cupped her breasts, skimmed over her bruised belly, teasing, making her skin come alive with fire.

His palm closed over the brand on her forearm, and her body convulsed with spirals of pleasure. His hips shifted to the side and his hand slid between her legs, his fingers sinking deep inside. "Oh, God, you're so ready for me." His voice was nothing more than a throaty groan, and she caught the words more in her mind then in her ears. The intimacy of the connection sent her spiraling toward the edge of control.

"Gideon," she gasped, unable to articulate the need building inside her as she moved her hips in desperate invitation.

"No, not yet." Gideon held her writhing hips to the bed with a heavy forearm across her belly. He dropped his head and bit her nipple, his teeth nearly closing through the skin.

Pain shot through Lily, morphing instantly into a pleasure so hot she couldn't think past the crackle of energy pulsing through her. His mouth closed on her breast again, this time with his tongue and his lips, while his fingers stretched her and teased her.

There was a loud crack somewhere in the distance, a crack that sounded like a Calydon weapon coming out. "Gideon—"

"Shh. It's okay. It was me." He worked his way back up her body, kissing and licking as he went, and she felt the cold steel of his axe on her belly.

Lily tensed, and he kissed her before she could protest. "I'm not going to hurt you," he whispered, his breath hot in her mouth. "I swear it. I'm going to keep you safe."

There was something dark in his tone that sent alarm spiraling through her, penetrating the lustful haze he was weaving around her. "Wait—"

"There's no waiting, Lily. There's no more time." His fingers began to work their magic again, sliding deep inside her, drawing her into their spell, even as she struggled not to succumb to the heat he was stoking within her. "Trust me, *sheva*. I can do you no harm. You know I can't."

His words touched a truth she'd long known about a Calydon and his *sheva*: a Calydon would die before he would hurt his mate. Steeped in the thrill of knowing this strong, deadly warrior was her ultimate protector, Lily's body refused to resist his touch, and desire began to build within her again.

Gideon's axe moved over her skin, a cold edge teasing dangerous fires within her. He pressed it to the underside of her breast, and she felt the pressure of the icy metal against her skin.

But there was no fear in her, just dangerous pleasure as Gideon took her to that edge, as she let her head fall back and arched her back, pressing her body against his blade as his fingers slid deeper within her. His thumb teasing over her folds as she gave herself over to him, even as his blade scraped across her breasts, so close to her heart.

"You're giving me the chance to kill you," he whispered.

"You won't."

"But I could." The blade slid over her throat, a sharp edge so close to cutting her, but not quite. "By trusting me with something so dear...your life, we just completed another stage of the bond. *Trust*."

His satisfied words penetrated the sensual fog clouding Lily's mind, and she realized he'd done it on purpose. *He was trying to tighten the bond*. She started to tense, then his fingers plunged deeper, tearing a gasp from her throat.

Gideon kissed her hard, knowing he had her where he needed her. Her mouth was warm and wet, her tongue desperate for him. Her need for him was burning deep inside him, matching his own, but he could feel her mind struggling to surface, trying to rationalize, trying to plan what was best for them.

Fuck that. He knew what was best, but he also knew they were both too damn cynical to let him do it, if he gave either of them time to think about it. He was riding the high of his instincts, and he didn't want to give either of them a chance to think about what he was about to do.

Lily moaned softly, her hips writhing beneath him as he found his rhythm, stroking her most sensitive spot with his fingers. His arm still pinning her to the bed, he could feel her belly tightening beneath his forearm as he coaxed her response. Still kissing her, he shifted his position to take his weight off the hand with his axe, and he moved the axe over his wrist, over the small white scar he carried.

Lily stirred beneath him. *What are you doing?* Her question was foggy, barely surfacing through the haze of desire he'd stirred up inside her.

*Protecting you.* He shoved the blade into his wrist as he thrust into her with his fingers again. He barely felt the prick as his skin split. Lily moaned with desire as the blood began to slide down his arm. He positioned the axe over the side of her neck, testing for the right spot. Minimal pain, maximum result. The cold metal pressed against her skin and Lily's eyes snapped open.

He hesitated for a split second, as she stared at the axe. At his arm. At the blood.

Realization dawned with instant clarity. "Bastard!" Lily grabbed his wrist, her fingers slipping on the blood. She dug deeper, her nails digging into the cut he'd made on his arm as she fought to get out from under him. "Get off me!"

Gideon grabbed her shoulders and pinned her to the bed, looming over her. "They're going to try to take you from me, Lily. I have to bind us to keep you safe. It's the only way I'll be able to find you."

"Damn you, Gideon! Let go of me!" Lily tried to bring her knee up between his legs, but he blocked her easily, not releasing her.

"No, dammit!" He could smell her panic, and guilt hit him. "Listen to me, Lily! They're going to take you! Do you want to be kidnapped again?"

His words seemed to register, and she stopped fighting. She stared at him with her chest heaving and her eyes wide. "I can't be kidnapped again," she whispered. "*I can't.*"

"I know, babe." He softened his grip. "If we do the blood bond, I'll be able to find you anywhere, no matter how far away we are. No matter how well hidden you are." He smoothed her damp hair off her forehead, letting his weight settle on her. "It's the only way I know I'll be able to find you."

"How could Frank get me here? How could he get past all of you?"

Gideon hesitated, having difficulty admitting it was the Order who'd been planning to take her, that it had been his own team he was planning to screw with. He'd been ready to risk the Order's vitally important plans to use Lily to keep Ezekiel from getting free. Where was his loyalty? Fuck. *Fuck*. Was he really going to make that choice? No, he wouldn't. He would find a way to fulfill both his missions. "I can't let you die," was all he said instead.

Lily's eyes held a wisdom he hadn't expected. He'd expected anger, retaliation, and fury that he'd planned to tighten their bond without her consent. But Lily wasn't that kind of woman. Logic was her tool to survival, and he saw her rapidly assess their situation and analyze it. "It's not just Frank, is it?" she asked. "You're worried about the Order as well. They're the ones who want to take me from you."

Gideon said nothing, feeling that any answer was a betrayal to his oath. To his team.

"Is it because I'm your *sheva*?"

"That, and more."

She pressed her lips together and let her head flop back on the pillow, staring at the ceiling. "You could have discussed it with me."

"I wouldn't have done it if I'd let myself think about it."

"Why not? Because it's a stupid idea? Because it's not necessary?"

He hesitated.

She lowered her gaze to look at him.

"Because it scares the shit out of me, Lily." He rubbed his finger over a bruise on her shoulder, as if he could wipe it away. "But I won't make the same mistake twice." His voice hardened as he met her gaze. "No way in hell am I going to let another *sheva* die for me."

"Well, at least you're smart enough to be scared about tightening the bond." She gave him a small smile. "And I do have to admit that I'm really kind of fond of your protective instincts."

He grinned. "Good, because they're not going anywhere." He had no clue how Lily could accept his dominance after she'd been the victim of it from others. How the hell could he be worthy of this woman? But as hell was his witness, he was going to try his damnedest.

"I know." Lily took the axe from him, turning it over in her hand. "I never thought you'd be the type to admit that."

"I'm not. I don't get scared."

"I do. Monsters sleep under my bed." She flicked her finger over the blade, testing its sharpness. "You swear you'd find me, no matter what?" She looked up at him. "You *swear*?"

Gideon's heart rate kicked into overdrive, both with fear and anticipation. Even though he knew the danger of tightening the bond, he couldn't stop the rise of male satisfaction at the thought of binding her tighter. "I swear on my Order oath that I'll find you. I swear on the oath I gave my first *sheva* that I will find you," he said fiercely. "I promise I will not let you down. Ever."

Lily looked up at him, her green eyes determined and scared. "I get protection from Frank and the Order and I get bonded tighter to you in exchange. Trading one evil for another."

"I'm not evil." Other things...yeah. Evil? No. He'd seen evil, and he wasn't it.

"Not at the moment. And the moment is what I have to live in." She pressed the blade to the side of his neck, her grip steady. "Okay, let's do this."

He raised his wrist. "I already made the cut—"

"I don't want blood from your old scar. This is about us, not her." She pulled the blade across his neck and hot warmth slid down his skin.

Anticipation licked through him as she handed the axe to him without a word, her green eyes huge and vulnerable.

He clasped her wrist and brought her arm up, laying the spiked handle of his axe against the brand coming to life on her skin. There were many marks now, so many lines. Silver and faint, but growing stronger. He realized that when he'd told her the truth about his first *sheva* dying, he'd satisfied the trust stage as well, by revealing his darkest secret to her. He tapped the silver lines on her skin. "I want blood from here. From my brand that you carry."

Lily nodded.

Gideon couldn't stop the dominant growl deep in his throat, and he kissed her hard. She grabbed his hair and held him tight as she kissed him desperately. He plunged deep and hard with his tongue at the same moment he sliced the blade through her skin. He caught her cry of pain with his mouth as carnal desire rose within him, tightening every muscle.

Lily shuddered beneath him and broke the kiss. For a moment, they simply looked at each other. He could feel her heart thudding against his chest, and her body was trembling.

Her gaze went to his neck, and the blood dripping down his skin suddenly became hot, searing him. He waited, unwilling to force it on her anymore, wanting her to be the one to make the choice.

She took a deep breath, then slipped her hands around his neck and pulled him toward her. The instant her lips closed over Gideon's wound, he felt his head spin, and the world began to blacken around him. His body flamed with desire, passion, and something so intense he could feel it pressing at him from all sides. Consuming him. Taking control of him.

Gideon clasped Lily's wrist and sank his mouth onto her skin, drinking in her lifeblood. His body sang with vitality as her blood slipped down his throat. The electricity took over his mind and uplifted his spirit as the words ripped out of his subconscious, as his hips began to move against hers. *Mine to you. Yours to me. Bonded by blood, by spirit and by soul, we are one. No distance too far, no enemy too powerful, no sacrifice too great. I will always find you. I will always protect you. No matter what the cost. I am yours as you are mine.*

Lily's response was instant, her soft voice filling his mind and his soul with her words, echoing with strength and conviction. *Mine to you. Yours to me. Bonded by blood, by spirit and by soul, we are one. No distance too far, no enemy too powerful, no sacrifice too great. I will always find you. I will always keep you safe. No matter what the cost. I am yours as you are mine.* There was a slight pause, and then she added his name. *Gideon.*

That addition, that personalization, that commitment to *him* tore through Gideon and he felt brilliant warmth in his gut that spread to his chest, his head, and his soul. He couldn't hold back and his hips began to thrust in earnest. He fumbled for the fly of his jeans. He tore his zipper free and yanked the denim down over his hips, needing to get closer to her, desperate to claim her and make her *his.*

*I'm yours already.*

Something exploded inside Gideon at her three simple words. He felt his world shatter, and everything he knew came crashing down around him. *I need you, Lily.* His jeans hit the floor, and he moved on top of her, skin to skin, nothing between them. He reared back to plunge himself deep inside her. To bind them so tightly they'd never be able to be apart.

*Yes.* Lily lifted her hips to meet him and suddenly there was a crash of music in his head, so loud his head felt like it would shatter.

Gideon felt Lily's magic leap into his body and ignite him. He froze, his erection hovering at the tip of her entrance as his Calydon powers lunged for her magic. "Hell, Lily," he croaked, his body shaking with the effort of trying to fight off his need to take all of her, to plunge deep and own her, to strip her of all her magic and suck it all into his body, giving him strength and power no Calydon had a right to have. "Pull it back."

"I can't," she gasped, her hips writhing beneath him. "I can't stop it. It needs you."

"Shit!" Her magic was feeding on their lust and their bond, getting more intense with every moment. In another second, Gideon would be *lost*, just like in the woods.

No. He would not betray her again.

With a roar, Gideon pulled his hips back and slid his hand between them, his mind burning with the haze of magic, need, and lust. *God, let this work.*

He pressed his palm against her folds as his fingers plunged deep. Lily shouted as she gripped his shoulders and her spine bowed under the force of the orgasm. Her release flooded his mind and body, but instead of her satisfaction lessening his need as he'd hoped, it catapulted him over the edge and snapped his control.

He had to take her. Now.

Gideon shifted into position above her, preparing to plunge deep, her magic filling him with greed and power and strength and...

"Shit!" He wrenched himself off her and threw himself off the bed.

He hit the floor hard and was on his feet in an instant. She was stretched out on the bed, glistening with sweat. His blood was streaked across her chest, his mark strong on her arm, the scent of her arousal driving through him, her music still ringing in his ears. One of Lily's legs was bent, and her back was arched. She was gloriously naked and still undulating from the climax. Her hair tousled in sexy waves, Lily turned toward him, her eyes decadently sensual. Her left hand opened and stretched toward him, calling him...

Gideon's hands fisted, his cock jerked, and he took a step toward the bed, desperate to bury himself in her, to take all that she was, to feed on her...

Then he saw a mark on her wrist. The faintest white line encircling her arm, visible only because of his enhanced senses. It was a scar from when she'd been tied up when she was seventeen, from when she'd been raped for her magic.

*I won't do that to you again, Lily. I won't be that man.*

He had to get out of there. Now.

He grabbed his pants off the floor and bolted for the door, as every instinct he had screamed at him to go back and finish what he'd started. To take her and claim her body, spirit, and soul, as he was meant to do as her mate. To steal her magic, as he was meant to do as her chosen—

He lunged out into the hall, colliding hard with Quinn who'd been sprinting for the bedroom door. Quinn was the only male alive who might be strong enough to stop Gideon from going back in there. Gideon grabbed his friend's shoulders. "Help me, Quinn—"

"I've got your back, man," Quinn said calmly, as he took Gideon to the floor with a move that sent brutal pain ricocheting through Gideon's body. "It's all good."

Ana hugged her knees to her chest as she sat on the small hill overlooking the fields that stretched to the south of Dante's estate. The ground was muddy from all the Oregon rain, so she'd duct taped a garbage bag to her cast and hobbled out there. It had taken her over an hour to walk that far, but she hadn't minded. It felt good to clear her head, and after being Nate's prisoner, it was a gift she'd always appreciate now, being able to go where she wanted, whenever she wanted.

Ana needed space from the hovering of her sister, from trying to pretend she was happy and recovering, but also to conceal the nightmares that haunted her and try to find her way around all the noise in her head. She wanted a break from the visits by the Order members asking about Elijah. She didn't want to have any more serious conversations about Ezekiel and Nate in which the Order asked her to recall every Calydon who had died at her hand, including Elijah. She needed a respite from reliving the nightmares of the last two months of her life when Nate had dragged her all over the Pacific Northwest, using her to kill warriors so he could strip their weapons out of their arms the moment they died. She needed time to process them without intrusion by everyone else.

Now that Lily was back, the Order would learn about Frank. They would want to know why Ana hadn't mentioned him when she'd told them about Lily and the stone. Why had she kept Frank a secret from them? She didn't know. She had no answers for those questions.

Ana rested her chin on her knees and stared out at the lush greenery. She watched the sunshine peek through a break in the dark clouds. A sucker hole, her mom used to call them. Just when you think the sun's coming out and head out for your picnic, the rains come and flood you out. *Sucker.*

That's what her rescue from Nate felt like. A sucker hole. She'd felt such relief and had thought her ordeal was over when she'd heard Grace's voice and Gideon had lifted her out of the mud.

But it wasn't over.

She sighed and rubbed her arm over Elijah's mark on her skin. She hadn't slept since she'd gotten to Dante's. Every time she closed her eyes, she saw Elijah die again. She relived the look of true horror on his face when he'd found out she was an Illusionist, a magical being who could create dark, twisted images that brought terrible things onto those who were exposed to them.

Yes, granted, Ana used to be the aberration who generated beautiful, happy moments, but Nate had destroyed that side of her. She had become exactly the monster Elijah had recoiled from. She wondered again what had been done to Elijah to make him react like that to an Illusionist. Who had hurt him? Yet despite whatever brutality he'd suffered from her kind, he'd stayed to protect her, and it had cost him his life. She'd killed him for protecting her. Not on purpose, but it was still her fault.

Ana squeezed her eyes shut as she heard his voice again in her head. Whispering her name.

*Ana. Ana. Ana.* Elijah's voice filled her mind, a desperate calling for her. What did he want? To save him? It was too late. She'd already condemned him. He had already died because of her.

*Ana.*

She pressed her hands to her ears, wanting to scream at him to stop haunting her, but at the same time, so desperately needing to hear his voice. It was as if he were still alive...calling to her...

A branch broke behind her and she tensed, not wanting to deal with Grace and her sisterly worries.

There was the sound of footsteps in the soft ground, coming up behind her, but she didn't turn around.

Then they stopped.

She waited, and when nothing else happened, her heart began to race. "Grace?"

"No."

She gasped and lurched to her feet, whirling around.

It was Frank Tully. He was wearing sunglasses, a pair of black pressed cotton pants, a button down shirt and an ankle length beige raincoat hanging loosely around his calves. There were silver flecks in his dark hair, and his lips were thin, stretched in an empty smile over his flawless teeth. "Ana."

Her heart started to race, and she glanced toward the house. It was over a mile away, perched on the knoll. So far away.

Too far.

Frank followed her glance. "This is as close as I can get. They're waiting for me." He looked at her. "Why are they waiting for me, little Ana? What have you told them about me?"

"I didn't tell them—" She stopped herself before she told him that Lily was the one who'd revealed his secrets. She sensed he didn't know Lily was at Dante's mansion, and she knew she had to protect Lily. She couldn't let him know Lily was there, knowing he meant her harm. True harm.

Yet at the same time, Ana felt the same pull toward him she'd felt the other two times she'd seen him. Like she knew him. Like he was safety. Like he was home. Granted, he brought to mind the image of a home perched on the edge of a steep cliff, swinging in a wild wind. Familiar and safe, but also dangerous and unknown.

Frank reached for her cheek and traced his finger down it, his touch so gentle and kind. "My dear Ana, I've been waiting for you for so long."

"You do know me," she whispered. She'd known it in her core since the first moment she'd seen him. His allure to her was something deep inside her, something that had been hidden for years and years. "Who are you?"

"I need Nate's knife, Ana."

She blinked. "What?"

"The knife. You took it from Nate. I came to get you and the knife."

Goosebumps popped up on her arms. "You came to get me?"

Frank smiled again, and this time there was warmth. "Of course I did. I've been waiting for you for years." His finger brushed over her cheek again, over a dark bruise from where Nate had punched her. "I wish I'd had the chance to kill Nate for hurting you," he mused.

Ana stiffened against the urge to press her face into his hand. What was wrong with her? She knew what Lily had said about him. She *knew* he was evil. She could feel it just standing this close to him.

But a part of her didn't care. He had answers for her. She knew it, somehow she knew it instinctively. Frank had something she wanted and needed.

It was something in the way he tilted his head, the secrets held in those merciless blue eyes. Frank Tully was what she'd been waiting for. Not just since she'd been rescued from Nate's.

For far, far longer than that.

And Ana knew, with absolute certainty, that he would never hurt her. Ever. Lily, yes, he would hurt her badly. Others, yes. Many others, yes. Ana, no. Whatever monster he was, he wasn't there to do her harm.

A slow smile spread across his face, as if he'd heard her thoughts. "You will come with me."

Ana didn't hesitate. "Yes." He had answers to questions, questions she couldn't think of right now, but she knew she needed them answered. Questions that would come to her...

"With the knife?" he asked.

"I don't have it. I gave it to the Order."

Frank dropped his hand, and there was a tic of aggravation in his cheek. "I need the knife, Ana. Bring it with you. I'll meet you here. An hour? Can you get it that quickly?"

"So soon?" That gave her no time to strategize, to figure out her plans. "I can't—"

*Ana.* Elijah's voice whispered through her mind. She clenched her fists against a sudden burning of Elijah's brands on her forearms, and she knew she had to find a way to get the knife for Frank. She didn't know why, not yet, but she knew she *had* to go. Her certainty resonated in every fiber of her being. "I'll come. Two hours."

Frank cupped the side of her face. "You were always the good girl, Ana."

She lifted her chin. "I'm not doing this for you."

One eyebrow went up above the tinted glasses. "And the games begin." Then he turned and strode away, the shadowed woods swallowing him up as he faded into the darkness, until even the sound of his footsteps faded.

# Chapter 16

Lily moaned as her music finally quieted a long time later. Her body was still on fire, and it felt like any touch to her skin would trigger another orgasm, sending her into an endless spiral toward her death. Was it the bond, the effect of the blood ritual, or her magic? Or a deadly combination of all three? How could her magic have come on so strongly indoors, away from the earth, when neither she nor Gideon had called it? She was earth magic, not blood magic.

Her forearms were searing hot, and she could practically feel her skin melting as the brand burned into her skin. She shifted on the bed and lifted her arm so she could look at the cut from Gideon's blade...and what she saw made her stomach turn. The outline of his throwing axe was complete, and much of the detail was filled in. The lines were bold and strong. "Dear God," she whispered. "How many stages have we done?"

She'd thought two. He'd killed for her and the blood bond. But this was so much more. She pressed her arm to her chest, against the dried blood still covering her. *Gideon. Can you hear me?*

There was no answer, and she felt a sudden aching loss, followed by sheer panic. Since they were blood bonded, they should be able to communicate over any distance. Why wasn't he answering? What if he was dead? She bolted upright in bed, her heart pounding. *Gideon! Are you there?*

A soothing warmth filled her, and she recognized Gideon's reassurance as he filled her mind. *I can hear you. You okay?*

Lily's throat thickened and she bowed her head with relief, pressing her palms to her eyes as her body shuddered. *I thought you were dead. It ripped me apart. What's going on? I shouldn't feel like this unless we were fully bonded.*

*Given the fact that Quinn had to chain me up in the basement to keep me from going back in that bedroom, I don't think I'm the one to ask.*

That stopped her. *You're chained up?*

*I was. I seem to have regained my mind again. Now I'm in the kitchen eating half a turkey to try to ease the most massive case of blue balls known to my race.*

She managed a small smile at his analogy. *I'll take that as a compliment for my irresistible sexuality.*

*You should.* His frustration pulsed over their connection. *You push me to places I've never been, Lily. I don't have control problems. Ever. This need I have for you isn't simply the bond. I've seen bonded warriors before, and this isn't it. Hell, I was afraid to go back into that bedroom to make sure you were okay.*

*That was probably smart. I wasn't...ready yet.*

There was a low moan. *Shit, Lily. Just the thought of what you might have meant by that comment's getting me hard again. What is it with you? Is it Satinka?*

Lily wanted to smile at how frustrated he sounded. He was aggravated that he wasn't in complete control. She'd studied Gideon enough to know that his tight rein on his emotions was his greatest pride and his best weapon. *I don't know. I'll have to look into it.*

*Research?*

She swung her feet off the bed, feeling comforted by his presence in her mind. *For you, your axe is your weapon. For me, it's my mind. It's all I have.* She walked across the room and realized the shower was still running. She stuck her hand in. Ice cold.

*Shit, Lily. I won't deny you're brilliant, but you're a hell of a lot more than your damn mind.*

She looked down at the crusted blood on her body, and sighed. It would have to be a cold shower. *You're referring to my fantastic sexual allure?* She stepped into the spray and let out a yelp when the icy water hit, driving her breath away.

*You're a warrior, Lily. Like me. It took a warrior mentality to do that blood bond with me today. You survived Nate. You have strength, Lily. Real strength.*

The genuine respect in his voice made her heart tighten. *Thank you for saying that. I appreciate it. Sometimes I need to be reminded.*

There was a pause, as if he'd shifted his attention somewhere else and she grabbed a washcloth and started scrubbing the blood off her, even as she started to shiver.

Then he was back. *Quinn wants to know how long until you can come downstairs and look at the knife.*

She hesitated. *Is it safe for me to be around the Order?*

*I'll make sure it is.* He didn't hesitate, and his words were honest and sure.

Lily smiled. As terrifying as the future implications of being his *sheva* were, it was an unbelievable gift to know that she could trust him entirely to keep her safe. She knew that only the *sheva* bond and Gideon's immense personal strength had enabled him to walk out that door when her magic had been calling to him. His need to keep her safe had been stronger than her irresistible siren call. An impossibility, but so unbelievably beautiful. Gideon, the warrior who'd been her nightmare her whole life, had turned out to be her salvation. Ironic, but she was too smart to turn down the gift he offered her. Granted, if they bonded, all hell would break loose, but until then he was a gift.

*I'm a gift? Sweetheart, you are going to be an easy woman to please if you think I'm a gift, but I really recommend you raise your standards. At least demand chocolate or diamonds. Take advantage of the* sheva *bond and milk me for all I'm worth. I have a shitload of money and I can't say no to my woman.*

She chuckled. *Gideon, I wouldn't even know what to do with diamonds. The way you make me feel is exactly what I need.*

*Damn, woman. That's a lot of pressure. Diamonds would be easier for me to deliver.*

She laughed then, and the laughter felt so foreign.

When was the last time she'd laughed? She hadn't thought she even remembered how to do it. *How on earth did you just make me laugh?*

*I'm a god. You're a lucky woman. Learn to deal with it.* His affection warmed her, and she could almost see his answering smile.

She laughed again, and this time she felt the lightness dance through her spirit. *Well, at least you're humble.*

*Humility is for wimps.*

She turned off the cold water and stepped out of the shower. A part of her wanted to spend an hour drying her hair, putting on makeup and making herself beautiful for him, the way she might have done in another life, a woman simply excited about a man.

*Sweetheart, you're the sexiest damn thing I've ever encountered and there's not a damn thing you could do to make me want you more than I already do. When are you coming down here? I need to get some time with my girl.*

She laughed. *Don't I get any privacy from you?*

*What? You want privacy from me?* He sounded shocked, but she could tell he was teasing. *Let me come up there right now and we can talk about that.*

She wasn't surprised by the sudden flush of desire that vibrated through her at the idea of Gideon walking into her bedroom again. *If you come up here, we'll never get down there. Leave me alone. I'll be down in ten minutes.*

*I'll be waiting. Just make sure you have clothes on and you're not singing.*

She smiled again, amazed that she had any smiles left in her body. *I promise.*

※ ※ ※

Lily paused in the hallway outside the living room. She could hear the murmur of male voices. The Order of the Blade was waiting for her. Men who had taken an oath to kill her on sight because she was Gideon's *sheva*. Warriors who were ready to take her from Gideon. Calydons who were at war in the battle that had resulted in her imprisonment for the last two years.

Suddenly, all Lily's courage and strength deserted her.

How could she summon up the energy to resume the battle? It had felt so good to flirt with Gideon, to wash her hair, to feel like a woman being excited about a new man. To be normal, or as close to normal as she could get.

She didn't want to resume her life again. She really didn't.

Lily leaned against the wall and closed her eyes. *I can't do this.*

"Yes, you can." Gideon walked out of the living room, apparently having sensed her presence before she'd reached out to him.

He was wearing a clean pair of jeans, a gray tee shirt, and a different pair of boots. This pair was black and worn. His hair was curling around the back of his neck, but there was a small mark on his skin where she'd cut him. There were angry red marks around both wrists...from the chains?

He followed her gaze to his wrists. "Yeah, it's the chains. I was a little crazed for a few minutes. Thankfully, Dante had the foresight to install them a long time ago to contain Order members after their *shevas* are killed. We had to put Ian in them after Elijah killed his *sheva*. I didn't think we'd get to let him go, actually..."

Lily swallowed, searching his blue eyes that were so serious now. "God, Gideon. What are we getting ourselves into?"

"I have no idea, and no one else does either. This is virgin territory, but we all understand now why Satinka are so rare."

"The Calydons killed us off."

"Yeah. Not on purpose, but that doesn't seem to matter." He flexed his wrists. "I'm under control now. You ready to go in?"

She shook her head. "The males in there are my enemies. I've spent my life—"

"I was the only Order member who was your enemy." He walked over to her and caught her wrist, his fingers just below the cut he'd made with his axe. "Just me."

"No, not just you. Cade was my enemy. Anyone in the Order would have come to kill him if you hadn't." She looked at his hand where he held her, his fingers loose around her wrist.

"If I hadn't been your *sheva*, I would have been someone else's. And now...now they want to kill me and—"

"This meeting in there isn't about you. It's about stopping Frank. That's the only focus right now. Any fate of yours is periphery right now."

She shivered. "Frank has to be stopped."

"He does." Gideon cocked his head. "Did I tell you we think he kidnapped a young Calydon? Nineteen years old? His name's Drew Cartland."

"Oh, God. You had to tell me that?" But she knew he did. It was too easy to forget the threat that Frank presented when she was behind these walls with Gideon by her side.

Frank was still out there, and he was still so dangerous. Far more dangerous than the bond building between Gideon and her. She took a deep breath, pulling herself together. *Just a little longer, Lily. You can keep it together for a little longer.*

She saw by the flicker of amusement on Gideon's face that he'd heard her silent pep talk. "No privacy even for my own neurotic moments?"

"Not anymore." There was a flicker of regret in his tone, but his face was heated, as if he was damned happy with how closely they were connected. "We've done almost half the stages. Trust has been completed by both of us. My half of the death stage was completed when I killed to save your life. We did the blood bond. We have only two and a half stages left: sex, transference and your half of the death stage."

Lily knew all about those stages. The death stage would be satisfied if she killed to save Gideon's life, or if she offered her life to save his. Transference occurred when his weapon recognized her as his mate and became hers to call from his arm, just as he could call it to life. And the final stage was sex. God. Sex with Gideon? Hello. How was she ever going to resist that?

Gideon's fingers brushed over the silver lines in her skin. "You okay with where we are?"

Lily managed a nod. "I have to be. There's no going back."

"No, there isn't." His hand closed over her wrist, and he lifted her hand to press a kiss to her palm. "You ready?"

"Absolutely. Frank has to die."

Gideon nodded and took her hand, then led her into Dante's luxuriously decorated living room. After all her years of researching the Order and reading so many descriptions of the team, now that they were all around her, brands revealed, she was able to quickly figure out who was who.

Quinn Masters was leaning against the empty fireplace. Ian was standing back against the wall, and he gave her a nod of recognition. He seemed to have recovered from the wounds he'd received after rescuing her, but his face was still haunted and bleak. There was a vast emptiness in his eyes, a gaping wound in his soul. Was it from the loss of his *sheva* as Gideon had said? She knew it was. She'd had the first hint of that loss when she'd woken up and Gideon wasn't with her. How awful would she feel if and when it ended between Gideon and her?

*Focus, sweetheart. No need to borrow trouble from the future. We've got enough to deal with right now.* Gideon squeezed her hand lightly, drawing her focus back into the room.

The rest of the men were present, most of them sprawled across the black leather couches. They were all there. Kane Santiago with his scars. The irreverent Thano Savakis with his smile. Ryland Samuels, the loose cannon whose pacing was making the other men wary. A restless dark energy was swirling around him, even more than she would have expected given what she knew about him. Was he getting worse now that his mentor, Dante, was gone?

Gabe Watson and Zach Roderick were sitting next to each other on the couch by the window, both of them watching her intently. She could feel the hum of energy in the room, the readiness of each warrior to call forth his weapon and end her life if they thought she was too dangerous. Um…yeah…

The conversation ceased the minute she and Gideon stepped inside. Gideon felt the tension level skyrocket as the males watched him carefully, analyzing his reaction to see if he was sane, or if Lily was dragging him over the line to rogue yet.

They'd all seen Quinn haul his ass down to the dungeons, and they were right to be on guard.

Lily's pulse was racing, and he felt her true fear at being confronted with the Order. Shit. He hadn't really realized how much her past would affect her. *I'm with you, Lily. You're safe.*

Her fingers tightened against his. *Keep telling me that, please.*

Quinn stood up. "Dr. Davenport."

"Call me Lily." She pulled her hand from Gideon's and stepped forward, setting her hands on her hips as she surveyed the males in the room. He could see the tension in her shoulders, and knew she was trying to be stronger than she felt. But that was Lily. She was about strength, and it didn't surprise him that she would need to face the room without leaning on him.

"Lily," Quinn agreed, his tone conversational, but his eyes sharp as he watched Lily and Gideon together. He nodded at the table. "What do you know about that, Lily?"

Lily followed his glance, and Gideon saw Nate's knife on the table. Ian's hand was resting on it. Her forehead furrowed. "That's Nate's knife."

She walked over and crouched next to the table, studying it carefully. Gideon sensed the angst ease from Lily's body as she inspected it. He smiled, realizing that Lily was indeed a scholar at heart, and her interest had been piqued by the knife. "How do you still have it?" she asked. "I thought Calydon weapons disappeared if they were outside the body for very long."

"They only disappear if they aren't touching a person. We keep touching it periodically to make sure it doesn't fade," Quinn explained.

Ian lifted his hand from the weapon, leaving the knife behind as Grace and Ana walked in and sat on chairs at the back of the room. Quinn raised his brows at Grace, and she smiled back, making something inside Gideon flicker with envy at their easy camaraderie.

Ana said nothing, and she looked even more strung out than she had been since she'd first arrived. Lily frowned at Ana, and then he felt Lily touch his mind. *We have to talk about Ana. I think Frank is messing with her mind.*

Gideon studied Ana more carefully. *Still? Even though she's here?*

Lily nodded. *I think she's in danger.*

*We'll put a guard on her.*

"Can you read the writing on the knife?" Quinn asked.

Lily glanced at Gideon, and then returned her attention

to the knife. She picked it up and turned it over in her hands, her touch careful, as if it were an ancient artifact she was afraid of breaking.

"It's a Calydon weapon," Gideon said. "You can't hurt it."

The room fell quiet, waiting for Lily to finish inspecting it. "The designs etched on this are incredible. It looks like it was crafted with the finest of modern technology, yet I know it's hundreds of years old." Her eyes were bright with interest, fresh energy flowing back into her face.

*Shit, you're beautiful.* Her eyes were brimming with an intelligence, curiosity, and warmth that shocked him. Lily had been brought back to life by her interest in the knife, and Gideon loved the excitement sparkling on her face. It pissed him off to think that two years with Nate had robbed her of this kind of pleasure, replacing this passion with a shadowed fear.

Lily shot a sharp glance at him, and then her face softened. *That's you talking, isn't it? Not the bond. You think I'm beautiful all on your own.*

*Yeah, I do,* he agreed. He didn't know how he knew, but he did.

A small smile played at the corners of Lily's mouth as she turned back to the knife. That one glimpse of her smile hit him hard, a symbol of the woman hidden beneath the stress and the trauma.

Lily chewed her lower lip as she studied the knife. "I've seen this language before. It's really ancient. I think I have some texts on it at my office." She passed her finger over it. "I think it describes a rite." She tapped her fingernail on a word. "This word is often used to indicate a ritual sacrifice."

"Human?" Quinn asked.

"No. Something more specific. Like an object with great power." She managed a wry smile. "Well, at least that's good to know he's not planning to sacrifice me." There was a murmur in the room, and Lily looked around. "What?"

Quinn answered. "Calydons are being murdered and their weapons are being harvested. If a Calydon weapon is ripped from the body at the moment of death, the weapon doesn't disappear. We think Nate was collecting them for the ritual he was going to conduct to free Ezekiel from his prison."

"A ritual." Lily sat down on the couch, barely noticing that Ian had to scramble out of the way to keep her from landing on him. She hummed under her breath as she traced the words, and Gideon could practically feel her mind turning over the possibilities. She looked up at Gideon. "You said that Ezekiel's prison walls are weakening, right?"

Gideon vaulted over the back of the couch to sit beside her, giving up trying to resist his need to be close to her. "Yeah. Does it mention him?"

She leaned next to him, her shoulder resting against his as she pointed to a small design on the handle. He bent his head beside hers to get a closer look at it, feeling strangely content as she leaned her elbow on his thigh, unconsciously, he was sure.

Her hair fell in the way and she shoved it aside impatiently, then pointed to a symbol that looked like three triangles superimposed over each other. "This is a symbol for strength, but it's been broken. That could reference the weakening walls."

Anticipation pulsed inside Gideon. "So, this is it, then? The stone has our answers to what's going on?"

"Maybe..." Lily continued to chew her lip as she studied the handle. "I need my texts. I can't remember what most of this means." Her finger traced over a symbol. "This one here. This is important. It's a location..." She faded off into silence as she studied the knife. "I need paper."

Anticipation hummed through the room as everyone scrambled for a pen and paper. It was Ryland who finally brought it from the kitchen. All the Order members tensed and readied to call their weapons when Ryland neared Lily, but all he did was set the paper and pen in her lap and walk away, shooting a scowl at everyone for not trusting him.

Gideon knew it was only a matter of time until Ryland went rogue, especially now that Dante was dead. Dante had been the only thing keeping Ryland on the right edge of rogue, and now that he was gone, the Order had to be ready to take Ryland out when he finally crossed the line.

But it wouldn't be yet. Right now, Ryland was too committed to avenging his mentor's death, and Gideon suspected that his goal would provide enough motivation to keep Ryland sane until he'd accomplished his mission.

Lily set the paper on Gideon's thigh and started to scratch notes, pausing every few minutes to inspect the knife again.

"Can you figure out the location of the rite?" Quinn's voice was brimming with anticipation. "If we can find where the rite is being performed we can stop it."

"Working on it," Lily muttered. "It's a map, but it's so old that once I translate it, we'll have to correlate the location to modern times. I need to go to my office and get my books."

Gideon rubbed her back as he spoke. "Do you think your office is still there?" he asked gently, not wanting to upset her. "You've been gone for two years."

"Of course it is. My parents would never have been able to let go of the hope I'd come back." Her conviction was apparent. "My office will be exactly as I left it."

Kane stood up. "I'll get them and bring them back. I'm fastest—"

"No." Lily was already shaking her head, and she *still* hadn't looked up from the knife. She was utterly focused on what she was doing. "I have thousands of books. I need to go and sort through them."

Oh, yeah, Gideon didn't like that suggestion. "Frank is probably waiting there for you."

She waved her hand dismissively, so caught up in her work that she didn't even react to the reminder of Frank. "My office is unlisted because I got too many threatening phone calls about my work. About tangling with the Calydons. He wouldn't be able to find it."

Gideon grinned and ruffled her still damp hair. Lily was a different woman when she was concentrating on her work. She simply shut everything else out. He could see now how she had survived all the hell she'd been through. She'd retreated into her mind and her work, into a world where she was powerful and in control. She'd found her place, and that gave her strength to rebuild whenever she revisited it.

*Uh, oh.* Lily went rigid beside him, and Gideon was instantly on alert.

His fingers stilled in her hair. *What's wrong?*

*I just found out why the Order thinks they may need to kill me to stop Frank. And they might be right.*

# Chapter 17

Gideon cursed silently, realizing the living room had fallen silent. Everyone was watching Lily intently. They'd picked up on her tension and knew she'd just learned something significant. Something she'd shared only with Gideon.

"What did she find?" Quinn's voice was soft...too soft. Dangerously soft, indicating that he knew full well that Lily didn't want to share. "Lily. What did you find?"

Lily didn't look up, but Gideon caught the scent of her sudden wariness. "These are instructions on how to bring down the walls of Ezekiel's prison." Her voice was careful. Modulated. Not giving anything away. "What's needed for the rite, where to do it, the words to say. That kind of thing."

Gideon felt the omission in her words and knew she wasn't telling them everything.

"And?" Quinn said.

*Gideon? If I tell them, they'll kill me.*

He closed his eyes for a second at her words. It was as he'd feared. *They'll know if you lie.*

*But will they kill me for lying?*

*Not for lying, no.* He studied the room, rapidly assessing the body language of his teammates. He felt their quiet intensity, their commitment to doing whatever it took to fulfill their oath of defending innocents, including the sacrifice of one to save many. Yeah, they'd do what it took. Gideon shifted closer to Lily, easing forward to the edge of the couch, readying himself for action. *But they won't hesitate if they figure out what you're not telling them, which they will.*

*Okay, then.* Lily slipped her hand into his, and then sat up. "The reason I can read this writing is because it's written..." Her fingers dug into Gideon's, and he flexed his arm, ready to call out his weapon. "It's written in my language. Ancient, but the longer I look at it, the more I can understand."

"Your language?" Ryland looked over at her, not slowing his pacing. "What are you talking about? What are you?"

"Satinka."

Ryland cursed and the other men grew still. Gideon set his hand on Lily's opposite thigh, using his arm as a shield between her and his team, making sure they knew where he stood.

Lily pulled herself more upright. "From what I can gather so far, the walls of Ezekiel's prison were originally created using Satinka magic, paired with a great Calydon warrior. The only way to bring them down is the same way: Satinka magic paired with a great Calydon warrior."

There was silence while the men absorbed that information and Gideon shifted so his upper body was in front of her. He reached out to Kane, who was leaning against the wall on the far side of the living room, his arms folded across his chest. They didn't have a blood connection, but they could still talk across short distances. *Kane? You feeling this?*

Kane looked at him. *I can sense it. I know. They're figuring that killing Lily will end the threat of Ezekiel getting out. A clean, easy, solution to protect thousands of innocents.*

*What side are you on?*

*Dante's.*

Dante had rescued Kane from a sewage-filled back alley three hundred years ago. Kane had been covered in scars, with no memory of his life before that moment. He'd been strung out and violent, and only Dante's counsel had helped Kane manage his anger and his sense of loss at not knowing who he was or why he was scarred.

Like Ryland, Kane had been heavily dependent on Dante and he was struggling with his mentor's death even more than the rest of the Order was. So, it was no surprise that Kane's only focus would be on revenge for Dante's death. But how did that translate into their Order's plans to kill Lily? *Which means what?*

*Still deciding.*

"So, Frank needs your magic to free Ezekiel?" Quinn asked, his voice deceptively casual.

Gideon tightened his grip on Lily's leg, watching Kane carefully. If Kane decided he was on Lily's side, he could teleport them out of there instantly to a safe zone. If he didn't decide to help them, there was going to be blood drawn, and Gideon did not want to go against his Order.

He really didn't.

But he would.

Kane's eyes were at half-mast and he looked bored, but his body was coiled. If all hell broke loose, Kane was their only chance to get out alive, because Gideon couldn't take down the whole Order at once and still protect Lily.

"It means that any Satinka could bring them down," Lily said, sliding ever so slightly toward Gideon, as if she could sense the rising threat in the air. "Not me specifically. Any of my kind."

Ryland had stopped pacing and was looking at her. "A Satinka hasn't been spotted for hundreds of years. You're the reason Frank and Nate started the process. Because they finally found you. Without you, he has no power."

"Without me, he will simply find another." Lily's voice was hard. Without fear, though Gideon could feel her pulse racing where he held her wrist. "You don't know of any Satinkas, but had Ana not sent Gideon for me, you still wouldn't know about me, either. We're out there. Plenty of us, and Frank knows how to find us."

"How do we find you?" Ryland leaned forward. "Tell us how."

"You want me to tell you so you can wipe out the last members of my race? I wouldn't do that to them." She lifted her chin, anger flashing in her eyes. "If you kill me, it will just be a race between you and him with you trying to kill off every Satinka before he can kidnap one for the rite. It's a race you'll lose eventually. There are too many of us."

"She lies." Ryland sat back. "I can smell it. She doesn't

know of any others. We kill her, and it's over."

"No, it's not." Gideon stood up, pulling Lily to her feet and shoving her behind him. "As long as Frank's still alive, it's not over. Killing Lily may not even slow him down. We have no idea if he has other Satinka on tap. He doesn't have to have Lily specifically, but we do. She can help us find the site of the rite, and she can draw Frank to us. She's our weapon, not a liability."

Ryland eyed her. "It would slow him down. He'd have to find another."

"It would slow us down as well. Drew could be dying right now. Ezekiel's walls could fall at any minute. Surely we're strong enough to keep one woman alive, aren't we?" Gideon threw out the challenge. "Since when do we fear one man so much that we slaughter an innocent rather than face him? Is this what the Order has become without Dante?"

"Dante held us together," Ryland snapped. "We aren't as strong without him. We all realize that, and we know that we're fucked if Ezekiel gets out. It's our job to kill one innocent if that will keep Ezekiel locked up! For hell's sake, if Grace hadn't been there to rescue us, we would have all been slaughtered a week ago by Frank's army of Calydons. We're alive because a woman saved us from a few Calydons, and you think we can protect Lily against more of Frank's army? Fuck that. There was a day when we could, but not now. Not without Dante."

"Grace is not just an ordinary woman—" Thano started.

"No. She's not. Which is why we're alive," Ryland retorted. "But when has the Order ever needed anyone to save them? Ever? It's never happened before, has it?"

He looked around the room, but no one had a rebuttal.

"What if Frank sends thousands of Calydons down on this house like Ezekiel did two thousand years ago before he was locked up? What then? We're *fucked!*" Ryland called out both machetes, and instantly every other warrior in the room had his weapons out, the cracks booming through the air. The room hummed with tension and violence. "And yeah, we wouldn't be able to protect a single woman in that situation. If you weren't so fucked up by her, Gideon, you'd realize it too. Just the fact you're standing there, telling us not to kill an innocent to save the world from the worst evil it has ever known, should tell us all exactly how screwed we all are. You're our true leader, Gideon, not Quinn, and when you fall, you take us all with you. Do you understand? We don't have shit anymore, and if that means that we're reduced to killing one innocent because we can't protect her, then it's better to realize that now and do it before Ezekiel ends up free because we were too deluded to realize we're *nothing* compared to what we used to be!"

His voice faded, and no one moved. No one even breathed.

Gideon finally spoke. "I don't believe we're weak. Dante still believes in us. He came back from the Afterlife to tell us that the future was up to us. He wouldn't have done that if we'd already lost."

"He also said it was time to create a new destiny, and maybe he meant we had to change our ways or die." Ryland's body was vibrating with rage now. "I will not let his death be for nothing. Ezekiel can't be allowed out. Lily is Ezekiel's ticket. That's all we need to know. We strike, and then we find Frank while he's trying to regroup. If we let Lily live, we risk failing Dante."

"Killing Lily doesn't end it," Gideon said. "Lily is our weapon to stop Frank forever. She needs to live."

The room was silent, and he felt everyone's attention on Quinn, who had been chosen by the weapons to be the leader for this mission. Until Ezekiel was stopped, or another leader chosen, it was Quinn who had the final word. He looked at Gideon with true regret in his eyes. *I'm sorry. I have to think about the greater good.*

Gideon felt his heart freeze. *Don't do this. It's the wrong decision.*

*It's the only one I can make. Step aside, Gideon. Don't die for her.*

Gideon felt Lily's hand on his back, and he looked across the room to Kane. *Decision time.*

Quinn held up his sword. "We will honor Lily Davenport in death, as a sacrifice to the greater goo—"

"Quinn!" Grace leapt in front of her mate and grabbed his raised arm. "Don't kill her! Are you insane?"

Ryland let out a scream of death and hurled his machete

at Lily.

"No!" Gideon threw up his axe to block the blow. "Ezekiel's winning if he breaks us up like this! We have to stand together!" He knocked aside Ryland's machete, then jumped in front of Lily as Quinn charged her. *Don't do it, Quinn. God help us both if you do.*

True pain flickered in Quinn's eyes, and Gideon realized Quinn was going to kill him to get to Lily. One of them was going to die.

Then there was a flash and Kane appeared in front of him. His arms went around both Gideon and Lily, and then the world fell away.

❦ ❦ ❦

Ana stumbled as she raced from the house, Nate's knife clenched in her fist. In the battle, no one had noticed her grab it when it had fallen to the carpet. She could still hear the shouts and the crashes as Ryland destroyed the house in his rage at losing the chance to kill Lily. Grace was shouting at Quinn for the choice he'd made. The men were arguing about what they should have done, what they were going to do. The Order was crumbling, and she knew it was because of the man she was going to meet.

Her cast caught on a root and she fell, wincing as the knife cut her hand. Tears filled her eyes as she pulled the blade away from her skin and saw the blood well up. So many times that knife had cut her when she'd been kidnapped by Nate. So many...

"You came." Frank kneeled beside her. "Are you crying because of Nate?"

She pulled back the tears. "I'm fine."

"You aren't fine." Frank helped her to her feet, his grip supportive, but not restraining, his voice kind. "But you will be. I'll help you heal."

She shrugged out of his grip. "Why? Why are you interested in me?"

He smiled, his eyes hidden behind his sunglasses. "You aren't ready to know yet, my dear." He held out his hand. "Come, it is time to go. Shall I carry the knife?"

Ana hesitated, her fist closing around the handle. Was she making a mistake? She knew Ezekiel couldn't be allowed to be freed. She understood that. She saw how evil Frank was. She knew he had to be stopped. If she gave Frank the knife, would the Order be able to stop him, or was she damning them all to a future worse than hell?

Frank waited.

*Ana.*

Elijah's voice whispered through her mind, and the marks on her arms pulsed. Certainty reverberated through her, and she knew she had to go with Frank. She didn't know why, not yet, but she had to trust her instincts and believe the answers would become clear. She set the knife in Frank's waiting hand. "It's yours."

He smiled and closed his hand around the knife. "Excellent. Let us go." He set his hand on her back and began to guide her through the woods.

She took a last glance back at the mansion, her heart tightening with fear as she left it behind. *God help them all if she was making a mistake.*

❦ ❦ ❦

"I need paper!" The moment Kane delivered them to their new location, Lily whirled around. "I need to write down what I remember about the knife before I lose it." They were in a huge studio apartment, furnished with only a mattress on the floor of the living room. Some clothes were piled in the corner.

The only other sign of its being inhabited was the card table in the corner that had a laptop and dozens of files piled all over it. So much paper. Notes.

Kane strode across the smoothly polished wood floor to the desk, rifled through the piles, grabbed a pen and a notebook and shoved it at her.

Lily sat on the floor and started to write, frantically scrawling words and notations, drawing pictures of the symbols. Her lower lip was clenched in her teeth as her hand flew across the page.

Gideon glanced around, moving closer to Lily. His brands were burning as he took inventory of their surroundings.

"This your place?"

Kane shrugged. "Yeah."

"And I thought my place was barren."

"Fuck off." Kane stalked over to an efficient fridge humming in the corner. "Got water. That's it."

"Works."

Kane tossed him a couple bottles and then propped his shoulder against the wall, watching Lily scribble. "You guys can't stay. Dante knew where I live. I'm sure Quinn will be able to find this place."

Gideon nodded. "Thanks for getting us out of there."

Kane's black eyes glittered. "I did it because I think we need Lily to find Frank and stop Ezekiel from being released. It wasn't an altruistic concession to the fact she gives you a hard-on."

Gideon tensed. "It isn't like that."

"I don't care what it's like. I just want answers." Kane's eyes went back to Lily, who seemed oblivious to the conversation. "Frank is targeting the Order. He's trying to fragment us, and it's working."

"I know." Gideon set his hand on Lily's head while she wrote, needing to touch her. "If he splits the Order up, we're history. Ryland was right about that."

"You're the leader. You need to pull everyone together."

Gideon shook his head. "The weapons chose Quinn. I won't interfere."

"You already interfered when you refused to let him kill Lily."

Gideon ground his teeth. "I wasn't—"

"The weapons chose him when we were pursuing Ana and trying to avenge Elijah's death. That mission is over. Even Dante said you're up next." Kane fastened his eyes on him. "You're the one the men most respect, and now you're breaking your oath and refusing to listen to Quinn. It's going to make everyone wonder who they should be listening to, or, like Ryland, thinking they can do whatever the hell they want. It's up to you to pull this shit together."

"I'm not a leader. I do my job, and that's it."

"Fuck the humility crap, Gideon. You step up, or we all

go down. You're the one everyone's waiting for." His gaze flicked to Lily. "Either she comes through and proves you were right to keep her alive, or..." He looked at Gideon. "Or I fear Ryland's explosion is just the start of the crumbling of the Order. We'll be no match for Ezekiel, or even Frank." He downed the rest of the water. "I'm going back. I have to see what's going on. You got a phone on you?"

Gideon nodded.

"Keep in touch." Kane's gaze went to Lily again, and Gideon saw a burning question in there, one that had nothing to do with the Order. Gideon realized that there was another reason Kane had stepped up for her, even if it was one he wouldn't acknowledge to himself. Lily was a researcher, and she might have answers about Kane's past that he'd been searching for. Or she might at least know where to go to look for them. She might be able to find out what the scars on his body meant.

"I'll ask her later," Gideon said quietly. "When this is over."

Kane gave him a sharp look. "Just help me avenge Dante. That's all I want."

Gideon nodded. "When you go back, tell them that I'm protecting Lily not because she's my *sheva* but because I believe we need her to stop Frank."

"They won't believe you."

"Tell them anyway. If I'm truly seen as the leader, as you say, it'll at least make them question the need to kill her."

"That's not going to be enough to pull everyone back together."

Gideon's fingers tightened in Lily's hair as she made a small noise of frustration and continued to write. "It's all I can do right now."

Kane ground his teeth. "You need to do more."

Gideon stiffened. "I'm doing what I can. Hell, Kane, you think I want Ezekiel to get free? You think I don't give a shit that Dante is dead? I spent my entire life dedicated to the Order, and my oath is what has given my life meaning for the last five hundred years. There's no way that I'm going to stand back and let this thing crash and burn around me. So back the hell off!"

A brief smile flashed across Kane's face. "That's all

I wanted to hear. *That's* the message I'll pass on." Then he shimmered and was gone.

# Chapter 18

Lily flipped on the overhead light as she stepped into her office, and a sense of utter completeness settled around her. Her books were everywhere and papers strewn about. It was exactly as she'd left it two years ago, except for the layer of dust all over everything. The grime on the one large window. And her plants. All eight of them dead.

She brushed her hand over one of the leaves, and the brittle brown leaf crumbled under her touch. No rejuvenation there. She picked up some of the soil and felt a sense of peace. The soil was still alive, still a source of power for her. Of strength.

Nature would always be good for her, but her true source of power was the earth. "God, it's good to be back."

The dirt bunched in her fist, she inhaled the scent of paper, leather from the old bindings, and mustiness from the office being closed up for so long. The futon she'd slept on so many nights was against the wall, her desk was buried under mounds of paper, and the small fridge still hummed in the corner.

It was as if she'd never left. As if time had stood still.

Lily walked over to the desk and sat down in her deep blue chair, specially ordered to match...she glanced guiltily at Gideon. Would he realize the chair was the exact shade of his eyes? She'd never seen a picture of him before she'd met him, but all accounts of his deadly attacks had recounted his blue eyes again and again, until she'd been certain she knew the exact shade.

Apparently, she had.

Gideon shut the door behind them, locking it carefully. He'd been tense ever since Kane had left. He'd been vigilantly searching for any threats coming after them, not pleased with Lily's insistence that she needed to go to her office. He wasn't nearly as confident as she was about it being unfindable, but she'd needed her texts to translate the rest of the knife, or as much of it as she could remember.

Lily spread her hands over the wooden desk she'd carefully selected when she'd first moved into this office. It had no coating on it, just linseed oil, so there was nothing between the wood and her skin. It wasn't the same as burying her feet in the earth, but it was elemental enough that she'd gained strength from it whenever she'd been overwhelmed by her research or her memories.

Or her nightmares.

Gideon paced the room, inspecting the window, the air vents and every other vulnerability where someone could gain access. "It's bigger than I expected."

Watching him assess her office so carefully, a tiny trickle of fear crept in past Lily's happiness to be home. Even in her office, she wasn't truly safe, was she? Would she ever feel safe again? "I needed a large office because I have so many books." It felt like such a mundane topic, her books, when the world was falling apart outside these walls, but at the same time, that's what she wanted to think about. For one minute, for ten minutes, to just pretend that her life was about books and academia again.

But as she watched Gideon's well-muscled body patrol her office, she knew it wasn't entirely true anymore. Did she really want to go back to a life of books and research, a life where there was no dangerous warrior stirring things inside her that were so intense, so powerful, and so *alive?*

God, no, she didn't. She wasn't the woman she'd been when she left here. Not anymore.

"I thought it would be in a university, not a random office building. Didn't you work for a college?" Gideon asked. He glanced over at her, and his eyes darkened at her expression. Lust flared hard and fast between them, like a blazing tension cutting through the air.

She cleared her throat, trying to ignore the surge of desire pulsing through her. Now was not the time, and they both knew it. And if they had sex, the bond would tighten, and heaven help her, the last thing they could afford was for Gideon to go rogue from the *sheva* bond. They both needed him sane right now. "I was a guest professor, but like I said, I needed my office to be kept private."

Lily felt the tension and stress easing away from her, the confidence building as she surrounded herself with the safe and familiar, her world before it was ripped apart. With Gideon there to keep her safe, and her well-ordered world surrounding her, it felt right. Better. She closed her eyes and leaned back in the chair, letting the peaceful vibes of the room soothe her, ease her rising desire for the man she'd allowed into her inner sanctum. "When I'm here, nothing else can bother me." How she'd dreamed of being back here when she was at Nate's. This place was her home more than her condo was. Here, she was in control. It was about academics and research. Her sanctuary.

Gideon walked around the room, peering at bookcases. "You have stuff in here that isn't about Calydons." He sounded surprised.

"It all relates to Calydons in some way." She listened to the sound of his footsteps, the heavy thud of each boot on her floor. She never allowed anyone into her space, but it felt right to have Gideon here, to let him see she was more than the terrified, bruised victim he'd found at Nate's. She was proud of who she was, of what she'd accomplished, and there was something so elementally satisfying to be sharing it with him.

Gideon fell silent, and she knew he'd paused to read something. She opened her eyes, then shot out of her chair when she realized what shelf he was inspecting. "Oh, um, don't read those—"

"You have three entire bookshelves of binders on me." His finger went to the spine of one them. "*Deaths Gideon Caused 1650-1687*," he read. He moved along and peered at another binder, a thin one. "*How Gideon Deprived the World of Hope: the Slaying of Juliette Pemberton*."

"Oh! Don't read that one!" She skirted around her desk and darted across her office, but Gideon had already swept it off the bookshelf.

"You tracked all the people I killed?" His voice was cold, devoid of emotion, which told her exactly how angry he was. "You made up stories about how the world would be different if I hadn't murdered those people? That's what you spent your time doing?"

"Gideon, I didn't know you. I didn't understand—" She grabbed for the binder, and he raised it out of her reach. "Don't read that one, please."

"Why not? I assume you never bothered to research how the world would have been affected if I hadn't interfered, did you? All the people who would have died if I hadn't acted?"

She felt her cheeks burn. "No," she admitted. "But I would now. Please give me that binder."

He turned away, flipped it open, and started to read. "The Calydon warrior Gideon is widely known for his brutal and vicious slaying of innocents throughout history. His ability to steal life from innocent young women without flinching is well-documented." He fell silent, reading, and then finally looked up. "You wrote and published this crap?"

She set her hands on her hips, unable to quell the guilt surging through her. "You told me earlier that it didn't matter if people thought you were cold and ruthless. You said you spent your life trying to foster that reputation. Why do you care?"

"Because you wrote it. That's why I care." Gideon held up the spiral bound document. "These are your beliefs. Your prejudices. Did you ever stop to think that it absolutely fucking broke me every time I had to kill an innocent? A woman?"

She swallowed. "No." She should have, though. How could Gideon have hidden who he really was so completely? If she'd been an unbiased researcher, she would have seen it. But she hadn't been. She'd been damaged and angry and trying to fix her life by hurting him. "I'm sorry, Gideon."

"Jesus, Lily." He stalked across the room, putting distance between them, the binder held tight in his fist. "You make me sound like a monster."

"I don't think you are one now."

He faced her. "How could you possibly change your mind? I feel your hatred for me in every word on this page." He turned the page. "Even more so than other Order members," he read. "Gideon can stand over the bleeding body of a young girl and not care. Instead, he is more likely to be seen beating his chest to declare yet another victory for the Order. Even when his own *sheva* fell at his feet, she meant nothing." His voice tightened.

"Gideon," she whispered. "Please stop reading that."

"Gideon's *sheva* was but another faceless sacrifice to this bogus mission of the Order," he continued, the stiff cardboard cover bending under his tight grip. "But to her family, Juliette Pemberton was—" He jerked his eyes off the page, staring at her in shock. "You found out her name?"

Lily walked over to him and set her hand on his arm. "Gideon, it won't do any good for you to read about her. Please stop."

"*Jesus.* You found out her name." His voice was a raw whisper, and he pulled out of Lily's grasp and stumbled over to the futon, sinking down on it, the binder clutched in his hands. "Juliette," he whispered. "Juliette Pemberton."

Lily's throat tightened. "I wrote that essay because I wanted to punish you. I wanted to make you suffer, to feel *something* for all the grief you'd caused others. I didn't believe you cared, or that you felt anything, and I hated you for that. I hated that I could suffer, and you felt nothing, so I wrote that essay as a letter to you, with the sole goal of finding a way to break through your wall and make you understand what effect you'd had on the lives you'd destroyed."

Gideon crushed the binder in his fists, his eyes bloodshot. "You have no idea—"

She dropped to her knees before him, grabbing his thighs. "But I do now. I didn't know before, but I do now." She laid her hand over his fists. "Please, Gideon, don't read that essay. I beg you."

His gaze flickered to her. "Is it true?"

"Is what true?"

"The essay. Her family. Her story. Did you make it up, or is it true?"

She hesitated. "Gideon—"

"Just tell me." His eyes were cold now. "Tell me the

damn truth."

"It's true. It's all true. I tried to write it in a way to hurt you, but the facts are accurate."

He looked at the notebook crushed in his hands. "I have to know."

"Then let me tell you about her."

"No. I need her story, and I need it the way you told it." His jaw was hard, his gaze unwavering.

"Why? Why would you torture yourself like this?"

He looked at her. "She was my *sheva*. She died to keep me alive. I owe her this much. I owe her my pain and my tears, if they will come." His gaze was fierce and unyielding. "And I owe it to you, as well, *sheva*. I need to know the pain I caused you. It is my duty." He jerked his head toward the desk. "Work on the knife. We don't have time for you to be telling tales to me, anyway."

Lily didn't need to ask him if he was certain. She knew he was. Instead, she leaned forward and pressed her lips to his. They were cold to the touch, and he didn't return the kiss. "Just so you know," she said quietly. "When you're done reading it, I'll be here for you."

Then she stood up and forced herself to walk back to her desk. She sat down in her blue chair and picked up the notes she'd scribbled at Kane's apartment, but she couldn't keep herself from looking at Gideon.

For a long time, he simply stared at the crumpled binder in his hands.

Then he set it beside his leg on the futon and pressed his palms to his eyes, his elbows propped on his knees.

Her throat tightened, and she pushed back her chair to go to him.

"No."

It was one word, but it stopped her. She pressed her lips together and pulled the chair back up to her desk.

"You need to work, Lily." Gideon didn't lift his head, and his voice was soft. "We're running out of time. You have to focus."

Lily took a deep breath. He was right. She picked up her notes and forced herself to read them, gradually shutting Gideon and everything else out of her mind, retreating into the academic world she knew so well.

It was many hours later before the rustle of paper penetrated her subconscious. She looked up to see Gideon smoothing out the crushed paper and flattening the pages. Then he settled back on the futon and finally began to read.

❧ ❧ ❧

Ana stopped as Frank flipped on the lights, flooding a massive pit with stark white light. They were deep underground, standing at the edge of the huge cavern looming below them, dug into rock hundreds or thousands of years ago. It looked like an ancient coliseum, with holes carved out of the walls at the base, as if they were tunnels leading off to prison cells. The walls were covered in archaic carvings. It was cold, damp, and brutally desolate, and Ana couldn't stop herself from shuddering. She felt like she should be in Greece, not underground in eastern Oregon. "What is this place?"

"You don't recognize it?" Frank walked forward, leaning over a hard clay railing to study the ground below. "It was our training ground."

"Ours? What do you mean?"

"This is where Illusionists were brought to refine their skills many centuries ago, and even far more recently than you would imagine."

Ana's belly twisted with discomfort when she realized what he meant.

Thousands of years ago, when Illusionists were first discovered, they were used by brutal leaders to torture prisoners. The Illusionists would create false images so real that the people seeing them were unable to convince themselves they were fake. The illusions were dark and terrifying ones that would leave the prisoners screaming and writhing as they clawed their neck to pieces, trying to pry the rabid dog off their throat. A dog that didn't exist, except as an illusion.

It wasn't just the horrors that the Illusionists could create that tortured the prisoners; it was the fact that the prisoners eventually went insane, unable to tell truth from reality, until everything was a terror.

Illusionists were the worst kind of torture, because they destroyed the mind and made the mind destroy the body. Over the years, Illusionists had been selectively bred. Only those with the worst, most deadly illusions were allowed to live, until the race became dark. So very deadly. They had become the harbingers of nightmares, the demons of the mind, making people insane with the sheer horrors that didn't even exist, except in their victim's mind.

Except Ana.

For some unknown reason, she'd been born with the capacity only for light, happy illusions. She had been the key to helping Grace cope with her own horrific illusions, ones that were so powerful that even Grace was affected by them, unable to see through her own nightmares. Through all that Ana had experienced, all the hell she and Grace had faced since childhood, Ana had relied so heavily on her happy illusions to stay sane. How many times had she created a peaceful meadow scene that had filled her and Grace with serenity and relief, pulling them both back from the edge of the horrors they were living?

But it had all ended when Nate had discovered that if he beat Ana badly enough, he could force dark illusions out of her. It was one of those dark illusions that had killed Elijah. Ana closed her eyes, remembering that horrific moment when Elijah had tried to save her, giving his life only to have her deadly illusion burst free. The way he'd called her name as he'd died—

Tears filled her eyes. She was such a monster. She was exactly what the Illusionists of the past had been: tools to murder innocents. She'd killed so many Calydons when Nate had kidnapped her, but the death that still haunted her most was Elijah's.

Since she'd been free from Nate, she'd tried three illusions, and all of them had been of Elijah dying. Her happy illusions were gone, replaced by her worst nightmare: the moment she'd killed Elijah.

Each time Ana had done an illusion and relived Elijah's death, she'd felt his blood on her hands, seen his eyes glaze with death, and felt the weight of his body as he fell on her. She'd relived his death again and again and again.

So Ana had stopped the illusions. She'd shut them down.

What used to be her greatest joy was now her hell. Without her happy illusions, Ana didn't even know who she was anymore, and she had no tools to cope with the nightmares.

And here, in this place of death and torture, Ana knew exactly what kind of illusion would be called forth. "I don't want to be here." She turned to leave, and Frank stopped her with a hand on her arm.

"But you are here, my dear. This is your world."

She shook her head. "No. It isn't." Lethal illusions would never be her world. She refused to be that person, that nightmare, that sadist.

"Yes, it is. This is your history." Frank took her arm and tugged her down the clay steps that were as hard as cement. He pointed her toward a massive throne made of red clay, with dark bits of volcanic rock pressed into the arms for decoration. "This is your future."

She tried to back up, frantic now. "No—"

He shoved her into the chair. "This is the seat for the Illusionist. Down below is her victim. Trapped." He gestured to the empty clay benches surrounding them, a balcony where observers had no doubt cheered on the illusion. "This is for the audience, who are always at risk of falling for the illusion as well. It is the game they play, like people of today who eat puffer fish. Risking their own death is half the fun."

Ana gripped the armrests, fighting against the images trying to fill her mind. Visions of crowds, of death, of torment, of her being the key to it all. "Why are you showing me this?"

"Because this is where you will heal."

Um, no. "This place won't heal me—"

"It will." Frank leaned over the railing, as if he were presiding over some festival of death. "In this place, you're free to do your illusions, with no fear of hurting anyone. It's here you can practice, until you learn to control them, to direct them to one person or thousands. You'll learn how to keep them from affecting yourself." He turned to look at her. "Here, you are free."

Ana stared at him as his words sank in. There would be no risk here. She could practice until she found her equilibrium again. Her happy illusions. There was no one to hurt here, except for herself.

He smiled. "Yes, Ana, I've been saving this place for you."

"Why?"

He pulled off his sunglasses and looked at her. His eyes were ice blue, like the frost of an icicle on a sunny day. Cold. "I promised your parents I would look out for you."

"My parents?" She cocked her head, finally realizing how she knew him. It was so long ago, she barely remembered him. "You were my father's best friend. I remember you. You went by another name back then—" She couldn't remember what it was... "I liked you. You were nice to me."

That's why she'd been drawn to him. Because she had memories of him rocking her on his knee, telling her jokes, and giving her candy. Because he made her think of her life before her parents had died and everything had fallen apart.

But he'd disappeared around the time of her parents' death, and she'd forgotten about him completely.

Frank nodded and slipped his sunglasses back on. "This is where your parents and I spent thousands of hours practicing. This is their legacy, and I give it to you." He gestured to the pit. "Try an illusion, Ana. For them."

No. She wasn't going to do an illusion for her parents, or for Frank. She was going to do one for Elijah. She'd sent him out of this world in a scream of terror, and it would end now. She would find her way back, and she would use her happy illusions to bring peace to people who were suffering.

She was taking herself back, and she was doing it now.

Ana faced the pit and leaned forward over it. She reached out with her mind, trying to picture a meadow with flowers...and suddenly her forearms burned and she felt Elijah's presence in her mind so vividly she spun around, expecting him to be standing behind her.

He wasn't.

She frowned. "Has anyone else been here lately?"

"No. Why do you ask?"

"Nothing." She knew Frank had been involved in Elijah's death. If he'd been working with Nate, Frank had to have been involved. Had he somehow brought Elijah's spirit to this place? Or...she recalled suddenly Elijah's revulsion when he'd learned she was an Illusionist. Was this where Elijah had learned to hate Illusionists? Had he once been tortured here?

She knew then that this was why she'd had to go with Frank. Because there were answers about Elijah here. Somewhere in this God-forsaken place that was stained with blood and nightmares, were answers she needed. "I'd like to be alone here."

Frank nodded. "As you wish. When you're ready to leave, just go up the stairs on the north side of the balcony. They lead to the living quarters."

She gave him a vague brush of her hand as she leaned over the railing, staring into the pit. There were so many dark stains on the hard clay, and she pictured Elijah, lying there bleeding.

An illusion crashed through her, rising so quickly and powerfully she was helpless to stop it. The wind rose with a howl, her hair lifted, and Ana screamed against the darkness rising within her. "No!"

But the wind stole her voice and the air pressure beat at her ears, and suddenly Elijah was on the ground in the middle of the pit, chained down, screaming as flames licked at his skin, burning him alive. Smoke rose from his body, charring him, his howl of agony blistering through her. She saw herself in the Illusionist chair, causing his pain, torturing him. She could smell the burning of his flesh, hear the popping of the flames as they turned his bones to ash, feel the scorching heat from the fire as it licked away at his life.

Ana fell to her knees, her hands pressed to her head, desperate to stop the illusion. "God, no! Don't do this!"

But his screams went on, and she heard her own laughter, laughing at his agony as she sat in the Illusionist chair and watched him writhe as his skin melted from his body.

"It's not true," Ana wrenched out, her fingers digging into her head as she tried to fight it. Tried to suppress it. But it was too strong, so much more powerful than anything she could control. "It's an illusion, dammit! You're not really killing him!" But she couldn't make her mind accept that. She couldn't block the horror as tears spilled from her eyes, as her soul broke with the horror of murdering her mate again. "God, Elijah, I'm so sorry!"

But it didn't matter. For the fifth time in two weeks, Ana killed him, and she had to live every moment of his agony along with him. The fact that the first death was the only real one, the only time she'd actually killed him, didn't matter. Just as her illusions were reality to whomever she was inflicting them upon, she couldn't escape them either. She knew they were fake, but her mind and her soul lived and suffered through them as if they were real.

It might be an illusion she was reliving now, but it was based in truth: she'd murdered the man who'd been destined to be her mate. She was every bit the demon as all those who had sat in that chair a hundred years ago and tortured strangers to their death.

Ana groaned as the illusion finally faded, and she slumped to the hard clay, her tears dampening the red rock. Was this why she'd come? To live her worst hell again and again? To punish herself? There had to be more. There had to be something else. There had to be a reason.

She rolled onto her back and stared at the stone ceiling, tears still trickling down her cheeks. *Elijah. Why am I here? This has something to do with you. I know it does.*

There was silence, and then she heard his voice, so faint, so broken, so weak in her mind. *Ana.*

She jerked upright. "Elijah?" It had sounded so close, so real, not a figment of her imagination.

But there was no one in the coliseum except her.

Of course Elijah wasn't there. She'd seen him die. The only place he still lived was in her heart. And in her nightmares.

# Chapter 19

Lily sat back in her chair and sighed with exhaustion. It was over. She'd done all she could with the knife. She had some answers, but not enough. "Gideon—" She looked up and stopped.

Gideon was bent over, elbow on one knee, supporting his forehead with his palm as he read the final page. His broad shoulders were hunched, his body language one of utter defeat.

It was exactly the image she'd held in her mind of him when she'd written it, and now... God, it was horrible to see. She'd stripped him of that which had made him a legend, of the strength that had enabled him to do what he'd had to do.

Lily quietly pushed her chair back and padded across the floor in her bare feet. She hesitated as she reached him, suddenly uncertain what his reaction would be. It was she who'd written those words, who'd worked so hard to break him.

Gideon looked up. His eyes were bloodshot and filled with such naked pain and regret that she wrapped her arms around him before she could stop to think. He pressed his face to her belly and his arms went around her waist, holding her tight.

"I'm sorry," she whispered.

"Don't talk. I don't want to talk." His voice was rough and harsh.

"Okay." She bit her lip against all she wanted to say.

He didn't move for a long time, but his grip on her never loosened. His ribs expanded with each breath, but that was his only movement.

The binder slid off his lap and hit the floor with the soft swish of paper, but he didn't move. She could feel his body shaking against hers, and she pressed her lips to his hair. "Gideon—"

"What did you find out?" He lifted his head to look at her, his eyes still so haunted. "About the knife?"

She frowned. "You don't want to talk about the—"

"No." His grip tightened around her waist. "I need to focus. Tell me what you found." His voice was almost desperate in its intensity, in its need to take action. "We're going to stop Frank, we're going to keep you safe, and we're going to make sure Ezekiel never leaves his prison. Nothing else matters."

She understood. Her interest in the Calydons had always been intense, but once her brother died, it had gone over the edge. She'd had a mission, and so did Gideon. They were both driven by the death of someone who'd mattered to them, someone they both felt they should have saved.

As Lily studied his blue eyes, she realized Juliette Pemberton would direct Gideon's actions from the grave forever. As Gideon's second *sheva*, Lily was nothing more than an opportunity for him to attempt to correct the past. Lily was not his future. She was not her own identity. She was Juliette reincarnated, a chance to change the way he'd played his hand the first time.

That's why he hadn't killed Lily. That's why he was protecting her from the Order. For Juliette. Not for her. How had she not realized that? How could she have been so foolish? Her heart ached with sudden pain and vulnerability, and she pulled herself out of his arms.

Gideon frowned. "What's wrong?"

Lily shook her head and hurried back to her desk while she swallowed the lump in her throat. Why did it matter? It wasn't as if she cared about him. But as she slid into her seat and picked up her notes, she knew she did.

She'd cared about him since the first time her mom had told the story. If she hadn't cared, she wouldn't have worked so hard to hurt him. She wouldn't have spent her life trying to find out everything she could. She wouldn't have fallen so hard into his arms even after she'd realized who he was. And now that she knew who he was and had connected with him so intimately?

She cared far too much.

No. She couldn't let it matter. This situation wasn't about them as a couple. This was about Frank, and the fact that he had to be stopped before Lily could get her life back and get away from Gideon and the Order. She cleared her throat. "The knife—"

Gideon slammed his hand down on the desk, making her jump back in surprise. His eyes were angry, his body coiled. "What's wrong?" he asked again.

Lily hadn't heard him approach the desk, not even a whisper of sound from him. "Why are you in my space? I'm about to translate the knife for you. What else do you want from me? You want me to be Juliette? I'm not. So back off!"

Gideon blinked, the fire gone from his eyes. "What are you talking about?"

"Nothing." Lily grabbed her notes and held them up. "The rite has to be completed tomorrow night. Once every thousand years. That's why Frank and Nate were acting now. Not because they finally found a Satinka, but because they have to do it now."

Something glittered in Gideon's eyes, as if he wasn't finished with the discussion on Juliette, but he took the bait. "What time?"

"Sunset. That's what time the walls went up the first time, so that's what time they have to go down."

He leaned against the pine file cabinet and folded his arms across his chest. "Tell me everything."

"I don't know everything, because I don't have the entire text in front of me. But there was a team of warriors who brought down Ezekiel originally—"

He nodded. "Ezekiel's brother, Caleb, teamed up with twenty other Calydons and they vanquished Ezekiel. Caleb couldn't bear to kill his own brother, so he locked him up instead."

Lily nodded. "It appears that all twenty-one of those men donated one weapon, and they were put in the prison walls as they were built. Those weapons are what give the structure its strength, and the Satinka magic sealed it."

He propped his boot up on her desk, listening.

"Apparently, the only way to bring the walls down is to reverse the spell that was woven into it originally. These instructions were written by the Satinka who enhanced the building. But to protect against a unilateral decision to free Ezekiel, all twenty-one men would have to agree to free him, and they would have to donate their matching weapon to reverse the rite."

Gideon nodded. "The weapons that have been harvested all belong to Calydons who were direct descendants of the original twenty-one men. Dante, our former leader, was the last one of his lineage...except his son, Drew, who Frank kidnapped."

"Is Drew still alive?"

Gideon's cheek twitched. "He was last time we saw him."

Lily scanned her notes. "He's probably the Calydon who's going to be used with the Satinka."

Gideon tensed. "How exactly is the Satinka going to be used?"

She didn't look up, trying to keep herself neutral. Not so easy when she was about to describe the fate Frank had planned for her. "As far as I can tell, her magic will feed the chosen Calydon, and she will say the words of the rite, and the walls will fall. Together, they will bring down the structure."

"The Satinka will die?" His voice was even, measured, as if he were trying to suppress intense fury.

She raised her gaze to look at him. "Most likely. It will take a lot of power to bring down those walls. She'll be drained." *God, please, don't let me die. Don't let Frank get me.*

His blue eyes glowed with fierceness. *You don't need God. You have me. When are you going to trust my commitment to keeping you safe?*

Lily stared at Gideon, unable to feel the same joy and exhilaration at his declaration anymore. "Do I have you? Really? Do you even see me standing here, or do you see Juliette?"

Gideon frowned. "What are you talking about?"

"Forget it! We don't have time for that." There was no point in the discussion. Gideon probably didn't even understand what he was doing. He was a male, right? What did men know about relationships anyway? Not that they had one. Yes, sure, she was his soul mate and he was her chosen one, but it wasn't like that translated into a normal, sane relationship anyway.

"Lily—"

"We need to find out where the rite is taking place." She tapped her finger on her notes. "The location of the ritual isn't written here. It says that the information on the location can be found where it all began..." She frowned. "I don't know what that means."

Gideon narrowed his eyes, unable to resist the lure of the mission, as she'd known he would. What warrior would rather talk about his soul mate's emotional upheaval instead of saving the world? "It could mean where the world was formed, where Ezekiel was born, where the prison was built..." He shook his head. "There could be dozens of 'it's.'"

Lily gestured at the books in her office. "If I know what the event is, I can find it. But we don't have time to chase down every location that is significant to Calydon history."

Gideon got a determined look on his face. "I'm checking with Quinn."

Oh, yeah, that sounded like a great idea, given how determined the warrior had been to kill her. "If you connect with him, will he be able to find us?"

"No. It's a different kind of blood bonding ritual than you and I did. Different ritual words. I wouldn't want to know where he was at all times. With a *sheva*..." Gideon's gaze flicked to her. "Different story."

She swallowed, her body suddenly springing to life at the hooded look in his eyes, and her gaze flicked to his wrists, which were healing from the chains.

He looked down and flexed his fist. "Yeah. Different story." Gideon would never forget those five minutes, when Quinn had called for reinforcements after Gideon had dragged himself out of Lily's room. It had taken four Order members to get Gideon down to that basement and chained up. He'd been ready to kill them all to get back to Lily and her allure of sex, of magic, of power, of...he thought of that moment in the bathroom, when he'd told her the truth about the day his *sheva*...the day *Juliette* had died. That was what Gideon had wanted to get back to as well: not just the sex and the magic, but also the intimacy of being in Lily's arms and having her listen to him as if he were a male of value instead of the monster...

Not that it mattered why Gideon had wanted back in that room. He would have killed Lily if he'd returned, and there was no one around to hold him back now. He had to keep his distance from her and focus on his mission.

Gideon unwove the shields he'd erected to keep Quinn out of his mind and reached out. *Quinn.*

*Where the hell have you been? We're under assault here.*

Gideon tensed, and he saw Lily frown, as if she were hearing the conversation. Of course she could. They were blood bonded now. Unless Gideon actively tried to block her, she'd be able to hear him. *What's going on, Quinn?*

*A bunch of Calydons showed up right after you left and they're hitting hard. The knife's missing and so is Ana. Ryland and a couple other guys took off, so there are only three of us trying to keep them off.* There was a grunt of pain from Quinn, followed by a roar of triumph, and Gideon knew he'd slain someone.

Gideon's forearms began to itch with the need to get back and help his team, to stand beside them. Where had Ryland and the others gone? Why had they left Quinn and the others in the lurch? Shit. The Order truly was crumbling.

*Ana went to Frank*, Lily said. *I know she did.*

Quinn cursed. *Did you translate the knife, Lily? Tell me you got a good enough look at it. Hell help us if you didn't. With Frank already in possession of it...*

Gideon looked at Lily. *She translated it.*

There was a rush of relief from Quinn. *Damn, I'm glad to hear you say that. Next time you challenge my authority in front of the team, I'll kill you, but this time, all I can say is, thank the Lord you're such an annoyingly stubborn son of a bitch.*

Gideon grinned. *So, we're good?*

*We're good.* There was a pause. *Gideon, I did what I felt I had to do. You know it would have haunted me.*

Gideon could feel Quinn's regret through their link, and he nodded. He would have known it anyway. *I know. It's all good. You got time to talk?*

*No. But do it anyway. What did the knife say?*

Lily gave Quinn the same recap she'd given Gideon. *So, do you know where 'it' all began?*

Quinn was silent, but Gideon could feel the energy of their connection humming. He came back after a minute. *I just checked around, and we think it might be the triggering event where Ezekiel went dark originally. Because that's truly where it all started, when he crossed over. But we don't know when it was—*

"I know!" Lily leapt out of her chair and raced across the office. She knelt in front of a shelf in the back corner, her finger tracing titles. The tip of her tongue was peeking out of the corner of her mouth as she concentrated, and Gideon caught the scent of her adrenaline, saw the energy in every feminine curve of her body.

That was Lily. Knowledge was her passion. Just watching her get fired up about her books made his body react.

*Gideon.*

He jerked his attention back to Quinn. *Yeah.*

*You holding up?*

*Lily's still alive, isn't she? I haven't drained her.*

*True.* Quinn cursed. *I have to go. We'll try to catch up as soon as we're clear here, but I get the feeling these Calydons are here to keep us pinned down. Follow up on Lily's findings and stay safe. Ryland, Gabe, and Zach are out hunting Lily so they can kill her, and there are rogue Calydons all over the damn place. You're on your own until I can get this place cleared out.*

Gideon ground his teeth, needing to go back and stand by Quinn's side.

*No. You have to stop Frank. We'll be fine. Grace is already working an illusion to bring them down. Just go!* There was a flash of pain, and Quinn abruptly cut off contact.

Gideon closed his eyes, trying to calm himself down. His adrenaline was raging, and his forearms were burning with the need to jump into the fray. It wasn't his style to do strategic work behind the scenes. He got in, did his job, and got out. It was easier that way. Less to get invested in.

"Got it." Lily was bent over a huge notebook, her hair falling onto the dusty pages. "It's thought that the triggering event for Ezekiel going dark was when he was fourteen years old and he saw his father attack his mother. He went after his father in retaliation and it took six men to pull him off." Her forehead furrowed. "They lived in the town of...hang on...I need to compare maps."

She set the book on the ground and hopped to her feet, not bothering to dust herself off as she crossed the room and thumbed through a few more books. She seemed oblivious to Gideon, just intent on her work.

She fell silent as she flipped through the pages, and suddenly Gideon realized she was humming to herself. A quiet, cheerful melody that spoke of contentment and satisfaction. Music that wove its way inside him and made desire thrum through him like the steady beat of a drum. "Lily."

She didn't even look up, and she hummed louder as she got to another page, her anticipation clearly building.

As was his own lust for her, responding to the music she was calling. "*Lily.*"

"*This is it.*" Her voice was a whisper under her breath, so sensual the way it slid off her lips, as she crouched and pulled another book off the shelf. He could feel the excited thudding of her heart as she quickly flipped through the pages, and his body began to ache with the need to respond.

"You need to stop singing." He couldn't keep the growl out of his voice, couldn't keep himself from leaning toward her.

Lily's eyes widened at whatever expression she saw on his face. Heated desire simmered in her eyes, and she swallowed. "You look like a predator," she whispered.

Something dark rumbled deep inside him. "Don't look at me as if you like it."

"I can't help it. I do." Her cheeks flushed. "The look on your face right now is why my magic responds to you. You're dangerous, you're deadly, and..." Her hand went to her throat. "This isn't good," she said.

"No." He pulled himself upright and stalked across the

office to the window. He gazed at the shadowed afternoon sky, heavy with rainclouds, and took a deep breath. "Stop humming, and I'll be fine."

"I didn't realize I was."

"I did." He turned to face her, needing to focus on anything other than the flush of her cheeks. "What did you find?"

"Right. I was working." Lily seemed to pull herself together, and she stood up, dropping the books on a card table. Dust flew up, and she waved the cloud aside. "There are two possible locations." She pointed to the map, and after a minute, Gideon grudgingly left the window to stand beside her, so he could see what she was pointing at.

Gideon caught a whiff of her scent, and his groin tightened, but it was simply lust, not magic. Without her singing, it was just his own need for her. He could handle his own desire for her. He took a deep breath and leaned forward, resting one hand on the table as he peered at the map.

"This map dates back to when Ezekiel was young, and this is where he was rumored to live." She pulled another book next to it, and her hair drifted across his arm. It looked so soft and inviting, just begging him to slide his fingers through it—

"This is a current map of Oregon. If you compare these natural landmarks..." Lily pointed to a couple rivers and a mountain. "Then this is where it happened. Southeast Oregon, near where the forest ends and the desert begins." She looked at Gideon. "Not that far from Nate's house. It could even be on his property, depending on how much land he has."

Gideon didn't miss the tremble in her voice, the slight paling of her skin, and his hand went to the back of her neck before he could stop himself, his fingers kneading gently. "We believe Nate had been working for Ezekiel since Ezekiel was initially imprisoned. It would make sense that Nate would set up his home at a place that was significant for Ezekiel."

Lily worked her jaw, her fingers clutching the table so hard her knuckles were white. "So, we need to go there. We need to find exactly where Ezekiel killed his father, and search for the information that will tell us where the actual rite has to occur."

"Yeah, we do." Gideon caught her shoulders and turned

her to face him. "Can you do that? Can you handle going back to Nate's?"

She lifted her chin. "Of course." Her voice was strong, her eyes were determined, but he could feel the terror in her mind, the panic trying to consume her.

"We're blood bonded now," he said. "I'll be able to find you no matter what."

She nodded. "I know." But there was no conviction in her voice.

His grip tightened, and his gaze bore into hers. "No, Lily. You don't understand. *I will find you.*"

She stared at him, her green eyes haunted. "What if they kill you?"

"God, Lily." He slid his other hand behind her neck, so that both were cupping her. "Don't you get it? Letting you get hurt isn't an option for me. It's just not. No one's been able to take me down for the last five hundred years, and I didn't even have you to keep safe. Now? Forget it. Me getting killed simply isn't an option."

She grabbed his forearms, her fingers icy cold. "Your arrogance will get you killed."

"It's not arrogance. It's reality." Gideon pulled her closer and bent his head to press a kiss to her mouth. Red-hot lust raged through him instantly, and he broke the kiss before it could take over. "I swear on my oath I'm going to stay alive long enough to ensure your safety. *I swear it.*"

She didn't take her gaze from his. "Okay, then. We'll go to Nate's."

He felt the conviction in her voice, in her body, and something eased inside him. Something that had been bound for five hundred years. She trusted him. *She trusted him.* She, who had every reason in the world to hate him, to fear him...she trusted him to take her into her worst nightmare and bring her out alive.

Hell, he hoped he didn't let her down.

But before he could think about it, there was a crash from the hallway. They both spun toward the door as a heavy thud sounded on it.

Gideon shoved Lily behind him. "I thought you said no

one could find this place."

He didn't bother to listen to her answer as he held out his forearms and called both axes out with a loud crack, the blades glistening in his hands as he backed Lily into a corner, reaching out with his senses to try to identify their assailants.

The dominant scent he caught was Calydons. Dozens of them.

Plus the three Order members who were hunting Lily.

# Chapter 20

The door of Lily's office flew open, and Gideon leapt in front of the doorway, rearing back to hurl his axes—

Son of a bitch! He aborted his attack at the last second when he realized it wasn't Calydons who had invaded his private time with Lily. An older woman in beige slacks and a beaded sweater hurried into the office. She had the same blond hair as Lily, and the man behind her was tall and lean. His brown slacks and crisply ironed shirt were far too intellectual for a Calydon, and he had Lily's dark green eyes.

Her damn parents, who hated him. Crap. Gideon did not have time for a meet-the-parents moment right now.

"Lily!" the woman shouted, her face radiating with joy and love so intense Gideon actually felt it hit him right in the chest. She looked past Gideon, clearly so excited about Lily that she hadn't even noticed the armed warrior standing in front of her. "We knew you wouldn't be able to stay away from your office."

"Mom! Dad!" Her voice brimming with emotion that leapt under Gideon's skin and slammed into his gut like a red hot fire, Lily tried to lunge past Gideon.

He blocked her. "Don't," he growled. This was not the time for a damned reunion.

"Lily!" Her mom's eyes filled with tears and she started to run across the office. She was less than two yards away when she finally realized Gideon had pinned Lily behind him. Her face blanched, and she stumbled to a stop. Her whole body was shaking, and the scent of her horror blasted through the musty office. *"Gideon."* Revulsion and terror spat at him.

"Yeah, it's me." Yeah, Gideon knew he shouldn't take it personally, but damn, it was hard not to notice the screaming horror emanating from her. Damn Lily for eradicating his emotional shields. He was completely empathic right now, and it pretty much sucked to feel her horror, and to realize it was directed right smack at him. "Nice to see you again," he offered awkwardly, having no damn clue what one was supposed to say to the child of someone he'd murdered. Especially when he was the soul mate and chosen one of the daughter she'd lost for so long.

Seemed a little late for a good impression.

Apparently not buying into the "let's try and put that hell behind us" approach, Lily's dad grabbed his wife and threw her back toward the door, his own face white. "Get the hell away from my daughter, you murdering bastard! I won't—"

"Dad! No! He's on our side." Lily tugged at Gideon's arm to get him to release her, but he tightened his grip on her, searching the door for the Calydons he'd scented. They were coming. He knew it. "Lily." Gideon turned her toward him, ignoring her blustering parents. Screw being pleasant. He had a *sheva* to protect, and that was all that mattered. "Calydons are coming. We have to get out of here."

"What?" Lily stared at him, and then *her* face went white. Hell, was he going to have to carry all three of them out of there? "They must have followed my parents." She whirled toward her parents, and Gideon winced to see her mom scrambling backwards on the floor, away from Gideon, and Lily's dad was trying to pull her to her feet. He was still shouting at Lily to run.

Their revulsion was palpable, and Gideon could feel it pressing against him and tainting the air. He could smell their horror in their sweat and he could feel the frantic thud of their heartbeats as they shrank from the monster who held their daughter.

Gideon clenched his jaw against the need to defend himself. Instead, he shoved Lily behind him and sprinted across the floor to pick up her mother. The woman screamed as he scooped her up, a sound of such brutal terror that he'd never heard before. She started pounding at him, and Lily's dad jumped on Gideon's back and started beating at his head with one of Lily's books. Lily started yelling at her parents, trying to get them to calm down.

"Let's go, Lily," Gideon commanded, his muscles straining with the effort of trying to hold Lily's mom still without hurting her. He grabbed Lily's wrist with his free hand as he felt blood streaming down his face from her mom's fingernails. He sprinted for the door, confident Lily's dad would be on his heels as Gideon took both women with him.

Gideon burst out into the hall and skidded to a stop as the scent of Calydons overwhelmed him. It was coming from all directions. Through the air vents, down the hall, and up through the floor. He could hear the rapid thud of heavy footsteps as they charged them. He heard the rasp of heavy breathing and felt the air pressure hum with their deadly intent.

"Oh, God, I can *feel* them." Lily stopped beside Gideon, her shoulder pressed against his arm. "They're everywhere."

"Back inside," Gideon ordered. He shoved Lily in the office and slammed his shoulder into Lily's dad to throw him back inside. Gideon kicked the door shut, didn't bother with the lock, and sprinted across the room to the window. He deflected Lily's mom as she went for his eye, then he slammed his axe into the thick glass of the picture window. The glass shattered, covering all of them.

Lily's mom paused in her attack, staring at the window. "Dear God," she whispered, her voice stark with horror. "He's going to throw us out."

"For hell's sake, what do you think I am?" Gideon snapped. "I'm trying to *save* you."

Lily's mom screamed like a freaking maniac and raked down his face with her claws again. "Let me go, you bastard!" Lily's mom screamed. "Run, Lily, *run!*"

Jesus. And he was the insane bad guy? Really? He dropped the woman. "Fine. Do whatever the hell you want."

Lily raced over to the window and looked out, catching her breath. "It's six stories, Gideon. It's too far."

Damn, it felt good to have Lily on board with him. Her

calm focus was steadying, and he appreciated the fact that her trust of him was firmly resistant to her parents' attempts to drive a wedge between them.

"Nah, six stories is nothing." He grabbed Lily and planted a hard kiss on her, needing to show her parents exactly what stood between them. He grinned when Lily just smiled at him, as if she understood exactly why he'd done it.

Damn, he could love that woman. She was as tough as any Order member, wasn't she? Calydons beating down her door, her parents on a rampage, a soul mate needing a boost to his pathetic male ego, and yet she was calm enough to smile. No wonder she'd survived all the hell in her life. She got tougher when things fell apart, and let herself fall apart only when she had the luxury. "You are fucking hot, woman."

Lily looked surprised, and then smiled. "You're insane."

"*I'm* the one who's insane? How about your parents?" Gideon whirled around and caught Lily's dad by the throat as the man charged him with a letter opener.

Okay, that was it. He wasn't going to accept any more interfering with his ability to keep Lily safe. Gideon shoved Lily's dad up against the wall, ignoring Lily shouting at him to put her dad down. "Listen, buddy," he snarled. "When you and your wife showed up here, you showed the bad guys how to find your daughter." Rage pulsed through Gideon at the thought of them endangering Lily. "And if you think I'm evil, wait until you see them."

Even as Gideon spoke, the scent of Calydons grew stronger and the footsteps got louder. Shit, he wanted to toss the man out on his ass and let him fend for himself, but he'd felt the love between Lily and her parents when they'd walked in. Yeah, Gideon was a monster, but there wasn't a chance on this green earth that he'd pound another nail into Lily's heart if he could help it. He was saving the whole damn family if he could.

"So, you have two choices," Gideon continued, spending way too much damn time talking when he should be vacating. "Either stop fighting me and let me save all of you, or I'm leaving you and your wife behind and I'm saving only your daughter. Make the choice," he snapped. "And make it right fucking now."

"Listen to Gideon," Lily urged her father. "We have

about five seconds. I'm going with him."

Her dad said nothing, his gaze going frantically between Lily and Gideon. Lily's mother had gone still, no longer trying to gouge his eyes out, but she wasn't exactly singing his praises either.

Fuck it. "We're out of here." Gideon grabbed Lily and tucked her against his hip. She threw her legs around his waist and her arms around his neck, total commitment to Gideon. Yeah, see? He wasn't that bad, not if Lily was willing to trust him.

"Lily!" her mom gasped in apparent horror at Lily's siding with Gideon.

Yeah, whatever. Gideon was so done here.

The door flew open and Calydons began to pour into the room, weapons out, their energy raising the temperature of the room almost instantly. Gideon barreled for the window with Lily in his arms.

Lily's mom's hand went to her chest as she faced them. "Dear *God*."

"Go get her, Gideon," Lily ordered. "Please!"

Shit. He couldn't say no to her. He simply couldn't.

Gideon raced back toward her parents and swept Lily's mom up against him as Lily's dad leapt on Gideon's back, nearly choking him. Then Gideon charged for the window, holding his cargo securely, but his grip was tightest on Lily. He dropped his head to clear the frame, and then flew out through the air.

Lily's mom screamed. Lily's dad swore and drew blood from Gideon, he was gripping so tightly. Lily, his courageous, confident, collected Lily, simply held onto him. She kept her gaze fixed on Gideon's face, her body pressed up against him. He concentrated on the warmth of her body, using Lily as his anchor as he fought to control their fall, trying to balance the three weights clinging so awkwardly to him. "Wrap your legs around my waist," he shouted at her dad. "I need to be the one to take the impact."

He tangled his legs around Gideon's.

"No!" Gideon shouted. "My waist." He kicked his legs free as the ground rushed up at them. Shit. His balance was off. "Everyone stop struggling for one goddamn second," he shouted.

For a split second, Lily's parents froze at his command,

and Gideon was able to straighten them out so his feet were hitting first. He smacked the ground hard and he staggered under the impact, fighting to keep his unbalanced, flailing load from slamming into the ground at the sudden stop. He lost his balance and they all tumbled. Lily's parents went flying, and Gideon cradled Lily against his chest, using his arms to block her body from the ground as he rolled over her.

He rebounded to his feet instantly, Lily still tight against him. Her parents were groaning, her dad was bleeding from his forehead, and Lily's mom was crying. But they were already climbing to their feet. A successful landing. Not so bad for a psychopathic bad guy, right?

"Mom!" Lily struggled out of Gideon's grasp and raced over to her parents. They were immediately hugging and crying, a tight trio of emotion and love into which Gideon was most definitely not invited.

Something pinged inside Gideon as he watched the tears flow, as the three held each other so tightly it looked as if they'd break. A sudden loneliness spread over him, a loneliness that burned deep and black. A yearning so strong he could barely keep himself from kneeling beside them and shoving his way into their embrace, to feel tears shed for him—

There was a loud crack from above, and he jerked his gaze upward, and then swore when he realized their pursuers had taken the same path he had.

The sky was raining Calydons.

⚜ ⚜ ⚜

Ana sat on the balcony of the coliseum, her body shaking and sweat dripping down her back. Frank was stretched out on the throne, his feet propped up while he studied her. "Not having success shaking the dark illusions?"

"No." She hugged her knees to her chest, exhausted. She'd called forth illusion after illusion since she'd arrived, and every one of them had been some version of Elijah being tortured to death. It had gotten to the point where his screams were reverberating in her mind even between illusions, as if he were truly alive and being tortured. She pressed her hands to her temples, trying to drown out his screams even now.

Frank cocked his head. "Perhaps this is because you have finally come into your own. Perhaps the happy illusions are a thing of the past."

"I'm not like that."

"No?" The heels of Frank's dress shoes scraped on the clay as he pulled his feet down from the ledge and set them in front of him. "You certainly seem to be like that. All I've heard are screams since I left you here. Doesn't sound like butterflies and puppies to me."

She leaned back, resting her head against the crumbling wall. "I'll get there."

"Where? To happy illusions? What power lies in offering cheerful emotions, Ana? None." Frank propped his elbows on his knees, leaning forward, his body language eager. "You're so powerful. You have a gift, Ana, and you should be embracing it, not suffering for it." He waved his arm. "This place is your playground. Think of the damage you could cause if you learn to control your darkness and use it as a targeted weapon."

Ana wearily lifted her head to look at him, her eyes narrowing. "Is that why you came to get me? To make me your protégé?"

"It's what your father wanted for you."

"Is it?" Her parents had been dark Illusionists, but they were good people. She couldn't imagine her dad would have wanted her to use her talents to murder. "Why me? Why not Grace?"

"Because you're more powerful, of course." He studied her, his icy blue eyes cold in his face. "I will need your help when I free Ezekiel, Ana. I need you by my side."

Her mind cleared as his words registered. Here it was. The information she'd been looking for. Anticipation raced through her, galvanizing her with fresh energy. "What are you talking about?"

Frank stood up and paced to the railing, leaning over to stare into the pit. "I've spent my life honing my Illusionist skills, using them to control Calydons. I'm very good at it." He turned his head to look at her. "I forced Elijah to murder his best friend. To break through that bond was immensely difficult, and yet I did it."

"Congratulations." She managed to keep the sarcasm out of her voice, her heart racing. *Keep talking. Tell me what I need to know.*

"Ezekiel is a Calydon, the founder of the race, as you know. He's the most powerful one who ever existed, except, of course, for his brother Caleb and their descendants. Ezekiel is pure evil, he's pure domination. If I can get him to work for me, I can do anything I want." He smiled. "I will have it all."

Oh...she understood now. "But you fear you can't control him by yourself. You need me to help you generate illusions strong enough to overpower him."

Frank nodded. "Even I acknowledge it would be dangerous for Ezekiel to be freed on his own terms. I was using Nate to help collect the weapons, but as soon as I was ready for the rite, I would have killed him anyway, because he believed Ezekiel should be truly free. I will free Ezekiel, of course, but I need to ensure I can control him. I need your help."

"If I don't help you?"

Frank looked at her. "If you don't help me, then Elijah dies."

Ana tensed. "What? He's already dead. I saw Nate—"

"Illusions, Ana. You, of anyone, should know not to trust what you see. Elijah is my backup plan, so I couldn't very well let him die, could I? Nate almost blew it by killing him, but I managed to bring him back."

Ana stopped listening to Frank, her lungs so tight she couldn't breathe. Elijah was alive? *Elijah! Can you hear me?*

There was nothing but the faint echo of his screams, and the hair on her neck suddenly stood straight up. "You're torturing him right now." She lurched to her feet, bile churning in her stomach. "He's really screaming."

"He'll keep screaming until Ezekiel is freed and in our control." Frank's eyes flashed. "By tomorrow at sunset, you need to have control over your illusions. I want you to be able to target one person at a time and to be able to control their emotions, the way I can. I'll show you how to do it, and then you'll practice until you've got it." He stood up. "I have things I need to prepare for the ritual. Your friend Lily, for one. Do you have any idea where she might be? I thought she was at the mansion, but the reports I'm getting indicate otherwise."

"Is Elijah here? Is he nearby?" Ana whirled around, searching the darkest shadows of the coliseum, as if they could be hiding a massive Calydon warrior.

"Ana!" Frank grabbed her wrist and spun her to face him. "Trust me when I say your only chance to save him is to help me. You'll never find him. Practice and get it right. You have one day, and if you fail me, Elijah is dead." His eyes glittered. "And I'll make sure he truly dies by your hand this time."

She stared at him, her stomach turning to lead at the threat in his eyes. "You weren't really friends with my father, were you?"

"I was his best friend for years. I am your godfather." Frank's eyes hardened. "Then he found out about my plans for Ezekiel, and my plans to use you, and he tried to stop me. He said I was taking things too far. So, I killed him. And your mother."

Ana's legs started to shake. "That was you? You murdered them?" She'd been in the woods that night, and she'd heard enough of the battle to know that someone had come for her, and her parents were protecting her. They'd died trying to keep her safe, just like Elijah had, and too many others. And how had she repaid her parents sacrifice? By turning herself over to the very man they'd died to protect her from. *Shit, I'm so sorry.*

"It was me." Frank leaned into her space and caught a lock of her hair. "Don't worry, Ana. You have nothing to fear from me. I value your talent, and I still regret that your parents had to die. I honor their death by raising their daughter to the highest levels. You're like me, Ana. I was never gifted with dark illusions, and my family thought I was useless because of it."

She stared at him. "So, we're the same because I was born to do happy ones?" Seriously? Was he that crazy to think they were similar?

"Yes." Anger flickered in Frank's face. "My father and brothers were Calydons. They were disgusted by the fact they'd spawned a male who wasn't a Calydon." He shoved up his sleeve and shoved his arm into her face. There were deep grooves in his forearms, like someone had used him for carving practice. "This is what they did to me and to countless others. They were sadistic bastards, like all Calydons, and they deserved to die."

Ana lifted her chin. "You're wrong. All Calydons aren't evil—"

"They are!" Frank's face twisted in insane fury. "They killed Mary! Do you understand that? My dear sweet Mary, the only one in the entire fucking world who realized that I wasn't a piece of shit. My father came home one night and found her with me and he killed her in a rage. My brothers came home and had to kill my father to stop him, and they blamed me! Me! For the fact my bastard father went insane!" He strode across the balcony and leaned over the edge, presiding over the arena below. "I had no abilities to defeat them back then. I didn't understand my power, so I came here and practiced."

Ana knew then what he was saying. "You came here with my parents. My father taught you how to tap into your illusions, even though they were different from typical dark illusions." Dear God, her father never would have helped a man like Frank if he'd known what he was like. Yes, her parents and Grace had been cursed with dark illusions, but they had been good people. Wonderful people. Loving parents.

"Yes. Your father showed me that the ability to manufacture emotions in people with illusions is actually very powerful." Frank was staring down into the pit, a grim smile on his face, as if he were watching some Calydon shrivel and die beneath his power. "I went back and murdered my brothers. Every one of them. I made them pay for being who they were."

Ana pressed her hand to her mouth as bile churned in her belly at the sadistic pleasure in Frank's voice. "So, why now? Why all these others?"

He spun back to her, his eyes glazing with frenzied power. "Do you really need to ask, Ana? All Calydons have a dark side. Eventually each one will go rogue and murder innocents. Even the precious Order has a standing order to murder the mate of other Order members. What kind of heroes murder innocent women?"

Ana hesitated, realizing that his argument made sense, in a perverse sort of way. The Order, and Calydons in general, weren't exactly angels in disguise. The Order had been ready to murder Lily in cold blood simply on the chance that it might slow Frank down. But how could Ana condemn them all, when she bore the brands of a man who'd given his life to save her? It was more complicated than how Frank saw it, even though there was an element of truth to his words. "They aren't all evil—"

"Aren't they?" He strode back over to her. "You know they are, Ana. No one can stop them, especially the Order. I can take them out one by one, but there are too many for me." He grinned. "But Ezekiel is more powerful than all of them. He is the ticket to destroying the monsters that his own insanity spawned."

Oh, dear God. Frank was going to free Ezekiel so he could wipe out the entire Calydon race? "You can't control him like that," she said. "He's too powerful—"

"No, I can't control him, but together, we can handle him." Frank's finger touched her cheek, and Ana recoiled sharply.

Yes, she understood the horror Frank had faced having his father murder his true love, and his brothers killing his father. Yes, it was awful, and she got that, and she wasn't blind to the failings of the Order and the darkness of Calydons in general. But Frank was wrong! The answer wasn't to unleash the worst evil in the history of the world to unilaterally wipe out an entire race. "I won't help you—"

"You will, and your parents will be so proud of you." Frank smiled, his eyes softening with genuine pleasure and love that was so perverse coming from a man talking about mass murder. "They will be smiling from the Afterlife to see you take over the legacy they rejected. It is how it should be, my dear."

He bent his head, as if to kiss her, and Ana stiffened and pulled back. Anger flickered in his eyes. "As you wish, Ana. Tomorrow night will come soon enough." He turned toward the pit and waved his hand. A Calydon stepped out from one of the tunnels, his shoulders broad and his head thrown back. He fixed a glittering stare on Frank, his face cold and impassive.

His white blond hair looked so much like Lily's, and she thought of her friend. *I hope you're someplace safe, Lily. You were so right about Frank. I don't know if I can stop him.*

"This is your victim," Frank said. "You will practice on him until you can control his actions with your illusions. I want you able to make him fall to the earth sobbing, because you have generated such sorrow inside him. I want you to make him dance and sing, because you have generated such happiness in him." He snapped his fingers and two more Calydons stepped out.

Both of these men were scarred, and one was limping. They looked beaten and battered. Weak. Vulnerable. "These are your foils. Any stray illusion will affect them, because they are too weak to fight. I want to see your victim bow to your illusions, while the other two weaklings remain unaffected." He looked at Ana, challenge glittering in his eyes. "One day, Ana. That's all you have. Then Elijah dies."

She knew she had no choice. She had to buy time for herself. Was Elijah really alive? She had to find out. She had to find him. The only way to do that was to play Frank's game. Ana clenched her fists against the urge to berate him for his insanity. "I'll do it."

"I knew you would." Frank turned away and began to explain how to do what he wanted, but Ana barely listened to him.

She was thinking about what he'd said. *Elijah was alive.*

She caught Frank watching her, and something about his expression made her stiffen. What if he was lying? Frank was all about illusions. Maybe she wasn't hearing Elijah scream at all. Maybe Frank was making her think she was. Maybe the truth wasn't a truth at all.

Even the men below, her victims, might not even really be there.

It could all be lies.

Or Elijah could be the one down in that pit. He could be her blond victim, waiting for her in the bowels of the earth, disguised as a stranger. She stared down into the pit and tried to summon her ability to detect illusions, but she couldn't access it. She looked at Frank. "What did you do?"

"You really think I would allow you to shield yourself against illusions while you're here?" He waved around the cavern. "This is my world, Ana, and you're a part of it. Join me. There's no other option." He smiled. "And trust me, when you finally learn to embrace your dark side, you will understand what it's like to truly be alive."

Ana ignored him, stepping forward to peer into the pit. *Elijah? Is that you?*

And then she heard it. *Ana.* A faint, faint echo of her name in her mind. Elijah's voice. So weak, so far in the distance, and she knew, with absolute certainty that he was alive, and in unbearable pain. Tears filled her eyes, and her chest screamed with agony for his suffering.

And then there was a humming in the pit and the wind began to rise, and she knew one of her illusions was starting to rise, brought on by her stress about Elijah's fate.

"That's it." Frank clapped her shoulder and faced her toward the pit. "Here is your first lesson in learning to control it."

She spun toward the pit, her fists clenched. *I will find you, Elijah.*

Then the illusion burst free, and all her attention was focused on trying to control it.

For now.

The minute Frank was gone, Ana was going to find the warrior who'd offered his life for hers.

# Chapter 21

"Lily!" Gideon shouted as he charged over to the huddled trio of Lily and her parents, his pulse skyrocketing. Shit. There were too many coming. They'd never make it on foot. "Where's your parents' car?"

She jerked her gaze up to the sky, saw the Calydons falling through the air toward them and leapt to her feet. "Gideon—"

"Go," he ordered her. "I'll stall them."

Her eyes widened. "Without you?"

Lily's parents looked up and then they were instantly in motion. Her dad grabbed Lily's arm and started dragging her toward a Volkswagen Golf parked down the street.

"Go," Gideon commanded. "Now!"

Lily hesitated for a long moment, her instincts telling her not to abandon him. "But—"

"I can fight better if you're safe. Go!" He pushed her away, and she finally turned and ran toward the car with her parents.

Gideon turned to face the onslaught, rage feeding his strength. He hurled his axes, cutting down the first Calydons before they even hit the earth. He called back his weapons and hurled them again, but more Calydons were falling. Too fast for him to keep up. He threw himself between the Calydons and Lily, using his body as a shield to prevent her pursuers from catching up to Lily and her parents, striking true with each blow, as Calydon after Calydon fell to his axe.

One got past him and Gideon lunged for him, hurling his blade as the Calydon reached for Lily's hair as it streamed out behind her. "Get the hell off her!" The blade sank deep into her assailant's kidney and the Calydon hit the dirt.

Then a brutal pain exploded in Gideon's back and he staggered. A Calydon sprinted past him and grabbed Lily's wrist, knocking her to the ground. Fury ripped through Gideon and he threw himself back onto his feet and hurled his axe. The Calydon dropped as Gideon's blade sliced through his neck, then Lily's parents pulled her to her feet and the three of them rushed toward the car.

*You need my music. Let me give you my music.* Lily glanced back at him as she ran.

Screw that. He wasn't risking that again. *No. Just get the hell out of here.*

Another burst of pain knocked Gideon to his knees and he jerked around, kicking aside a spiked hammer on its way to his head. He slammed his foot into his assailant's gut and then sank his blade into his throat the instant his axe returned to his hand.

Gideon rolled to his knees and hurled both axes, taking out two more Calydons closing fast on Lily. But there were dozens streaming past Gideon, taking advantage of the fact he'd stopped to fight. There were too many for Gideon to stop.

Crap. They had to run. It was their only chance.

With a roar, Gideon leapt to his feet and charged through the throngs in a dead heat to reach Lily first. He dug harder, his legs pistoning on the cement as he ran, gaining ground on her. Lily looked back, and her eyes widened with horror as she saw the throng closing in on her, then her gaze met Gideon's. *Behind you, Gideon!*

Gideon put on a burst of speed, and a sword whizzed by his head, the blade nicking his ear. He tucked his weapons and ran, not bothering to try to take down the other Calydons. He knew Lily's only chance was for him to make it to her first and outrun them. Her parents were screaming as her dad fumbled to unlock the car, the shadows growing darker as the mob closed in on them.

Gideon reached the front of the throng and knew he

was going to get to her before the others did. Unless they were Runners, he'd be able to outrun them. He *had* to outrun them. There was no other option.

Then he felt a shift in the focus of the Calydons closest to him. They turned their attention from Lily and directed it toward him. They were going to try to detain him so the others could get to Lily.

"Oh, *hell*." Gideon got his axe up just in time to block the sudden blow from his left, and then suddenly all the Calydons near him attacked, blades flying fast and hard, dozens of them, teaming up, slashing, stabbing, chopping. He was surrounded, and he threw his axe straight up as a Flier came hurtling down from above at him. The assault was relentless, like a frenzied mob, and he fought desperately. *Lily!*

There was no reply, and anger roared through him. Adrenaline kicked into overload and Gideon went on a rampage, cutting down everyone he could reach. But more kept coming.

Then suddenly there was a shout he recognized as belonging to Gabe, one of his Order members, and one of the Calydons who Quinn had said was on his way to kill Lily. But Gabe was Order, and Gideon sure as hell hoped that would take priority. *What side are you on, Gabe?*

*Yours. Quinn made you and Lily sound too valuable. Zach and Ryland are here, too. We're coming in from the outside, but the next time you have a party, you really ought to screen your guest list better.*

Gideon grinned and fought with renewed strength, taking down warriors as he felt their attention shift outward, to the threats coming at them from his team.

It took twenty minutes before the four of them were the only ones left standing. Bodies were everywhere. Blood streaming down the street, even as the bodies began to disappear, the extremely old ones vanishing almost instantly. The young ones would take weeks to be reclaimed by the earth.

All the Order members were bleeding badly, and Ryland had a deep slice across his throat that he was pressing his palm against to stem the flow of blood.

Sirens began to wail, and Gideon jerked his head around. The street was empty. All pedestrians had fled... Even

Lily's parents' car was gone. Hope sprung in his chest. Had they made it? *Lily? Are you safe?*

Silence.

Gideon's gut began to turn. *Lily. Talk to me.* He reached out over their connection, and felt a pulse from her. She was alive, but unable to respond. Which had to mean she was unconscious.

They'd gotten her.

Bile churned in Gideon's stomach, but he shoved it aside, ruthlessly crushing his emotions and retreating into the singular focus of a warrior. He lifted his face to the sky and opened his mind to her, reaching out to determine which direction she'd gone.

Sirens were growing louder, and his team was already piling up bodies, moving so fast that a human would barely be able to discern their movements.

But Gideon didn't move. He turned south, searching. His mind was racing and his heart was pumping, but he had to pull his shit together. He took a deep breath, forcing himself to calm so he could sense Lily's vibration and figure out where she was.

He heard the hiss as Zach knelt beside the pile of bodies and called in the wind, oxygen, and heat. Gideon glanced over as Zach laid his mouth on the shoulder of the body on top of the pile. For a moment, nothing happened, then the shoulder of the dead Calydon turned black, smoke began to spiral, then the body exploded in a flash of flames. Gideon and the others stood back, but Zach remained in the fire, letting the flames consume him as he fed the fire with the very oxygen that sustained him, until the entire stack of bodies was burning with a flame so hot it was as white as pure snow.

The flames shot so high Gideon couldn't see the top, even with his enhanced eyesight, and then the flames exploded, feeding on the blood strewn over the pavement. Gideon checked his location to make sure he was standing on clean pavement and shielded his eyes against the explosive white glow.

Then the fire vanished.

Gideon dropped his arm and the pavement was clean, devoid of any sign of the attack. The fire had consumed the blood until there was nothing left. Zach was pale and shuddering as Gabe helped him to his feet.

The police cars spun around the corner, lights flashing.

Gideon whirled away and headed down the street, letting his mind soften, thinking only of Lily, her scent, her energy, and her aura. He brought her essence into his soul, until his blood began to hum with her energy, until her blood came alive within him.

Suddenly he felt her presence.

Gideon turned to the southeast, his entire being thudding with the power of his connection to her. She'd headed toward the desert, and she was moving fast. He'd never catch her on foot.

"We're all in separate cars." Ryland was right behind him. "We'll go after her."

"No." Gideon's pulse was racing, and he was so strung out, it was all he could do to focus, to be strategic. "You need to head to Nate's place and find the marker that will tell us where the ritual is occurring."

Gideon quickly explained the situation, keeping his mind focused on Lily, on keeping that link active. "I have no idea what it is, and I never got a chance to ask Lily what form she thought the information would be in. Hell, for all I know, it's more shit she'll have to translate." He cursed as he felt her continue to get even further away from him. "I gotta go. You guys good?"

Ryland tossed Gideon his keys. "Go get the girl and meet us at Nate's so she can seal the deal. We'll be in touch."

Gideon snatched the keys out of mid-air and sprinted for the black Explorer parked down the street, his whole body vibrating with Lily's energy. He held his focus tight as he leapt into the truck, jammed the keys in the ignition and peeled out. *I'm coming, Lily.* He shoved the thought at her as hard as he could, hard enough to penetrate her mind, even though she was unconscious. *I swear to you, I'm on my way.*

Empty words, if he was too late.

⚅ ⚅ ⚅

Lily jerked back to consciousness as her head smacked

into something hard. She moaned, cringing against the pain as hands grabbed her and roughly shoved her to the side. She tried to catch herself, and felt the deep bite of cords around her wrists and ankles as she tried to move. Dear God. She was bound, just like before. "No!" She screamed and her eyes snapped open in horror.

She was in the back seat of an SUV, and three huge Calydons were in the truck with her. Two were in the front, and the third was in the back with her. Lily fought to sit up, pressing herself back against the door, her mind screaming in denial. It couldn't be happening again. Not again. Not again. *Not again.*

The SUV lurched as the driver floored it and skidded around a corner. The momentum threw her across the seat and she crashed into the Calydon sitting beside her. His body was hard and powerful, and nausea churned through her at the contact.

He shoved her away from him, his palm bracing against her chest as he pinned her against the opposite door. "Call Frank."

He was pressing so hard she couldn't breathe. She was trapped again. At their mercy. She couldn't do it. She couldn't go through this again. It couldn't be happening again.

"Call Frank," he ordered again.

Frank. Dear God, *Frank.* He knew she was Satinka, which meant these men would too. Would they be able to resist her? Would they even try? Or were they intending to steal from her that which kept her alive?

Frantically, she checked them out, trying to ascertain how much immediate danger she was in, trying to focus her mind away from the debilitating panic and into the sanity of self-preservation. Her captors were all wearing black, with heavy boots and dark leather pants. Thick, rugged leather, like it was designed to protect them if they went skidding across concrete. They were not of a more delicate persona like the Runner who'd chased her down outside Nate's. These were thugs, males hired because they were willing to do the ugly stuff.

The driver hit a couple buttons, and then a voice echoed through the truck. "You got her?"

A chill crawled over Lily at the gravelly sound of Frank's

voice, thin and flat, almost disembodied, yet so full of evil that she felt it prickling at her arms. She shuddered, trying to shake off the cloying darkness.

"Yeah." The Calydon driving the truck glanced in the rearview mirror at her, his eyes black, little bottomless pits of doom. "We got her."

"Let me speak with her."

The Calydon holding Lily against the door, dug his fingers into her flesh, bruising her. "Talk."

She coughed as his fingers squeezed off her air, her mind spinning as she tried to think of what to say. Frank didn't know she'd translated the knife, or that she'd had time to study it. Maybe she could work it to her advantage if he thought she was clueless. Anything to buy time, to make him underestimate her. "What do you want? Why are you after me?"

"Ahh...Lily." Frank's voice drifted through the car. "I'm so glad to hear your voice."

She could feel the sweat beading on her forehead, and her palms were clammy. "Why? What do you want from me?"

"To sacrifice you, of course."

Sacrifice? Was that what he called draining her dry for her magic? "For what?"

"I have plans, my dear. You are my ticket. You and Nate's stone."

She closed her eyes. "Do you have it?" Lily wasn't sure how much to reveal she knew, but couldn't keep herself from asking, "Is Ana with you?"

"Yes, she sought me out. My darling Ana thrives under my tutelage even as I speak."

Lily's head began to ache. *Oh, Ana, what have you gotten yourself into?* "Is she okay?"

"She's making me proud." There was no hiding the smugness in his voice, and Lily grimaced.

Anything Ana could be doing to make Frank happy was not a good thing.

"I assume you know how to read ancient scripts?" he asked.

She glanced at the Calydon in the back with her. He was watching her like a predator scenting his prey, and she shrank back against the door. "Well, some of them..."

"Excellent. I'll be waiting for you."

"Wait!" she interrupted.

There was a pause. "What?" There was a flicker of irritation in his voice.

"You want to free Ezekiel, don't you? Is that what you're doing?"

There was a longer pause. "Why do you ask?"

"I won't help you do it. You'll never be able to harvest my magic. Find someone else. Don't waste your time with me." A last ditch effort, but it was all she could think of. It wasn't as if she had any leverage.

There was a murmur of amusement. "Oh, Lily. I look forward to the challenge you present. For your information, I figured out the earth component to Satinka magic, so I'll make sure you have plenty of Mother Nature at your disposal."

Of course he would have figured that out since the failed attempt to harvest her magic at Nate's. If he had earth and a Calydon, it would be practically impossible for Lily not to respond. Her magic wouldn't be that powerful, but Frank could force it out of her on some level.

Her mind flicked back to those horrifying five days when she was seventeen, to that feeling of having her magic stripped from her, of being helpless to stop it, of seeing those males coming at her, with that gleam in their eyes—

"Not only will you help me free Ezekiel," Frank interrupted, jerking her back to the present, "but you'll also help me murder a young Calydon named Drew who looks almost exactly like your dead brother."

Lily's stomach turned. "Did you kill Trig?" she whispered. "Was it you?"

There was another chuckle that made her shiver. "Did it ever occur to you that you might have killed him yourself, Lily?"

"Me?" she echoed, unable to stop the rise of horror at his question, as he breathed life into the fear that she'd been carrying for so long.

"You. You played with your magic, Satinka, and you interfered in an ancient Calydon rite. Did you really think you could do that and not kill him?"

Her stomach lurched, her body seizing as her deepest fear slammed into her. "No," she protested in a strangled voice. "I didn't kill him."

"Didn't you?"

Lily clenched her fists, fighting so hard not to lose control. She scrunched her eyes shut, but she could still hear Frank chuckling. It couldn't be true that she'd killed her brother. It couldn't. Could it? Memories of that night started to crash back into her mind, and she winced, trying to keep them at bay, unable to cope with remembering. Not right now. "How do you know about me?"

"I've been studying Calydons far longer than you have, my dear. And everywhere I turned, there you were. So interesting when you showed up at Nate's that day. So very interesting. Did you ever wonder how you got his name?"

She blinked, trying to understand what Frank was saying. "You set that up?"

"You think major plans such as mine occur overnight? It takes decades of planning."

Lily went cold at the thought that he'd been manipulating her for years, that he'd been stalking her for so long. "Gideon will stop you. The Order knows about you."

"The Order is being taken care of. As powerful as they are, they're no match for the number of warriors I have under my control right now. Even as we speak, the Order is falling."

"You'll never defeat them." Lily immediately reached for Gideon over their bond. *Gideon? Can you hear me?*

Silence. Nothing but an empty void where Gideon's presence should be. Bitter loss, overwhelming loneliness, and utter desolation assaulted her. *Please, Gideon, don't be dead.*

"How many of you are in the car?" Frank asked.

"Three of us," the driver said.

"One to drive, two to rape her. It's the ultimate psychological torture. Should work well on her."

Lily sucked in her breath, and her body went rigid. The Calydon in the front passenger seat jerked his head back to look at her. There was something in his eyes...regret? Reluctance? Anticipation? Cold fingers of fear beat at her, and panic fought to take over her mind.

"I expect Lily to be thoroughly beaten down by the time she arrives here," Frank said. "Do whatever you want to her. My only stipulation is that her mind is working fine because I will need her to translate the stone and do the rite when she gets here. Other than that, break her will."

The Calydon in the passenger seat ground his jaw. "What if she agrees to help?" he asked. "Then can we leave her alone?"

There was a pause. "Lily? Do you agree to help me?"

The Calydon in the front seat gave her a hard look, and she could feel him willing for her to agree. She looked at the one sitting next to her, and she tensed at the sight of his dark eyes fastened on her. They were brimming with lust, violence and anger. Not rogue. Perfectly sane, yet brutal.

The Calydon in the front passenger seat reached back and touched her shoulder. He gave her an emphatic nod.

Lily swallowed hard and knew she had no choice. Keeping her eyes fastened on his face, she nodded, knowing she was lying. Anything to buy her time. "I agree. I'll help."

Some of the tension left his shoulders.

"You lie," Frank said, sounding disgusted. "Do you really think I'm that naïve? I know you, Lily, and I know you don't give in. Ever."

"No, I survive," she retorted, furious that this psychopath thought he knew her so well. "I know when to fight and when to give in. I'm giving in. You win, you bastard."

"She lies," Frank said to her captors. "I need her so beaten down that she can't resist me by the time she gets here. You three have approximately eight hours until you arrive. Get on it."

Then there was a click, and he was gone.

The Calydon in the front dropped his head back against the headrest and closed his eyes. She saw his hand flex, and she prayed he was about to call out his weapon to protect her and not slay her. She hoped that his Calydon instincts to protect an innocent were overriding whatever hold Frank had over him.

Lily shifted, testing the bonds that held her wrists, her heart thudding. If he moved in defense of her, she had to be ready. He looked over at her, then inclined his head slightly.

She tensed, ready to move.

There was a loud crack, black light flashed above his arm, and a dagger appeared in his hand. She lunged for the door—

The Calydon in the back seat grabbed her and hauled her into his lap as the driver slammed a mace into the chest of the Calydon in the passenger seat. Lily screamed as his body convulsed. Blood splattered over the windshield and the dash, and then he slumped back against the seat.

She covered her mouth as the driver yanked his mace out of the Calydon's chest, and then the dead Calydon shimmered and disappeared, his splattered blood vanishing with him, leaving no trace behind. Dead. A very old Calydon, for him to have vanished so quickly after death. Was that why he'd been able to fight off Frank's influence?

The driver glanced in his rearview mirror at Lily. "And then there were two."

There was no reluctance in his eyes. He wasn't rogue, but his instinct to protect innocents was gone. Frank had done something to them. Somehow, he'd completely overridden the most basic tenet of what defined a Calydon: to protect innocents.

The warrior in the back with her grabbed her ankles and ripped the binding holding her feet together. His eyes were dark, burning with his intent to destroy her.

She knew in that instant that she'd never survive the next eight hours with them. Even if she lived, she would be dead. Forever. She didn't have enough left to survive it again.

He yanked at her jeans and they came easily over her hips as he jerked them down to her ankles. Panic screamed through her mind, but she forced herself not to move, to wait. Like she'd done in the basement. *One chance, Lily. You'll have one chance.* She clenched her fists, willing her trembling body not to move. Not yet.

"What are you waiting for? Start already," the driver ordered.

"She's not struggling. I can't hit her if she doesn't fight."

She jerked her gaze to his face at the revealing comment. He wasn't totally lost to Frank's influence. Not totally. Something inside was resisting what he had to do, even as his conscious mind was telling him to rape her.

"Oh, she'll struggle. They always do. Free her. Make her feel like she has a chance."

The Calydon in back grabbed the cords binding her wrist and ripped them, freeing her arms. "Fight me."

Lily stopped resisting the tears and let them fall, forcing him to see her as the innocent he was born to protect.

He glanced at her face and his eyes darkened. "Hell. She's crying."

"For hell's sake. I'll do it." The driver slammed on the brakes, and Lily rolled off the seat onto the floor.

She scrambled back up as the predatory instincts of the male in back with her rose to the surface. "Fuck that. I get her first."

Lily saw the moment his natural need to protect lost the battle. His shoulders flexed and his jaw hardened as he committed to what Frank wanted him to do. Lust rose in his eyes, and the front of his jeans swelled in anticipation. She fought back nausea, her body shaking as he released her to free himself from his pants.

The Calydon in the front seat gave a grunt of satisfaction as he kicked the truck into drive again. The instant her assailant's hand went to his zipper, Lily slammed her feet into his crotch and shoved off him, grabbing for the door handle. She got it open, then he grabbed her feet and hauled her back across the seat.

"No!" She threw up her hand, and suddenly there was a loud crack and Gideon's axe appeared in her hand.

For a split second, they both stared at the axe in shock, then she tightened her grip around it and swung as hard as she could. The blade slammed into the side of his neck with a sickening thud, disappearing several inches into his flesh. He screamed, yanked the axe out of his neck, and slammed it at her chest as blood poured down his shoulder.

But the axe diverted itself and harmlessly hit the seat next to her shoulder. She held up her hand and the axe flew out of his hand and slammed into hers. "Calydon weapons don't work for other Calydons," she snapped as she drove the spiked handle straight into his heart.

He screamed and his hands went to his chest, trying to pull the axe out. The driver was shouting, and Lily planted a foot on the end of the axe and shoved as hard as she could, pushing the axe deeper and thrusting herself out the open door in the same movement.

She tumbled out of the moving vehicle, hitting her head on the pavement so hard her teeth shook and she felt like her skull had split open. She skidded across the pavement, the abrasive ground shredding her skin like sandpaper. The tires screeched as the truck careened to a stop, then the driver jumped out of the car and raced toward her.

Lily pulled herself up on her knees, her feet slipping on the asphalt as she tried to scramble to her feet. The ground dipped and wove, and she stumbled, trying to fight the dizziness.

Suddenly there was an outraged roar and a loud crack that shuddered through her body. Metal flashed by her head and then an axe slammed into the approaching Calydon. His death screams rattled through her, and she covered her head as blood spewed from his chest and his body crashed to the ground. The axe ripped from his flesh and whizzed past her again. Everything blurred, and darkness fluttered at the edges of her vision.

"Lily!"

The sound of Gideon's shout brought her head up. "Gideon?" She turned, her mind numb with disbelief as he ran toward her, confusion swimming through her pounding head. "You're alive?" She blinked, trying to clear the black spots out of her vision. "I thought—"

Gideon fell to his knees beside her and hauled her against him, holding her so tight she couldn't breathe. "Jesus, Lily. I'm so fucking sorry."

His muscles were hard, the heat from his body wrapping around her, his scent so familiar...safe. She was *safe*. She stopped fighting the dizziness and slumped against him, letting the darkness take over.

# Chapter 22

Gideon cradled Lily as she passed out, her body so small and fragile as she tumbled trustingly in his arms. He scooped her up, breathing in the feel of her body against him. She was alive. He'd made it in time. He'd found her—

He suddenly noticed her jeans around her ankles. "Son of a bitch," he whispered as raw horror raced through him. He'd been too late. His hands shaking, he shifted her position and pulled her jeans back over her hips. There was a fresh bruise on her inner thigh. "Jesus." Self-loathing iced through him, like the blackest poison.

Agony ripped through his chest, and he laid his palm over the bruise, as if he could erase it and make everything go away. As if a desperate prayer could change what had happened. He was her protector. He'd sworn to keep her safe. His duty was to be that buffer against anything that could cause her harm, and instead, her worst nightmare had come to life and claimed her. God! He was a bastard! How could he have let this happen to her? He'd made her a promise and he'd broken it.

He'd betrayed her on levels beyond comprehension.

Gideon's jaw tightened as he fastened her jeans, his hands trembling violently as he tugged the zipper closed, images whirling through his mind about what had happened in that truck. He stood up, cradling Lily to his chest, then threw back his head and released a cry of such anguish, such loss, such self-hatred. Five hundred years of suppression and guilt burst out of him, a twisted evil that he'd been holding inside for so long. His torment shook the trees around them, shriveled the leaves, and wrapped around his heart like a black vice of hate. He screamed again.

And again.

And again.

*And again.*

Clutching Lily against him, Gideon stood on that abandoned road, tears streaming down his face for the women who had suffered at his hand.

He was a failure in everything he stood for as a man, as a Calydon, as an Order member, and as a mate. Honor was an illusion. It was the lie he'd used for the last five hundred years to justify the way he'd failed Juliette, to give meaning to his brutality, and his need to kill and slaughter.

There was no way to make it up to Lily. To Juliette. To Lily's mom. The past couldn't be changed. There was no way to make it all right. God, Gideon could still see the visceral hatred in Lily's mom's eyes as she'd pounded on him, the unbearable agony and loss...

He screamed again and despised even the sound of his own voice as it bounced off the trees.

His entire existence was a lie.

※ ※ ※

Lily awoke to the scent of mothballs, musty air, damp earth, and Gideon. Gideon! She sat up quickly and looked around. She was in a small cabin...no, more like a shed. There was a dirt floor, and she was on a portable cot in the corner. There was a single light bulb hanging from the ceiling, a small fridge humming, and a few shelves with some non-perishable foods.

Gideon was standing at a small window, his shoulder propped against the wall. His arms were folded across his chest, his muscles bunched, and his forehead furrowed. His body was tense, and his leather jacket was tossed on the floor in the corner. Lily's heart swelled with warmth as she saw him, and she remembered that moment when she'd seen him standing there on that desolate highway, with his broad shoulders, his gleaming axe, and that fire raging in his eyes.

He'd found her just like he'd promised. Lily knew in that moment, she would never be alone again. Gideon would always be there for her. Always. Her strong, powerful mate. He wasn't intimidated by who she was, and he was strong enough to cope with her and the enemies she brought with her. He empowered her, but he also treasured her and made her feel like the sensual woman she'd fought so hard not to acknowledge her entire life. No wonder her magic had chosen him. Of course, he was the one. There was no one else. There never would be. "Gideon," she said, unable to keep the smile out of her voice. "You found me."

"How do you feel?" He didn't even look at her when he asked the question, and he didn't move a muscle.

Frowning at his lack of warmth, Lily pulled her arm out from under the old faded quilt, and there were no scrapes from the pavement. She touched her head where she'd banged it on the asphalt, but there was no soreness. No cut. She frowned, confused. "What happened?"

"I healed you while you slept." Gideon still didn't look at her, and his voice sounded odd. Distant. Estranged. "Now that we're blood bonded, I can take you into my healing sleep and clear up all your problems." Yes, there was definite bitterness in his voice. "Hope you don't mind that I did it without asking. It pissed me off to leave that bruise on your leg."

"It's fine. I appreciate you healing me." Lily tried not to think about how intimate it must have been for him to bring her into his mind and his spirit during the healing sleep of the Calydon. She found herself wishing she'd been conscious for it, able to share in the connection of such a special moment. She sighed. All she wanted to do was hold up her arms and beg him to come over to the cot, but of course, they couldn't afford to tighten the bond any more. They were so dangerously close already. Frank was out there, and he had to be stopped. Now was not the time.

So, instead of succumbing to her desire, Lily threw off the blanket and kicked her feet over the edge of the bed, her bare feet sinking into the earth. She sighed and wiggled her toes in the dirt, feeling peace steal over her body. "Where are we?"

"My place. It's safe. No one knows I have it." Gideon turned to face her finally, and she was shocked by how drawn his face was. His cheeks were hollow, his eyes sunken, and there was no fire in his gaze at all. Just emptiness. He simply looked like a man who had no more strength left in him.

"Gideon! What's wrong?" She started to hurry over to him, but he held up his hand to stop her.

"You'll be safe in my cabin," he said. "I'm heading out to deal with Frank, and you're staying here. When it's over, one of the Order will come back to get you and you can go home. I called your parents and told them you're fine." His voice tightened, and she could only imagine what her parents had said to him.

She frowned, confused by the distance he'd erected between them. "Gideon—"

"Bathroom's in there. It's not much, but it works." He jerked his head toward the wall, and she noticed a door she hadn't seen. "There's some food in the fridge and on the shelves. It's all you need for now. I just wanted to stay long enough to make sure you were okay." He levered himself off the wall and headed toward the door. "Someone will be back for you when it's over."

Lily stared after him. "Are you kidding? You're leaving?"

Gideon didn't even turn around as he yanked open the door and stepped outside, slamming it behind him.

☙ ☙ ☙

Gideon hadn't even made it halfway across the forest floor before he heard the door behind him open. He tensed as Lily's earthy scent drifted to him but he didn't stop walking. If he didn't leave now, he knew he'd never tear himself away from her. It had been all he could do to stop himself from opening his arms to her when she'd come running toward him, worried about him.

He had to honor her by letting her go. He had to give her that much. He had to keep walking. He hadn't walked away from Juliette because he'd wanted to feel what it was like to have a *sheva* adore him. All he'd had to do was walk away from her, but he hadn't.

He was doing it this time. This time, he was going to be strong enough to give Lily her freedom.

"Hey!" she shouted.

"Go back inside, Lily. You're—" He stumbled as she tackled him from behind.

"Don't you dare dismiss me!" She wrapped her arms around his neck and her legs encircled his waist.

His body hardened instantly at the feel of her pressed against him, and he fisted his hands against the need to grasp her thighs and lose himself in the gift of beauty, peace, and sanity she gave him. "Get. Off."

"How can you leave me?" She punched him lightly on the shoulder. "You swore you'd be my guardian. You can't just abandon me in the middle of the woods."

Fury roared through Gideon. He tugged her legs off his waist and set her on the ground, his body vibrating with the effort of keeping control. How dare he even acknowledge how badly he wanted her? He didn't deserve her, not even for one damn minute.

He could feel the darkness pulsing at him, a darkness he knew was the precursor of his rogue side. It was so close to turning him. "I fucked up," he ground out. "Yeah, I promised to keep you safe, and look what happened? They fucking *raped*—" He stopped as his throat closed up, unable to get the words out.

"Oh." Her face softened in understanding. "Gideon, they didn't touch me. Your axe came to me in time."

He blinked. "My axe?"

"I called it. I used it. It worked." Lily refused to think about what she'd done with that axe. It had to be that way. She could not torment herself over it. If Gideon could live with five hundred years of slaying, she had to be okay with what she'd done to save herself. "I'm fine."

Gideon's brow wrinkled in confusion, as if he were struggling to understand what she'd said. "But the bruise on your thigh—"

"I dove out of a moving truck," she said. "I got a little banged up."

Still he stared at her, and she could see his resistance, his refusal to exonerate himself. "They didn't touch me," she repeated more firmly, realizing that he was using it as an excuse to punish himself for the guilt he'd been carrying for so many centuries. "Gideon, your axe saved me from the first one, and then you arrived in time to rescue me from the second one. *You saved me.*"

Gideon finally registered her words. He hadn't been too late—

No. He would not let himself off the hook. Not this time. He lifted his face to the trees, fighting off the need to succumb to her words. To let her comfort him.

The soft touch of her hands slid around his waist, and he jerked free, unable to allow himself to accept her forgiveness. "Don't you get it? Your mother's right. I'm a monster." He couldn't stop his fingers from trailing through her hair, for one last touch. God, it was so soft. She was like an angel of light that had been gifted into his life, and he'd blown it.

"You're not a monster," Lily said, her voice clear and true, her gaze unwavering.

"There have been only two women that my soul required me to protect more than any others, and I failed you both. Juliette is dead, and you were kidnapped by a psychopath." Gideon swore softly at the utter lack of judgment in her green eyes. "Don't look at me like that, Lily. I'm not a hero. I'm a demon, and the longer you hang out with me, the more your life is at risk." He grabbed her arm and pressed his palm to her mark. "The bond's almost complete, or did you forget? When it finalizes—"

"Nate raped me."

Gideon went rigid, and his vision momentarily went white with rage. "Jesus, Lily."

She didn't look away. "Frank wanted Nate to call out my magic, so he made my mind forget I hated Nate." She swallowed, the tendons in her neck strained. "I broke Frank's hold on me before, and I thought I'd won."

Gideon couldn't keep himself from reaching for her, and she let him take her hand, but she kept her body stiff, holding tight to her emotions.

She lifted her chin and pulled her shoulders back, and he could feel her trying to lock down the pain of her memories. "Nate had never touched me sexually until Frank convinced him they had to break me to get me to do what they wanted, to get to my magic." She met his gaze, and he was stunned at the strength in her eyes, even though they were laced with such pain.

Gideon's throat thickened. "Lily—"

"They didn't break me, Gideon. I refused to let them." She held up her hand to block him as he tried to pull her against him. "Don't give me sympathy, Gideon. I won't crumble for them. I need to stay strong. I need to move forward. I need to kill Frank."

Darkness raced through Gideon, and he welcomed it. He embraced the rage, the fury, and the need to kill. He let that deadliness surge to the surface and invited it to consume him. "He's mine." His voice was so lethal and deadly he didn't even recognize it. He was crossing the line. He was becoming the demon he'd tried so hard to convince himself he wasn't.

"Gideon! Stop!" Lily grabbed him, her grip tight on his arm. "Don't you dare go rogue on me, Gideon! Don't you get it? The reason I told you about that was so you'd understand the truth! You're not the monster! Nate was! Frank is! Not you!"

A faint red glow began to shield Gideon's vision, tainting everything he could see. Violence crept through him, like the insidious crawl of insanity, death, and merciless destruction. "I almost did the same thing as Nate did. I drained you for your magic in the woods. I almost made love to you at the mansion and I would have stolen your magic there, as well."

"No!" Lily grabbed his shoulders. "No! It wasn't the same thing, Gideon! I was right there with you! I gave you my magic in the woods. At the mansion, I wanted it as much as you did—"

"Stop it!" His voice was gritty, and he didn't even recognize it. The world began to glow as if a fire was consuming it. He knew his eyes were glowing red now, and he felt the darkness tighten its grip. It would be over soon. He'd be consumed by the darkness. No more guilt. Nothing but the need to destroy.

"I know what I've done," he rasped. "To you, to Juliette, to your grandmother. I *know*. I'm not a hero. I'm not honorable, and I'm not lying to myself anymore. How can I, when I look at you and see all the goodness I'm going to destroy, one way or the other." His mind began to spin, and he started to stagger. He fumbled for his keys and threw them at her. "Get out of here. Once I succumb, I'll take you out, too. I'll go after Frank and he will die. Suffer." Images flashed in his mind of Frank's body. Of Gideon slamming his fist into the bastard's stomach and ripping out his intestines, raising them to the sun, letting them burst into flames—

"Damn you, Gideon!" Lily grabbed his shoulders and pushed him backwards so hard he stumbled and fell on his ass. She jumped on him, her knees landing on his stomach.

The air slammed out of his gut with a whoosh, and Lily leaned over him, her green eyes blazing. "Frank's men will find me here! You know they will. And when they kidnap me, it'll be your damn fault for being a damned martyr and leaving me behind."

Gideon bellowed his rage as her words burst through the fiery haze surrounding him. The truth of her statement broke through his denial, yanking him back from the dark precipice. She was right. Frank would come after her. "Fuck, Lily! I'm trying to do something right for a change."

"No, you aren't." Her hands were on either side of his head, bracing her as her knees continued to dig into his gut. "You're trying to pull some macho warrior crap instead of facing some tough emotions. For hell's sake, Gideon, going rogue and killing Frank isn't going to make the pain inside you go away and it's not going to change the fact that Juliette's dead!"

Guilt swelled through him, and he shoved her off him.

She sat in the dirt, her eyes blazing with fury. "Juliette's dead, Gideon. She's dead! It's over! No matter what you do, you'll never change that! No matter how hard you adhere to your oath, she'll still be dead!"

Gideon staggered to his feet, his head reeling. Agony beat at his mind, denial screamed at him. "Stop it!"

"Juliette's dead, but I'm not! I'm right here!" Lily shouted it so loud it burst through the storm raging through him, and he stared at her.

Her chest was heaving, tears were streaming down her cheeks, and her face was red with heat and fury. Lily saw that he'd finally noticed her, and her voice quieted. "The future doesn't have to repeat the past. Don't you understand? I'm your life now, Gideon. It can be different this time, but you have to drop your baggage and deal with me." She held out her hand to him. "This time, be strong enough to fight the way the battle should be fought. I need you, Gideon. I need you by my side, not leaving me behind."

His body started to shake, and he dropped to his knees in the dirt beside her. "I can't. I can't bring you into this. I can't risk you for the Order's goals. I—"

"They aren't only the Order's goals, Gideon. They're mine, too. I have to make sure Frank is stopped or I'll never be free. If you shut me out and Frank succeeds, we all lose. Let me fight for myself, Gideon. Stand by me, keep me safe, but please, let me fight. You need me. You know you do." Her eyes were aching with pain but also with the strength he'd always admired about her. She crawled across the dirt to him. "Please, Gideon, don't give Frank the victory because you're letting your guilt about the past keep you from doing what's right today."

He closed his eyes. "I can't risk you—"

"You can." Her hands went to his waist again, and this time he didn't push her away. "I'm not dead, Gideon. Say it."

He opened his eyes to look into her face. "Juliette's dead," he said. "Dead because of me."

Lily nodded. "She is."

He lifted one hand to her hair, her brilliant, golden hair. "But you're not dead. I haven't killed you yet."

She smiled softly. "No, not yet. I know what you are, Gideon, and I'm asking you to stay with me. Unlike Juliette, I accept the risks. This isn't about some unilateral decision you made to change my life. I know exactly what I'm doing and what the risks are, and I want you."

"Lily." Gideon was overwhelmed by her words, by her truth. He was in awe that this woman, this incredible woman, could see him for who he was and accept him. She smiled and grasped his hand, and he saw his marks on her arm, evidence of how he'd taken away her choices.

Gideon dropped his hand, disgusted with himself for even thinking he had a right to her. "You've been through too much because of me. I can't keep you safe. I tried. And I failed—"

Lily put her finger over his lips, silencing him. "Do you remember the night in the woods, when you held me while I cried, after we'd survived the river?"

The moment came back to him instantly, the way he'd held her for so long while the sobs wracked her body. He recalled his consuming need to protect her, to keep her safe. He remembered the utter satisfaction he'd felt at having her body tucked against his, at having her drop her defenses for him. Unbidden, his hand crept back to her hip, his fingers slipping beneath the hem of her shirt and over her skin, the way he'd done that night. "I remember." God, he remembered. He'd never felt more right in his life.

"I cried because for the first time in a long time, someone was there to protect me, and it was okay for me to be vulnerable." Lily met his gaze, those enormous green eyes looking at him with a warmth and compassion he didn't understand. "I try to be tough, Gideon. I really do. But I can't do it by myself. I know my limits, and I need you." She raised herself up on her knees until she was level with him. "You chase all the nightmares away when you hold me in your arms," she whispered. "Your hands have killed so many, but when you touch me, it's all good. It's only good."

God, she was beautiful. A gift. An angel. How could she be looking at him like he was worthy? He didn't understand. "Lily—"

"Not only do you chase away the bad, but you give me new memories. You give me hope." Her hands went to his shoulders, her breath warm against his lips. "I need hope, Gideon. Hope for change. Hope that we can win. Hope that someday, somewhere, I'll be able to crawl into bed, snuggle into your arms and find peace."

He touched the pad of his index finger to her cheek. "You make me feel..."

"What?"

Gideon had no words to express the soft emotions rolling around inside him, and he knew, in that moment, he would give anything to be the man she believed him to be. He wasn't, and he never would be. But for this instant, he wanted it too badly to walk away. He wanted to hide in the fantasy she'd created and live it, for one minute. He burned to look into her eyes and see himself as she saw him. He had no idea how she'd come to view him in that light. It blew his mind, but he didn't give a shit right now.

Right now, he wanted to be the man she thought he was.

He knew it was wrong. He knew they had no time. And he knew it would endanger them both by tightening their bond. But he simply could not tear himself away from the oasis that she offered him, a moment so beautiful and so honest that he knew it would sustain him for the rest of his life.

He swept her up against him and kissed her.

Not just a kiss.

It was a penetrating connection that was far more than foreplay; it was a hot, wet, sinfully erotic promise and a dominating, demanding commitment, all tangled up in a mixture of unrepentant burning need.

When Lily opened her mouth under his assault and arched her back so her breasts pressed against his chest, Gideon knew they weren't going to stop until he'd gotten what he needed.

Which was her. Every last inch of her body, her mind, and her soul.

*Now.*

# Chapter 23

Lily tasted the desperation in Gideon's kiss as he lowered her onto the nurturing earth, his mouth hot and frenzied against hers. It wasn't a kiss. It was a statement of possession, controlled anger, frustration, and such raw, blistering hunger as she'd never felt before. It thrilled her, the way he needed her, his inability to pry himself away from their connection.

His hands raced over her belly, palming her stomach, her hips, her ribs, as he continued to kiss her, his mouth so demanding, she felt as if he'd inhale her right into his soul. The kiss was everything she wanted. She wanted Gideon to lose control, to go so crazy with his need for her that he forgot to hold back. Lily wanted to burst through those cold walls he hid behind. This kind of intensity was what she wanted from him. Heat, passion, craving, and intimacy, so many tumbling emotions that no doubt scared him to death. She wanted him to *live*.

Gideon yanked her shirt over her head, tugged her bra aside, and his mouth closed down on her nipple so hard she yelped.

He froze instantly, his body going rigid. *I hurt you.*

There was such raw, exposed pain in those three words that she couldn't have stopped him even if he *had* hurt her. But he hadn't. It had been the perfect synergy of unbridled passion, uncontained need, and unrivaled connection. "Not even close." She wrapped her arms around his head, and pulled him down to her breast. "Lose control, Gideon. I want to feel you lose control."

She almost laughed with giddiness as she said those words. How her life had changed since Gideon had come into it. She was actually telling a Calydon to lose control with her? Where was the reserved, fearful woman she'd kept locked down so rigidly her whole life? Gloriously free, because she knew that her bond with Gideon was so strong that he was incapable of hurting her. He would do whatever it took to make sure she was safe. His instincts were her safety net, the gift that allowed her to embrace him so completely and coax him to do the same. Together, they could both fully live in a way neither of them ever had before.

After a moment, Gideon slid his hand over her skin and cupped her breast. He was being careful now, but she could feel his urgency pulsing at her, driving at him even as he strived to be tender with her. Lily smiled, her heart warming at his internal struggle. This was a monster? This man who honored her so completely that he refused to allow his passionate nature to surface? No chance.

Gideon's tongue swept over the tender peak of her nipple, and she released a breath of delight. His touch was so light. So careful. He wasn't giving her any of the need, passion, and desperation that had driven him a split second ago. After that moment when he'd thought he'd hurt her, he'd slammed a rigid lock on his passions.

The dark fingers of loss slid through her mind, and she knew what he was giving her wasn't enough, not anymore. She didn't want the reserved, controlled Gideon of the last five hundred years. She couldn't accept the man who was crumbling inside while his stoic veneer held the world at bay. She wanted the visceral heat, the total wildness, the dark, heated passion that rode so strongly beneath the surface.

Nothing else would do.

Gideon lifted his head, his blue eyes fastening on hers with regret, clearly sensing her withdrawal. "I understand—"

"No, you don't." Lily fisted his hair and yanked him down on top of her, kissing him the way he'd kissed her. So hard, so deep, so desperate. She uncorked all her pent-up emotions of fear, anger, loss, loneliness, hopelessness and channeled them into her need for him, his kiss, his body, and his complete capitulation to what was between them.

She needed to feel him fall into the fire. She ached to have him lose his control and bow under his need. She put all of that into her kiss, until Gideon was kissing her back just as hard, his tongue thrusting so deep she thought she'd explode from the sensations ripping through her.

Then his palm was at her chest and he deftly flicked the front of her bra. Cold air swept over her raised nipples, and she caught her breath in anticipation as he broke the kiss. She opened her eyes to find his heated gaze drinking in her breasts, such unguarded desire in his eyes that her heart tightened.

Darkness flickered in his eyes, and he moved faster than she could see, but suddenly his mouth was on her breast again, sucking while his tongue swirled and his teeth grazed her skin in a tantalizing rhythm that had her hips writhing under him. His fingers pinched her other nipple, mimicking the movement of his mouth, while his other hand cupped between her legs, drawing heat and wetness through her jeans.

His movements increased in intensity, his mouth working, his hands teasing, faster and faster. He growled fiercely, and then he yanked down her pants and shed his, again moving so quickly she didn't have time to miss him before his hips settled between her thighs, his hot skin so smooth against hers.

For an instant, she froze as a flashback of Nate knifed through her mind. Her stomach churned, and panic assaulted her. She shoved at his shoulders in sudden panic. "No, wait. I can't—"

"Lily." Gideon's voice was soft, yet firm as his hand skimmed her hip, his touch so light, and teasing. "Look at me."

She opened her eyes to look into his blue ones and saw the raging need for her burning in them. Not just lust, but a deep-seated yearning that was so far beyond anything he could even articulate. In his face was the intimacy reserved only for her, and she knew the desire raging between them had nothing to do with the *sheva* bond or her magic. Right now, it was just them, just this passionate, wonderful man who was so burdened with guilt and self-hate, and yet somehow managed to commit himself so completely to her.

Lily felt Gideon withdraw and realized he was about to stop, summoning immense willpower to keep her safe. He could do nothing else other than protect her, no matter how badly he wanted her. She felt the warmth of his concern for her filling her like the beautiful sunshine on a spring day, his commitment to her evident in the heat of his spirit as it wrapped around her like a protective shield. There were no words for him to speak, she felt his commitment to her in every breath, in the steady rhythm of his heart, and in the beauty of his spirit.

That realization, that truth made all her fear vanish, chased away by her complete and total trust in him. This wasn't Nate, or any of the other bastards she'd fought off in her life. This was *Gideon*, the man who'd been a part of her life since before she was born, destined for her since the beginning. She laid her hand on his face, feeling the prickle of his whiskers and the warmth of his skin. "You," she whispered softly. "It's always been you."

Gideon gave a quiet smile, then gently kissed her, a tender kiss of sensuality and desire, of protection, of promise.

Desire rose hot and fast within her, chasing away the memories until all that was between them was unadulterated need. *Give me new memories, Gideon.*

*You're sure? We don't have to—*

Lily wrapped her legs around his hips and pulled him tight against her, feeling his erection pressing into her belly. *I'm so sure.*

Gideon groaned and the rhythm of his kiss changed again, spiraling into the same dark descent he'd gone into before until control didn't exist for either of them, until he was kissing her so fiercely, his hips moving against hers with a franticness that reflected her own desperation.

His hand slid between her legs, and his fingers sank deep inside, a deliciously erotic invasion that tore a throaty moan from her.

*That's right. Let it go, sweetheart. I'm here to catch you.* Gideon's voice was husky and aroused in her mind, and his presence ignited spiraling desire inside her.

Lily felt his arousal, his burning ache for her, the confusion in his mind at the intensity of the emotions racing through him, driving him, consuming him even as he stoked the pulsing need within her. His skin was hot and slick, his muscles rigid. His fingers were delightfully skilled where they sifted through her folds and teased deep within her, bringing her to a point where sanity and control didn't exist. Fire raced through her body, her nerve endings screaming, her body yearning for his, teetering at the precipice—

Then he shifted, his hips thrust, and he sank deep inside her.

He stilled for a minute and met her gaze. There was such utter male satisfaction on his angular face, but there was so much more as well. Awe, possessiveness, and a tenderness that made her eyes fill with tears. Then he slid out, ever so slowly and deliberately, the friction from his hot flesh singeing every single inch of her body, his gaze never leaving hers, as if he couldn't get enough, as if he were memorizing every moment to keep with him forever.

Gideon sank deep again, harder this time, further, and her hips came off the ground as fire exploded inside her, not just in her body, but in her mind and her soul. The look in his eyes was so intense she felt like he'd strip her raw as he pulled out again, his eyes darkening when she wrapped her legs around his hips to try to keep him inside her.

Then he plunged again, so hard their bodies smacked together, and this time he didn't stop, his hips moving in a steady rhythm, harder and faster with each thrust, his blue eyes never leaving her face. His eyes were turbulent cauldrons of emotion, the complete antithesis of the man she'd once thought him to be. He was heat, he was fire, he was a lethal warrior, but he was so vulnerable, so damaged, so desperate for *her*.

He caught her mouth in his, a hot, wet kiss as frenzied as the movement of his hips as he drove so deep inside her, and flames began to lick at her, searing her body, her arms...her forearms were on fire—

*The bond.*

*Yes, Lily. The bond. You are mine. Forever.*

The utter possessiveness in his voice sank deep into her heart and tumbled her right over the edge. Her body exploded, and she screamed as the orgasm consumed her. Gideon stiffened and he threw back his head, bellowing her name to the world in utter and complete capitulation to everything he fought so hard not to be.

❦ ❦ ❦

Gideon buried his face in Lily's neck, breathing hard. Her arms and legs were wrapped around him, her chest rising and falling as she fought to regain her breath.

He was afraid to move, not willing to lose the moment yet. It had been...it had been everything he'd never thought he wanted, and it had stripped him bare.

Lily was stroking the back of his neck, playing with his hair. Her touch was light and delicate, a casual affection that spoke of so much more than sex or lust. He closed his eyes, focusing on the gentle play of her fingers against his skin, trying to imprint the moment in his mind forever.

Because the minute they got up, it was over. It had to be.

"There's one stage left now," Lily said.

Gideon lifted his head to look at Lily. Her green eyes were at half-mast, drowsy from the lovemaking, but there was a hard reality beneath those thick lashes. "I know." He caught her arm and flipped it over so he could look at the brand. The silver lines were dark and bold, and all that was left to appear was a small design on the handle of his axe. The symbol of his lineage. "All that's left is for you to kill to defend me, or to risk your life for me. Your half of the death ritual."

All the other stages had been satisfied. Sex. Blood ritual. Transference, when his weapon responded to her call. The Death ritual, his part satisfied when he'd killed to save her life. Trust had occurred when she'd given him the power to kill her at the mansion, and when he'd bared his soul and told her the truth about the day his first *sheva* died.

They were so close now, and even though Gideon knew it was dangerous and wrong, it felt so damn good to see his brand on her skin.

Lily rubbed her fingers over the mark. "When this first happened, all I could think about was going insane and murdering my children."

He worked his jaw. "I remember."

"But now..." She fell quiet.

"Now, what?"

Her gaze went to his. "Did I ever tell you that I think I killed my brother?"

He frowned at the change in topic, but it also made him smile. Hell, his woman was so complex. She had such a full life, so full of challenges and heartache, but somehow, she was lying here with him, inviting him into her soul and herself. "No, you didn't. Tell me."

Lily nodded, her fingers still tangled in his hair. "I knew that many Calydons don't survive their dream, so I spent my life researching the dream to see if there was a way I could ensure he survived." She sighed. "I knew that the dream entailed them getting involved in some deadly battle in a dream, or in another world, and I worried about him because he didn't have a mentor who'd taught him how to fight."

Gideon recalled his own dream. He'd been in a barren field, armed with only his axe, and he'd been faced by a huge warrior in all black, with a hood over his face and a sword in his hand. Gideon had known instantly it was Death, and he'd realized that to win would take far more than battle skills. It wasn't a test of physical strength. It was a test of emotional strength, conviction, ruthlessness, intelligence, and toughness.

Gideon's dream had been over in less than a minute, and he'd awoken with his brands and his weapons.

Lily rubbed her hand over the brand on Gideon's arm, and satisfaction rumbled deep inside him at the action. It was a statement of acceptance of who he was, and he loved it. "When Trig got close to the age to have his dream," she said, "I slept in his bedroom every night with a bucket of dirt to feed my magic. One night, he woke me up with his screaming. He was convulsing on the bed, and he was bleeding from deep gashes all over his body."

Gideon winced. "He was losing."

She nodded, her grip on his arm tightening. "I panicked, and I started dancing, calling my magic to make him stronger. I held his hand and gave him everything I had until I passed out. When I woke up, he was dead. My magic wasn't enough.

The one thing I wanted to do with my magic, and I couldn't do it." Her voice was quiet, muted with the ache of old pain as she looked at him. "I've spent my life torturing myself over that night, wondering if I'd done something differently, whether he'd still be alive."

Gideon managed a wry grin as he took her hand and entwined his fingers through hers. "I'm familiar with that sentiment."

"I was so envious of you," she said quietly. "You'd killed people you cared about, and it didn't bother you. I wanted to be like you. I wanted to be spared the pain of what I'd done. I wanted to stop feeling, because it hurt so much to lose Trig, to know I might have killed him because I interfered."

Gideon gave a harsh laugh. "You were envious of me?"

"Yes." She looked at him. "But I'm not anymore."

He felt something tighten in his chest. "No?"

"No." She slid her hands over his shoulders. "Because I see what it's done to you."

"And what is that?"

Her green eyes were so intense as she looked at him. "It broke you."

Gideon tensed. "I'm not—"

"You've spent five hundred years crumbling inside because of the choice you made with Juliette. After I met you and realized that, I saw I'd done the same thing. I'd tormented myself with my brother and wasted my energy hating a man who had simply done his job. When I was kidnapped today, Frank mentioned my past with Trig, and it broke me." She smiled softly and rubbed her hand over his chest, an intimate, natural touch that in some ways, was even more stirring than the sex had been. "A few minutes later, when I couldn't reach you, I thought you were dead. In the light of that, the whole thing with my brother simply faded into the past, into something that could never be changed, no matter how hard I tried. You are my present, and you are what matters to me today."

Gideon closed his eyes, basking in the feel of her gentle touch. He understood her words, but he knew he couldn't live by them. "I know I can't change the past," he said. "But I need to keep it alive. By remembering, I can do things to try to atone for it."

"What things? Like being dead even while you're alive?" Lily's grip tightened on him, and her voice became fierce. "I loved my brother and I will treasure the time I had with him, but I'm wasting my life obsessing about his death." Her gaze met Gideon's. "Right now, you're here, and if I fight our connection and make myself miserable, then, when I lose you, I'll never have had any joy at all." She smiled, a beautiful, warm smile full of such love. "You give me peace, Gideon. I've never had that before, and I treasure it. Whatever time we have before destiny rips us to shreds..." She lifted her chin. "I'm in."

He cursed. "Lily—"

She put her hand over his mouth. "Don't say it, Gideon. I just wanted you to know I'm here with you." She held up her arm, showing him the mark. "It feels so right to be connected with you right now, and I know we can hold off the final stage of the bond long enough to kill Frank. After that..." She shrugged. "After that, I vote that we enjoy what we have until we don't have it anymore."

His throat tightened up and something ached in his chest. "How can you say that? How can you just give in? The *sheva* destiny means we will both die. *Die.*"

"I'm not immortal, so I'm going to die anyway, unless we complete the bond." Her green eyes were unwavering. "But while I'm alive, I'll be damned if I'm going to let a fear of loss haunt me. Been there, done that, and for the first time in forever..." She looked at him. "You make me happy, Gideon. Even when you make me mad, you make me so happy."

Gideon dropped his head to the curve of her neck, blinking hard against the stinging in his eyes. "Jesus," he whispered, his voice hoarse. "Like I didn't have enough reason to feel like shit for not keeping you safe."

Her arms went around him and she hugged him tight, so tightly, with no reservation, total forgiveness for the fact he'd already failed to protect her, for his being who he was, and somewhere, deep, deep inside him, hope flickered.

*You aren't a monster, Gideon.*

He pressed his face into her skin, desperately fighting off his need to believe her, to fall into what she offered. He'd never be able to stand the loss if he bought into it and then had it ripped away from him. Never. *Your parents think I'm a monster. You can't have them and me in your life. They'd never survive it.*

But the truth was, he was the one who wouldn't survive it. He'd gone so long not caring about what other people thought about him, and Lily had broken through that. She'd made him feel, and now there was no way he could sit there, on the outside of her family's circle and not be affected by their hatred.

Not anymore.

And Gideon could never take Lily away from her family and thrust her into a life with the man who had brought nothing but death to her and her family.

Lily would die if she stayed with him, and he couldn't live with that. *So many reasons, Lily. There are so many reasons.*

He felt her pause, felt her flicker of sadness for the truth he spoke. Sudden grief slammed him so hard he lost his breath. He gritted his jaw and summoned up the cold walls he'd held around himself for so long, his gaze boring into Lily's face. "They're your world, Lily. I felt the love between all of you. It was—" No. He couldn't think about how intense their emotions had been, how much he'd yearned to be a part of it. "They're family, for hell's sake. Family is..." He had to stop to fend off the thickness in his voice. "Family is the foundation of life. You can't walk away from them, not for me. You'd never forgive yourself, and I wouldn't either."

"Gideon—"

"No." He made his voice as harsh as he could. "We have one goal: to stop Frank. We do that, you go back to your family and I go back to my life, and we never do that last stage. I'm strong enough to fight the need to consummate the bond, because my need to keep you alive is stronger than anything else."

"But—"

"Don't even start, Lily. I can't take it." His voice cracked and for a split second, he lost the cold façade he'd erected, and he saw Lily's eyes widen at the pain she saw on his face. He struggled to regain his control. "You have to let me go, because if you hang onto me, and then walk away later or die because of me..." He closed his eyes against the disclosure it was so against his nature to make, but that Lily deserved. *Only then will I truly be broken.*

There was silence, and she laid her palm on his cheek. He pressed his face against it, absorbing her touch. Needing it this one last time.

# Chapter 24

Gideon glanced over at Lily as they neared Nate's land. For most of the eight-hour drive from his cabin, their conversation had been targeted to problem-solving the situation with Frank, and she'd filled him in on what she'd learned when she'd been in the truck with Frank's men. Gideon was relieved to learn that Drew was still alive. Lily had spent much of the ride using a satellite computer the Order kept in the truck to research Ezekiel and try to find the exact location of the site where he'd turned on his father.

They hadn't discussed their lovemaking, the bond, or their relationship.

Gideon knew Lily had retreated into her world of academia as a defense against the distance he'd erected between them, and he was glad she had that option. When she was lost in her research, he could tell she separated herself from the real world, almost as if she were in a trance.

It was the same kind of reserved existence he'd woven around himself for the last five hundred years, a respite he couldn't find his way back to since Lily had broken through his shields.

He kept inhaling her scent, watching the curves of her throat each time she swallowed, smiling at the frustrated noises she made whenever she ran into a dead end.

Shit. He was lost to her.

He gritted his teeth at the thought. Did he really have time to be mooning over her? He needed to be focused on the damn mission. He'd checked in with Quinn, who'd reported that Frank's Calydons had retreated from the mansion once they'd started to lose, disappearing as quickly as they'd arrived. Regrouping for another assault, he and Quinn were both certain.

Quinn had taken the rest of the team over to Nate's property and everyone was searching for the information about where the rite was to occur. So far, no results.

Lily looked up at Gideon and he realized she hadn't been in a fog at all. There was determined awareness in her eyes, and she was fully aware of the danger they were driving into. "On the plus side," she said, "worrying about the Order deciding to kill me when we get there, and the fact Frank might have a team waiting to attack us is distracting me from the trauma of returning to Nate's."

He lifted his brows, then smiled at her grittiness. "Facing death is always a bonus."

"That it is." She sighed and looked out the window. "Just try not to get yourself in a position where I have to kill for you and complete the bond, okay? I'd really love for things to stay the way they are with us and not descend into a living hell, you know?"

"No worries." He rubbed her thigh, offering reassurance. "There's a reason I'm one of the oldest surviving Order members. I'm impossible to kill."

Lily raised her eyebrows. "You've almost died a couple times since I met you."

"Almost is everything when you're talking about death." He drummed his fingers on the steering wheel as the truck bounced over the rutted road. "Can I ask you something?"

She folded down the lid of the computer. "Sure."

"How come your magic didn't rise when we...ah..." He couldn't revisit the intimacy of their lovemaking. Not yet. It brought to the surface emotions that were too intense for him to be feeling when he was on the edge of battle. "Earlier. At my cabin?" He'd been so into her at the time that he hadn't even thought of it, but the thought had occurred to him since. He'd nearly driven off the road when he'd realized the risk he'd taken by making love to her when there'd been no one there to stop him if he'd lost it.

"I was thinking about that, too." Lily hugged her knees to her chest, rubbing her chin on her knees. "My magic doesn't come on its own. It has to be intentionally called up by me or a Calydon. Most Calydons can't call it in me if I don't want them to, though I think you could."

"I would never do that," he said quickly.

Lily smiled and patted his arm. "I know you wouldn't. My point was that I would expect my magic to stay quiet like it did in the woods. That's more normal. What's unusual is that my magic came when we were at the mansion, even though neither of us called it. It's never done that before."

Gideon rolled that idea around in his mind. "So, what do you think happened?"

She shrugged. "My best guess is that it reacted to the blood ritual and the intensity of our emotions at the time. We were both worried about the Order and Frank coming after me, and we did the ritual to protect me. I think we were both so in tune with the threat to me, that we actually did call my magic, at least subconsciously, because we were working so hard to keep me safe. My magic felt the threats we were sensing and rose in response. To protect us."

Gideon considered that. She was absolutely correct about what was driving their connection at the mansion. "Whereas, at my place, there were no threats."

"Neither of us called it, and the moment wasn't about danger." She smiled, her face relaxed and happy. "When we made love, it was just about us and how we felt about each other. It was beautiful and passionate, an expression of all good things, so there was no reason for my magic to be summoned."

Gideon's chest tightened again at her description of their lovemaking. Had he really been a part of something that was beautiful and an expression of all good things? Had he really helped create that kind of moment? For a split second, he had hope, a glimmer of hope that maybe there was more to him than he'd always believed, that there was a chance for a life he'd never thought about.

Then he sobered. He was a warrior, a killer, not some angel of beauty. He had to remember that. He couldn't get lost in some delusional vision that he was something he wasn't. He had to be a warrior right now. "So, how's Frank going to try to call it up to free Ezekiel? Is he going to try to force you to have sex with Drew?" He couldn't get the grit out of his voice at his question.

Lily shot him a slightly confused look at his change in topic, but she let it go. "My power is heightened by sex, definitely. But it's fueled by earth, music, and the Calydon spirit." She rubbed the brand on her arm. "If Frank influences me again with an illusion, he might be able to call it up, but would it be enough power to make the walls fall?" She shrugged. "Maybe. I don't know." She looked at Gideon. "If it was with you, it would bring down the walls in a heartbeat. Together, we're extraordinary."

Yeah, they were. He agreed with that, and he liked it. "Then we make sure Frank doesn't get us together." Hell, what was he saying? He was making damn sure Frank didn't get Lily at all. End of story. "After we figure out where the rite is taking place, you take my truck back to my cabin and wait it out there. I—"

"No." Lily folded her arms over her chest. "Gideon, I know you need to protect me, and I'm all for that, but you have to let me fight."

Yeah, there was no chance of that. "You're not a warrior."

"I am. I don't have weapons like you do, but this is my battle. You need me. My brains. And my magic. And you may need to use me as bait to lure Frank—"

"No!" No damn way would he ever allow that to happen. *Never.*

"This is my war as much as it is yours," Lily continued, ignoring him completely. "Frank was behind my abduction by Nate, he's the reason Nate raped me, and he's still stalking me." Her eyes glittered. "I will not stand back and hide. I need to be a part of it. It's my right to reclaim my life."

"I don't give a shit. The thought of you—" He shot a glare at her. "It would seriously fuck me up if I let you join us and you got killed."

She smiled, her eyes softening at his confession. "So keep me alive, then. Let me do what I have to do, but keep me alive."

He cursed softly and thudded his fist on the steering wheel. She was right. They needed her, but God help him if he let anything happen to her. "You make me want to walk away from my duty. I never thought it would be possible, but you do. I want to turn this truck around and drive you so far away that none of this shit will ever find you again."

"But then Ezekiel would get free and we'd all die anyway."

His jaw tightened. "But Ezekiel would get free and we'd all die anyway," he agreed. Damn. He hated logic sometimes.

"So, it's done." She held out her hand to him. "Teammates?"

"Soul mates." Gideon wrapped his hand around hers and held tight. This time, for once in his goddamn life, let him not screw up keeping his *sheva* safe. One. Damn. Time. *Let me get this right.*

※ ※ ※

Lily's heart rate accelerated as Gideon pulled onto a sandy road going off into the desert. It was the road that led to Nate's, and suddenly she could recall with vivid clarity the moment she'd stepped into his house, reeling with shock when he'd grabbed her and she'd realized he was going to keep her—

"Lily." Gideon's thumb rubbed over her palm. "You with me?"

"Yes." She clenched his hand as the truck bumped over the uneven road and Nate's house came into view.

It was the same brown ranch house, standing so starkly among the harsh high desert scrubs and trees. Her gaze drifted to those tiny basement windows, the one on the far right that had been her only glimpse of freedom for so long. She could see the sunlight glinting off the glass, making it impossible to see the bars over the windows. Her cell.

Movement caught her eye, and her attention jumped back to the front door as it opened. Quinn stepped out onto the stoop, and Kane walked out behind him, his scars so visible in the sun.

Gideon pulled the truck up in front of them, and she felt him reach out to touch his friend's mind. He didn't open the car door or turn off the engine. *What's the status?*

Quinn answered. *We haven't turned anything up, but the team is willing to wait to see if Lily can help them find the information. I've convinced Ryland that his bloodthirsty need to avenge Dante's death will be better served if he actually draws the blood of the enemy instead of simply making it more difficult for Frank and Ezekiel to succeed, and the others are following suit. They're not planning to kill her at the moment. She's safe.*

Safe. Hah.

*Good.* Gideon shut off the engine and kicked open his door. He climbed out and then turned to help Lily get out. For a moment, she couldn't move. All she wanted to do was have Gideon turn the truck around and drive her away from all of this. What if it was a trap? What if Frank was waiting for her to show up, and then he was going to ambush them? "Oh, God," she whispered, her hands starting to tremble.

"Hey, sweetheart." Gideon's voice was soft, understanding. "We're all here for you. We won't let anything happen to you."

"I know." God, she didn't want to be controlled by her fear. She had to face this. She had to be stronger than this. "I'm coming." She released the seatbelt and scooted across toward Gideon's door.

He gave her an intimate smile, just for them, as he helped her out. The moment her feet were on the dirt, he pulled her close and slightly behind him as he approached the two Order members, using his body as a shield to protect her. "What progress has been made?"

"We've searched the entire area that Lily suggested, and now we're looking in Nate's house. We haven't turned up anything, though." Quinn's gaze went to Lily. "We're hoping you have a miracle in you."

Lily nodded distractedly, her heart pounding as she looked at the house. A Calydon passed by one of the windows. Ian. He glanced down at her and nodded. She clung to her memory of him driving the truck that had taken her away from Nate's. He'd saved her once. He was on her side. See? She wasn't going to be trapped here again. These warriors were on her team this time, at least for the moment.

"Lily?" Gideon's voice was gentle and sympathetic, laced with a hardness that made her relax. He was on guard. They were all on guard. "You don't have to do this."

"No. I do." She took a deep breath and headed into the house that had been her own personal hell for two years.

❧ ❧ ❧

Gideon kept his hand on Lily's back as he followed her through the house. Quinn and Kane were trailing behind them, weapons out, senses humming. He knew they were all waiting for this to be a trap, for Frank to send his team after them.

Gideon's blood was boiling at the thought of what had happened to Lily in this place. He was disgusted that he'd spent two years oblivious that his *sheva* had been trapped. Her scent was everywhere, deep in the carpets from her years of imprisonment. Her blood hummed at him from the walls where it had sunk into the wood. He couldn't see it anymore, but he could feel it. He could taste it. He could breathe it.

Her terror was soaking into every pore of his soul. His mind was screaming with rage, with the need to destroy, to annihilate Nate, Frank, and the house. To wipe all of them from the earth so Lily would never have to dream of any of it again.

*Gideon.* Quinn's mind touched his. *You're not going to do any of us any good if you go rogue. It was in the past, and you can't change it. All you can do is go forward. You have her now.*

*You sound like Lily.*

*Then she's a smart gal. Listen to her.*

Gideon looked at his mate, at her blond hair cascading over her shoulders and the stray pine needles still in her hair from their lovemaking on the forest floor. He raged inside for her, for the injustice that had stolen so much from her, and for the brutality that had left her blood on these walls. *I should have known, Quinn. I should have known she needed me.*

*She needs you now. Be there for her.*

Lily stopped suddenly, and her muscles went rigid under his touch.

Gideon immediately called out his axe, and Quinn and

Kane stepped up beside him, weapons raised and ready.

She grabbed Gideon's arm, her fingers digging in. *This is where Nate raped me. This is the room.*

Fury spewed through Gideon as he stared into the library. Beautiful mahogany bookshelves, fancy Oriental carpet, and a huge oak desk with solid brass fixtures. His gaze was drawn to the floor, and he could see it. Her blood. He knew it was there. Knew that's where Nate had raped her. He felt his control snapping, spinning away, spiraling as the room began to take on a reddish glare—

Lily's fingers slipped into his grasp, her hand shaking and icy cold. *Come inside with me, Gideon. I can't do it without you.*

And just like that, her need for him caged his fury, slamming it back with a force that had him staggering. He gripped her hand tightly, able to think of nothing other than giving her whatever she needed from him. That was all that mattered. *I'm here. I'm with you.*

He felt Quinn's nod of approval, but he ignored his friend, focusing all of his attention on the woman by his side. She took a deep breath, gripped his hand tighter and then stepped inside.

Even an appearance by Ezekiel himself wouldn't have pried Gideon away from her side in that moment.

In that moment, Lily was his *entire* world. There simply was nothing else.

# Chapter 25

Lily's stomach churned as she stepped into the room, her feet sinking into the thick Oriental carpet. This room had been Nate's favorite place to hurt her. The cloying scent of air freshener floated through the air and she jerked her gaze to the corner, where the little blue flower was plugged into the outlet.

She hated that scent. *Hated it.*

Gideon's axe flew through the air and the air freshener shattered as the blade slammed into it. Blue plastic pieces exploded over the room, falling with a soft clatter on the wood floor by the wall. Gideon called back his axe and set it in her palm. "In case there's anything else you don't like."

Her fist folded around the handle, the cold metal so hard and strong in her hand. "I wish I'd had this when I was here before."

"So do I."

Lily's throat tightened at the expression of barely contained fury and deep concern for her on Gideon's face. She truly wasn't alone. Not anymore.

The tension in her belly eased, and she felt her shoulders relax. She gave Gideon a quick smile, then walked over to the stereo that Nate had used to play all different kinds of music to try to force her magic.

The only music that had worked for even a minute had been the music Frank had brought.

She glared at the CD player. "Frank tainted my music." For some reason, it was the CD player she wanted to destroy.

Music was her special gift, her life, and he'd exploited it and used it to abuse her. What should have been her power had become her noose.

She fisted Gideon's axe and brought it back to slam it into the CD player, then stopped.

Frowning, she cocked her head at the stereo cabinet, recalling the night Frank had played that music for her. The music had come alive for her...but had it been the tunes he'd selected, or something else?

At the time, she'd assumed it was simply the music selection, or the way he'd worked her over with an illusion. But was that all it had been? She chewed her lower lip, thinking.

The men were standing behind her, quietly waiting. Gideon's hand was still on her back, supporting, but not demanding. The warmth of his touch helped ground Lily, enabling her to relax enough to focus on the question skittering around the edges of her mind, just out of her reach.

Lily handed the axe to Gideon and walked up to the stereo cabinet. She slid her hands over the metal casing of the CD player. The metal was too new to have been harvested from the days of Ezekiel's youth. She tapped her fingernails on the wooden shelf. What had been different that night when Frank had played the music?

She closed her eyes, trying to recall it...then suddenly she *knew*. "It wasn't the music! It was where I'd been standing! I wasn't on the earth, but something was working just like that!" She raced across the floor past the men to where she'd been standing behind Nate's desk, and pulled back the carpet. The wood looked like any other wood, but she knew Satinka magic was there somewhere. "Pull back the floorboards," she said excitedly. "Pull them back!"

The three males were down at her feet instantly, and she grinned at the sight of their heavily muscled shoulders straining as they ripped back the floorboards after Gideon loosened them with his axe. Order members. Working for her. With her. A miracle.

"This has been pulled up recently," Kane said. "The nails are new." He tossed a board over his shoulder and it shattered the glass of a painting.

No one cared.

"Holy shit," Quinn breathed. "She was right."

"I was? Let me see!" She squeezed in between Gideon and Kane. Gideon slid his arm around her as Lily peered into the hole in the floor. Nestled between the support beams was a wooden slab, with writing on it.

"The tablet." Quinn grabbed it and lifted it out of the floor. "I can't believe it. This has to be the actual tablet created at the time Caleb imprisoned Ezekiel."

The wood was shiny, as if it had been polished by many hands, smoothing the tablet over long years. Words were burned into the wood, branded into it, like the weapons the men carried in their arms. It looked so old, so significant that Lily itched to touch it. To study it. To lock herself in her office with it for a month so she could decipher all its stories.

Quinn handed it to her. "Tell us where the rite's taking place. Tell us where Frank is."

She carefully accepted it, and she felt the Satinka magic the minute her fingers touched it. Tingling spread through her body, and music danced in her mind. Happy music, music that was so ancient and powerful that she knew it was her ancestors' songs. Music she'd never heard, but that she knew in her heart and in her soul.

"I hear bells," Gideon said.

She nodded. "This script is written for me. For a Satinka." She traced her finger over the symbols, over the wealth of information contained in the tablet. There was so much power in the scripture. She could practically feel it seeping into her.

Gideon set his hand over hers, laying his palm on the wood. "It feels hot. It's tingling."

Quinn frowned. "I didn't feel it."

"My magic chose Gideon. He's connected to my legacy." Lily was so tempted to peruse the tablet in great detail, but instead, she traced her fingers quickly over the symbols, skimming past the information carved on Nate's stone that she'd already read. "Some of this is exactly what was on Nate's stone. I think he lifted it from here, so he wouldn't have to keep accessing the wood."

She paused as she got to carvings that hadn't been on

the stone, her mind whirling through the translation easily, as if she'd written it herself, the magic of her heritage clearing her mind. "It's describing an ancient place of magic. The rite was performed in a place of Otherworld magic." She frowned, trying to think of a place nearby that was so drenched in power, and then she knew. "Oh!" She jumped to her feet. "It's where the elders used to gather."

The men stared at her blankly. "Elders?" Gideon asked.

"Elders. Two thousand years ago, certain members of the different races of the Otherworld joined together, seeking to discover a path toward harmony between the races. They created a hidden meeting place where they shared secrets about themselves to try to find a way to keep peace. Ezekiel's mother was one of the founding members, and Caleb became part of it too. By the time Ezekiel was going crazy, the Elders had disbanded, but it was where Caleb and his team of twenty-one met to make plans for taking Ezekiel down. It was the only place where they knew Ezekiel wouldn't have little spies lurking to report back. It would make sense that Caleb would have done the rite there, as a symbol of peace."

Quinn was frowning. "I've never heard of this place."

"Of course not. Only the members of the committee knew about it."

Gideon raised his brows, and the pride on his face was evident. "And you."

She smiled. "Of course. If it has to do with Calydon history, I know about it."

"So? Where is it?"

"Southern Oregon. It's a meeting room hidden deep beneath the surface. A chamber. Justice was administered there, but it was really more like a pit of quicksand. People went in and didn't come out. It's been used for other things since..." She caught her breath. "It's been used for Illusionist training. That's how Frank learned about Ezekiel. He was probably trained there. It makes sense!"

Quinn was on his feet now. "Can you get us the exact location?"

"I can get us close. I don't know where the entrance to it is, but I'm sure we can find it."

The door slammed open and she jumped as more Order members came inside. It was Ian, and four others. Their weapons were out, muscles bunched, their eyes hard with battle. She tensed at the hostile glare from Ryland and Gideon carefully slid her behind him.

"Lily came through," Quinn said. "We know where Frank will be doing the rite tonight."

Ian gave her a quiet nod. "Right on."

Ryland gave her another hostile glare, and she lifted her chin. With the tablet in her hands, her magic, when combined with Gideon's strength, would be impenetrable. But it would corrupt Gideon, and everyone in the room would die. Including herself. So, yeah, not the best option if it could be avoided, but at least she wouldn't die a victim. No more victim for her.

Gideon's hand went to her shoulder. *We won't need that. Everyone's focused on Frank.*

She didn't look at him. *For now.*

His fingers tightened in acknowledgement. Until Frank was dead, the Order still might be forced to make the kind of choice that had haunted Gideon for so long. Until Frank was dead, she wasn't safe.

*I will do it right this time*, Gideon growled. *I will not fail you.*

Lily saw the determination in his eyes and prayed he wouldn't be tested.

❧ ❧ ❧

Ana bit her lower lip as she stared down at the three Calydons passed out on the floor of the pit. They were all bleeding and bruised from her illusions. It was less than four hours until Frank would need her for the rite, and she knew she was going to fail. She hadn't learned to control her illusions, which meant Elijah would die for her failure, if he were still alive.

But if he wasn't alive, then she still had to stop Frank... but how would she do that? She hadn't learned a single useful thing since she'd arrived.

She braced her arms on the clay railing, her fingers digging in so hard her knuckles ached. *Elijah. Are you there? Please, give me something.*

But once again, all she heard was the faint echo of his voice in her mind, whispering her name again and again. Her imagination? Or his answer?

She needed to know. Time was running out, and she seriously doubted the reason she'd come here was to help Frank control Ezekiel. She was still certain there was a *reason* she'd gone with him, and she was running out of time to find it.

Ana had already searched the small house he'd built on the surface, and there was nothing in there relating to Ezekiel or Elijah or any of it.

The answers had to be down below in one of those tunnels.

Ana eyed the descent, a good forty feet to the hard ground.

Obviously, there was some other way to get down there, but she hadn't found it yet, and she didn't have time.

She took a deep breath, then swung one leg over the railing.

Then the other, so she was sitting on the railing, her feet dangling toward the pit. Ana eyed the distant floor, then rolled over onto her stomach and slid down, until she was hanging onto the railing by only her hands. Then she closed her eyes and let go.

❧ ❧ ❧

Kane transported the team from Nate's house to their destination in southern Oregon, delivering them into a small cluster of trees. Their arrival was dead silent, utter stillness, until the air began to hum as the Order members searched for threats with their senses.

Gideon set his hand on Lily's arm, and he wasn't about to let go. He caught not a single scent or sound in the forest. Total silence. *Anyone sense anything?*

Negatives from everyone.

*It might be an illusion*, Quinn said. *Everyone still have their bracelets?*

Gideon looked down at Lily's wrist and realized she didn't have one. When they'd been going after Nate to rescue Ana, Grace had given them all copper bands that protected them from Frank's illusions. Yeah, Frank couldn't create illusions like Ana and Grace, but his ability to create false emotions was just as powerful. He'd created murderous hate between Order blood brothers, and he'd already messed with Lily. The arm bling didn't work for external illusions, but they sure as hell kept Frank from messing with their heads.

He wasn't getting to Lily. Not again.

Gideon peeled one of his wristbands off and fastened it around her arm, but as he did, he became increasingly aware of how quiet the forest was. Something had to be very, very wrong.

The forest was never silent.

※ ※ ※

Ana yelped as she landed on the clay floor, pain shooting up through her broken ankle, her knees smacking against the hard ground. She staggered to her feet, ignoring the pain as she quickly inspected the area.

Six tunnels.

She grimaced, knowing she had time only to check out one or two of them at most. She quickly paced the circumference of the pit, limping past each tunnel and peering inside. Each one was carved out of hard rock, with stains on the walls and the ground. Stains that made her shudder.

But they were all the same—

The marks on her forearms burned suddenly and she stopped, turning to face the tunnel that headed dead east.

That was the right tunnel. She was sure of it.

She glanced behind her to make sure the Calydons were still down and Frank was nowhere in sight, then she turned and sprinted down the tunnel, the thud of her cast echoing with each step she took.

※ ※ ※

The attack came at them so suddenly, from all sides, that the Order barely had time to get their weapons up before the blades came flying out of the forest. Dozens of blades, so many that the sky was a mass of streaking gray metal.

Lily didn't even bother to duck as she continued to search for the landmarks, letting Gideon fend off the blades while she frantically scanned the landscape for markers that would tell her where the underground coliseum was. She could see the two rocks that were supposed to form the entrance, but there was a hill between them, when there should have been a field instead... Oh, right. Duh. "It's an illusion," she said. "The hill's not really there. It can't be."

"Go!" Quinn shouted, as a spear grazed his shoulder. "We'll hold them off."

Gideon grabbed her and they sprinted for the hill. Calydons fell in their wake, taken down by Order blades as they chased after Gideon and Lily.

Lily focused her mind as she ran, knowing that the only way to break through an illusion was to convince herself that it was a lie, to know it with absolute certainty in her heart. "The hill's not there. I know it. *There's no hill.*" She forced her mind into the truth, until she knew without doubt that the hill didn't exist.

"I believe you." Gideon whipped his axe through the air and knocked down a hatchet aimed for his heart. "I've seen enough illusions lately to question everything I see. Let's do it."

They reached the base of the hill and ran right at it. They burst through the illusion and then Lily found herself running beside Gideon across a flat field. "I was right! We did it—" A huge wooden structure suddenly appeared in front of them, and she crashed into it before she could stop herself, hitting so hard she was flung onto her back, the wind knocked out of her completely.

"Well, I'll be damned." Gideon grabbed her arm and helped her to her feet, throwing up another block as weapons sang through the air, blades clashed and warriors screamed in pain. "It's a building."

The illusion had vanished when they'd burst through it, so it was no longer obscuring what was really there. It was a house, a quaint little cottage. *Quinn? You see this?*

*It looks like you disappeared into the hill.*

So, he and Lily were the only ones who could see past the illusion. *There's a building here. We're going in. You coming?*

*Not a chance. We're a little busy. It's all you, buddy.*

Gideon tried the doorknob, found it locked, then threw

his shoulder into the wood and shoved the door out of the frame with the loud crack of splintering wood. He stepped inside and was hit instantly with unbearable agony in his gut. He staggered, his eyesight blanking out with pain, his head spinning, his body screaming with soul-deep torment as he felt like he was being skinned alive.

Lily grabbed his arm as he went down. "Gideon!"

He looked at her worried face and for a split second, he was consumed with such a mind-bending *terror* he couldn't think. Couldn't breathe.

And then he started screaming.

# Chapter 26

"Gideon!" Lily scrambled after Gideon as he ripped his arm out of her grasp and stumbled across the room. He was screaming, an unearthly horrifying noise that no living creature could possibly make. It was death. It was the sound of specters being tortured in the bowels of hell. It was the kind of torment that made a man slice his own throat instead of facing it.

Gideon's eyes were whited out, sweat was streaming down his face, and his hands were clawing at his arms, drawing blood.

"Whatever it is, it's not real! Gideon! It's an illusion!" Lily caught up to him when he stumbled over a couch and fell, clawing at his stomach, still screaming...not a scream... something so much worse.

He called out his axe and raised it, and she realized he was going to slam it into his stomach to kill whatever he thought had him. "God, no!" She lunged for him as he brought the axe down, throwing herself in front of it before she could even think about what she was doing, her eyes squeezing shut instinctively, waiting for the blow.

It didn't come.

After a second, she opened her eyes. Gideon was clutching the axe, a look of absolute horror on his face. "I almost killed you." His eyes were blue again, she noticed with relief. He'd shaken the illusion. "Jesus Christ, Lily! *Never* do that again! What if I hadn't broken through the illusion? Are you insane?" His hands were shaking, and his face was coiled with fury.

She realized she was shaking too. "You couldn't kill me. That's why you broke the illusion. Your instincts to keep me alive are stronger than anything else."

Recognition dawned on his face. "You saved me. You risked your life to save me—" He grabbed her arm before she could move and shoved her sleeve up.

She stared at her arm and watched the final design appear, as if someone were drawing it with a silver marker. "It's done. The bond's complete."

His hand closed over her mark. "It is."

"Why don't I feel any diff—"

Gideon yanked her against him and slammed his mouth down on hers, and suddenly she was flooded with such intense longing for him that she knew, with absolute certainty, that he was her life, her death, her oxygen. Without him, *nothing mattered.*

He couldn't think. Couldn't kiss her hard enough. Couldn't touch her enough. The need for her was so great, so intense that he couldn't stop it. They had no time, no privacy, and it didn't matter.

*It didn't fucking matter.*

Nothing mattered except being inside her. *Nothing.*

He had both their pants off in less than a second, and then he was sinking deep inside her. Her body was so hot and wet, so perfect for him. He groaned as she molded around him. *Dear God, Lily. This is what I've been waiting for my whole life.* It was perfection. It was right. *It was home.*

He didn't give a shit about her parents. About whether he fit in anywhere. Because he was home.

*You belong with me, Gideon.*

Her arms tightened around him as the total conviction of her words sank deep into his heart, and suddenly he was moving so fast inside her he couldn't control it. His hips pumped, his body roared with the rightness of it. Tears filled his eyes as an intense sense of belonging consumed him, then the climax took them both. He clung to her as his body bucked, completely out of his control, his heart aching, his soul healing, truly healing—

*I love you, Gideon.*

The moment he heard those words, he knew they both

were damned. But the words felt so good, and so right that at this moment, he absolutely didn't care. He held her tight against him, while the final twinges of the orgasm left, knowing he had to let go, but not able to bring himself to do it. Not yet.

Because they'd just brought destiny to her feet, and she'd be coming for them hard and fast now.

❦ ❦ ❦

Ana reached a row of cells, and she shivered at the sight of all the steel doors with their tiny barred windows near the top. Was this truly what she was descended from? People who kept victims like animals, to be brought out for torture?

No. She didn't have time to think about that. "Elijah! Are you in here?"

"Hello?" A male voice echoed through the hall, and a hand stuck out into the hallway, between the bars, about halfway down the corridor on the right. His arm was torn open like he'd been flayed, the skin raw and serrated.

It wasn't Elijah, but Ana ran down the hall anyway and grabbed his hand, which was covered in caked blood. "I'm here."

His hand tightened around hers in a grip that was almost desperate, making the blood ooze from his forearm again. "Thank God," he croaked, his voice raw. "I'm Drew Cartland. Can you get me out of here?"

"I don't know." Ana stood on her tiptoes to peer through the bars. A Calydon in his early twenties or late teens had his face pressed against the metal. He was covered in filth and barely healed gashes. One of his eyes was swollen shut, and his shoulder was so crooked she knew it had been dislocated. "Oh, God. Are you okay?"

"Frank killed me, stole my weapons in the split second I crossed over, and then helped me revive." Drew's eyes were so haunted, she felt her heart ache for him. "He's got my weapons, and if he uses them, we're screwed. We have to get them back before the rite. If I can get close enough to them, I can call them back into my arms—"

"Where's the rite taking place? Where are all the weapons?"

"I don't know." Drew jerked his head to the right. "But

† 305 †

he always goes in that direction after he comes to see me."

Ana nodded and started to turn away, then turned back. "Have you seen a Calydon named Elijah since you've been here?"

"Elijah?" Drew frowned. "He's dead."

Ana's throat tightened. "Well, if he is, then my job is easy. I'll be back!" She turned and ran down the corridor, searching frantically for keys or Frank or *anything*. She made it around the corner and stopped dead when she saw the open door in front of her. There was a table piled high with documents, plus a computer and filing cabinets. Frank's office?

She stepped to the door, looking around carefully to make sure no one was lurking, then peered inside. She sucked in her breath when she saw the wall on the right was a collage of photos.

Photos of her from as far back as when she was a baby, tracking her life. The most recent one was of Nate abducting her off the street. Frank had been there? He'd watched it happen? He'd handed her over to Nate? He'd stalked her since she was born...waiting for the right time to come after her.

She shuddered, and tore her gaze off the wall, thinking of Drew with his shredded arms and the clock ticking on the rite. There had to be something...she looked around the office at the piles of documents and the computer sitting on the desk. Frank's secrets.

Here were her answers. This is why she'd come. She didn't know what she'd find, but she knew it was in this room.

She stepped inside, locked the door behind her, pulled open the top drawer of the filing cabinet, and started to search.

☙ ☙ ☙

Gideon yanked on his jeans, his mind racing as he tried to figure out what had happened to him, what illusion had gotten him, but he couldn't remember anything from his brief trip to hell. "You didn't see anything on me?"

"No." Lily was getting dressed as fast as he was, the sounds of battle raging outside. "There was no illusion visible, but I swear, you completely lost it. Can't you remember anything about what it was?"

He shook his head. "All I remember is thinking of

Elijah. That was my whole thought—"

Her head whipped up, her eyes sharp. "You've done a bond with Elijah."

"Yeah, long time ago. Why?" He buttoned his jeans, then he grabbed her hand. Together, they raced through the house, searching for a door that would lead into the ground.

"I've read stories about the Calydon blood bond," she said. "Can you feel his pain when he's hurt?"

Gideon shot a look at her. "Yeah, sometimes. I mean, I could before he...died."

Lily nodded. "I'm guessing that what you felt was Elijah's experience. That he's been here and been tortured, and you felt what he was going through."

Gideon frowned. "But he's dead. I've never heard of picking up on the aftermath of an experience through a blood bond. It's not as if the image hangs around waiting for me to pick it up—" He stopped suddenly, the enormity of his words blossoming before him. "You think he's still alive? And being tortured right now? Here?" Son of a bitch! Elation and disbelief rushed through him, followed by the dark realization of the extent that his blood brother was suffering, if he truly was alive.

Lily yanked open a door and found only a closet. "Is there another explanation?"

Shit. He couldn't think of one. *Elijah?* Gideon reached out over their connection, throwing all his mental energy into the link. *Where the hell are you?*

No response. That had to mean Elijah was dead. Their connection was too strong. He would at least feel something if Elijah was nearby. It had been nothing but a false alarm. A brutal one, at that.

Lily was still moving quickly through the house, and he rushed to catch up to her, yanking open a door as he passed. Another closet, not stairs to a basement.

"I couldn't reach him," he told her. "He must be dead."

"When I was in the truck, when Frank's men had me, Frank implied you were dead." Lily looked over at him, and he saw the flash of pain in her eyes at the memory of what it had felt like to be disconnected from him. "I tried to contact you with my mind, but there was no response. Yet, it turned out you were after us and closing fast."

Gideon frowned as he walked into a den with a huge flat screen television hanging on one wall. "I was trying to reach you, too."

"So, despite the blood ritual, which should have allowed us to connect over any distance, we got nothing." Lily ran over to a bookshelf and peered behind it, looking for a hidden door. "Frank must have done something to block our connection. Maybe the car itself was specially designed to block those kinds of communications between Calydons."

"Son of a bitch. You think?" Gideon walked over to the flat screen television and studied it. Frank didn't seem like the type to kick back and watch television. His goals were too lofty to spend time doing something that unproductive. "And you think Elijah might be here? Now? But blocked, like you and I were?" *Elijah, if you can hear me, I'm coming for you. Hang in there, buddy. You're about to get your life back.*

"Maybe."

"Then it ends now." Gideon backed up a few steps, then he charged the television and slammed his shoulder into it. Sparks flew, the sound of shattering wood filled the room and then he was through the wall, standing in a tunnel built of clay. Bingo. He fisted his hands, his mind going into the singular warrior focus. "I'm going to find him and bring him home." His voice was colder than he'd intended and he realized he was falling into battle mode. Hell, it was about damned time he figured out how to be a warrior when he was with Lily.

Lily hurried into the tunnel after him. "Gideon—"

"What?" He started jogging through the passageway, his senses on high alert for any threat. Damn, it felt good to be focused. His mind was humming with intensity, his muscles were firing with adrenaline, and he could hear every sound as if it were magnified a thousand fold.

"What do you want most? What's the most important thing to you right now?"

He glanced at her. "You're thinking about our destiny? Now that we've bonded, we're both destined to lose that which we care most about? Utter destruction and all that shit?" He heard the faint skitter of cockroach feet in the distance, quickly cataloguing it and dismissing it with the efficiency he hadn't felt since he'd met Lily. It was as if completing the bond and knowing Lily was his forever had given him the freedom to accept it and let his connection to her weave seamlessly into his being. He could be both her mate and the warrior he needed to be. Feel and fight at the same damn time.

Who the hell knew that could be possible? But it was. He was brimming with rage for Elijah's fate. He was so connected to Lily that his heart was beating in synch with hers, he was one damned flood of emotion, and yet he was focused and intent in his mission. He felt like he could take down the damn world, which was good, because that's about what it was going to take to keep Ezekiel locked down.

Lily nodded. "Yes, what is destiny going to try to destroy now that we're bonded?"

Gideon thought about it as they ran down the hall, their feet crunching over clay pebbles and grinding on centuries of dirt and grime. What mattered to him most right now? Stopping Frank from freeing Ezekiel, definitely. It was the culmination of his life's goal. But finding a way to save Lily...shit. Gideon would never survive if something happened to her. And if Elijah was alive...the guy was his best friend. "It's a tossup. You?"

Her green eyes were heavy with emotion. "I have a number of things on my plate right now. A lot of things to lose."

"Yeah, me, too." They fell silent as they ran, and he felt her rising tension, mirroring his own. "Quinn and Grace beat it," he said. "They survived."

"For now."

"Now is enough for me."

She glanced at him and he saw the fierceness in her eyes. "I wish I'd had time to analyze what was different about them that made them survive."

"Screw analysis, Professor. This one's got to come from the gut."

Lily raised her brows at him. "You're telling me to do this from my heart? You're the one who doesn't believe in emotions."

"How I feel about you kept me from killing you, so yeah, I think our connection is our weapon." It had to be. He might be a bastard, but he was a damned good warrior, and he knew a weapon when he saw one. "It's us, Lily. You and I. We're the key. Got it?" He tapped her heart. "Fight from here. That's our chance."

Lily lifted her chin, her eyes flashing with determination. "I won't give up on us," she said. "I swear I'll fight destiny. I don't get defeated easily."

He grinned and ruffled her hair. Was it any wonder bonding with this amazing woman made him stronger? "And that's why we're going to make it—" Gideon felt a sudden shift in the air pressure and felt a rising threat. He called out his axes and grabbed Lily and pushed her behind him in one motion. *Quinn? How's the shit going down? I think I'm going to need you soon.*

There was no response, and Gideon realized Lily's guess was right. They were cut off from communication with the surface.

The loud crack of a weapon being called out echoed through the tunnel, and Gideon backed Lily up against the wall. It sounded like only one Calydon was approaching, and that would be easy for Gideon to dispatch.

The approaching footsteps were loud and uneven, as if their assailant was dragging a leg behind him. "Stay there, Lily."

Gideon stepped out into the center of the passageway and raised both weapons, ready to face what came around the corner. But when he finally saw what it was, he knew he was in deep shit.

# Chapter 27

"Elijah!" Gideon's heart leapt with disbelief and joy when the man he'd thought was dead stumbled around the corner. It was Elijah, his blood brother, *alive.* He lowered his weapons instantly. "My God, man! You're alive!"

Then Gideon saw the state Elijah was in, and his soul broke for him. Elijah's body was beaten and bloodied, his eyes were glazed with terror and pain, and his face was contorted in a mask of true insanity. He was stark naked, every inch of him carved raw, and dark blood was streaming from a set of fresh puncture wounds in his stomach, wounds that exactly matched the points of Elijah's throwing star.

Lily sucked in her breath. "Oh, God. He stabbed himself, exactly what you tried to do with your axe. You were living his experience."

Jesus. If what Gideon had experienced had truly been what Elijah was living, then Elijah's scrambled mind was nothing more than a mass of terror and pain. There was no sanity left. Gideon strode down the passageway toward him. "Elijah! It's me. Gideon." Elijah, along with Quinn, was one of the only two opponents who might actually be able to take Gideon down in a one-on-one, and with Elijah insane, the odds shifted in Elijah's favor because Gideon would hesitate to deliver a killing blow to his friend. "Hey, man, I'm here for you."

A shudder shook Elijah's body, and then he let out a scream of such inhuman terror and pain that Gideon paused. "Jesus, buddy. What did he do to you?"

Elijah raised his throwing star and charged, emitting a shrieking howl of deadly intent and desperation. It was the kind of noise a creature makes when they know they are facing the battle of their lives: die brutally, or take your opponent down first. No in-between.

"I'm not going to kill you," Gideon shouted as he threw his axe at Elijah's thigh to disable him.

Elijah blocked it with his throwing star and hurled his weapon so hard and so fast with the force of true desperation that Gideon couldn't block it and it sank deep into his own leg. "Shit!" He yanked it out then dove to the dirt to dodge a throwing star slicing toward his head.

Then Elijah was on top of him, fists pounding, stabbing with his weapons, still screaming that god-awful noise. Gideon's cheekbone shattered under the first blow and his head rang as the throwing star cut his neck. "Jesus!" He slammed his axe upwards against Elijah's chest, using the flat of his blade to throw Elijah off balance before he could finish the deadly slice.

Shit. Elijah was his best friend, but if Gideon didn't start fighting for real, he'd be dead in a heartbeat. "Come on, Elijah," he shouted. "Pull your shit together—"

"Frank's behind you," Lily shouted suddenly, her terror sucker-punching Gideon in the gut.

He lost his focus, and Elijah slammed his fist into Gideon's face. Gideon swore and hurled his axe at Elijah. It slammed hard into Elijah's side, a disabling blow, but not fatal. Blood spewed everywhere. Elijah rolled off him with a scream of agony that twisted in Gideon's gut as his brain went numb against the pain in his head. "Hell man, I'm sorr—"

Elijah slammed his throwing star into Gideon's heart, with a final scream of defiance. Gideon jerked under the blow, gasping as he felt his heart stutter. He ripped the throwing star out of his chest and let his arm drop to the side as Elijah lay gasping beside him. Hot blood ran down his side under his arm, and he groaned, trying to press his palm over his chest to staunch the flow of blood. "Good to see you, too, my friend," he gasped.

Elijah rose up beside him, his face so bloodied he was unrecognizable, his eyes staring out from the mask of blood, so full of rage, terror, and desperation. Of deadly intent.

Gideon tightened his grip on his axe. "Don't make me do it," Gideon warned. "Don't make me do it, Elijah—"

But the bastard did, thrusting his throwing star down toward Gideon's face in a deathblow. Gideon had no choice but to defend himself, and he slammed his axe into the front of Elijah's throat. The blows hit at the same time, and Elijah's mouth opened in silent protest, his hands going to his neck as he fell on top of Gideon, his body hitting hard as agony burst through Gideon's head and darkness consumed him.

❃ ❃ ❃

Lily was shaking violently as Frank's Calydons dragged her past Gideon and Elijah's immobile bodies, both of them drenched in blood. "Gideon!"

There was no movement from either warrior.

The Calydons thrust Lily in front of Frank, who was wearing an all-black suit. His hair was slicked back and his shoes were polished. There were two spots of blood marring his perfect white shirt, residual from the fight. He smiled. "So nice of you to come."

"I won't help you—"

A Calydon slapped a piece of duct tape over her mouth, and she inhaled in panic when it went over her nose too. Frank's eyes narrowed and he tugged the tape down from her nostrils as someone bound her wrists behind her back. "I'm tired of your attitude, Lily. We don't have time for this. The ritual is starting now." He snapped his fingers, and several more Calydons emerged from the tunnel behind him. "Deal with Elijah and make sure the other one's dead—"

Lily squealed in protest and tried to rip herself out of her captor's grasp as a tall blond Calydon called out a war hammer and walked over toward Gideon. She slammed her foot into her captor's shin and lunged for Gideon, throwing herself across the two downed Order members before the war hammer could find its mark.

"Bitch!" Her captor grabbed her to haul her off, then stopped when Frank held up his hand.

"Everyone hold." He walked over and grabbed her wrist, spinning her around so he could look at her arm. Gideon's brand glowed silver on her skin. Frank raised his eyebrows at her, then snapped his fingers.

The Calydon with the war hammer pried Gideon's arm out from under Elijah's body and held it up. Frank jerked Lily's arm next to Gideon's, and she saw that it was a full and complete match now. Every last design was perfect.

"I'll be damned. You're bonded." Frank released her arm and her captor yanked her to her feet. Her entire front was covered with blood now, but part of it was Gideon's, and it tingled where it touched her skin. Could she raise him with her magic?

"Bring her mate with us," Frank said. "See that he lives."

Lily nearly sagged with relief at his words, then stiffened when she realized Frank had noticed her response. He smiled, a thin smile that made her stomach turn. "Knock Lily out. I don't want her bringing her dead boyfriend to life before we're ready. And find Ana, for hell's sake. I need her."

Pain exploded in her head and then there was nothing.

❦ ❦ ❦

Lily woke up with a start, agony blistering through her shoulders. She peeled her eyes open to discover she was in the bottom of the pit she'd read about, lying on her side, bound hand and foot on a thick pile of rich, fertile dirt. Naked. She was surrounded by Calydon weapons, laid carefully on the ground around her in a precise circle. For a split second, her mind flashed to the past, to that moment when she'd woken up by the garbage dump with all those Calydons around her, but the familiar panic didn't take hold. All she could think about was Gideon. Where was he?

A young Calydon was facing her, trussed up the same as she was, also naked. His eyes were fixed on her face, and they were wide with terror, but also determination. "I'm Drew Cartland," he whispered, the moment her gaze fastened on his. "Dante's son."

"Lily Davenport." She was relieved to discover the duct tape was off her mouth. *Gideon? Can you hear me?*

The silence had her starting to panic, until she remembered that there was limited mental contact down here, and she lifted her head up to scan the area. They were surrounded by Calydons, and Frank was conferring with two of them. She caught sight of a slumped body off to the side, and her heart stuttered at the sight of the man she loved. He was still caked in blood, and he wasn't moving. He was chained down with heavy links that she was sure had been proven strong enough to hold a Calydon, which was a good sign. That meant he was still alive. Tears filled her eyes and her vision blurred. *He was alive.*

"Lily." Frank turned toward her.

She blinked several times to clear her eyes, then dragged her gaze off Gideon and looked at Frank. The look on his face was so evil, so anticipatory, that she couldn't stop herself from shuddering.

He walked over to her, stepping carefully over the weapons. He set Nate's knife in front of her, so she could read the writing. "You will bring the music to life, empower Drew, and then you will invoke the rite. Do you understand?"

"You can't possibly think I'm going to—"

Frank snapped his fingers and she stared in horror as the Calydon with the war hammer walked over to Gideon and held the weapon over Gideon's head.

"No, don't—"

She screamed as he slammed it into Gideon's head. Blood spattered, and the sharp crack of bones splitting ripped through the air. "Don't, God, don't! I'll do it!"

"Don't do it," Drew hissed. "Do you have any idea—"

She was shaking so hard she could barely think. "Shut up, Drew. God, shut the hell up! I know the risks, but I can't let him die!" *Gideon, please, please, please wake up. I love you, dammit! Don't let him kill you!*

Frank nodded and stood up and used his foot to shove Drew toward her so they were skin to skin from shoulder to feet. "Begin."

There was no tingle from the touch of his Calydon skin, no response from her magic at all. Just revulsion from having another male pressed up against her breasts.

"Gideon wouldn't want you to free Ezekiel just to save him," Drew said. "He's Order. He's supposed to sacrifice himself—"

"Shut up!" Tears were streaming down her cheeks, and she didn't care. She closed her eyes and tried to imagine the body pressed against hers belonged to Gideon. That the warm skin was his, alive and breathing.

But it wasn't. It was just empty flesh she didn't care about, and her magic was silent.

"Hit Gideon again," Frank snapped. "She's stalling."

"No!" She shouted, her eyes snapping open. "Don't! I'll do it! I swear!"

The war hammer stopped just short of Gideon's skull, and she scrunched her eyes, trying to focus. She started to hum... and there was no magic. Nothing.

"Don't do it," Drew whispered. "You're betraying all he represents if you do it."

Lily shut him out and started to sing, the same melody Gideon had sung to her in the woods, an ancient song of seduction and power.

And nothing happened.

She jerked her eyes open, her heart pounding. "I swear to God, I'm trying. I really am. I don't know why it's not working. It worked with Gideon..." She and Frank both looked at Gideon, and then she knew. "Oh, God. It'll only work with him now."

Frank narrowed his eyes. "Why?"

"Because he's my chosen one. He heard my bells. He's the one my magic has been seeking, and now that it's found him, no one else will do. I can't do it without him. I swear I'm not lying—" She screamed, tears pouring from her eyes as the Calydon hit Gideon again. "I'm not lying! I can't do it! I can't! God, stop beating him. Stop!"

Frank held up his hand and the war hammer disappeared into the Calydon's arm. "Bring Gideon into the circle. Strip him first."

Lily barely stifled a cry as two Calydons sliced Gideon's clothes off, their blades sinking deep into his skin as they cut through his jeans. Then they grabbed him and dragged him along the rock floor. His body was limp, his head lolling to the side as blood oozed out of it. God, how could he possibly survive that level of damage?

They hoisted him over the circle of weapons so his feet didn't dislodge them, then they dumped him on top of Drew and Lily.

The tingle from his skin was instant, and her magic came alive as he sank onto her, his body so heavy and thick. And warm. The kind of warm that meant he was still alive. Her body shuddered with relief and for a moment she was too overwhelmed to do anything but press her face against his bloody cheek. "Gideon," she whispered. "Don't you dare give up."

Drew's eyes went wide and she saw the first hint of true panic. "I can't move," Drew said. "He's pinning us to the ground. What they did to him—"

"Stay with me, Drew," she said. "Don't freak out." She realized Drew hadn't been able to see Gideon before now and he'd had no idea what they'd done to him. The shock of seeing Gideon's terrible condition was unnerving him. "The rest of the Order is outside. They're coming."

"They are?" Drew looked shocked as he whispered his question? "Really?"

She couldn't look Drew in the eye, knowing she was lying. There had been hundreds of Calydons outside fighting the small group of Order members. Even if they were still alive, they'd still be fighting, not free to come after them. Quinn had told them they were on their own, and she knew he meant it.

Frank bent over them, his face so close she could smell the mustiness of his breath. "Use Gideon to call your magic, but give the power to Drew. His weapon is involved in the rite, so he has to be the one."

Drew's eyes widened. "I won't do it."

"You want to end up like Gideon?" Frank's voice was conversational. "I don't actually need you conscious. Alive is all I need. Lily will do all the hard work."

Lily met the young Calydon's gaze. "Just be quiet. You're no help to any of us if you're knocked out." She gave him a hard look, and he finally shut his mouth. She saw on his young face the realization that he had no choice. They had no option but to go forward and hope an opportunity arose.

If it didn't, there was plenty of time to die later.

Frank stood up. "Let me get out of the circle before you

begin."

He strode out, the heels of his dress shoes clicking on the rock as he strode across the circle and stepped carefully over the weapons. He took a stance between two Calydons, shooting a glare around the pit. "No one can find Ana? She has to be down here somewhere. Check the tunnels again. Check the cells. Kick down locked doors. I need her here by the time this rite's finished."

More than half the Calydons who had been standing around him vacated, streaming out through a maze of tunnels.

Frank set his gaze on Lily. "Begin."

"Lily—" Drew whispered, shifting against her, so she felt his nakedness against her body. Her stomach started to turn, so she pressed her cheek against Gideon's face and focused on the feel of his body draped over hers, the stickiness of his blood holding them together, bonding them as they were meant to be.

The panic eased from her chest and her shoulders relaxed as she concentrated on Gideon. On his vanilla scent, on his hard body, on his whiskers prickling against her cheek.

Then she closed her eyes and began to sing.

# Chapter 28

Ana froze when she heard the doorknob rattle on the door of Frank's office, and her gaze slid to the deadbolt she'd thrown.

"It's locked," a male said.

"He said break the doors down to find her."

Ana stopped breathing, holding absolutely still.

"We can't break down this door. He specifically built it to keep us out."

*Thank you, God.*

"You want to go back there and tell him that?"

The male cursed. "Fine. I'll get the key. You wait here. I'll be back in a minute."

*Shit.* Ana frantically scanned the room but there were no other exits. It was sealed, and there was one of Frank's Calydons on the other side of the only way out.

There was no way to escape. Okay, then. If they were going to get her anyway, there was no point in wasting what little time she had left. Fighting panic, she yanked open the drawer of the last filing cabinet, and the wheels rattled over the sliders.

"I hear her! She's in his office! Hurry up!" There was a slam against the door that made her jump. "Open the door!" He shouted as his weapon thudded against the door. "Now!"

Her heart pounding, Ana rifled through the folders, then Elijah's name flashed past. She quickly backed up, trying to find the paper with his name on it, her hands shaking, sweat trickling down her back as she tried to hurry. There! She yanked the file out and flipped it open.

It was a file on Elijah.

This had to be what she was looking for. It had to, because she was out of time if it wasn't.

Ana sat down on the floor and started reading as quickly as she could.

❦ ❦ ❦

Lily's magic surged as she began to sing the melody Gideon had sung to her in the woods, and her hips began to move as she tried to dance.

Drew sucked in his breath and tried to pull back as she writhed against him. She shut him out, taking herself back to the woods. She basked in the memory of the dirt under her feet, Gideon's hands on her body, sliding over her breasts, along her inner thighs, his face against hers, his rough voice making the music so lyrical and beautiful, rising to such heights.

Her body began to tingle and hum, and she felt the magic growing stronger, reaching out for Gideon everywhere they touched. She sent her magic into him the same way she'd done in the woods, giving him her strength, giving him her power.

Drew moaned and moved closer, and she realized he was getting the high from her magic as well.

She ignored him, continuing to focus on Gideon, sending her magic into him, touching his heart, his mind, his warrior strength...and then suddenly she felt his arm tighten against her. It was working! "Yes," she whispered. "Take my magic. Let it make you strong."

His lips moved against her cheek, and she realized he was trying to sing with her. She pressed her lips against his and sang, softly, for him and for him alone. The brands on her forearms began to burn, and her skin began to sizzle everywhere they touched. Her chest felt like it was expanding as strength and energy flowed through her.

Then Gideon's eyelashes moved against her cheek, and she opened her eyes to see him looking at her. His lips were still moving against hers, mimicking the words, though he couldn't speak yet.

She held his gaze as they sang, his beautiful blue gaze clinging to hers as if she were his anchor, his life force. She felt the intensity of his commitment to her, the truth of their connection, and she knew in that moment that she could trust him with her magic, every last bit of it. Gideon would never hurt her. He would protect and honor her magic, and he would use the depth of his feelings for her to make sure he didn't hurt her. And with that, she let go of all her restraint, and she gave him everything of who she was. She opened all her magic and gave it to him.

Gideon smiled softly, and he gave a single, small nod, and she knew then that he believed the same. He had accepted the intensity of his feelings for her, and that gave him the power to be the warrior she knew he was.

She smiled back, and her heart tightened just a little bit more for the man who had won her heart.

Drew shifted against her, and she saw Gideon's gaze flick to the youth. Drew's eyes widened, and he froze. "I didn't mean to touch her," he whispered.

Gideon shook his head once, ever so slightly, and then his gaze returned to Lily, holding the focus so tight. She tugged at her bound wrists in frustration, wanting to slide her arms around him, stroke the hard planes of his body, and feel his muscles clench under her touch. She moved her hips again, trying to dance, her body needing an outlet for the music.

Gideon's deep voice melded with hers, his words so quiet she knew Frank wouldn't be able to hear him. The rumble of his voice touched her deep in her heart, and her magic raced to meet him. She felt the power building around all three of them. Gideon's eyes became bright and focused. The rhythm of his breathing changed, becoming deeper and steadier, and his stomach muscles flexed where he was draped over her hips.

She raised her brows at him in question as she kept singing, and he gave a quick shake of his head that he wasn't ready yet.

"Do you feel that power?" Frank's voice echoed through the room, and she could imagine him lifting his arms to the ceiling, embracing the magic swirling around them and through them.

But she didn't look at Frank. She kept her energy centered on Gideon and felt it the minute he began to pull on her magic, instead of simply accepting what she was giving him.

She nodded and summoned more strength, more magic, more power, until suddenly Drew rose to his knees, as if the chains holding him weighed nothing.

"Yes!" Frank shouted. "Read the words! Read them now!"

She glanced over at Frank and saw the Calydon with the war hammer watching Gideon eagerly, his weapon clutched in his fist. She knew they'd hit Gideon again if she didn't do it. She raised her eyebrows at Gideon, and he grimaced.

"I just need another few seconds," he whispered.

She looked over at Frank again as she continued to sing, and saw him nod at the Calydon, who yanked his arm back to hurl the war hammer at Gideon's head.

No! She had to give Gideon more time! She immediately started chanting the ritual words, not even understanding them or knowing what they meant, but they flew off her tongue, a mixture of sounds that meant nothing, but at the same time, meant everything. The air sizzled with energy and sparks ignited around them, popping with frenzied light.

Drew raised his arms, snapping the chains and holding his arms out as she chanted. The weapons lifted off the ground and began slamming into his arms with loud cracks, one at a time. Each weapon vanished in a flash of black light when it made contact with his forearm. They weren't his weapons that he was sheathing. He was taking control of the other weapons, ones that weren't his and shouldn't have responded to his call. And yet, they were settling in his forearms as if he'd called his own weapons home.

Oh, yeah, that couldn't be good.

The music rose in a loud crescendo, taking on a life of its own, swelling through the room, echoing and pounding, like a thunderstorm of the gods.

Gideon's muscles bunched, and Lily braced herself a split second before he leapt off her with a roar of fury. His chains shattered and he charged through the circle of weapons at Frank. He called his axes out and hurled them both with deadly accuracy straight toward Frank's heart. His Calydons leapt in front of him to block the blows, and Gideon's axes tore through their bodies and thudded into Frank's chest, taking out all three of them at the same time.

Frank screamed and went down to his knees, blood pouring from his wounds as his bodyguards fell, gaping holes in their bodies from the axes that had blistered straight through them. Gideon called back his axes as he sprinted toward them. He reached Frank and slammed his axe down in a lethal blow.

The man fell to the ground, dead. It was over.

Gideon turned and met Lily's eyes, and her heart swelled. *I love you, Gideon.*

He flashed her a smile as if he'd heard her words, then whirled, taking out Calydons as they attacked. Gideon was moving so fast, he was a mere blur.

Then there was another loud crack and she jerked her gaze back to Drew. He was hovering in the air now, just off the ground, his arms outstretched. His irises were a faint pink that almost looked white, and his hair was now long and wiry, a coarse yellow. Holy crap. "Drew!"

She rolled onto her knees and shoved her shoulder against his legs, trying to knock him down. But he didn't move, didn't even notice her, his gaze looking past her. She turned and saw he was focused on the only set of weapons that hadn't yet settled in his arms.

His own.

They were in the air now and spinning in a violent circle, like a baton twirler on speed, and they were racing toward him. "Gideon! Get his weapons."

Gideon whirled around, his eyes narrowed and he sprinted toward the weapons.

Weakness shot through Lily's body as Gideon drew ruthlessly on her magic, and she sagged to the floor as he bore down on the speeding weapons. His legs were moving so fast she couldn't even see them anymore. Drew saw him coming, his eyes widened, and then his weapons picked up speed, hurtling toward his arms.

"No!" Gideon leapt through the air and lunged for the weapons, his fingers closing around them a split second before they hit Drew's forearms. His momentum sent him crashing hard into Drew. Both Calydons careened out of the circle and smashed into the stone wall. The wall shuddered at the impact and a huge crack split the clay and shot upwards, racing toward the ceiling as if it were alive.

The floor shook and suddenly the ground cracked open beneath Lily, splitting wide and creating a bottomless cavern below her. "Gideon!" She began to slide over the edge, unable to stop herself with her bound feet and wrists. "Gideon!"

Her back scraped over the sharp edge, and suddenly she was over the precipice—

Gideon's hand latched onto her arm, catching her in midair. He hauled her back up, shielding her body with his as rocks started to tumble from the ceiling. Both of Drew's polearms were clenched in his fist, and he used the spiked tip to slice through the tape binding her.

"You got Drew's weapons?" she asked.

"Sure did—" He grunted as Drew tackled him. Gideon threw Lily to the side and away from the crack in the floor as Drew's momentum carried him across the coliseum.

She scrambled to her feet as Drew attacked Gideon with a power and fierceness no young Calydon should ever possess. He was stronger than Gideon. So much stronger. Faster. Bigger. And he had dozens of weapons at his disposal, blades flashing and slicing and stabbing. As fast as Gideon was, Drew was more than twice as quick.

Drew was no longer himself. He had become something more.

Lily started singing again, sending her magic into Gideon. He drew on it instantly, and the fight exploded with energy and fire and such dizzying speed as she'd never seen before.

Her legs became weak from Gideon's drain on her, and she eased herself to the floor as Gideon and Drew battled. With the strength of her magic and their bond, Gideon was a warrior far beyond what he'd been in the woods when he'd taken out all those Calydons in less than a heartbeat using her magic. He was so much stronger and faster than was even possible, and yet Drew was beating him.

"Dear God," she whispered, as realization finally dawned on her. She'd completed the rite. It was too late. Ezekiel had been freed, and he had taken over Drew.

Gideon wasn't fighting Dante's son anymore.

He was fighting the warrior who no one could defeat, the man who had almost destroyed the world two thousand years ago. And he was losing.

# Chapter 29

There was a shout from above. Lily looked up and nearly cheered with relief when she saw Quinn and the rest of the Order leaping over the balcony railing of the coliseum, jumping into the pit. They charged into the fight with Drew and Gideon as rocks pummeled down on them from the ceiling. The walls were shaking and cracks were shooting up and down the sides, through the floors, the earth roaring its rage as it shattered under the violence.

Drew struck Quinn, and the Order member was flung backwards into the wall. Then another Order member went down, and another, until Gideon was the only one still standing against Drew.

Drew had taken down the Order in less than a second.

Drew slugged Gideon with a club and Gideon fell to the ground, immobile. He whirled toward Lily, not even flinching as the rocks pummeled him. His eyes were still a whitish pink, and she tensed when he focused on her.

"I will take you." He strode across the floor, stepping over gaping cracks in the ground as if they were slivers, not yards wide.

Lily scrambled backwards, trying to find the strength in her body, even as she kept the music going, sending her magic to Gideon, who was prone on the ground. "Gideon!" He didn't move, and she quickly found herself teetering on the edge of a giant crevice.

Drew grinned, a boyish grin that didn't reflect the ages-old-evil in his eyes. "Gideon cannot stop me. Don't you see?" He held up the polearms that he'd apparently retrieved from Gideon. "The world is mine now. *Mine.* As are you." His eyes shifted, whiting out entirely. "Nate did well to select you for me." His voice was hard now, dark and full of malevolence as he reached Lily. He grabbed her hair and wrenched her to her knees. "By the time I finish with you, I'll be at full power. Your body and your magic will be the last key."

Oh, God. She couldn't let this happen. This couldn't be how it ended. *Gideon!*

There was movement behind him, and Drew casually tossed his polearm over his shoulder. The weapon sped across the pit and pierced Ryland's gut. He sank back to the ground with a groan, clutching his stomach.

Lily started to sing, calling to Gideon, sending her magic out to all the Order members strewn on the floor like cast-aside garbage. She felt Gideon catch her magic and feed on it, draining her so hard and so fast she slumped to the ground.

"You raise them, I kill them. Boring game." Drew slammed his other hand around her throat, cutting off her air. "I have much more important things to do. My list grew long in the two thousand years I was locked up."

He threw her limp body over his shoulder. Her mind screamed in protest, but she was too weak to fight, too weak to do anything but keep singing, to keep feeding Gideon.

Drew leapt easily to the balcony surrounding the pit, and spots began to dance in Lily's vision. *Gideon. I can't go with him. I can't—*

Suddenly, there was a roar of such uncontained fury that Drew whirled around just as Gideon flew up from the pit and slammed both axes into Drew's chest, his eyes glowing bright red with the true rage of a Calydon gone rogue. Destiny had taken him. *Gideon was rogue.*

Drew shouted with rage and dropped Lily to yank the axes out of his torso.

Gideon charged Drew as Lily fell, bouncing over the edge of the balcony and falling straight toward one of the giant cracks in the floor. "Gideon!"

The wind raced past her as she plummeted down toward

the gaping crevasse in the earth, as the pit shuddered and the ceiling began to fall for real. Weapons clashed on the balcony as Gideon and Drew engaged, and she knew he was too consumed by the rogue to hear her.

Destiny was taking over. The bond complete, Gideon's destiny was to lose his woman, go rogue and destroy all they cared about. It was all unfolding exactly as it had thousands of times before. Screw destiny. This was not acceptable! "Gideon! For God's sake, *help me!*" She fell past the floor of the pit into the crevasse—

A firm grip suddenly grabbed her wrist, and she was yanked to a stop. Gideon's grim face stared down at her from the top edge of the crevasse.

His eyes were blue. Not red. Not rogue. He was back.

"You broke through," she gasped. Destiny required that once he lost his *sheva*, he would go rogue and never recover, and she'd have to kill him to stop him. But he'd come back on his own. He'd beaten destiny for them both, and he'd cut himself from the high of her magic. He'd triumphed over both of them, for her. She knew in that moment that her big, strong warrior loved her. So deeply. So passionately. Lily knew it in her heart, even if he would never be able to acknowledge it or understand it. She did, and that was enough.

His eyes were soft and full of love. "I couldn't let you die, *sheva.*" His muscles flexed, and he hauled her back up on the ledge, tumbling backwards with her on his chest as the ground shook violently.

Lily sagged against him, content to feel the hardness of his muscles under hers. She was too weak to do anything other than collapse on top of him. "You saved me because I'm your *sheva?*"

"Hell, no." He framed her face and kissed her hard, his kiss so full of love and commitment she felt her heart swell with passion. "The mere fact you're my *sheva* wouldn't be enough to pull me back from the edge, or other Calydons would have done it too. I broke through the curse because my heart shattered into a million pieces when I saw you falling." His grip tightened on her, his gaze searching hers desperately. "I love you, Lily, and I'll be damned if I'm going to let destiny take you away from me."

She smiled at him, her heart filling with warmth and happiness. This warrior, this courageous, amazing man was the gift she'd been seeking her whole life. He was her everything, her oasis from a past that could no longer torment her, not with Gideon's love surrounding her. "That must be a very powerful love if it's enough to defeat a fate that has been unstoppable for two thousand years," she teased.

He hugged her. "Yeah, well, what can I say? You won me over." There was a loud crash as another piece of the ceiling fell to the ground. Gideon rolled over, tucking her beneath him as rubble showered them, rocks beating at his body. "Let's get the hell out of here." He jumped to his feet and tucked her against him, using his body to shield her.

Lily wrapped her arms around his neck and buried her face against his chest as the debris continued to shower down on them. "Did you kill Drew?"

"No." Gideon broke into a run, sprinting toward the other Order members, who were staggering to their feet, helping each other up. "He took off when I came after you."

She closed her eyes in dismay. Dear God, he got away? "He's Ezekiel."

"I know." Gideon sounded grim.

"How can you stop him?"

He looked down at her. "You saw it, Lily. We can't."

☙ ☙ ☙

Ana flinched as rocks pummeled her, dropping down from the ceiling of Frank's office as she continued to scan Elijah's folder. She brushed the dirt off with her sleeve, trying to clear it enough to read. The Calydons guarding her door had bolted when the first earthquake had hit, and she had remained behind.

*Go.*

She jerked her head up as Elijah's voice rang in her mind, so solid and certain that she knew instantly it wasn't her imagination. Elation leapt through her heart. *Elijah!* It was as if whatever had been keeping him at a distance had shattered, and now she could hear him so clearly. *You're alive!* She clutched the folder to her chest as tears filled her eyes.

*Get out.* His voice was laced with torment, with agony,

and hatred for her. Such brutal, intense hatred, directed at her, but also at himself. It felt as if he couldn't help himself from warning her and caring about her, but he despised both of them for that fact. Ana knew in that moment that his hatred for her ran too deep. There would never be redemption.

But for all that, she couldn't leave him here. He died for her once, and she couldn't let it happen again. *Where are you? Are you here?*

*Ceiling... Falling.*

She looked up at the ceiling and saw the cracks spider-webbing through the rock as another loud rumble made her shudder. A boulder dropped from the ceiling and she dove to the right a split second before it crashed down on where she'd been sitting, trapping Elijah's folder beneath it. She cursed and tried to tug it out as the ground shook again.

*Go.* Elijah's voice was trembling and she could feel his pain.

*No! I need the folder!* She sat down, braced her feet against the boulder and yanked on the folder. The rock didn't move, but the papers tore. She fell backwards, smacking into the desk. She stared at the folder now hidden under the boulder. "Dammit!" She ran over to the rock and shoved her shoulder against it, her feet sliding on the rubble as more debris rained down. She had no chance of freeing the folder.

Nearly sobbing, she gave up and leaned against the boulder. "After all this, I'm going to fail? Dammit!" She stared at the torn pages in her hand. "Like this is going to do me any good—" She frowned suddenly and started reading more carefully.

Then her heart started racing. "Oh my God. This is it!" She had what she needed!

Clutching the paper to her chest, she ran to the door, threw the lock and ran down the hall toward the main pit, stumbling as her cast knocked into fallen rocks. *Elijah! Where are you?*

There was no answer, but she knew he had to be in one of the nearby tunnels.

"Elijah!" She shouted his name as she tripped again, and the paper fell out of her hand.

It didn't matter. She'd already read it. She already knew what it said.

*Elijah! Talk to me! Where are you? I'm coming to get you!*

But there was silence again, as if he'd never been.

But she knew he had. She *knew* he'd spoken to her. He was here. In the pit. Somewhere.

A rock landed on her shoulder and she staggered, trying to pick around the debris raining down around her. "Elijah!"

"Ana!"

She looked up to see Ian limping toward her. He was bloody and his leg didn't appear to be working right. "Ian!" she shouted. "Elijah's here! We have to find him!"

"We don't have time. The place is caving in." He reached her, swept her up, and whirled around, limping back toward the pit far faster than she could run with her cast, despite his injury.

"No!" She fought against his iron grip. "We have to get Elijah!"

Kane appeared in front of them, and the blood was so thick on his shoulders she couldn't even see his scars. "I got everyone else out, and the pit's collapsing. We can't get back to the coliseum."

Ana realized Kane was going to transport them out. "We can't leave without Elijah! We need him! It's on the paper." She kicked hard, and Ian grunted but didn't let go as Kane reached them. "Take me back and I'll show you."

The ground bucked under their feet and they all looked up to see the ceiling implode down toward them, tons and tons of earth pouring down.

Her heart dropped and she realized they were going to die.

Kane grabbed them, and they faded just as the earth smothered the spot where they'd been standing.

🐾 🐾 🐾

Lily leaned against Gideon as she watched the house that had been Frank's collapse into a sinkhole more than a mile wide. Dirt and dust flew up in a giant cloud, contaminating the air as the entire underground structure collapsed and the earth filled in.

Lily was wearing Quinn's shirt, but Gideon hadn't bothered to find clothes. His body had healed miraculously from her magic, but he was the only one in decent condition. The rest of the team was damaged and weak. Decimated would be a better word.

The air was thick with the mood of the Order as they silently surveyed the devastation.

"Frank's dead." Gideon rested his cheek against hers while the other Order members sat in stunned silence, waiting for Kane to reappear with Ana and Ian. "Neither of us died. Destiny didn't win. We beat it."

His arms were secure around her waist, and she was holding him just as tightly. "But Ezekiel is free." The huge fir trees that had towered over them when they had arrived were brown and shriveled. There were several dead squirrels hanging from the branches, as if they'd died mid-run. There were no birds at all on the land, but flocks of them darkened the sky, the creatures squawking as they fled the area.

Lily dug her toes into the earth, and it felt acrid and dead. It made her skin tighten and her stomach turn. "All this is from him?"

"All this is from him." Gideon's voice was quiet. "It's the first step to the world's descent into hell."

"We're fucked." Ryland wrapped a tourniquet around his heavily muscled thigh, trying to cut off the fountain of blood spewing from his leg. "We're completely fucked. How the hell are we going to take Ezekiel down?"

"Get us each our own Satinka and attack at the same time?" Thano said. "How did they bring him down before?"

"They had Ezekiel's brother, Caleb," Quinn said. "Caleb was the only one as strong as Ezekiel."

"Well, what was so special about him?" Ryland demanded. "Why could *he* beat Ezekiel when no one else could?"

"Because they shared blood," Lily said. "They were brothers."

Gideon rested his chin on her head, and she snuggled deeper against him, needing the reassurance of his touch.

"So?" Ryland sounded frustrated, and she didn't blame

him. "What difference did that make? If we find that out, maybe we can recreate it somehow."

"They shared the same bloodlines," Lily explained. "That made them equals in combat. The rest of the original twenty-one took down Ezekiel's men, but it was Caleb himself who defeated Ezekiel."

"So, we become as powerful as Caleb," Thano said. "That's our only option."

"But how?" Quinn asked, pressing his palm to the side of his head as blood squeezed between his fingers and trailed down his arm. "Even Gideon wasn't strong enough with Lily's help. I've never seen anyone fight the way Gideon and Drew did, and it wasn't even a challenge for Drew."

Kane appeared in front of them with Ian and Ana, who was shouting and pummeling at Ian's arms. The minute he let go of her, she whirled away from him and ran straight for Quinn and Gideon. "We have to go back and get Elijah!"

Lily touched Ana's arm, her heart breaking for her anguish. She could only imagine how she felt losing her mate. Lily knew it would destroy her to lose Gideon. "I'm so sorry, Ana, but he's dead." If he hadn't been killed by Gideon, he was certainly dead now after that collapse.

"No, he's not!" Ana protested. "He spoke to me! I heard it in my mind."

Lily and Gideon exchanged glances. "Something about the way that place was built prevented mind to mind contact," Lily quietly told Ana. "He couldn't have talked to you that way."

"But I heard him!"

Quinn set his hand on her shoulder. "I'm sorry, Ana. He's gone."

They'd already told Quinn how Elijah had been crazed, and Lily knew neither of them wanted to tell Ana the ugly truth about how Elijah had died fighting his own teammate. Gideon's pain pulsed at her, his regret and guilt for his role in Elijah's death. She patted his hand. *It's not your fault.*

*I loved him.* His voice was quiet, but so heavy with pain that Lily turned in his arms to face him.

His blue eyes were haunted, and she slipped her arms around his waist. This Gideon was so different from the man she'd first met. No longer was he trying to be the stoic warrior. He was pulsing with emotions, with love, heartache, and passion. It was beautiful, and she felt her own soul blossom in response. Pain was hard, for sure. But without it, the soul was empty, and love was elusive. She knew neither of them would ever be willing to trade the beauty of their love to retreat back into their ordered, emotionless worlds of survival and duty. *I know you did. I'm so sorry.*

Gideon gave a small nod and pulled her against him, resting his forehead against hers. *Just your touch gives me comfort.*

*As does yours.*

He kissed her softly, his lips warm against hers. *I love you, Lily. Everything I've been through for the last five hundred years...it was all to take me to this place. To your arms. To bring you into my life.*

She smiled up at him, her heart expanding with joy. Was it crazy that she could feel happy after all that had happened? No, it wasn't. All the hardships in their lives were what had enabled them to feel this kind of love. She knew all too well that you had to take the good when you got it, even when things were crumbling all around you. *I feel the same way.*

"Listen to me," Ana shouted, drawing Lily's attention back to her. "For God's sake, will all of you just listen for one minute?" Her face was streaked with dirt, and she had smears of blood on her clothes. "Elijah can't be dead."

Gideon sighed. "Ana—"

"He can't be dead, because I found out the truth about him. I found out why Frank brought him here and kept him alive." She glanced around at the Order, all of them silent, all watching, all weary. "When I first arrived, Frank said he couldn't afford to have Elijah die. Why couldn't he afford to have Elijah die? Does anyone know?" Her face was angry, as if she thought people had been lying to her.

Quinn was the one who shook his head. "Tell us." He sounded exhausted and strained, too tired for games.

"Because Elijah is descended from Caleb," she announced.

The Order went still, and Lily sat up, catching her

breath. "You're sure?"

Gideon tensed against Lily. "The original Caleb, who brought down Ezekiel? That's who Elijah is descended from?"

"Yes! He's not a direct descendent, but he has his blood." Ana shot challenging looks at the team. "Frank needed Elijah to stay alive in case he couldn't control Ezekiel after all. Elijah was his insurance to take Ezekiel out, because Elijah is the one who could kill him. Did you hear? Elijah is the one who can stop him!"

As a unit, the team turned to look down at the rubble still settling. The carnage and destruction was so fast, so brutal, so complete, that the hope died instantly in Lily's heart.

"There's no way he survived that," Gideon said. "Assuming he was still alive when it went down."

"Even if he were still alive..." Gideon's voice was laced with pain he couldn't hide and wasn't even trying to suppress, and Lily hugged him tighter. "He was insane, Ana. There's no way he would be a weapon now. He'd kill us all."

"He's not insane!" Ana marched over to the rim of the sinkhole and surveyed it, as if she were already assessing how she was going to get down into the cavern and start digging. Passion was radiating off her, a fierce determination that reminded Lily so much of herself, of all those times when she'd summoned the will to survive.

"He was perfectly lucid when he ordered me to get out. He told me the ceiling was falling." Ana's fists clenched. "We have to go back for him."

Lily sat up in surprise. "He spoke to you? And he sounded sane?"

"Well, he sounded tormented and he hates..." Evasiveness flickered in Ana's eyes. "...Frank. But yes, he was completely aware of what was going on, and that I was in danger."

Lily looked at Gideon, excitement building in her at the possibilities. "Since Ana is his *sheva*, maybe she could make him sane when nothing else could."

Gideon exchanged looks with Quinn. "Who the hell knows what a *sheva* can do? At this point anything's possible."

Ryland moved to stand beside Ana, his face hard with determination. "I'm going after Elijah. If there's any chance he's alive and able to function, we have to get him back."

Ana grinned and threw her arms around him. "Thank you, Ryland! I know he's there!"

The warrior didn't hug her back, and Lily knew he was thinking only about avenging Dante's death. Unlike Gideon, Lily suspected there was very little humanity and warmth hidden beneath Ryland's abrasive and violent exterior, which was no doubt why he was treading so close to rogue. There was nothing anchoring him to sanity. "I'm going in now," he said. "Is anyone with me?" he challenged.

Lily glanced past him at the sinkhole. The ground was still shifting and buckling.

"We can't go back yet. We'll get crushed," Quinn said. "It'll take days for the earth to settle enough for us to start digging."

Ryland ground his jaw, but he nodded in acknowledgement. He turned toward the pit and sat down, as if he were holding vigil over the crater. "I'll wait here, and I'll call you the minute it's safe to search for him." He called out his machete and rested it across his lap. "You all go back and heal while you can." He lifted his face to the wind, to the acrid smell of rotting vegetation. "We'll need all our strength for the battle that lies ahead." He raised his machete. "I will not fail Dante. I will not let his son be used to destroy all that he worked so hard to preserve."

The rest of the Order raised their weapons and shouted Dante's name and their promise to win.

There was no other option.

# Chapter 30

Gideon stopped his truck outside the small red house. It had a quaint little lawn that was mostly weeds, but was freshly mowed. The flowerbeds were half-weeded, as if someone was in the middle of restoring them. It looked domestic and suburban, and he knew he didn't belong there, in this kind of neighborhood, in that kind of house. "This was a mistake to come here."

"No, it wasn't." Lily leaned past him, her hand on his shoulder. "My parents used to be amazing landscapers. They let it go over the last two years." Her voice was jubilant and excited, so full of life and vitality. "But I can see they're out here again. They're taking their life back now. Isn't it great?"

Gideon slid his hand around Lily's waist, more to comfort himself than her. "It's because you've come back to them."

"Yes." She looked at him, her eyes brimming with delight. "Let's go in. My mom's making lasagna. You'll love it. She's the best cook on this side of the Mississippi. I used to dream of her meals when I was locked up at Nate's. Come on!" She gave him a quick kiss and hopped out of the truck.

Gideon didn't move.

While they were waiting for the ground to settle so they could search for Elijah, Gideon had agreed to take Lily back to see her parents. She'd promised Gideon that she'd talk to them about him, and he'd heard the hours of conversation she'd had with them, trying to convince them he wasn't a monster, but last he heard, they hadn't sounded convinced.

All he could think about was how much her parents hated him. How Lily's mom had watched him slay her own mother.

Shit. It had been a bad idea to come. Sweat beaded on his forehead. "I can't do this."

Lily walked around to his door and opened it. Her eyes were dancing with happiness. "Come on, Gideon. Remember, my mom's name is Maggie and my dad is Gerry."

He shook his head. "I can't—"

Her smile faded, and she wrapped her hands around his. "You can. They forgive you."

"They couldn't possibly, and why should they? I did exactly what they think I did."

"Yes, but you also saved their only child." She smiled at him, her green eyes so full of warmth and affection. "You love their daughter, and their daughter loves you. That has to be enough for them."

"What do I say to them?" He paused as he heard the front door click, then snapped his gaze to the front porch.

Lily's parents opened the door and stepped out onto the porch. Maggie was holding tightly to Gerry's hand, and her face was white.

Gideon cursed, feeling the pain he was causing them by his mere presence. "I can't—"

"You can." Lily didn't even turn around to look at her parents. She climbed up on the running board, wrapped her arms around his neck and kissed him, a full mouth kiss that told anyone who was watching that she was staking a claim to him.

His throat tightened as she pulled back, and he brushed a strand of her beautiful hair off her face. Hell, how could this amazing woman be his? How could she love him like that? But she did. It was evident in everything she did, in every word she spoke, in the way she watched him with those beautiful green eyes, as if she were drinking him into her soul. "You might have just broken their hearts with that move."

Lily grinned. "They'll learn to love you, because I love you." She hopped down to the street and tugged his hand. "Now, come. It's time for everyone I love to meet each other properly."

Gideon winced and let her pull him out of the truck. His

boots thudded on the asphalt, and he felt clumsy and awkward as Lily shut the car door behind him and led him across the grass.

As they neared, Maggie retreated into Gerry's side, and both their gazes were fixed on Gideon's face, so stark with pain and fear and distrust.

He stopped at the bottom of the stairs. "I'm sorry," he blurted out. "I'm so sorry for the pain I've caused you, for what I did to your family. I don't deserve your daughter, and I would walk away from her to spare you the pain of seeing my face. I swear I'd do it in a heartbeat if I could, but I can't live without her. She's my life, my oxygen…" His voice broke, but he kept going. "She's made me alive again, and I can't survive without her." He went down on one knee and dropped his head. "I would never seek your forgiveness for all I've stolen from you, because I don't deserve it and I don't forgive myself. But by all that's good in the world, I give you my oath that I will love Lily and treasure her for all eternity. I extend my protection to you as well, and never again will you or your family ever have to fear the Order no matter what happens. I am your servant forever." His throat tightened. "Hell help me, but I love her too damn much to walk away. I'm so, so sorry, but it's true."

And then he ran out of things to say. He had nothing more to offer.

There was a heavy silence.

Then Lily set her hand on his shoulder. "Can you see why I love him so much?" Her voice was soft, so full of love and emotion, that he looked up at her.

But she wasn't looking at him.

She was looking at her parents.

Then she smiled, and Gideon slowly turned his head to look at them as well.

Tears were streaming down Maggie's face, and even Gerry's eyes looked a little bloodshot.

Maggie released her husband's hand and walked over to the edge of the porch, her gaze fastened on Gideon. She walked down the steps, and he stiffened, but didn't rise off his knee.

Maggie came to a stop in front of him and looked down at him.

For what felt like an eternity, she stared at him and said nothing. He felt his heart begin to shrivel up. There was no place for him in their world. Lily might love him, but she would always be torn. He would never be a part of the light that was such a part of her—

Maggie touched his shoulder lightly, and she smiled. "Welcome to our family, Gideon."

His eyes immediately filled up, and his vision got blurry. "What?"

Lily's arms went around them both and hugged them together. "Thank you, Mom."

Gideon stiffened when he felt Lily pull her mom against him, and then suddenly Maggie's arms slipped around his shoulders and hugged him too, and then Gerry was there and hugging them all, and Gideon was in the middle of it.

He was home.

# Sneak Peek: Darkness Surrendered

## An *Order of the Blade* Novel

Ana felt Elijah tense beneath her. He was awake.

His body hadn't so much as twitched, his breathing hadn't changed, and his heart rate hadn't sped up. But there was a vibrating tension about him, a readiness.... A warrior in battle, not giving away anything.

She lifted her head to look at him, trying to move slowly so as not to trigger him into another manic episode. His scarred brown eyes were glazed, unseeing, but they were focused on her face, as if he could see her through some deeper force than his vision.

Her heart started to race and she hesitated, not sure what to do. Was he about to freak out again? Or was he sane? "Um..." She licked her lips nervously. "I'm Ana Matthews... but I guess you already know that."

Elijah blinked several times, the movement awkward and jerky, as if his eyelids were rasping painfully over his damaged eyes. Her heart ached at the sight of all those raw scars on his face, as if he'd tried to claw out his own eyes rather than see the hell he'd been facing. Was she responsible for that? Had it been her illusions that he'd tried to defend against by blinding himself?

Tears filled her eyes, tears of guilt, regret and empathy, and she instinctively laid her hand on his cheek. "Oh, Elijah," she whispered, forgetting to fear him, ignoring all Gideon's warnings about how Elijah might be so violent and insane when he finally awoke from his coma. "I'm so sorry."

He blinked again, wincing at the agonizing movement as he tried to see her.

"No, no," she whispered. "Don't torment yourself. Here." She clasped his wrist and placed his palm against her cheek. "See me this way."

He closed his eyes and let his hand drift across her face. He moved his fingers over her skin, over her cheekbone, her eyelashes, the bridge of her nose, his callused fingers so light against her skin.

Elijah touched her mouth, tracing the outline of her lips. Heat began to swirl inside Ana as he gave a small nod. "Good." The word came out as a grinding noise, and her heart tightened at the grimace of pain on his face.

But God, to hear his voice again, his real voice, not the whisper in her mind. It burned right to her soul, like the forbidden heat of a sensual danger designed to strip her defenses and possess her completely. She swallowed, suddenly nervous, no longer feeling like a woman trying to protect a man. Instead, she felt like a female being drawn ruthlessly into the spell of the male destined to consume her. "Elijah—"

His arm snaked around her, trapping her he pulled her down against him. He buried his face in the curve of her neck with a deep groan of contentment that made desire pulse through her relentlessly.

Ana froze as he inhaled deeply, and she knew he was examining her scent, memorizing every detail about her body. "It's me," she whispered. "You know me."

He blew out, his lips feathering her neck with heat.

Her skin felt like it was on fire. She became aware of his scent, the raw, fierce pulse of danger and death, mixed with something softer. Vulnerability. Fear. Desperation. Dear God, his suffering was so intense, filling her with the agony of his despair, of his confusion. Had she done that to him? Was all of that her fault? How much worse would she make it if she stayed with him, if he realized who she was? "This really isn't a good idea." She set her hands on his shoulders and gently tried to push him away. "It's the *sheva* bond making you want me. You actually hate—" She stumbled over the words, regret thick and bitter. "You hate me, Elijah. As soon as your mind settles again, you'll remember."

His hands snapped to her hips, trapping her against him. "Mine," he growled. His eyes were still closed, unable to defeat the pain of the scar tissue, but his hands were burning over her, as if he were stripping her clothes off and branding her with every touch.

"Oh, God," she whispered. "Don't pull me into this. I don't have many defenses left." Her heart had bled for this man so many times, and now he held her like she was his salvation, his anchor, the only thing he had to hold onto.

She'd already seen the way he looked at her, with pure revulsion for who she was and what she'd done to him. She knew it would come again the moment he regained his senses. She couldn't let herself fall into his touch, into his need, and then survive it when he took it away from her. He wouldn't survive it either, being sucked into her nightmare. "We can't lie to each other," she whispered as she grabbed his wrist, trying to stop him. "This isn't real. Please, don't do this to me. To us."

"Real," he whispered, sliding his hands beneath her shirt, flattening one palm over her belly. "You're not real?" His voice cracked, and he gripped her sides with sudden intensity. "You have to be real—"

"I am, I am," she soothed quickly. "You're not having illusions. I'm right here." She knew he'd been tormented by illusions. He'd been thrust mercilessly into the world of uncertainty, unable to know what nightmares were real, and which were fake. Men had died from the insanity the illusions caused, from the inability to know truth from delusion, and she knew Elijah's greatest tool right now was reality. She couldn't take that away from him. "I'm not your imagination," she said.

Elijah opened his eyes again, straining to see her, but there was no recognition in those scarred eyes. "I can't see you," he croaked. "You're not real—"

"I am!" Ana grabbed his hands and squeezed. "Feel my touch," she ordered. "Hear my voice. I'm here, dammit! You're not being messed with anymore!"

"You're real?" His voice softened with awe and disbelief. "This is you?" He ran his hands over her stomach, her ribs, and desire leapt through her.

Ana leaned her head back and closed her eyes, her body trembling at the sensation of his hands on her body. God, how long had it been since a man's hands had touched her with kindness? Not just kindness. Reverence. Adoration. Callused hands that would never hurt her, no matter what she did. Hands that would wrap around her at night and keep her safe. Strong, masculine hands that would seduce her until she was his, forever...

Oh, God. What was she thinking? She couldn't do this, not to him, not to herself. Her only job was to help him regain his sanity, to bring him back so he could fulfill the mission he was meant to do. She had to stop him from weaving this web around them, from drawing them both into the dangerous attraction between them, the one that was only about their *sheva* bond, not reality, not the truth about how much damage there was between them.

"Elijah! We don't have time for this. Your team needs you upstairs. You have to save the damn world." She winced at how she sounded a little too breathless and sensual. Desperate and panicked, yes, but also... intimate. She cleared her throat and leaned back, away from his face still nuzzling her throat. "If you were in your right mind, you'd never touch me like this. You despise me and I—"

"No," he growled. His hands slid up her back beneath her shirt, and he pressed against her bare shoulder blades, pulling her toward him. Toward his mouth.

Anticipation hummed through Ana even as she stiffened, fighting the urges racing through her. God, how she wanted to lose herself in him. "Dammit, Elijah. Stop!"

Her body was trembling with desire, with nervousness, and the need to leap off his lap and bolt. But she knew he'd snap if she broke physical contact with him, and she didn't know if she'd be able to bring him back from his delusions and insanity again. She owed him, and she knew that her soul was already too black to survive causing Elijah's death for a second time. "Elijah—" Her palms went to his bare chest to try to block him from pulling her any closer, and the heated spark was almost instant.

They both froze, and she could feel his heart pounding beneath her palms.

*Mine.* His possessive growl echoed in her mind, sending spirals of fire and heat racing through her.

*Yours.* The word popped into Ana's mind before she could stop it.

The moment the word formed in her head, Elijah jerked upright and yanked her against him. His hand roughly palmed the back of her head to bring her down at the right angle, not giving her a chance to resist or to stop him. He sank his mouth onto hers, and her lips parted instantly for him... and then she felt the beast consume him. His need pulsed at her, shredding all her resistance in a heartbeat.

She barely stifled a scream as Elijah shifted and rolled her beneath him, covering her with his body. His kisses were frantic, his mouth almost violent in its assault on her. His hands were all over her, her stomach, her breasts, his fingers bruising and desperate. She could feel his *desperation* for her, and she knew he might hurt her.

And she didn't care.

Hot desire rose hard and fast inside her, and she threw her arms around his neck, holding him tightly as her own need met his. God, she'd needed this for so long. Not just any touch. *His touch.* She knew it in every fiber of her being that he had been inside her soul since they'd met. *We will destroy each other.* The thought was like a cold hit to her gut and she tried to break the kiss. "I can't—"

He tugged her shirt up and caught her breast in his mouth, a decadent, raging kiss of desperate desire that eviscerated her resistance to him. His fervent passion for her was tearing at her soul with every kiss.

Darkness slithered along the edges of her mind, a danger so vivid and poisonous that her soul recoiled and she tried to pull back. Elijah growled and deepened his kiss, and she realized that the hell she'd sensed was in Elijah's mind, a demonic darkness trying to overtake his sanity. She knew Elijah was trying to outrun it by sinking himself into her body and her mind, seeking solace in their touch, in the kisses.

She was the oasis, the sanity, the beauty that could bring him back from his insanity, from the demons in his mind. A sense of absolute rightness filled Ana with heat and warmth at the realization that she could help him. The hell she would face later didn't matter anymore. Elijah needed her, and as his soul mate, she could help him. *I'm here for you.*

His energy reached for her through the nightmare that beat at him. His soul wrapped itself around her as he fought for his sanity and control. His relentless need for her consumed both his mind and hers...

*Yes, Elijah. Take me. Whatever you need from me, it's yours.* She wrapped her arms around his neck, gasping as he kissed her breasts. A growl ripped from this throat, an untamed sound of possession and domination as he lowered his hips between her thighs. His hips began to pump, his erection slamming into her through her jeans.

Desire raged through her, sweeping her up and away from all the anguish she'd been carrying for so long. In his arms, there was nothing left of the woman who'd hurt so many people. Gone was the debilitating guilt and grim awareness of the monster she was. The aching loneliness, the constant fear, the incessant terrors…all gone, cradled in the strong palms of this courageous warrior. Instead, there was simply beauty and passion, a sense of being loved and desired, of being treasured. *Yes,* she whispered, her heart too full of emotion to dare stop him. She wanted more of this moment, even though she knew she didn't deserve it, even though she knew it would all be torn apart the moment he recovered enough to remember who she was.

His body was rigid under her touch, and she felt every cut, every wound under her hands. There was nowhere to hold him without hurting him more. He shouted and thrust harder, and suddenly she couldn't think anymore, his need for her calling out an answering yearning in her. His body was so hot, his skin serrated and broken, his muscles rock hard beneath her touch, sliding under his skin.

Ana arched her back, her body reaching for him, for his touch, for the heat in his hands and the fire in his kisses until it wasn't just about his desperation, but hers as well. His hand went to her jeans and he fumbled with them, trying to get them undone as his thrusts grew more frantic, more forceful, his erection slamming through the denim into her most sensitive spot.

Utter rightness swelled inside her, consuming her, until the fire began to lick down her limbs, igniting every inch of her until the sensations exploded, overwhelming her soul and her body. She screamed Elijah's name and his deep roar mixed with hers, his body convulsing against her as he drove again and again, his hands braced on the floor by her head, his attempt to get her pants off lost in the blazing inferno consuming them both. He went rigid above her, and then he collapsed, his body sinking onto hers, his chest flush against the bare skin of her breasts, his hips stilled between hers, his breathing raw and harsh on her neck.

She locked her arms around his shredded back and entwined her feet along his thighs, holding him as tightly as she could as the final tremors faded.

Elijah shuddered against her and then his body finally went quiet.

Neither of them moved or spoke, though she was certain he was awake. They just lay together, intertwined, on the steel floor, recovering.

After a moment, she rested her elbow on his shoulder and pressed her hand to her eyes. Dear God. What had she done?

Elijah shifted suddenly. He rose swiftly to his hands and knees, his body going rigid. He straddled her, his palms braced on either side of her head, his legs outside hers. It was the position of a male defending his woman with his body. He stopped breathing, going utterly still, a predator waiting for the enemy to attack.

Ana froze, her heart pounding. What had he seen? Had his mind snapped? *Elijah? What's wrong?*

*They're coming.* His head was up and he was staring blindly past her with the intensity of an assassin who had targeted his mark.

*Who?* Demons? Some figment of his ravaged mind? Ana carefully twisted her head to look where he was looking. Relief rushed through her when she saw Quinn and Gideon standing inside the door. Elijah wasn't imagining things. He was all right! "I'm fine," she quickly told them, her cheeks heating with embarrassment at being caught in such an intimate position. Her pants were still on, but it was obvious what they'd been doing.

Neither warrior moved, and Elijah lowered himself slightly, his chest resting protectively against hers. She noticed then that Gideon and Quinn had their weapons out, and they were pointing them at Elijah. Oh, crap! No wonder Elijah was on the defensive. "Put your weapons away," she said quickly.

"He's—"

Elijah's hand went to her mouth, silencing her.

Gideon swore and didn't sheathe his weapon. "We're going to grab you and pull you out from under him."

Oh, Dear God, that would make Elijah snap if they went after her! "No! Don't touch me! Don't take me away from him!"

Elijah tensed at her sharp tone, and he immediately shifted his weight to free his right arm. "No, Elijah." She fought to keep her voice calm. "They're your friends—"

He called out his throwing star with a crack that reverberated against the steel wall, and she knew they were a split second away from a full battle, a battle which she knew would end only in death.

# Sneak Peek: Not Quite Dead

## A *NightHunter* Novel

With a sigh, Jordyn spun her chair toward the dining tables, propped her elbows on the counter of the bar, and leaned back against the battered wood. Slowly, she examined every person in the room, going through the same process she'd used at every other bar she'd visited in the last three hours to see if the man she was looking for was present.

Even as she did it, she was aware of the low odds of success. Did she really think she'd find Tristan this way? No, but he'd lived here for at least six months, and he had to have had an impact, right? Somewhere in this town, he'd left a clue before he'd disappeared. According to Eric, this was the last place he'd been seen.

Her gaze wandered over to the Gaston brothers, and then the door to the bar swung open, drawing her attention. The screen door slammed against the wall, and a dark shadow filled the doorway. The man who stepped inside was tall and broad-shouldered, with dark hair. His presence was so powerful that the energy in the room actually shifted, rippling as it tried to accommodate the sheer force of his being. She sucked in her breath and sat up, chills racing down her spine.

*Eric.*

He was there.

She stared at him, her fingers clenching the seat of her stool. He was so much bigger than she remembered. Taller, wider shoulders, a more dominating presence. He seemed to loom over the entire bar, an unstoppable force of power. He scanned the room slowly, starting with the Gaston brothers.

A part of her wanted to leap up, race over to him, and throw herself into his arms. She was riveted by the raw strength of his body, and she knew exactly how much power radiated from him. He'd been wild and untamed in the jungle, but here, it was as if he were part predator, a feral beast constrained by no one and nothing, stalking through civilization in search of the prey that he would conquer. She recalled his claim that he wasn't a man, and she suddenly believed him. Yes, a man, but there was something else as well. Something more visceral and dangerous. Something so graceful and lethal, physicality far beyond that of an ordinary man.

His hair was longer now, disheveled and ragged as it hung over his forehead. His eyes were blazing and dark, his jaw taut, his muscles flexed. The man standing in the doorway was nothing like the flirtatious, irreverent man she'd met a month ago. This man was moody, dark, and pulsing with an energy so intense that it slid down her spine and settled right in her lower belly. This man was a warrior, and he was pure, unfettered *male*.

Her heart started to hammer, thundering against her ribs, as she watched his gaze slide over the patrons, moving inexorably toward her. She knew then why she was still wearing her business suit. It hadn't been to prove herself to the town that had once been her home. It had been for Eric.

The only time she'd met him, they'd been deep in the Brazilian jungle, and she'd been wearing boots, jeans, and a ponytail. He'd overpowered her with the sheer force of his person, and she'd wanted to reinforce her shields this time by putting on her work persona, the one that was about the power and strength of a woman.

It wasn't working.

She felt sucked into the vortex of his power, every cell in her body tightening with each passing second as she waited for him to notice her. In the jungle, she'd been so worried about finding her friend that she'd had no emotional space to really let Eric affect her, but now it was different.

Now, she was so deeply aware of him that she couldn't stop thinking about how it had felt during that brief moment when he'd kissed her in the jungle. Fast. Passionate. Intense.

His gaze penetrated the darkest corner of the bar, his brown eyes alert and vibrant. He'd looked rugged and athletic before, but now, he looked rougher, like he'd been spawned by the earth itself. His jeans sat low on his hips, dripping wet, as if he'd been submerged in the bayou for hours. His boots were thick with mud, and there was dirt streaked across his face. His dark hair was damp and tangled, shoved ruthlessly aside so it was spiked and messy. Droplets slid in a wet sheen across his forehead, the sweat of a man who'd been working hard at something, even though it was the middle of the night. Whiskers were heavy on his jaw, and she had a sudden ridiculous urge to run her fingers over them.

So much for thinking that four weeks in Boston was going to make her immune to the effect he had on her. It had gotten worse, exponentially more intense, since they'd parted ways.

She wasn't ready for this.

She wasn't ready for him.

She wasn't ready for any of it.

Jordyn swallowed, her heart almost leaping out of her chest as he turned his head toward her. His eyes met hers, and she knew instantly that, unlike the town that had known her for the first sixteen years of her life, *he* didn't have any trouble recognizing her. The flash of awareness was instant, and she felt like her skin was on fire. She swallowed, her mouth suddenly dry, and her fingers tightened around her stool, as if she could keep herself from tumbling off it and into his arms.

Instantly, he shoved away from the doorway and headed straight toward her. His jaw was tense, and his stride was long and purposeful, rippling with languid strength. His gaze was fixed on hers so intently that she wanted to look away...except she couldn't take her eyes off him.

She tensed as he neared, sitting up straighter and trying to get a cool expression on her face. "Where have you been—?"

He gave her no time to finish her sentence. He just swung his arm behind her lower back, hauled her up against him, and kissed her.

# Sneak Peek: Prince Charming Can Wait

## An *Ever After* Novel

Clouds were thick in the sky, blocking the moon. The lake and the woods were dark, swallowing up light and life, like a soothing blanket of nothingness coating the night. Emma needed to get away from the world she didn't belong to, the one that held no place for her. Tears were thick in her throat, her eyes stinging as she ran. The stones were wet from the rain earlier in the day, and the cool dampness sent chills through her.

She reached the dock and leapt out onto the damp wood. Her foot slipped, and she yelped as she lost her balance—

Strong hands shot out and grabbed her around the waist, catching her before she fell into the water. Shrieking in surprise, she jerked free, twisting out of range. The evasive move sent her off balance again, her feet went out from under her, and she was falling—

And again, someone grabbed her. "Hey," a low voice said. "I'm not going to hurt you."

Emma froze at the sound of the voice she knew so well, the one that had haunted her for so many sleepless nights. The voice she thought she'd never hear again, because he'd been gone for so long. "Harlan?"

"Yeah."

Emma spun around in his grasp, and her breath caught as she saw his shadowed face. His eyes were dark and hooded in the filtered light, his cheek bones more prominent than they had been the last time she'd seen him. Heavy stubble framed his face, and his hair was long and ragged around the base of his neck. He was leaner than she remembered, but his muscles were more defined, straining at his tee shirt. He looked grungy and real, a man who lived by the earth every day of his life. He exuded pure strength and raw appeal that ignited something deep within her. She instinctively leaned toward him, into the strength that emanated from him. His hands felt hot and dangerous where they clasped her hips, but she had no urge to push him away.

Damn him. After not seeing him for nearly a year, he

still affected her beyond reason.

"You're back," she managed.

"Yeah."

Again, the one word answer. He had never said much more than that to her, but she'd seen him watching her intently on countless occasions, his piercing blue eyes roiling with so much unspoken emotion and turbulence. She managed a small smile, trying to hide the intensity of her reaction to seeing him. "Astrid didn't mention you would be here."

"She doesn't know." Again, he fell silent, but he raised one hand and lifted a lock of her hair, thumbing it gently. "Like silk," he said softly. "Just as I always thought it would feel."

Her heart began to pound now. There was no way to stop it, not when she was so close to him, not when she could feel his hands on her, a touch she'd craved since the first time she'd seen him. It had been two years ago, the day she'd walked back into her life in Birch Crossing. He had been leaning against the deli counter in Wright's, his arms folded over his chest, his piercing blue eyes watching her so intently.

And now he was here, in these woods, holding onto her.

His grip was strong, but his touch was gentle in her hair as he filtered the strands through his fingers. "You've thought about my hair before?" she asked. Ridiculous question, but it tumbled out anyway. And she wanted to know. Had he really thought about her before? Was she not alone in the way her mind had wandered to him so many nights when she hadn't been able to sleep?

His gaze met hers, and for a second, heat seemed to explode between them. Then he dropped his hands and stepped back. The loss of his touch was like ice cold water drenching her, and she had to hug herself to keep from reaching out for him.

"Tell Astrid I was here," he said. "I'm leaving again—"

"What?" She couldn't hold back the protest. "Already? Why?"

"I have a job."

That job. That mysterious job. He had never told Astrid, or anyone else in town, where he went when he disappeared. Sometimes, he was in town for months, playing at his real estate business, taking off for only a few days at a time. Other times, he was absent for longer. This last time, he'd been gone for almost a year, which was the longest that anyone could remember him being away. And he was leaving again already? "Astrid misses you," Emma said quickly, instinctively trying to give him a reason not to disappear again. "You can't leave without at least saying hi."

Harlan's gaze flickered to the house, and his mouth tightened. He made no move to join the celebration, and suddenly she realized that he felt the same way she did about invading that happy little world. He didn't belong to it any more than she did. Empathy tightened her chest, and she looked more carefully at the independent man who no one in town had ever been able to get close to. "You can stop by and see her tomorrow," she said softly.

He didn't move, and he didn't take his eyes off the house. "She's happy? Jason's good to her?"

Emma nodded. "He treasures her. They're so in love." She couldn't quite keep the ache out of her voice, and she saw Harlan look sharply at her.

"What's wrong?" he asked. "Why did you say it like that?"

"No, no, they're great. Really." She swallowed and pulled back her shoulders, refusing to let herself yearn for that which she did not want or need in her life. "She would kill me if she found out I let you leave town without seeing her. How long until you have to go?"

He shifted. "Forty-eight hours." The confession was reluctant.

"So, then, come back here tomorrow and see her," she said, relief rushing through her at the idea that he wasn't leaving town immediately. For at least two nights, she could sleep knowing that he was breathing the same air as she was.

"No, not here." He ran his hand through his hair, and she saw a dark bruise on the underside of his triceps. "You guys still go to Wright's in the morning for coffee?"

Emma's heart fluttered at his question. For a man who had held himself aloof, he seemed endearingly aware of what his sister did every day...and he knew that she was always there as well. "Yes. We'll be there at eight thirty."

He nodded. "Yeah, okay, I'll try to make it then." He glanced at her again, and just like before, heat seemed to rush through her—

Then he turned away, stealing that warmth from her before she'd had time to finish savoring it. "No." She grabbed his arm, her fingers sliding over his hard muscles. Shocked by the feel of his body beneath her palm, she jerked back, but not soon enough.

He froze under her touch, sucking in his breath. Slowly, he turned his head to look back at her. "No?"

"Don't *try* to make it tomorrow morning," she said quickly, trying to pretend her panic had been on Astrid's behalf, not her own. "You *have* to make it. Astrid needs to see you. She wants you to meet Rosie. She's happy, Harlan, but she needs her brother, too. Jason is her family, but so are you, and you know how she needs to be connected."

Harlan closed his eyes for a long moment, and she saw emotions warring within him. For a man so stoic and aloof, he was fermenting with emotions in a way that she'd never seen before. She looked again at the bruise on his arm. "Are you okay, Harlan? What happened while you were gone?" There was no way to keep the concern out of her voice, no way to hide that her heart ached at the thought of him being hurt.

His eyes opened again. He said nothing, but he suddenly wrapped his hand around the back of her neck.

She stiffened, her heart pounding as he drew her close to him. "What are you doing?"

"I need this." Then he captured her mouth with his.

She had no time to be afraid, no time to fear. His kiss was too desperate for her to be afraid. It wasn't a kiss to seduce or dominate. It was a burning, aching need for connection, for humanity, for something to chase away the darkness hunting him...everything she needed in a kiss as well.

Her hands went instinctively to his chest, bracing, protecting, but at the same time, connecting. She kissed him back, needing the same touch that he did, desperate for that feeling of being wanted. She didn't know this man, and yet, on some level, she'd known him for so long. She'd seen his torment, she'd felt his isolation, and she'd witnessed his unfailing need to protect Astrid, even if he had never inserted himself fully into her life.

Somehow, Harlan's kiss wasn't a threat the way other men's were. He was leaving town, so he was no more than a shadow that would ease into her life and then disappear. He wouldn't try to take her, to trick her, to consume her. He wouldn't make promises and then betray them. All he wanted was the same thing she did, a break from the isolation that locked him down, a fragile whisper of human connection to fill the gaping hole in his heart.

"Emma!" Astrid's voice rang out in the night, shattering the moment. "Are you out here?"

Harlan broke the kiss, but he didn't move away, keeping his lips against hers. One of his hands was tangled lightly in her hair, the other was locked around her waist. Somehow, he'd pulled them close, until her breasts were against his chest, their bodies melted together. It felt so right, but at the same time, a familiar anxiety began to build inside Emma at the intimacy.

"Do not fear me, sweet Emma," Harlan whispered against her lips. "I would only treasure what you give."

His voice was so soft and tender that her throat tightened. How she'd yearned for so many years, for a lifetime, for someone to speak to her like that…until she'd finally become smart enough to relinquish that dream. And now, here it was, in the form of a man who would disappear from her life in forty-eight hours, maybe never to return. Which was why it was okay, because she didn't have to worry that he would want more than she could give, or that she would give him more than she could afford. Maybe she didn't belong in the room of couples and families, but for this brief moment, she belonged out in the night, with a man who lived the same existence that she did.

"Emma?" Astrid's footsteps sounded on the deck, and Harlan released her.

"Don't tell her I was here," he said. "I'll come by Wright's in the morning. Now is not the time." Then, without a sound, he faded into the darkness, vanishing so quickly she almost wondered whether she'd imagined him.

# Sneak Peek: Chill

## An *Alaska Heat* Novel

"Yeah." Luke looked away from his friend. He didn't want to talk about his past. He didn't feel like opening doors with Cort that had stayed firmly closed during their long friendship. They'd been partners for eight years, but he'd hired Cort on several occasions prior when he'd come to Alaska to do research.

He shifted in his chair as he surveyed the bar. The juke box was blaring. A few pilots were hanging around. Some locals. Place was gloomy as hell.

It had never bothered him before. But right now, the moody atmosphere was grating on him big time.

"I'm going outside." He shoved his chair back to stand up, and then the front door opened. In walked a woman of the ilk he hadn't seen in eight years, since he left Boston. Her dark hair cascaded down her back. Even in the dim light of the bar it was glistening.

It looked as soft as the fur on a Husky pup.

It reminded him of the kind of hair women shelled out a thousand bucks a week to maintain. Women in Alaska didn't bother. Women in Alaska let their true beauty speak for themselves.

This woman was not from Alaska.

She strode up to the bartender and began hammering him with questions. She was gesturing furiously, her hands flying around like she was agitated beyond hell.

The bartender nodded in Luke's direction, and she turned and looked directly at Luke.

He immediately sat up, his body responding when he felt the heat of her inspection. Her eyes were black as the sky during a stormy night, but they were alive and dangerous. Sensuous and passionate. He knew instantly that this was a woman who ran hot, who didn't hold back from whatever was in her heart. She sort of reminded him of how he used to be, before he'd realized living that way made too many people die.

Her jaw was out, and she looked fiercely determined.

Yet there was a weariness to her posture, and dark circles under her eyes, visible even in the dim light. She rubbed her shoulder and winced, her body jerking with pain.

Her vulnerability made him want to get up and haul ass over there and offer her help.

Her eyes widened at his expression, and a hint of red flushed her cheeks. The she plunked herself wearily down on a barstool and turned away from him.

Just as well. Luke still had issues when it came to woman in need. Big issues. The kind of issues that haunted his dreams and brought him screaming to consciousness, his body drenched in sweat.

His skin began to feel hot, and it wasn't just from the strip of smooth skin peeking out between the bottom of her sweater and the waistband of her very low-cut jeans... He peered closer and caught a glimpse of a bit of lacy black thong above her jeans.

He'd seen that action on plenty of women and it didn't do much for him, but on her...shit. All his blood was heading south at full speed. Despite her attire, there was a level of innocent sensuality that was drawing him like a grizzly to a picnic basket.

He inspected her more closely, needing to assimilate as much information about her as possible to explain his reaction to her. Her shoulder blades were strong, and her back narrowed into a trim waist and toned hips. The woman took care of herself. Yoga? Most of those wealthy women seemed to have so much time on their hands, they did nothing but spend hours in the gym to try to attract the powerful, rich men they had their sights set on.

Was that her? It didn't feel accurate. She was more than that. The fancy clothes were window dressing, meant to obscure a deeper truth she was trying to hide.

He narrowed his eyes, quickly tabulating all the data so he could make an accurate assessment. It was difficult to tell from this distance, but the sweater appeared to be cashmere. High quality, given its lines. He'd guess upwards of a thousand bucks for it. And her jeans...he recognized the designer brand on that fine ass of hers. His gaze dropped to her boots...heels were low and practical, but the leather was clearly soft and supple, and the seams had that extra bit of style he recognized from his own mother's closet. In fact, she seemed to be wearing exactly the kind of outfit all his dad's women used to wear, once he got finished dressing them up like the Barbie dolls they were willing to be for a chance at his money and his power.

From the brief glance Luke had at had her face, however, this woman was beautiful in a natural way. She didn't need all the glam to look good, but she apparently went in for it anyway. She was refined and beautiful, she was as far from Alaska and carnage as a woman got, and she was exactly what he wanted to bury himself in right now to forget the hell he'd been in for the last fifteen hours.

She turned toward him suddenly, as if sensing his continued perusal. When she saw him watching her, she sat up straighter, and he saw in her something he hadn't expected. Courage. Strength. The woman was a survivor. Not a weak female. She was strong, and that put him over the top.

After what had happened eight years ago, weak, scared, defenseless woman scared the shit out of him. But a woman who was a survivor? Hot as hell. The cashmere? It was escape from Alaskan hell he'd been crawling in the last two days.

Her gaze dropped to his mouth, but then she quickly averted her gaze, shutting him out.

"Too late, my dear," he whispered under his breath. "Too damn late."

He shoved back his chair and stood.

"You heading out?" Then Cort followed Luke's gaze, and he grinned. "She's a little too prettied-up for these parts, isn't she?"

"Damn straight she is." And then Luke headed right for her.

# Select List of Other Books by Stephanie Rowe

(For a complete book list, please visit www.stephanierowe.com)

## PARANORMAL ROMANCE

The *Heart of the Shifter* Series

Dark Wolf Rising
*12/15/15*

The *Shadow Guardians* Series

Leopard's Kiss
*Early 2016*

The *NightHunter* Series

Not Quite Dead

The *Order of the Blade* Series

Darkness Awakened
Darkness Seduced
Darkness Surrendered
Forever in Darkness
Darkness Reborn
Darkness Arisen
Darkness Unleashed
Inferno of Darkness
Darkness Possessed
Shadows of Darkness
Hunt the Darkness
*2016*
Order of the Blade Box Set Books 1 - 3

The *Soulfire* Series

Kiss at Your Own Risk
Touch if You Dare
Hold Me if You Can

The *Immortally Sexy* Series

Date Me Baby, One More Time
Must Love Dragons
He Loves Me, He Loves Me Hot
Sex & the Immortal Bad Boy


## ROMANTIC SUSPENSE

The *Alaska Heat* Series

Ice
Chill
Ghost


## CONTEMPORARY ROMANCE

The *Wyoming Rebels* Series

A Real Cowboy Never Says No
A Real Cowboy Knows How to Kiss
A Real Cowboy Rides a Motorcyc;e

The *Ever After* Series

No Knight Needed
Fairy Tale Not Required
Prince Charming Can Wait

Stand Alone Novels

Jingle This!


## NONFICTION

Essays
The Feel Good Life


## FOR TEENS

The *A Girlfriend's Guide to Boys* Series

Putting Boys on the Ledge
Studying Boys

Who Needs Boys?
Smart Boys & Fast Girls

## Stand Alone Novels

The Fake Boyfriend Experiment

# FOR PRE-TEENS

The *Forgotten* Series

Penelope Moonswoggle, The Girl Who Could Not Ride a Dragon
Penelope Moonswoggle & the Accidental Doppelganger
*Release Date TBD*

## Collections

Box Sets

Alpha Immortals
Alphas Unwrapped
*12/1/15*
Last Hero Standing
Mischief Under the Mistletoe
*11/17/15*
Wicked After Dark
*10/6/15*

# Stephanie Rowe Bio

*USA Today* bestselling author Stephanie Rowe is the author of more than 40 novels, including her popular Order of the Blade and NightHunter paranormal romance series. Stephanie is a four-time nominee of the RITA® Award, the highest award in romance fiction. She has won many awards for her novels, including the prestigious Golden Heart® Award. She has received coveted starred reviews from Booklist, and Publishers Weekly has called her work "[a] genre-twister that will make readers...rabid for more." Stephanie also writes a thrilling romantic suspense series set in Alaska. Publisher's Weekly praised the series debut, ICE, as a "thrilling entry into romantic suspense," and Fresh Fiction called ICE an "edgy, sexy and gripping thriller." Equally as intense and sexy are Stephanie's contemporary romance novels, set in the fictional town of Birch Crossing, Maine. All of Stephanie's books, regardless of the genre, deliver the same intense, passionate, and emotional experience that has delighted so many readers.

www.stephanierowe.com

http://twitter.com/stephanierowe2

http://www.pinterest.com/StephanieRowe2/

https://www.facebook.com/StephanieRoweAuthor

Made in the USA
Las Vegas, NV
11 February 2021